Lots of L

"Luna Marina and the McMachina tells the heart-warming story of an emotionally troubled American teenage girl who travels to 1950's southern Italy. In this wondrous new/old world where everyone is depended upon to be busy and productive, and some of the most treasured possessions and pastimes are hand-made, young Luna's behavior and personality are instantly transformed.
This book is a real page-turner for young readers and for the young at heart, as well as everyone interested in exploring southern Italy of the 1950's.

Highly recommended!' --

Cynthia Sue Larson
www.realityshifters.com

Great Cross in front of St. Bartholomew Cathedral

Luna Marina and the McMachina™

Book 1 of The Adventures of Luna Marina Blue

By G. A. Costa and A. R. Costa

To Nonno and Nonna,
(The Hatter and his Lady)
And their way of life in 1950 Pontecorvo, Italy –

Gino and Sandra

Nonno, the Hatter, was a soldier in Africa
His first day back as a civilian, he decided
to buy himself a Borsalino hat.

Nonna sold him the most expensive Borsalino in her father's shop,
but he didn't care;
all he could see were her blue eyes.
They married a year later and lived together in love for the rest of
their lives.

With many, many thanks to Adele for her invaluable help. Without her, this book would not have been what it is now.

Gino and Sandra

With many thanks to my friends Angela, Cathy, Maria, Dave, Lorie, Wendy, Rochelle, Lena, Matt, Liz, Karen, Mike, Lisa, Tabitha, Gloudie and her family, and all of my other wonderful friends, who have shown me confidence and support, whether they reside close by or halfway around the world!

Lastly, I wish to say Thank You to a dear friend and adviser, Cynthia Sue Larson, for her unwavering confidence in me, for taking me under her wing, and for her excellent advice on life, gaining confidence and getting exposure.
She can be found on www.realityshifters.com and Cynthia Sue Larson or RealityShifters on facebook.
Her favorite saying: "How Good Can it GET?"

Gino

To Elena and Sergio, thank you for the wonderful gifts and ideas; they made this book complete.
To Maria, thank you for always being there throughout my life and for just being you.

Sandra

Cover
La Cannata (The water jug)
Watercolor by Filippo Indoni (1800-1884)
Private Collection

Illustrations
Vintage Postcards and Photos

15. Cartolina, bollo post. 6 V 1913 Retro "27880" Garioni Piacenza".

Thoughts from Pontecorvo 1913
Garioni, Piacenza

7

Table of contents

71. *Bagnanti*. Foto montata su cartoncino pesante con decorazioni floreali. Fot. Macioce, "Pontecorvo - 30 Agosto 1903".

River Liri bathing beauty 1903.
Lorenzo Macioce

1: Wrong Side of the Bed

Luna Marina Blue is dreaming the most perfect dream ever! On her head she's wearing a jeweled crown made from solid gold and inlaid with delicate silver designs, passed down through the ages, waiting for the moment it could rest on her pretty head. Her long, dark, and lustrous hair (in real life her hair is short and dark) hangs nearly to her waist beautifully. She's wearing a long and soft gown of blue velvet which seems to glow with its own inner light, matching her eyes perfectly. Hundreds of people are there, and they all love, adore and admire her and every last one of them looks at her with great expectation. Luna Marina Blue is celebrating her fourteenth birthday and she's having the time of her life at this unbelievable party. Her birthday party was organized by her Fairy Godmother, Giselle, and everything was done in pink and blue, Luna's favorite colors. There are fluffy clouds of pink and white, with red and blue roses growing out of them on long, leafy stems. There are big, bright balloons of bright yellow and green (and of course blue and pink as well). The multilayered birthday cake is pink, white, and frosted silver, taller than Luna herself, with fourteen bright candles and sugar flowers in all the colors of the rainbow. Besides her entire family and all her friends, the guests are very famous and important people, all dressed beautifully in every color imaginable and all are happy just to be invited. But the best one would be the secret guest. Giselle had kept quiet about the biggest surprise of all. She said that his last name was Charming and she had laughed joyfully, her tinkling laugh making everyone smile. Luna doesn't dare say who she thinks this guest would be, but she's hoping. Then the secret guest finally reveals himself, and she meets THE PRINCE! She looks up into his beautiful eyes and falls completely in love at first sight. This Gorgeous Prince is humble, charming, tall and dashing. He looks admiringly into her deep blue eyes, kisses her tiny hand, and then he wants to kiss HER. Luna is anticipating the loveliest kiss in the world, drinking him in eagerly. Then she goes for the kiss slowly, jubilantly, their lips getting closer and closer. Just when their lips start to touch and JUST as they start what Luna knows FOR SURE is the most WONDERFUL kiss ever..........she hears someone yelling in the background:

"LUNA, WAKE UP SWEETHEART! FIRST DAY OF SCHOOL!!......."
Somebody is shaking her awake. Her Mom is pretty and petite, with short dark hair and blue eyes, perky and sporty, always wearing white sneakers and white cotton shirts on the outside of her slim, neat tailored jeans. She's usually kind, gentle and loving, and today she's really proud of her Little Luna Blue for graduating to the 9th grade. While she bustles around Luna's room, she keeps telling her how much she will enjoy seeing her friends, meeting new teachers and maybe even meeting a nice boy to date. But Luna is grumpy, tired and irritable. Slow to wake up, she just wants to stay in bed, blast her music and forget about everyone and everything. She was in the middle of the most perfect dream ever, when Mom unknowingly woke her up AT THE WORST POSSIBLE MOMENT!! And even if she hadn't, she would have awoken some time anyway, it was just a dream and not real after all. Bummer!

It's the First Day of School, and summer vacation is over. How can her Mom be so cheerful, so sweet, so nice, so HAPPY, while Luna is so grumpy?! How can she be that CHIPPER on an awful day like this? Doesn't she know that Luna just wants to be left alone and revel in her bad moods? Luna blames everything on her parents, but actually she's just being her usual grumpy, spoiled, pouty, pissed-off little self. Let's face it, petite little Luna Marina Blue has the temper and disposition of a sailor (with the manners and the language to match)! On this particular morning she desperately wants to stay in her rumpled bed and talk to her friends about how bad things are at home and how pissed off she is that Mom makes her clean her room while continuously telling her to be respectful to her elders. Not all of them command respect, as Luna and her friends well know; some of these ELDERS are pretty mean and stupid, like the cross guard in front of the school. She's forty if she's a day, and she hollers at them to stay put, even when everyone could see that there are no cars coming. If Mom tells her to do stupid things, dad talks at her like she's a child. He demands that she help with chores, while saying:

"No!" To her spoiled-brat wishes, wants and ravings. Her brother Kyle is another story all by himself. The chubby, blondish, spiky-haired eight-years-old is the bane of Luna's life. This morning, when she comes down to breakfast, Kyle is already installed at the kitchen table, the smile on his pudgy little face a prelude of things to come. Luna scrunches her face at the good and nutritious breakfast Mom made:

"Why can't we have pastries, brownies, strawberries in clotted cream and other good stuff for breakfast?" She says. And then, with a little snobbish look, she demands: "I would like a continental breakfast, if you please! A chocolate croissant and a cappuccino, thank you!" Mom giggles while she serves her a bowl of creamy oatmeal with a bunch of fresh blueberries sprinkled on top, and a fluffy biscuit split and decorated with a pat of butter and a spoon of marmalade. Mom puts the food on the table with a flourish:

"You are being served, Ms. Blue!" She snaps the white kitchen towel she carries over her arm, and she says with a smile: "Luna, Honey, please don't scrunch up your face like that or it will freeze that way!" Luna's blue eyes flash in anger, and her black hair sticking up everywhere gives her the look of an angry little Medusa. This morning she wore her tightest cropped jeans full of holes, and she tied her already short shirt around her waist. Her midriff is bare, and her petite little figure is showing curves she doesn't even have yet. She looks much older than fourteen. Her dad, tall, slim and handsome, with blondish brown hair and brown eyes, an esteemed podiatrist, frowns at her, and sternly says:

"Show your Mom some respect, Luna Marina Blue! And go change your clothes! You're going to school, not a beauty contest!" Then he pecks all their collective cheeks quickly, checks his neat suit in the hallway mirror, grabs his leather bag and runs off to work without another word. While this was going on, Kyle had been trying to kick her under the table the whole time, forcing her to sit sideways. So, just before she leaves, Luna drops her spoon, bends down to pick it up, and pinches his leg meanly. Then Luna runs out to the bus (in the same clothes) with a quick:

"Bye!" Accompanied by Kyle's howls and her mother's soft and reassuring voice.

On the bus, the little Rug Rat Brats, who get dropped off at the kindergarten in the basement of her school, start getting under her skin immediately, and she's just mean to them, telling them to shut up and disappear. She gets even madder as the little brats start making fun of her in response to her Stone Face, calling out:

"Luna-Tic, Luna-Tic, my Big Sister's a Luna-Tic!" Making faces and sticking out their tongues, making her get redder and redder, whereupon they laugh even harder:

"Kyle, you are SOOOO going to be TOAST when I get home! I Promise You!" Of course that was one of Kyle's little ditties, Luna figures, as she fumes all the way to school.

Cathedral of St. Bartholomew

Front stairs to the Cathedral of St. Bartholomew
The sexton's house is attached on the left.

First Day of School

On the way to the school building, Luna walks by a teacher, responding to his 'Good Morning' by sticking her tongue out, making him ask what he did to so upset her on this fine, lovely day.

In homeroom she puts her Mad Face on display for all to see, says "HUMPH" when called, and generally acts like a surly little brat. Her old, jovial homeroom teacher has been replaced by a mean, stern old lady (she's probably at least fifty) who takes none of her crap, calls her out in front of the entire class, and asks her embarrassing questions, like:

"Are you having a bad day, My Dear?"

Luna sees her friends at lunchtime, and they all have great stories about their vacations. Plump little Maria went to Italy with her mother to see her grandparents:

"The boys there are great," she says, "they worship American girls!" The rest of the time was like being dropped off in the 1950's, Maria says. And then:

"At my grandparents' farm, it's like time stood still, it's almost in black and white. But it was lots of fun! We had hayrides, family reunions, and my aunts, uncles and cousins ate, drank, danced, sang and partied like there was no tomorrow. I did anything I wanted. In the whole confusion no one knew or cared what I did. I hid in a haystack and kissed a boy. CHE BELLO!" She sighted and closed her eyes dreamily. Luna remembered her grandmother, Grammeva, who was originally from Italy, telling her at one time that when she was young, growing up in Italy, in the 1950's, she had a ball. Luna didn't even want to talk about her silly little dream. Compared to Maria and Grammeva's reality, she felt like a baby:

"I wish I could go back in time to Italy in the 1950's" Luna whispered, dreaming of dances, haystacks and boys, and dreaming of herself in cute peasant blouses and dirndl skirts, and of long kisses and languid looks. She would be the girl from faraway, beautiful and mysterious, intelligent and stylish, whom all the boys worshipped from afar, and sometimes from not so far!

Tall, lanky Myrna went to Greece with her parents, but they just traveled the country as tourists, visiting all the ancient places and learning about the past. Their trip sounded more like another learning experience to Luna, and she had no desire to learn anything new. She knew enough already, thank you very much!

The girls all talked about how happy they'd be to have Mickey D. for lunch: Big Macs, fries, cokes, giant shakes, all their favorites! Maria says that everything was fine in Italy, except for the farm food. Some of it was ok, but some was downright strange. At times she was even forced to make her own food! All the girls shuddered at that. Luna went ahead in search of lunch, but when she got to the lunchroom and looked for the soothingly familiar Golden Arches, Helga the Lunch Lady explained, in a condescending voice, that over the summer the school switched to more 'wholesome and natural lunch selections'. She said that there were plenty of good lunches to choose from. Like boring good-for-you crap, strange good-for-you crap, and gross good-for-you crap. Crap, Crap, CRAP!

"I might as well be in Italy in the 1950's," thought Luna, pouting and moody as usual, "maybe they've got better crap over there!"

After spending an entire morning being talked down to, being yelled at, and being told what to do and what to eat by dummies who know nothing of her needs and wants, she couldn't take it anymore. Her dark mood won out (as it always did) and set her off Big Time! She yells at the jolly, fat Lunch Lady, telling her that she can stuff that oh-so-good-for-you junk up her you-know-what, loud enough for the entire lunchroom to hear. When Helga gets stern at her about showing common decency, Luna completely loses it. After all, what does this smelly, 'rotund' cow know about common anything? Helga shakes her head at Luna and her short, brassy hair fans out like a helmet, while she makes a disapproving sound aimed at her. At that time Luna takes a heaping dish full of smelly-old crap and throws it at the Lunch Lady. When other people come to watch, she throws crap at them as well, all the while making fun of Helga. She laughs joyfully and evilly, making 'oink-oink' noises and yelling:

"Go check out Wendy's Russian commercial on the Internet, Fat Lady, 'cause YOU'RE IN IT!"

When she starts spraying teachers and students alike with water and juice (no soda here --- way too fattening, dont'cha'know!) other students join in the fun, and start throwing things as well. In a few seconds flat, a full-fledged food fight is underway, and Luna is laughing even more joyfully and maniacally at what she started. She keeps making rude jokes about the Lunch Lady, her homeroom teacher and even her parents who made her get up this morning. For all this she is dragged to the Principal's office, where she is left alone and silent, while everyone else has gym outside.

When the Principal finally shows up, he lectures at her in a droning, flat and monotonous voice, telling her that she's earned the distinction of being the first student to behave so badly that she's earned a detention on the First Day of School, as well as a conference with both her parents. All on her First Day of School!!

In English class the teacher, Mr. Wheeler, introduces himself, and then tells them that on the First Day of School he always starts the class with a favorite reading, to illustrate the beauty of the English language. He starts reading a poem about some black bird, written by a guy named Edgar Allan Poe, and after the long, depressing and dreary thing is over, he asks them to write one page on their summer vacation, as well as how they feel about being back on their First Day of School. While Luna rudely starts to write her paper, she thinks how stupid the teacher is. She renames him Mr. Weenie, while spending a long time pouting, answering a cranky:

"No!" When asked if she enjoyed her summer vacation, and once again displaying her Mad Face for all to witness. She can't stop thinking how everyone around her are all know-nothings, how all she ever wanted was to stay home and be cranky, and how her Mom always ruins her dreams on purpose.

Soon, the teacher collected all the papers, and when he got to her, he read some of her work, laughed out loud, complimented Luna on her originality, and proceeded to read everything she wrote in front of the entire class. All the better to humiliate her as much as humanly possible; of that, Luna was absolutely sure. Then he complimented her again and smiled at her, making her feel even angrier and more embarrassed. So this is the paper Luna wrote in a fit of pique.

My Summer Vacation: by Luna Marina Blue.

My summer vacation was crud. We took crappy day trips to both sets of grandparents, one set of grandparents is Italian, so we had to eat Italian crud, and the other set is English, so we had to eat English crud. My Italian grandmother tries especially hard to give me crud for dinner every time we go there. I love Grammeva, but when she tries to give me Italian gunk for dinner I just tell her that lips that touch gunk will never touch mine, and when she tries to kiss me good bye, I turn my face. One day she tried to give me some crazy concoction that looked like a piece of bread with pieces of fat stuck in it, and when I recoiled, she said something strange to me:

"This will be one of your favorite things ever; just you wait and see my pretty!" And she cackled like a witch. It sounded almost like a threat, or a prediction. Sometimes I think she's losing it. She's always talking about things I know nothing about.

At least my English grandmother, Grandmum, never tries to touch me, and I like that much better. Then, since we live outside of Boston, we went to New Hampshire and Maine to see 'The Outlets', as well as the numerous malls around New England. (I Hate New England, I want to be in California!) I wanted to go to Disney, but my mother said:

"Luna, dear, we can't leave the cat alone, and we don't trust anyone to take really good care of her. You know how attached she is, if we leave her she'll probably run away and we'll never see her again!" It seems as if it's always 'The Cat this, The Cat that!' Well, let her run away, and good riddance, I say! But nooooo! That mangy Gattina is more important than their little darling daughter who wants to run wild and party in the hallowed halls of Mickey Mouse and Donald Duck. We went on lots of day trips to antique villages and museums, to more malls and outlets. The antique villages and museums stunk! I know more history now than a body has the capacity to hold and I might add that I hate the good, bad old days, but the malls and outlets weren't that bad, only I had to sit in the back seat next to my brother Kyle, and he would continuously chant:

"Luna-Tic, Luna-Tic, my big sister's a Luna-Tic!" I'm so fed up with him; I think he'll be lucky if he makes it to the ripe-old age of

nine alive. And to top it all off, my mother absolutely REFUSED to buy me anything that I like. I wanted a bikini, but she would not buy me one, even though my friend Myrna got one. My friend looks like a bean pole wearing it, but I would look precious. All the boys would be stunned if they saw me walk down to the beach looking like a goddess. But my mother says:

"No, dear, you're too young. Wait until you're a few years older." Sometimes I think that under all that cheerfulness she really hates me, and doesn't want me to be popular. Just because she wasn't popular (I saw her pictures, she was a geek) she wants me to be just like she was, and to become an old maid. And my dad says:

"No, Luna, No! You cannot have high heels. Your mother never wore high heels (What did I tell you? A geek!). And look how perfect her feet are!" Great! My Mom's the poster girl for 'Your mother wears combat boots', and my Dad's the poster child for 'Mad-and-Upset'. He doesn't care about anything except his Job, his newspaper, and his various sports and, of course, how green the grass is! He only comes alive when I'm taking a shower. You can always hear him hollering all the way from the living room:

"What the hell are you doing in there??!! Five minutes should be enough for anyone!" He thinks half an hour is too long for the shower, so meanest of all: he simply shuts off the hot water in the middle of my shampoo. What does HE think I am? A hobo or something? Doesn't he know I mind freezing to death? Five minutes enough? Ha! My hair alone takes at least fifteen. All in all, my summer vacation was crap, and what is my reward for going through that hell without going completely nuts? My FIRST DAY OF SCHOOL!!

The End,
Luna Marina Blue

Later that day, at loose ends and angry without even realizing why, Luna was sitting in the back of her science class not listening or taking part. Her teacher, Mrs. Fudgebudge, was droning on and on in her weird accent, and finally got through to Luna that she was being called by name:

"Ms Blue, did you understand the experiments we were discussing?" Luna answered angrily:

"Yes, I did! I'm not stupid, you know!" The teacher replied:

"I'm very glad you did! Would you please come up and help me demonstrate?" Luna got up hesitantly, and slowly walked to the front of the class. All the kids were looking at her expectantly, and Mrs. Fudgbudge showed her some glass containers and some bottles of chemicals on her desk, and asked Luna to proceed. She looked at the teacher, looked at the containers, and gave a good imitation of a deer caught in the headlights. Slowly the kids started laughing. First sporadically, and then more and more; to Luna it felt like a roar. The teacher was pressing her and pressing her, and that's when Luna decided:

"I'm blowing this joint; I'm walking out of here forever!" But before she did just that, full of rage and determined to liven things up a bit, she pushed all the bottles of chemicals off the desk in one fell swoop. All at once the stuff reacted together, and started to eat up the rug; the smell was awful and there was smoke coming up off the floor. This made the fire alarm go off shrilly, as the teacher ran screaming from the room. While all the kids were laughing and clapping, the janitor ran in with a fire extinguisher. Luna was pushed into the principal's office, and the second conference was much different than the first one; her parents were there too. Everyone was talking at once, and her parents were upset and silent. After the principal stated that Luna put the entire class in jeopardy, and could have set the school on fire, (Luna thought that he was just exaggerating) he pronounced Luna suspended for a week. Her father walked out without saying a word, and her mother grabbed her by the arm, and dragged her out of the building. And all of this on Luna's First Day of School!

10. *Donna in costume locale.* Cartolina postale.: timbro 7/1V/
1922. Retro: "55359 Edit. L. Macioce".

Woman in Pontecorvo local dress 1922.
Lorenzo Macioce

At home, with everyone all angry and fighting, screaming at each other (especially at her), no one talking calmly, and even Kyle looking scared, Luna screamed at them to just leave her alone:

"And don't bother me ever again! I Hate You! All of you! I hope I never have to see you again! I don't care where I go or what I do as long as none of you are there with me! Now, please just leave me the HELL alone and don't bother me anymore!" With that she shook her fist at them all, spun on her heel, ran into her room, and slammed the door hard enough to make the house shake. With her heart beating a mile a minute, with sweat pouring down like crazy, Luna wondered why she always felt so alone and un-cared for at home. She wanted so much to talk to her friends and tell them what jerks everyone was being right now, how everyone seemed to hate her. They would understand what Luna was going through, while no one else seemed to even try. All her 'family' ever did was scream at her and tell her, never ask how she was or how she felt. But Luna was grounded for a month, and on top of that, they took her phone away. Even her Mom, who this morning was waking her up so happily, ruining dreams and making her go to school, was upset. Her father simply ignored her as usual, except when he yelled at her to do, or not to do, this-or-that. And her little 'brother' did nothing but laugh at her, calling her 'Luna-Tic', 'Luna-Tic'. Why was everyone so hateful to her, Luna couldn't imagine. Maybe, Luna thought, it was because she was not their real daughter. Could she be adopted, or did someone drop her off as a baby, to a mean family who never cared one thing about her like in the Cinderella story? Did Luna even belong here at all? If she didn't belong here, where did Luna belong? And since no one wanted her around anyway, would anyone mind if Luna just up and left them, to go somewhere else? Or maybe she could just hole up in her room without talking to anyone ever again, and without eating ever again! Everyone will be sorry when they eventually broke down the door and found her cold, pale and dead. She envisioned herself in a white casket, with loads of white flowers (Luna loved white flowers) and everyone crying their eyes out and being very sorry they had been mean to her. Would any of her friends cry for her, or would they just reveal themselves to be shallow and uncaring, just pretending to like a girl who was unlikable? After all, for as long as she could remember, Luna's mother had always been bossy and demanding, her father aloof and distant, and Kyle had always laughed at her. Luna knew that the dream of being taken away to a huge castle by a handsome Prince was only that; a dream. But she just wanted to be somewhere she belonged, and it was obviously not here!

As Luna lay on her bed, not thinking or feeling, a quiet, inner voice asked her:

"Where do you think you DO belong, Luna Blue?" Luna was startled, asking

"Who's there?" At first, Luna thought she was imagining things, but the voice continued:

"Do you feel you don't belong here? Do you wish to be somewhere else?" It pushed and pushed at her:

"YES!" Luna answered, feeling sad and angry, with tears streaming down her face. "I – I feel like a stranger here. No one cares for me, no one understands me, and no one knows me at all. Even my friends don't care, unless I'm doing something to entertain them. And my family HATES me!" Luna wondered what this voice wanted, and why it was talking to her now. After all, the only thing to happen to her was that she got suspended from school:

"Who are you, and why are you talking to me?" Luna asked, but all she got was more questions:

"Where do you think you belong, if not your original time?" The voice continued. "Are you sure you would be happier somewhere else away from your family and friends?"

"I told you! My family cannot stand me, I'm nothing to them." Luna said in a broken voice. "Unless I do something to get into trouble, they just leave me alone. And unless I'm doing something outrageous, everyone else does the same. No one would miss me; I might as well disappear forever and never come back." And then Luna complained. "Am I even their real child? Or did they take me from somewhere?"

"Where would you rather be, Luna Blue?" the voice insisted:

"I have some distant relatives from Old Italy, and I've heard that it used to be nice there, quiet and peaceful. I wonder what it would be like to live when they were young, like in the 1950's. I've heard how wonderful it was there and then." After a minute, when something, the voice maybe, seemed to poke and probe around inside her, it asked:

"Are you sure about this, Luna Marina Blue? Do you really want to live in Italy back in the 1950's?" Luna simply wanted to be anywhere away from here, and she wanted no part of her family, her school, or even the friends who never asked about her feelings, either. "If you're absolutely sure, Luna Marina Blue, look behind you and then step into the light."

After a few seconds, wondering what the hell this voice was asking her and why, she got up off the bed, turned around, and was extremely surprised to see a very bright, white light in her bedroom! This light shimmered silver and pure white and it seemed to come from the ceiling, although there was no light there. It was strangely inviting, as if it knew what was inside her and exactly how to get her to step into it. Luna knew in the back of her head that she should get her parents first thing, but what would they say to her? Nothing but yelling and anger, that's what. Assuming they even believed her and came, which they probably wouldn't in any case.

Thinking of all the bad things said to her, how no one even wanted her, knowing that everyone would be happier without her, Luna hesitantly stepped into the light...and was suddenly surrounded by the brightest light she'd ever seen. Within seconds, this too dissipated, and Luna found herself standing, wearing her pajamas and robe, in a strange room, which was definitely NOT her bedroom at home. What had happened to her? This new room was large and brightly lit, with stone walls and circles painted and carved onto the hard stone floor, one of which she now stood in. She was the only person in this room at the moment, but many others could be heard outside. Suddenly, a tall man wearing a glowing, blue-violet robe strode in, saying:

"Welcome to the Machine of Time and Space, otherwise known as the McMachina if you will, Luna Marina Blue! My name is Balthazar, and you came here because you believe there's no place for you back home." Balthazar was over six feet tall, looked like he was of great age, and had a wizened look on his wrinkled face. With large, blue eyes that twinkled, a hooked nose, a long, white beard that trailed almost to his waist, and an impish, all-seeing expression, he regarded Luna quizzically:

"Who ARE you, and why am I here and not in my bedroom?" Asked Luna nervously:

"You seem to think you're not meant for where you come from, Luna Blue. After all, you told us in such great detail how unhappy you are there, how you seem to have it so hard in your time and place, and how no one likes you or even cares if you're there. So we've decided to see if there's a place where you would be happy living, somewhere you belonged." Luna, dumbfounded, just said:

"What's this 'here', some kind of dream?"

"No, you're not dreaming at all, my dear!" Balthazar assured her. "This is completely real, and this place is for children who, like you, think they have it worse than anyone else in the Universe! Unfortunately, Luna Blue, since you made the choice to step into that light, what we call your Grand Odyssey has already begun. We cannot send you back home as if nothing happened. You have to see your Grand Odyssey to its end, and then decide how you feel about your life afterwards."

"What do you mean by 'My Grand Odyssey has already begun'? And where are my parents, and what would they say to your kidnapping me?" Luna asked in a surprised and scared voice. Of course, Luna wasn't sure IF her parents would be angry or not, depending on how they felt about her, or whether they even cared one way or the other:

"Don't worry about a thing, Ms. Blue. You WILL be back in your room, at EXACTLY the time you left, and no one will ever know you were anywhere else. There will be nothing to prove where you were, and you'll be wearing your clothes, exactly as before. But hopefully, Ms. Blue, you'll come back a wiser, more mature young lady, who cares for and appreciates others. Now, come with me, Luna Marina Blue. Your Grand Odyssey awaits!" As Luna started sobbing, suddenly and unbelievably homesick, Balthazar took her hand, and in a fast walk, led her in tow out of the large room and down a series of long, winding, stone-covered hallways, with large, circular windows that looked outside. Luna noticed how there was no grass or scenery to be seen, just space and sky the color of dark violet all around them, and lots of big, bright stars. As they ran along, Luna noticed that Balthazar's long robe reached nearly to the floor, how it seemed to glow wherever they went, with a shimmering blue and white metallic light that looked eerie and strange. Similarly, Balthazar's turban glowed with that same, strange glow, making him look otherworldly and haunting. Balthazar's manner was brisk and businesslike, not speaking much and not giving away any details. Didn't he realize that Luna STILL didn't believe this was real? After all, this was too fast and too unusual. Luna stopped and looked up at Balthazar:

"Where are we now?" She asked him. "What's outside the windows?"

"Outer space, my dear." Balthazar replied:

"You mean like not on Earth at all?"

"Of course, Luna." As he stroked his beard up and down, he said: "Miss Blue, have you ever heard of 'Deus ex Machina'?" Luna looked bewildered and said:

"No!" Balthazar shook his head:

"Of course, these days children are not as erudite as we were in the olden days; 'Deus ex Machina' is Latin and it literally means 'The God from the Machine', The Universal machine that is. In all the Greek tragedies, when all seemed lost, a God would appear, to fix all things and solve all plots and conundrums. Here we call this God 'The Powers That Be' and this is the Universal Machine. Like I explained already, this is The Machine of Time and Space, so what better place to have it than between the stars?"

"But who runs everything here? Who kidnapped me?"

"Why, The Powers That Be, of course!" Replied Balthazar, "Who else?"

"And you mean to tell me you're just a strange guy who kidnapped me and brought me here for no reason?"

"I told you what this place is and why you're here, Ms. Blue!" Balthazar said in a businesslike manner. "But there is not much time to waste. We must get you ready for your trip to Italy in the year 1950!"

"Can't I just go home?" Luna asked again in a scared voice. "I didn't really think I would go back in time like that!"

"I'm very sorry, Ms. Blue, but that's just not possible. Like I said, after this trip, you'll return home, and no one will ever know,

I promise you. You will not be away any time at all. Hopefully, it's you who will be different."

"I want to go home!" Luna said with tears. "I just want to be where I was and forget that I ever wanted to go away! Please, Balthazar, just take me home!"

"I can't Luna," he said with a sad voice: "It's not up to me, and this cannot be undone without you going through and coming out at the other end. But fear not, Luna Blue, you will be taken care of, and nothing could ever happen to you!" As they continued to walk down more twisting hallways, Luna lowered her head down and once more started crying softly, as Balthazar repeated how safe she would be, and how Luna would learn valuable life lessons from this trip through time.

Eventually the pair came upon a huge stone room filled with several large portals set into the walls, all of different shapes and styles. Within the room, there were tall, running waterfalls that emptied into ponds with giant lily pads and softly glowing rocks, and several mysterious hallways which led off the room in unknown directions. There were also a large number of children in here, some of whom sat quietly in alcoves set into the wall, while others ran or swam in the inviting water, laughing and making loud splashing noises as they played. Along with the children were older people, much like Balthazar himself, but younger looking and not as tall, acting as guides. There were children from every race, including Japanese, Chinese, Indian, African, European and American, just to name a few, but many of them were in rags and looked like they've been mistreated or were starving:

"See those children, Luna?" Balthazar asked. "They're here from other places and other times. But they're here for an entirely different reason than you. Understand, Luna, these children will NEVER see their original homes again, and for that they're eternally happy!"

"How?! Why?!" Cried Luna suddenly: "I could NEVER stand to be away from home forever!" Balthazar looked at Luna sadly and continued:

"Unlike you, Miss Luna Blue, the 'homes' these children came from were extremely hostile to them. They have been starved, abused, tortured, and made to work as slaves. See how they're thin and dressed in rags? They've had nothing to eat, have never been loved or cared for, and have never felt warm or safe. Luna, they've had it much, much harder than you've ever even imagined. No modern toys, nothing to play with, no cell phones, no friends to complain with over being punished by teachers or parents. No school. No homework. No teen pressure. No Facebook; nothing! Luna, remember that, no matter how bad things may have seemed to you, someone's had it much worse! Further, these kids are from various times in the past, some from hundreds of years ago or more. When they were taken here, they had no idea what was happening to them or why. If they had stayed in their original place and time, they wouldn't have survived. But even coming here has frightened them greatly! Since they've been brought here, they now have a chance for a good life." Silent and staring, with sudden understanding about the ways of the world, Luna simply nodded and remained quiet: "Some of these children didn't come from bad homes, but from natural disasters, such as earthquakes, giant forest fires, or volcano eruptions, which destroyed their homeland. Have you ever heard of the ancient Italian city of Pompeii, Luna?" Speaking for the first time in a while, she answered:

"They talked a little about it in History class, I forget when. It's really old, isn't it?"

"Truly ancient, Luna! Pompeii was located not far from where Naples is today, and it dates from the Roman Empire. It was buried in a gigantic eruption from the volcano Mount Vesuvius, almost two *thousand* years ago!"

"Is there anyone from Pompeii here now?" Luna asked, suddenly excited:

"Actually, there are a few. Think about it, Luna. To these children, Pompeii is simply all they've ever known, and the eruption is as new and as fresh to them as the argument you had with your parents is to you. They are still scared to death, and all we can do is try to calm them down and find a good place for them to live. And being from that time, they have no way of knowing that in your time Pompeii had been buried and undiscovered for over 1,500 years (and it was just an accident that it was even discovered at all)."

"Wow!! I never knew this much about any place that old!!" Luna cried in awe. "Did people really live entire lives back then?"

"Yes, Luna, they did. History is full of people living and dying, long, long before you, or even your entire family, were ever born!" Balthazar told her. It was one thing to read about it in boring history class, but quite another to see and hear about it for yourself. At that, Luna responded:

"When I get back home, and I WILL get back home, I promise you Balthazar, I WILL study more, especially places like Pompeii. And I can say I actually know people from there as well!" Balthazar smiled approvingly at Luna, putting a gentle hand on her trembling shoulder:

"You're finally starting to learn more about how the universe works, Luna Blue; not everything revolves around you or those close to you. Each of us has his or her own experiences, all different from the rest. And just as going back to Italy in the 1950's scares you, others would be homesick coming to you from their own time."

As Luna looked around at the children coming out of the portals, the other helpers who were sort of like younger versions of Balthazar himself, and everything else, she became transfixed by her strange and new surroundings. Hearing the sounds of laughter, strange languages and water splashing, Luna almost forgot how scared she was, far from home, and as far as she could tell, with no way to get back, especially on her own:

"Can I meet someone from another time?!" Luna asked tentatively:

"Sure! Let's go down to meet someone right now." Balthazar assured her. Putting his hand on her shoulder and leading her towards a solitary little girl sitting quietly in an alcove, Balthazar said reassuringly:

"Remember, Luna, no matter how different their languages may be, these children are in many ways just like you. They have the same feelings, and in many ways, the same experiences. They just come from different homes and times. Don't be afraid to talk and become friends." As they came to the sad little girl, Luna noticed how little clothes she wore, and what little she did have was charred and burnt. The girl herself also had burns across her entire body, and tears were coming out of her eyes. Looking at about the same age and height as Luna herself, with European features, olive skin, deep, dark eyes and long dark hair, the girl had a haunted and frightened look about her, as if she'd just seen something awesome, scary and unbelievable. Luna immediately went to her and gave the girl a giant hug, putting her own quilted blue robe over the girl's trembling shoulders. The girl instantly hugged her back, just for the affection of a kindred spirit, though one from a totally different place and time, and said:

"Gratias tibi." Looking at the girl's face, Luna shyly said:

"Hello. My name is Luna Marina Blue. Who are you?"

"Salve te, Luna Marina Blue. Mihi nomen est Valeria." The girl said softly, sounding incredibly sad:

"What did she say?" Luna asked:

"She said Hello and gave you her first name, Valeria."Balthazar said: "She speaks Old Latin."

"How do you know?" Asked Luna with big eyes:

"My dear Ms. Blue, you will find out that I know everything there is to know!" And at Luna's skeptical look he amended:

"Well! Almost everything!"

"How do I talk to her?" Luna asked:

"Don't worry, My Dear, that as well as everything else, has all been taken care of! Speak to her again, and you'll see." Balthazar assured her brightly. Turning back to the frightened little girl, who was busy touching the large gold buttons on the robe like she had never seen buttons, Luna asked:

"Where are you from, Valeria? Is that your real name?"

"Yes, it is." Valeria answered. "And I am from Pompeii, A VERY large city! I've lived there with my family as far back as I can remember." It was with a sudden start that Luna realized that she understood the foreign words, similarly, but not exactly like her understanding of her own English. And then Luna realized again that Valeria had just named Pompeii as her home town:

"Did I suddenly just learn Latin?" Luna asked Balthazar. "And did I hear right? Did she *really* say she came from Pompeii!?"

"Yes, she did come from Pompeii, Luna. And the reason she's here in the first place is because she saw the eruption of Mount Vesuvius, and the complete destruction of all she's ever known, first hand. Luna, I know this may sound harsh, but you've *never* had to go through anything like what Valeria just experienced.

And although to you it's many years ago, to her it *just* happened! Imagine one summer morning all hell breaks loose, without warning whatsoever. And without any way to know what's happening, you find yourself in this strange place, only to be left alone, with time to think and realize that you'll never see your family again, ever! Luna, you WILL see your home and family again. Valeria never will! We've got to find her a good place to live, because if we had left her there, she would have died also. Even with our efforts, you can see she'll need a lot of attention. And the best thing for her, especially right now, is for you to be a friend and comfort her. I know this place scares you. Trust me; it scares her a whole lot more!" As Luna looked in alarm, realizing for the first time what this meant, Balthazar continued: "As for you learning Latin, we've taken care of that for you. You'll find that you understand everything very easily, as if you've spoken it all your short life."

"Really?" Luna asked unbelievingly:

"Try it for yourself and see." Balthazar said confidently. "Go on, speak to her." Next, Luna asked Valeria:

"Where were you from again?"

"Pompeii." Valeria answered in tears. "My family, my home, all gone! Why? What did we do to offend the Gods?" Suddenly, Luna realized that while she was talking with Balthazar, Valeria was sobbing and sadder than anyone she'd ever seen in her life. Holding Valeria while she wept quietly, Luna felt at once very sad and very close to her and wanted to take Valeria home to make her happy. But how would she explain Valeria's appearance in her modern time and place? Luna was afraid everyone would ask her constant questions. Turning back to Balthazar, Luna asked:

"Where will you send her? What time and place will she go to? Could she come live with me in my time?" Luna said excitedly:

"We're still deciding that right now." Balthazar said gravely. "We have the ultimate responsibility for her life, and we must choose her future very wisely! We cannot send anyone anywhere on a whim or a plea."

"Why not?" Luna asked angrily: "I could use a sister who would be nice to me and never call me "Luna-Tic!"

"For one thing, Luna, Valeria would not survive in your time, certainly not like you do. She is from a totally different home after all, and everything which you take for normal would scare and terrify her." As Luna's face fell, Balthazar continued: "Valeria wouldn't know what to do or where to turn, any more than if you were transported to the year 3010 (I've been there myself, so I know whereof I speak). First, she would have an extremely rough time at school, and everyone would laugh and make fun of her, constantly hurting her feelings. Second, differences in conditions between your time and hers could kill her, such as diseases that she would be susceptible of catching. Third, how would you explain where Valeria came from? Even in your time, someone cannot simply pop out of thin air and be made part of society. And there are other reasons as well. I am sorry, Luna, but as I said before, we are taking great care in placing Valeria where she will live a good life."

"So have you decided yet where she will go?" Luna asked sadly:

"Yes we have, as a matter of fact."

"Where will she live?" Luna asked just as sadly. "Will she remember me at all?"

"Yes she will, actually. What we have decided is that Valeria will be one of many survivors who escaped Pompeii and were rescued by good Samaritans, a family of which took her into their home in a nearby city. This is very believable because just after Pompeii was destroyed, many people, including entire families, were seen walking dazedly out of the rubble and were rescued by those wanting to help those in need. Just like in your time, people have always helped others during an emergency. Think of the news stories and subjects I'm sure you've studied in school, and know the same happened all those years ago with Pompeii."

"We studied recent earthquakes in school." Luna said. "It was so sad, I was glad I wasn't there!" Balthazar said:

"Valeria will be in safe hands, she'll stay near where she was born, and she'll remember you as a friend who helped and comforted her when she needed it most." Somehow, Luna felt a little better. If Valeria could not come home with her, at least Luna had made a difference in her life. Suddenly, just as Luna was starting to really like her new friend, two of the younger helpers, both females looking younger than Luna's teachers at school, came up and asked for Valeria to come with them. Suddenly, Luna started crying, screaming:

"No! You can't take her! I'll never see her again! NO! Let her stay with me!" Valeria also started crying, hugging Luna fiercely, and putting her head on Luna's shoulder. Although they only met a few minutes earlier, the two girls felt a strong kinship and had found some security in each other's presence, and now that that security was going to be ripped off just like that, they tried to hang onto each other fiercely. But between Balthazar and his two helpers, who were just as functional and impassive as Balthazar himself, they got the two girls apart. As Luna watched, tears streaming down her own face, Valeria was led down a far corridor by the two helpers, her own head down, obviously sad. Before they disappeared around a corner and went out of sight for the last time, Luna waved to Valeria, saying a sad and plaintive:

"Bye Valeria! Please remember me! I Love You!" And Valeria turned around, waved at her and said:

"I love you too, Luna Marina, I'll never forget you!" And then she left. Balthazar made an attempt to put his arm around Luna to calm her, but Luna just jerked out of his way, asking:

"Why couldn't we at least have some time together? Why?"

"Luna, what would that do for either of you? It would only make parting even harder than it is for both of you, and could ultimately make it much harder for Valeria to survive even in her own time. I wish there was a way for you two to be together, but in time you'll understand that this is the best we can do for both of you. Rescuing people is never easy, and there are always hard choices that must be made. As I told you before, we simply cannot make life-altering decisions on a whim, no matter how good the intentions; we simply made the best choices with what we have, and letting you two stay together would most likely end up in disaster." After about a minute, the two female helpers came back, and as Luna looked up anxiously, one of them said:

"Done!" To Balthazar. In response, he nodded back at them in acknowledgement. After another minute of silence, Balthazar suddenly looked up, a distant look in his eyes, then back at Luna, and said:

"Luna, you might want to know that our decision was indeed for the best. Valeria was taken in by a very wealthy family and had a good life where she belonged, without danger or major stress." Luna cried:

"What! She's already dead?" Balthazar looked at her sadly:

"Yes, Dear, for hundreds of years. That's how time works, I'm afraid! Right here and now, she's gone, but back there, in ancient Roma, she is still living and enjoying life. She never forgot you, and she lived to be a very old and successful woman, with a large family herself. Also, even though she loved you for befriending her, she did come to realize the wisdom of what we did. Not without a few tears, mind you, but then life is often lived with tears as well as happiness. And ultimately, Luna, Valeria became very happy. And your help made it all possible! Without your support, things would have been much tougher for her."

"Thank you, Balthazar." Luna said, still tearful. "I hope you didn't just lie to me."

"No, I didn't, Luna. What I told you is absolutely the truth. You can revisit those days and see how it was."

"How, Balthazar?" Asked Luna:

"History, My Dear, history! The Internet allows you to look up anything you want, remember?" Luna thanked him again, glad that Valeria was saved, and that Luna herself had made a difference.

Balthazar tapped Luna on her shoulder:

"It's time for your own Odyssey to commence, Luna." She had almost forgotten that she was far, far from home, that she would not be going back until her 'Odyssey' was done, and that she was still very much scared and alone. Valeria was the only person who made her feel cared for, and all of a sudden, she was gone, back to where she belonged. Luna just wanted to go back to her bedroom and family, and forget all about everything here, but Balthazar again reminded her that this just wasn't possible:

"Once you've come here, Luna, you must complete your 'Odyssey'. There is no turning back." Briskly, Balthazar stood up, taking Luna by the elbow, and started leading her towards a dark hallway, different than the one where Valeria went. With light sobs and sadness, Luna asked why Balthazar himself led her.

"You're a very special case, Luna. Because of who and what you are, and because of what your future might hold, it was decided that I should lead you on your 'Odyssey' myself."

"So this 'Odyssey' is what I must go through to get back home?" Luna asked. As they walked down the long, strangely winding corridor, the lights and sounds of the large room fell away, turning to near-silence. Only a very soft, low-pitched sound could be heard, like moving earth. Balthazar answered softly and severely:

"Yes, Luna. You thought you were so unique and 'modern', that no one could ever comprehend you. So to show you how others have lived, we decided to grant you your wish; to live in Italy in the early 1950s for a time. After you complete your stay there, if and when you get back home, you'll have learned some valuable life lessons which, it's hoped, will guide you in your own future." Unlike the rest of the 'Machine' in outer space, this corridor was dark, with no windows, lit only by a dim, blue-violet light that seemed to come from everywhere. In the frightening near-silence, Luna's soft footsteps and occasional whimper could be heard clearly, but Balthazar had taken on a quiet, businesslike demeanor, guiding but not comforting her. As they continued down the many twists and turns of the strange hallway, the silence became deafening, making Luna feel scared and alone all over again. Eventually they came to a dead end, and while Luna watched, Balthazar's face took on a look of intense concentration. A second or two later, a portal winked into existence on the wall ahead, looking like a pale whirlpool. Making a soft swirling and tinkling sound, this portal lead into complete darkness:

"Luna, it is time." Balthazar said in a low voice: "Come." He motioned her forward, and as Luna steeled herself and stepped through the portal, Balthazar came in behind her. As the portal disappeared behind them, Balthazar continued guiding Luna forward:

"W-w-where are we going now?" She asked as they walked through the darkness:

"Through one last portal, then we will be at your destination." Balthazar answered: "Your 'Odyssey' starts very soon, Ms. Blue. I suggest you prepare yourself for it."

"Why so many portals?" Whined Luna.

"The corridors of time have their own rules, Ms Blue, and we must obey them just as you must do back home." Responded Balthazar. Less than a minute later, the very last portal, similar to the others, opened in front of them, and Luna knew that her time in the 'Machine of Time and Space' was at an end. What she had no idea of was what lay on the other side of that last portal. Would she go back home? End up somewhere else and never see home again? She had no idea! But what she did know was that she was scared, sad and alone. And she wanted it all to be over so she could forget it like it never happened.

11. *Donna in costume locale*. Cartolina, bollo post. 2/XI/1935 [foto ritoccata a mano]. Retro: "Prop. ris. Ed. G. Quagliozzi - Libreria e Cartoleria / EIS".

Woman in Pontecorvo local dress 1935.
G. Quagliozzi

Balthazar stepped through the portal and motioned Luna to follow him. She hesitantly stepped out of the 'Machine', and suddenly she was plunged into complete darkness. The only thing guiding her was the shimmer from Balthazar's robe. As far as Luna could tell, they were in a long, narrow tunnel, and after a while Luna started to breathe hard, feeling like she didn't have enough air. But soon she felt the tunnel enlarge, and she felt it start to rock, rattle and roll. Right after that, lights appeared on both sides of the tunnel, and she could see pastoral scenes rolling past. Luna soon realized she was looking at windows, and the scenery rolling past was the outside, and that she and Balthazar were on a train. She looked at Balthazar and he turned around and said:

"Come, child, let's not dawdle, we are on a time frame." They walked some more, and Balthazar opened a door. Luna hung back, scared, as she heard voices. She didn't know what they were saying, as the words were incomprehensible to her, but they had a very musical sound, and someone was laughing. She told Balthazar:

"You're not going to leave, are you?" Balthazar replied, sadly:

"I'm sorry to say, but my part is almost over for now." He smiled kindly, and petted Luna gently on her head. She cried:

"But I don't understand what they're talking about, and I'm still in my pajamas, and I'm not wearing any shoes, I'm still in my slippers!" Balthazar laughed:

"Adjustments are being made, don't worry, and in fact look at your clothes." Luna looked down and she was stupefied; her pajamas had changed into a little black skirt, white cotton shirt, and a little grey sweater. On her feet she was wearing white knee high socks, and flat black shoes with tick leather soles. To Luna's astonishment, Balthazar put his hand in his robe and produced a small cardboard suitcase which he handed to her:

"Here is your gear for 1950's Italy, my dear, everything is authentic and made to fit. You will find no trousers in the lot, but they were not standard equipment for a female of your station in those days, and we wanted you to belong. You are part of Italy

1950, like you requested. Now I will find you a seat and then I must leave."

"Leave?" Shouted Luna, "you're leaving me here all by myself? What will I do? And how will I go home again?" She was shaking and scared, and Balthazar caressed her tousled black hair:

"Don't be afraid, dear, precautions have been taken and you will be fine. There is someone watching over you the whole time, and if you need something, all you have to do is ask."

"Who shall I ask, I don't know anyone." Balthazar laughed:

"You will have aunts and uncles and cousins, like you wanted, and they are going to be kind, so ask for anything you want." Luna looked up at Balthazar:

"When will I go home?"

"When you are done!" And with that Balthazar opened the compartment door and walked right in. There were hard wooden seats all in a row on both sides, and a narrow isle in the middle. On top of the seats luggage racks held baskets, bags and bundles. The floor of the train was made of large, old planks of wood, and in between the planks Luna could see the tracks fly by. Balthazar slid Luna's suitcase under a seat near the window, and motioned for her to sit. The only other occupants of the compartment were two men sleeping in their seats, and an older woman, also sleeping in her seat. Luna sat and looked up to thank Balthazar and say good bye, but with a smile he handed her a cardboard ticket, turned around and started to walk away. Luna choked-up and wanted to get up and run after him, but he turned slightly, motioned 'no' with his finger and with a wave of his hand saluted her and disappeared through the compartment door. Luna ran after him, opened the door, but the long compartment was empty. Luna ran all the way to the end, but the end of the compartment was also the end of the train. He was gone! Luna went back to her seat and putting her head down, started to sob quietly. The woman seating across from her woke up and said something, but Luna didn't know what she said, and shook her head. She looked outside, and was surprised that it was daytime. She had left in the middle of the night, as far as she knew. She was so weary! The woman took one of the baskets from the luggage rack, took something out and put the basket back. She unrolled a white napkin, and inside was a sort of sandwich. She was going to start eating, when she saw Luna look at her and stopped. Whatever the woman had, it smelled delicious, and Luna realized that she hadn't eaten for a long time. Usually she would not touch other people's food with a ten foot pole, and the woman did not look like she enjoyed bathing, but she forgot all that. The woman showed Luna the food and made a motion to break it in two, and Luna gratefully nodded yes. The woman broke the small loaf in two and handed her half. Luna accepted it, and said:

"Thank you very much!" But to her surprise, it came out in a different language. The woman said:

"I didn't think you could speak, I guess you were just upset. Are you traveling alone?" Luna nodded while she bit into the two pieces of bread that held a thin piece of cold cut:

"This is delicious! What is it?"

"Bread and mortadella! Haven't you ever had some?"

"No" Answered Luna. And the woman said:

"You must be from the North of Italy. They eat all kinds of different stuff there." Not knowing what to say Luna kept on eating. The friendly woman pulled out a small flask, and handed it to Luna. Not knowing what to do with it, Luna looked at the woman questioningly, and the woman said:

"Drink, drink, or you'll choke on that bread, it's a little stale." Luna looked for a cup, but when she saw the woman look at her expectantly, brought the small flask to her mouth and hesitantly took a small sip. It was wine, and Luna was never allowed wine at home. Come to think of it, no one in the house drank wine very much. But it was sweet and fresh, almost as frizzy as seltzer, and Luna took a long swallow and handed the flask back:

"It's new wine!" The woman said. "It's the best!" With that, the woman wiped the end of the flask with the white napkin she still had on her lap, and took a swallow herself. Luna started to feel better. The little old woman was mostly dressed in black with some white, her hair covered by a kerchief tied on the back of her neck. Luna was transfixed by the little old lady's shoes. They seemed to be made of a large piece of leather, and the leather was curved on the sides to cradle the foot. The front was longer than it should have been, and the corners curved a lot on both sides to form a point that stuck up almost like the shoes of a genie. This contraption was strapped to the foot by long strings that wound around the leg all the way to the knee. Under the strings you could see some heavy, white cloth wrapped around the leg. Luna had never seen anything like it, and for a moment she was fascinated. The old lady was wearing a white shirt made up of hundreds of small horizontal pleats, and she had a large, black shawl over her shoulders. The rest of her attire was a heavy black skirt, and from the bottom of her skirt peaked a bit of heavy white lace, which Luna took to be a petticoat of sorts. The woman's small face crinkled in a smile, and she said:

"My name's Anna, what's your name?" Luna all at once realized she had been rude but the woman didn't seem to mind. Regularly she would have said that it was no one's business, what her name was, but she wanted to find out more, and the only way to do it was by making friends:

"My name is Luna!" She said. And at the same time that she said it, she instantly knew that her name meant moon, in Italian. Anna smiled:

"What a pretty name! " Luna said:

"My name is Luna Blue!" Anna said:

"Your name is Blue Moon! How wonderful." And she started to sing "Blue Moon" in Italian. At the sound, the two guys woke up and stared at Luna. Her new friend asked:

"Where are you getting off?" At that Luna looked at the cardboard ticket Balthazar had given her, but couldn't make heads or tails of it. She looked up, perplexed, and Anna took the ticket from her and looked at it:

"You are going to get off in Aquino, like me. Is anybody waiting for you?" Luna found that, all at once, she knew the answer to that question:

"My uncle is going to be there. I'm to spend some time at his farm, with his family."

"What's his name?" Asked Anna, "I might know him!" Luna was saved from answering by the entrance of a small man in some kind of uniform:

"Tickets, please!" He intoned, and proceeded to take the two tickets from the guys, and punching a hole in them. He then walked to Anna and took the ticket she was holding:

"How is it going, dear girl, are you going to your daughter's then?"

"Yes," and she smiled a flirty smile up at him, "they're slaughtering a large pig tomorrow, and I'm going to lend a hand."

"Bring me a blood sausage on the way back, will you?"

"If I can, Alfredo, I'll bring you a large one." Then he turned to Luna who had watched this exchange with growing horror on the mention first of slaughtering a pig and then of blood sausages:

"So, what do we have here, a young lady traveling alone?" Anna came to her rescue:

"Her name is Luna, she's from the North, and she's going to stay with her uncle and his family for a while." Alfredo smiled at her, and she handed the cardboard ticket to him:

"Strange ticket," he commented, "but valid." He punched a hole in it, and gave it back to her. Luna put it back in her small handbag. Wait a minute! She had a bag? She looked at the small, round, felt bag. It resembled a small hatbox with a handle, and it had a small bunch of flowers also made of felt attached on top. It was a beautiful buttercup yellow, and the flowers were a small bunch of violets with bright green leaves. The strap was just long enough to carry it around on your arm or in your hand, and the circular top was closed by a small zipper that went all around the bag. Luna opened it and she saw a small wallet, a coin purse and a small envelope with an elastic band around it. Other odds and ends were stuck in a small pocket to the side. There was also a square compartment with a zipper, and that is where Luna put her ticket. The gaily decorated bag was almost an anachronism in the dreary compartment, next to people all dressed in somber colors, including Luna herself, but it made Luna happy, and she was glad it was hers, at least for the time being. At one time that bag wouldn't have meant anything to her, but what was once a throwaway item was now a precious gift to cling to. The small bag looked to be handmade, and in her heart, Luna knew her new aunt had made it. Her eyes started to mist, but at that moment the clickety-clack sound of the heavy, black, rusty train started to slow, and Luna's heart started beating fast. She looked outside, and saw a gray, dusty train station appear. It was surprisingly large, and there were a lot of people milling around. She looked at Anna expectantly, but her friend shook her head:

"It's not our stop; this is Cassino. We get off on the next one; Aquino. It will be about fifteen minutes." Luna couldn't relax, she started to fidget, she opened and closed her bag, and she took her suitcase and put it on the seat next to her. A lot of people boarded the train, and soon the compartment was full. Everyone squeezed on the wooden seats, and Anna said:

"A lot of these people are going to Frosinone, some to Roma, but not too many, it's quite a trip. At Roma the train turns around, that is as far as it goes." Luna nodded, but didn't say much. After a few minutes more, the train started to slow down again, and Anna got up and started to pick up her bundles. Luna did likewise, and clutched her little yellow bag while holding her small suitcase between her legs. When the train stopped, Luna followed Anna off the train. She jumped off the high steel step, and started to walk away on wobbly legs. Anna turned and said:

"Follow me to the waiting room; I'll wait with you until your uncle gets here." Grateful, Luna followed her, and they soon entered a small room with wooden benches. It was dusty and dark, but there was a wonderful smell around. Luna knew it was a coffee smell, but not the coffee she was used to; it was pungent and exotic, almost like the smell in a Starbucks, but different. At one end of the room there was a small alcove, and in front of it there was a small counter with a girl standing behind it. In the back of the girl there was a coffee machine and a small shelf that held a large plate of goodies covered by a transparent cupola of some kind of glass. Luna shyly sat down on one of the seats, clutching her bag and suitcase still. She had never been shy in her life but found that she did not have the desire to shout and be heard. She just wanted to hide from everyone. She leaned her head on Anna's shoulder and started to sob quietly. Anna caressed her hair and whispered:

"You have never been away from home alone, have you?" And Luna smiled through her tears:

"No, not this far!"

At this point, a well-dressed gentleman in a grey suit entered the small, dusty room and made straight for the small counter as if he had been there before. He carried a leather bag, had a black wool coat over his shoulders and was wearing very shiny, pointy shoes. Anna cackled under her breath:

"Well! Well! Well! I'm so elegant while I get my food; I'm just too beautiful for my own good!" And she laughed. Luna looked at her with questions, and Anna said: "I've seen him before, he's a big shot lawyer from Roma; he thinks he's the best thing since white bread. Just wait and see; our country lawyers will have him on the run so fast he wouldn't know what hit him!" As Luna watched curiously, the man approached the girl and ordered imperiously:

"A chocolate croissant and a cappuccino, please!" At that Luna started to laugh loudly in the quiet, dark, dusty room and had to hide her face in Anna's shawl at the curious looks from the bystanders.

Sometime later, a figure appeared at the door. Outside it was bright and sunny, and the figure was limned by the light. You could tell it was a man wearing a cap low over his eyes, but his face was in the shadows. He looked around the small room and his eyes fixed on Luna:

"Luna Blue?" He asked, and you could sense a smile in his voice when he said that. Luna clung to Anna, and the woman regarded the man and asked:

"Who wants to know?"

"I'm her uncle Pasquale Sargento. I'm here to pick her up and take her home to my farm. I have here a letter from her parents." He showed Anna the letter he pulled out from his pocket, and looked at her curiously. Anna said, defiantly:

"Where is this farm." Her uncle said:

"It's right at the beginning of the Saint Lucia District, right outside of Pontecorvo proper." And Anna said:

"I'm going to be in the same district, and right at the beginning too; tomorrow I'll come and see how Luna is doing." Luna looked up and smiled at Anna:

"You will?"

"I certainly will!" Said the old lady. "I'm going to be almost up the street from you, and I'll get my son-in-law to drive me."

"How are you going to get there now?" Asked Uncle Pasquale:

"I'm taking the bus to Pontecorvo and my son-in-law will be waiting for me there."

"I'm going to pass right through Pontecorvo," Uncle Pasquale said, "hop in my truck and I'll give you a ride." They all walked outside, and Luna clung to Anna's hand while the little old lady beamed at her. As Luna's uncle led the way, Anna leaned down and whispered in Luna's ear:

"I can't read, but I was curious to see if he really had a letter or just a blank piece of paper; it was a letter!" Luna giggled and followed her uncle. He was a tall, wiry guy, a little stooped, almost gaunt, and he had a leathery brown face with deep grooves on each side of his mouth. Luna's uncle had a kind and intelligent face. He took his cap off, and carried it in his hand. He looked to be in his thirties, with brown hair and surprisingly very light grey eyes which he had a tendency to squint. He was quite handsome in a rugged sort of way. He looked to be a very nice man and he had a courtly manner about him. Luna felt better; maybe this stay was not going to be so bad after all!

They made their way to a huge, black truck and her uncle opened the cab and let Luna go in first, then Anna. He secured their door, then walked around and sat in the driver's seat. The truck started up with loud pops and clanging noises, but her uncle didn't seem worried, so Luna wasn't either. After a while, Uncle Pasquale engaged the shift, and they drove off in a cloud of smoke. Luna's eyes and lungs burned, but she tried not to cough. After all, if they could stand it, so could she.   They eventually drove through a small town, Aquino, made up of colorful houses with flowers spilling everywhere, from window boxes, gardens, and outside pots stationed on the sidewalks. There were people walking everywhere, children playing outside and small stores with signs like: 'Butcher' 'Bakery' 'Fruits and Vegetables' 'Coffee shop' etc. Luna was amazed that they did not have one store that sold everything all in one place, like their supermarkets at home. The streets were very narrow, and all twists and turns, and Luna was very worried when they practically brushed vehicles coming the other way on the road. But after a while she realized that her uncle was a very good driver, shifting the heavy machine and turning the rusty steering wheel with ease, so she relaxed again. It hit her all at once that here and there, amongst all the nice houses, some appeared to have been demolished by a big blow. She asked Anna why some of the houses were broken to pieces, and Anna replied:

"They have been like that since the war. Eventually all of the houses will be reconstructed, and then we can finally forget about the war."

"What war was it?" Asked Luna and Anna said:

"The Second World War." They drove on a short stretch of highway before turning into a smaller side road. After about ten minutes they started to see houses along the road, also with flowers spilling from every available spot. There were also cactus plants, fig and pomegranate trees, and large bushes covered with flowers, some white, some red and some purple. Anna said, pointing at them:

"Do you like the Oleanders?"

"They are pretty," said Luna, "but I never saw one before." Anna shook her head:

"I forget, you come from the North, they wouldn't grow there."

"You wouldn't believe how far north I come from!" Said Luna.

Her uncle didn't speak at all, he just gave her an encouraging smile once in a while, and she felt comforted by that. At last they drove into Pontecorvo, and stopped at a large plaza right in the center of town. There were buses stopped on the side, and small restaurants and coffee shops lined up on one side of the street. There were newspaper booths, a bakery and a hairdresser with a large sign that advertised Perms.   'Get the curls you were supposed to be born with, by Gaetana the hairdresser' it said and it looked to be a very busy place. Uncle Pasquale stopped near the buses, and from the truck Luna could see that on the other side of the street there was nothing but a sheer drop down.   At the bottom of this drop there seemed to be a whole other town. There were other roads and houses covered in flowers, and lots of people walking about and more demolished houses too. They came out of the truck, and a couple minutes later a young man wearing a coverall exited the coffee shop and crossed the street. He took the bundles out of Anna's hands, and said:

"Hello' Ma. Did you get a ride?" Anna explained how she met Luna on the train, and this was her uncle who came to pick her up. She then said:

"I want to go see my little friend tomorrow, to see how she's getting along. She's from the North and not used to these parts. I don't think they live too far up from you. Meet her uncle and get directions to their farm; you're driving me there tomorrow afternoon." The young man talked to Luna's uncle. His name was Mario Merolli. He asked directions to her uncle's farm and they agreed on a time. Luna's uncle asked him why they still hadn't met, as they lived so close. Mario said he was a sharecropper from up near Frosinone, had been for almost fifteen years, but his father, Giovanni Merolli, had decided to retire and Mario and his family came down some months ago to run the farm for him. Luna's uncle said that he knew the farm and his owner, and both were in great need of help:

"I should say so!" Said Mario. "I haven't stopped working since I got here!" Uncle Pasquale asked him if he needed any help, and Mario told him that they were raising a barn the following week, and could use another pair of hands. Good-natured Uncle Pasquale said:

"Don't worry, I'll be there." Anna crushed Luna to her bosom, and said:

"See you tomorrow Luna Blue!" She got into a Model T-like car and they drove off in a puff of smoke. Uncle Pasquale said:

"Let's go, Little Luna. Your cousin Ivana has been waiting for you anxiously, not to mention your Aunt Esther. And we don't want to keep them waiting."

Luna sat next to the kind man almost happily, although she had a permanent knot in her stomach. In fact, she was almost getting used to that uncomfortable feeling, hoping it would go away when she was finally at the end of her journey. The thought that her parents did not exist in this time and place, and that she was all alone in a strange universe of so long ago, gave her a chilling hurt. She would have welcomed with opened arms even that little brat; Kyle. They drove in silence through the town, with the road taking a downward path. Everywhere you looked, there were beautiful, colorful houses and some ruined ones about to fall apart, also from the war, no doubt. At one point, they crossed a bridge, and Luna could see brown, turbulent waters under it. Her Uncle said that it was the bridge that gave the town its name. In olden times, the town was called Pontecurvo, because of the curved bridge, but over the centuries, the name had changed to Pontecorvo. There were many legends as to why, but his favorite was that of the ravens. He said that every evening at twilight, dozens of ravens would flock to the bridge, and from that, Luna suddenly knew that bridge was Ponte in Italian, and raven was corvo, hence Pontecorvo. Unbidden, Luna whispered to herself:

"Open here I flung the shutter, when with many a flirt and flutter, in there stepped a stately raven, of the saintly days of yore."

Edgar Allan Poe's lines gave Luna a chill. She didn't remember listening when Mr. Wheenie read that on the First Day of School. Was it only yesterday when things were still 'normal'? She must remember to read the whole thing when, or if, she got home. Wait a minute! Read the whole thing? What the heck was happening to her? She didn't like reading, unless it was magazines with lots of pictures:

"Something's happening to me." Thought Luna, but she was not sorry, life was a lot more exciting when you don't know what is going to happen to you, and you fear for your life! It was scary too, though.

They traveled across the bridge, where they met several roads going different ways. Uncle Pasquale took a far right, and bypassed a large church on his left. The road he took was kind of narrow, and it had small storefronts where they sold just about everything you could want; from gold to cloth to vegetables. The streets were crowded, and Uncle Pasquale said that this was the Pastine quarters, the lower part of town, where the more common folk lived; it was a great, friendly place. The wealthy, important people all lived uptown, in the Civita quarters: it was also a great, friendly place, in a high class sort of way, of course! In about five minutes, they left the town behind, travelling down a small, winding country road. They passed solitary farmsteads, where they saw the odd person working in the fields here and there. Luna asked her uncle:

"Uncle, that lady, Anna, was wearing some funny shoes. I've never seen anything like them!" Her uncle looked at her and smiled:

"They're called Cioce or Cioci, I prefer Cioci, and people have been wearing them over here for hundreds of years, when only rich town folks had real shoes. My own parents wore them, but now only the old folks do. Because of the Cioci this region is not only called Lazio, the official name, but it's also known as Ciociaria. During the war, when there was no leather to be had, folks made Cioci with rubber cut out from old truck tires. They were very interesting and unusually sturdy." Luna was thoughtful, imagining how tough things must have been if people were making their shoes out of truck tires. She felt lucky that at home nothing like that had ever happened. She had heard of wars, of course, there was always one going on in some place or other, but hearing it from the people who were there, it kind of gave you the shivers. She had never given a thought to wars or conflicts, but she now realized how bad they were, and hoped that she would never have to go through one in her lifetime.

IL COSTUME LOCALE

6. *Uomo e donna in costume locale*. Foto montata su cartoncino pesante retrointestato. Circa 1890. Fotografo: P A. Esposito & Figli, Napoli.

Man and woman in Pontecorvo local dress 1890.
P. A. Esposito & Sons

Finally they arrived at a large driveway. Uncle Pas turned to the right into it, and said:

"We're home!" The driveway veered to the left, and on her right Luna saw a small cluster of houses, while Uncle Pasquale made for a big house all the way to the left. He beeped, and the front door of the big house opened and out spilled a young girl probably Luna's age, who ran towards the truck. Uncle Pasquale stopped the truck in front of the house, and stepped out of it to go around and open the door for Luna.

The girl was taller than Luna, and had brown hair and brown eyes. Her hair was in two long braids that flew out behind her like banners.   Her beautiful, suntanned face had a large smile plastered on it, and she threw herself at Luna and hugged the bejezees out of her. She smacked both her cheeks with big sloppy kisses, and cried joyfully:

"Finally! Finally you're here, Luna Blue! I do so love saying your name, it's wonderful, and it's so different than any name I know. You people really are smart, up North; my little cousin!"

"Let your cousin breathe, Ivana." Said Uncle Pasquale. Luna disentangled herself from this alien show of affection, and looked up. Near the front door, standing quietly was a woman. She was severe looking, tall and angular in a shapeless cotton dress. Her dark hair was braided tightly, and the braid was rolled up like a coronet on top of her head. As Luna looked up at her, a welcoming smile softened her features, and for a few seconds she was just beautiful. Luna walked shyly up to her and her Aunt Esther bent down and hugged her briefly:

"Come in! Come in Luna, you must be very tired. I'll show you your room, and after you change into clean clothes, you can come down to dinner." Ivana eagerly asked:

"Can I show her, Mom?"

"Yes, but don't tire her with your chatter," said Aunt Esther, "Luna has traveled very far to get here, and she's probably very tired." Luna kept looking at Ivana and Aunt Esther; something very strange was happening, she could have sworn that she had seen them before, or at least they looked very familiar to her. She shook her head as if to clear it; it was probably the shock of being so far from home, because there was no way she could have ever seen either one of them before. Uncle kept looking at her, but he just smiled every time she threw a questioning look at him.

Inside, the house was all bricks, tiles and stonework, and a large tiled staircase went from the entrance to the second floor. Luna followed Ivana, who ran up agilely carrying Luna's suitcase. On the second floor there was a long hallway, and at the end of it small wooden stairs went up to what was probably an attic. That's where Ivana headed, and at the top of the stairs there was a small landing with two doors. Ivana opened the door on the right, and they walked into a small, whitewashed room:

"Here we go! This is your room, right across from mine. You have the better view, all I see from mine is the barn." Said Ivana. Luna looked out of the window and saw unlimited, peaceful green fields. She then looked around at the plain, almost Spartan room, and desultorily thought how different this room was from her room at home. There was no TV, no frilly curtains, no homework desk, no large shelf filled to overflowing with plush animals, no large closet overflowing with shoes and clothes, no big bed with pink sheets and coverlet to match, no CD or DVD shelf, no bookshelf and, of course, no computer. This was more like a nun's cell, with a small, austere bed, a small table and chair, and a small bureau with a large pitcher and bowl on it. On the wall a large picture of Saint Maria Goretti, the child Virgin Saint, (how she knew this was a big surprise to Luna) was the only decoration in the room. But somehow this room fitted Luna's mood very well, and with a sigh she sat on the hard little bed. Ivana touched Luna's hair and sighted:

"I wish my mother would let me cut my hair short, like yours. I so would love to look different than anybody, like you, but she wouldn't let me do anything fun."

"Welcome to the club!" Said Luna, "my mother doesn't let me do anything I want either. I guess parents are all the same everywhere." She stopped talking, embarrassed. She didn't know what else to say to her cousin, and Ivana shook herself and said:

"Well, get changed into your everyday clothes, and then come down to eat. Mama made some special food just because you're here." Luna was baffled, she thought she was already wearing everyday clothes, but she put her small suitcase on the bed and opened it. Inside she saw three pairs of cotton underwear, three cotton undershirts, three little long sleeved cotton shirts in different colors, and three little skirts in different colors, one was a plaid. There were three little plain housedresses in subdued colors, three pairs of white socks, three small nightgowns, and a small, cotton robe. She also had three little slips, the kind her grandmother wore under her dresses. For shoes she had a brown pair exactly like the black ones she was wearing, a pair of slippers and a pair of leather sandals. Luna was immensely relieved that she didn't see some shoes-contraptions in her suitcase that resembled Anna's footwear. What surprised Luna was the fact that all of her possessions were not brand new; they had a slightly used look to them, although everything was scrupulously clean. Luna picked a light blue housedress, changed her underclothes, wore the dress over the slip and clean undies, and slipped the sandals on her feet. She looked for a hamper, but saw none, so she just threw her dirty clothes on the floor, next to her bed, and looked in her bag for a brush. She didn't find a brush, but found a comb, and pulled it through her hair carelessly. She went out of her bedroom and retraced her steps to the first floor. She heard voices through a door, and pulled it open, ready to face her new time and place as bravely as she could.

When Luna showed up at the door, Ivana ran to help her get her seat at the table, and Luna whispered in her ear:

"I was looking for the ………you know……..the restroom, and couldn't find it upstairs, can you show me where it is?" Ivana wrinkled her forehead and said:

"The rest room? You rest in your bedroom, that's what we do here." Luna colored a little and stammered:

"The place where you take a bath and do other things, you know?" Ivana suddenly understood, and exclaimed:

"Oh, I know! You're talking about the Water Closet. We don't have indoor toilets here yet, they have them in town, and papa' will build one very soon, as soon as he can get the plumbing, the tub and some people to help him dig up the cesspool, and the tiles and all the other stuff you need for an indoor place. For now we use the one outside. Come with me, I'll show you where it is." She ran outside, and Luna followed her, embarrassed. Right in front of the house there was a gigantic mulberry tree with a swing hanging high up, and underneath stood a small, wooden structure, like a shed. Ivana opened the small door and showed Luna what was inside. Needless to say, she realized that this was the barebones toilet they were looking for. She asked Ivana:

"This is it? Where's the toilet paper, how do you flush this?" Ivana giggled:

"The paper is there, hanging on the wall, and you do not flush it, every few days papa' turns the dirt in there." Luna stepped inside and closed the door. There was a small latch to hold it in place and on the wall there was a nail with some squares of cut up newspaper stuck there. The seat was a makeshift wooden round shape with a hole in the middle, and underneath it lurked a dark and dank space. Luna was thankful that it didn't smell as bad as she expected. She quickly used it:

"A square of newspaper? Really!" And she was quickly out of there. Walking back to the house, she asked Ivana:

"How long do you think it will take your father to build one in the house?"

"Oh, I don't know, two, three years maybe!" Luna sighed:

"How about washing up? Is it too much to expect that you maybe have a tub in the house someplace?" Ivana cheerfully answered:

"Of course we do! It's in the pantry, every Saturday night papa' gets it down from its hook, and mama fills it up with warm water for our baths." Luna just stopped asking questions, for now she was just so hungry that she could eat a raven, and no doubt she was going to be served one.

When they went back inside, Ivana's parents were already settled at the table, and the platters of food were already out. Luna looked around for a television. She knew that they existed somewhere in the 1950's, but obviously not on this farm. In front of Luna sat a large plate of homemade pasta, with red sauce and cheese on top. She asked:

"Is this all mine?"

"Of course!" Said Aunt Esther. "You're a growing girl; you need to eat!"

"Wow!" Thought Luna, "no diet warnings here; maybe this Italian pasta has no calories." The food smelled great, and Luna tucked in with gusto. After she finished her pasta, she sat back replete and hoped there wasn't much more food coming out because she couldn't eat another bite. After everyone had finished their pasta, nobody moved to get more food, they just sat there talking to each other about their day. Uncle Pas (as Luna renamed him) was telling Aunt Esther about Mario Merolli and the proposed visit on the following day, and Ivana asked Luna what class she was in. Luna said ninth grade, and Ivana was very surprised and asked her a lot of questions about her school. She told Luna that they only had up to fifth grade, after that, they had three years of junior high, and four years of high school. Ivana said that in town they had all the classes and the teachers in a big school building, but on the farm there were so few students that they only had one teacher, only one schoolroom, and they were thought all together:

"You'll be going to school with me in the morning, and then you'll see for yourself." Luna was astounded:

"I have to go to school? I thought I was on vacation." Aunt Esther turned to Luna and said:

"It's against the law not to send you to school at your age. The police would come and we would be in trouble."

"How the police even know that I'm here?" Asked Luna arrogantly:

"Because we have notified them of your arrival dear!" Said Aunt Esther. Luna started to get really angry:

"Why?" She said. Aunt Esther responded pacifically:

"Because it's the law, dear! You'll be staying with us for at least three months, if not more, and that's not considered a vacation; it's residency. The police will be here soon to check your papers." Luna's face started to get red. Not only was she stuck here in the boondocks of a hundred years ago, she had to submit to the stupid laws of this place that didn't even exist anymore. And she was going to be here three months? Over her dead body! She felt a temper tantrum coming on; she was not going to stand for this! Just wait and see! If that Balthazar showed up, she was going to tell him a thing or two! Ivana was obviously getting nervous and started to fidget, and Luna shouted:

"I don't have any papers!"

"Yes you do, Luna Blue." At Uncle Pas' words she remembered the envelope in her handbag, the one she didn't even bother to look at. She looked up and saw him look at her impassively, his eyes impenetrable, like he was watching an experiment. She saw something else in his enigmatic look; Uncle Pas knew about her! She realized that Uncle Pas knew when and where she came from, and why, and he was assessing her behavior. All at once Luna's eyes moistened and she looked at her uncle with regret. He smiled slightly at her and said:

"I think that we are ready for the rest of our meal, Estherina." Aunt Esther got up and went to get the rest of the food. She had a platter of very, very thin, wrinkly slices of meat; they were peppered with some kind of herb, and smelled great! But the most curious thing to Luna was the stove. It wasn't a stove at all, but a kind of brick structure, almost like a built-in barbeque, and at the top it had four separate chambers, opened in the front and topped by a grid. There was a small fire smoldering in the four chambers, and once in a while Aunt Esther poked the coals in the chambers and tried to disperse them in an obvious attempt to turn them off. The kitchen was large and sunny, and it contained the large table where they were sitting, topped by a humongous slab of marble covered by a snow white tablecloth, a great hutch filled with plates and glasses, and a large wooden chest on four chubby feet. Luna saw her aunt open the top of the chest and bring out a large item wrapped in a white napkin. It turned out to be a substantially large piece of bread, and Auntie sliced some of it and put it in the middle of the table, then rewrapped the loaf and put it back in the gargantuan bread box. It was like a kind of pie safe, bread box and general storage for all the baked goods. A heavenly smell came out of it every time someone opened it. At one end of the room, an immense fireplace stood guard, complete with hanging iron pot, and several tripods in different sizes. On the wall on one side of the fireplace were pots of every size hanging in a row, and on the other side there was a large assortment of utensils hanging in a row, from small to extremely large. Big hams, links of dried sausages, flats of bacon, some things that looked like heavy, white balloons and other assorted things that Luna couldn't place were hanging on the rafters of the kitchen, right along with bundles of herbs and braids of onions and garlic. After her assessment of the cheerful country kitchen, she turned back to her plate:

"What is this?" She asked Ivana:

"Sliced beef fried in olive oil and sprinkled with oregano." Luna cut off a small piece and tested it. It was the best meat she had ever eaten, and being so thin, it didn't make her sick to her stomach, as all meat did. She cut a small piece off the large, thick slice of dark, supple bread, and dunked it in the juice, like she saw Uncle do. She looked up at him and saw him watching her with a small, approving smile on his face. And this food was so very good! She started to feel better. Maybe three months won't be so bad! Next to her plate, she had a small earthen bowl with bits of greens and bits of tomatoes and cucumbers; this she recognized; it was a salad, of course. Luna looked for the salad dressing, and Ivana said:

"The oil and vinegar are next to the pitcher of water." In fact, to drink they had a large pitcher of spring water, and a large pitcher of red wine. Luna watched Ivana put a little wine in her glass and add some spring water to it. So she did the same. Somehow she knew that asking for ice was just a waste of time:

"Lukewarm wine cooler! It wasn't that bad!" The salad was really good, even with just oil and vinegar on top; in fact, it was actually better, not so greasy. After the meal, Ivana and Aunt Esther got up and started to put things away, and Luna got up and helped a bit, even thought she didn't know where anything went. While the women worked, Uncle Pas pulled out a small pouch and a small box. He put them down on the table, and took out a tiny piece of very thin, white paper; he held it in the palm of his left hand, and with his right hand shook something out of the pouch onto the paper. He then lifted his left hand to his mouth, and licked the edge of the paper to moisten it. After that, he put the pouch down and with his right hand he rolled the white paper up tight and topped one end of it on the table to settle the content. Luna was mesmerized; Uncle Pas had just made a cigarette. In fact her uncle put it in his mouth and sparked a match to light up the cigarette he just made. After that he leaned back on his chair and with a sigh inhaled deeply and let out a small cloud of smoke. Luna pulled Ivana to the side and whispered to her:

"Your father is smoking."

"I know," whispered Ivana back, "he deserves it. He works very hard all day; a little relaxation is good for him!" Luna realized that in this time and place, cigarettes were not considered bad, and actually the smell from it wasn't as bad as she remembered:

"Where does he get that kind of tobacco?" Luna asked Ivana:

"From the storehouse."

"What storehouse?"

"Ours!"

"You have a storehouse of tobacco?"

"Of course we do." And at Luna's puzzled look, she added:

"This is a tobacco farm, silly, didn't you know?"

Luna couldn't believe it; she had never seen people grow and make their own anything, let alone cigarettes. Everything she saw came from big companies with Big Brand Names, and all anyone ever worried about was whether some stupid picture or this-or-that slogan would affect their children or not. Yet here was Uncle Pas growing his own tobacco and making his own cigarettes, without a care in the world. Luna wondered what all the stupid Snobs and Uptights she was used to would think of that.

After dinner, when all of the dishes and pots were stocked up in the sink, and everything else put away, Uncle Pas made a small pot of espresso, put it on a small tray with two small cups on small saucers and two small spoons, and carried it outside. On his way out, Uncle Pas put his free arm around Aunt's waist, and Aunt Esther, the sugar bowl in her hand, leaned her head on his shoulder while they were walking out. At this point, uncle Pas bend down a bit and whispered something in her ear. Aunt Esther looked up and whispered something back softly, and Uncle Pas threw his head back and laughed while Aunt Esther colored a little. Luna had not seen Uncle Pas laughing so carefree since she had met him, and then she saw him look at Aunt Esther with a look of such tenderness, that it almost made her cry. Luna realized that the two adults were just standing over there flirting like teenagers, and she stood there in a trance. Ivana turned to Luna and said:

"Oh, never mind them. They love each other, they're always doing that! When papa' feels sweet on her, he calls her Estherina, that's his pet name for mama. When I hear that, I stay away from them, who wants to see that! Let's have our own coffee and dessert." She picked up another small pot, and quickly made some very dark coffee:

"We are having some chicory coffee, we're too young to have the real espresso, but it's not bad, it's better than nothing." After she had put the two very small cups and saucers on the table, with small spoons and a small container of sugar, she went to Gargantua (as Luna called the bread box) and pulled out a dish covered by another dish. After she removed the top dish, she displayed an assortment of cookies in various colors and shapes. She took three cookies for herself, and laid them on the side of the small dish that held her espresso cup. She then pushed the cookie dish to Luna. The cookies looked delicious and different, and Luna (who had a sweet tooth) would have liked to try them all, but she looked at Ivana with only three little cookies on her plate, and took just three for herself also. Ivana put the dish back on top of the cookies, and replaced the plate inside of Gargantua. She then put a large spoon of sugar in her coffee, and took a small sip. Luna said smiling:

"Ivana, are you having a little bit of coffee with your sugar?" Ivana laughed:

"Chicory coffee is quite bitter, you have to add a lot of sugar to it." And proceeded to add another bit of sugar to her small cup. Luna took a small sip, and the coffee was so bitter, she had never tested anything so bitter in her life. She then realized that Ivana knew what she was talking about, and added just as much sugar to her cup. After that, the coffee wasn't that bad, and mingled with small bites of cookies, was in fact quite pleasant. While they were having their coffee, Luna had followed the goings on outside with Uncle Pas and Aunt Esther. There was a small table with two chairs under a gnarled fig tree in the back of the house. Uncle Pas had chivalrously served the coffee to Aunt Esther and then reached up and plucked two juicy, plump figs from the tree and put one on Aunt Esther's dish, keeping one for himself. After that, they sipped their coffee, and ate their fruit while talking pleasantly to each other. You could see how much they enjoyed each other's company. After the coffee and dessert was done, the girls got up and did the dishes in the large, stone sink that sported a hand pump. Luna had learned to pump up and done to get the water to rinse the dishes, after Ivana had washed them with a bucket of hot water she had gotten off a kettle from one of the four barbeque-like pits in the kitchen. When everything had been put away, Ivana suggested they go to their room and get some rest. Luna was exhausted, and welcomed the idea, but first they visited the Black Hole, as Luna had renamed the outhouse. Back in her room, Luna lay down on the bed and fell asleep as soon as her head hit the pillow. She dreamed of having to walk with very large Cioci on her feet, and they were not even made of leather, hers were made of tire rubber. The worst thing was that she was wearing them on her way to school back home, and a group of people were following her, pointing at her shoes and laughing out loud. But slowly the people melted away one by one, and she was back here, and no one took any exception to her wearing pieces of tires on her feet, in fact they smiled at her and nodded approvingly.

When Luna woke up about two hours later, she felt much better. Ivana knocked on her door, telling Luna that if she was up to it, she would take her around to meet the other inhabitants of their little hamlet. It was late afternoon, and Luna had all of her energy back, so she agreed readily. They changed into fresh clothes (Luna had never changed so many times in one day) and after telling Aunt Esther where they were going, they were off. They walked off the front door, and took a left, to the first house in the small cluster of buildings. Ivana said that that was the house of Great Aunt and Uncle Marianna and Biagio. She told Luna that this couple's children were their aunts and uncles as they were her father's cousins:

"You'll meet them later." Ivana said. "One of their sons is married to the teacher." When they showed up at the door, a tiny old lady opened the door for them, and a small, wrinkled gentleman with long handlebar mustaches came to greet them. They were hugged, kissed, and made to sit in the good dining room. While Great-Aunt Marianna laid a white napkin on each of their places, and gently served them some small sweet buns, Great-Uncle Biagio asked about Luna's parents. Luna said that they were fine and her brother too. Great-Uncle Biagio said he had often wondered about them, they had left so long ago, and when he heard they were sending their daughter to spend three months, he was overjoyed:

"That proves that blood is thicker than water!" He said: "That they trusted their precious daughter to us for that long period of time, proved that they had not forgotten their roots, and that they trusted their family still." He then leaned over and caressed Luna's cheek. Luna was overwhelmed by this welcome, and wondered who they were talking about, but said nothing; this was probably one of Balthazar's adjustments. The small, fluffy buns were light as a feather (Luna knew in her mind that they were called maritozzi) and barely sweet, but they went very well with the small glass of thick, rich milk that was served with them. They left with the promise of further visits, and walked to the next building, which was very close, almost attached, with only a small space in-between the two buildings; just enough for a person to pass through. Ivana said that this was the house of Uncle Luigi and Aunt Nannina, two children of great uncle and aunt next door, and Luigi's daughter Giustina. Luigi was a widower, and he made his home with his sister. Aunt Nannina was home, with Giustina, who at sixteen was Ivana's and Luna's cousin. Nannina was a teacher in town. She had never married, and she drove her own car. She was pretty advanced for this time and place. She was a good-looking, solid blonde woman, and Giustina was almost a younger copy of her; you could see that her aunt was her idol. While Ivana was talking to Giustina about some boy they both knew, Aunt Nannina asked Luna questions about her mother:

"Is she still pretty, or serving a man for twenty years has taken its toll?" Luna could answer with complete honesty that her mother was still the same girl as she always was, and that her father didn't expect to be served or anything, in fact he was always asking her mother to hire people to clean the house, but her mother always said:

"Thank you, dear, but I don't like strangers touching my things, I much rather do it myself." Nannina sniffed:

"The same silly woman as she always was, I see! She plays right into his hands. I would love to see his reaction if she said yes!" At this point so would have Luna. This was something her parents always argued about. They were sitting on a lovely little terrace on one side of the house, and the whole place was a riot of flowers. The sweet fragrance of flowers, mostly giant carnations of all different colors, hanging geraniums and small white roses was everywhere, and added to the sweet fragrance of homemade chocolate truffles shining on a small plate, made Luna long to share all this with her family back home. She wondered how they were. But then, Balthazar had said that she would be returned home at the same instant that she had left, so she already knew how they were: mad and angry, of course! But sitting on this small terrace, talking quietly while chewing on sweets with the droning of yellow bees hovering over the flowers, was very pleasant, if sweetly melancholy. They left the welcoming little place, and walked to the end of the little group of houses. At the very end stood a small two story house, it looked to be only two rooms, one at street level, and another on top. Ivana said:

"This is the last house we will visit. Aunt Palma lives here. We all call her Aunt, but I don't really know what she is to everyone. I think she's Great-Uncle Biagio's sister, but I'm not entirely sure. She's ninety years old. Her husband died many, many years ago, and she never had any children." They knocked at the tiny front door, and the tiniest old woman Luna had ever seen opened it and welcomed them. She was plump and pink, and her piercing blue eyes looked them over from a finely wrinkled, round little face. She was wearing a plain cotton blouse and a gathered skirt, and she had a small kerchief tied around her head. All Luna could think of was the munchkins from the Wizard of Oz. On her feet she wore the 'Anna' shoes, all wrapped around her legs. Aunt Palma was expecting them; she knew by word of mouth that they were visiting, so she had waited impatiently on her little window until they arrived. She hugged and kissed the two girls with surprising strength, and ushered them into the small dining room in the front of the house. The bottom floor consisted of a tiny kitchen and the dining room, and the top floor was one bedroom with a tiny storage room attached. This she explained to Luna, because, obviously Ivana already knew. She flitted about the little dining room saying that they must have gotten all kinds of sweet and fat stuff in the other houses, and she was going to settle their stomachs with some medicinal elixir of her own making. She poured them each the smallest glass of some gold colored nectar, and Luna was very curious to know what it was. She sipped it a bit, and came out sputtering. The stuff was very strong, and it had some bitter tang to it. Ivana looked over at Luna and mouthed, behind Aunt Palma's back:

"It's made with walnut husks, it's called nocello, it really settles your stomach, and it grows on you. You better drink it, or Aunt Palma will give you Cynar, artichoke brandy, and that's really bitter!" Luna sipped it slowly, and found that it left a pleasant aftertaste in her mouth. She finished it, and started to listen to Aunt Palma's diatribe about food:

"I know the others gave you girls fat and tasty food. They always do. If you eat stuff like that all the time you'll die young, at seventy or eighty. Look at me, I'm over ninety, and I'm still going strong. I never eat anything fat or sweet; I never eat anything good, never! All I ever eat are beans, never anything good….." She sniffed self righteously: "Of course, I drink a good dose of my elixir morning, noon and night." Finally, she started to ask questions about Uncle Pas and Aunt Esther, and knowing that her turn came right after that, Luna sat quietly and enjoyed the slow pace. Culture shock was wearing off, and she started to accept these strange people, almost feeling rested and peaceful, without the constant rage she felt at home most of the time. Even though they were all so strange, and different from each other, they all had one thing in common; they were genuinely interested in her, and they were all very kind, in their unique and different way. When they left Aunt Palma with promises of future visits, Ivana asked Luna if she wanted to go home or if she felt a little adventurous. Luna felt adventurous, and Ivana said:

"I want to show you the river that runs through our farm. It's called The River Liri; it's fast and dangerous, but I love to look at it. I imagine all kinds of adventures when I do. I know it's getting kind of late and the sky's getting red and soon it will be dark, but if we hurry, we can make it." From the little house, they took a right and walked down a barely discernible path. There were fields on both sides, which soon turned to bramble, and on both sides there were ancient, tall trees branching out on both sides of

the path. Under the trees Luna could hear water running, and
Ivana said that there was a small brook under the giant trees.
There was one especially, on their right, which towered over
everything else. Ivana said:
"Walnut trees! We're almost ready to harvest our walnuts.
That's when Aunt Palma gets the husks, when they're still green
and juicy. We got some 'nocello' from last year's batch. The new
stuff will strangle you on the first sip!" They kept walking, and
soon they were picking their way through overgrown bushes and
small trees. Then they started to go downward, and suddenly
Luna heard it! The sound of fast running water made them start
running, and all at once the river was in front of them. Ivana
explained that it was the same river that went through the town,
but in town it was quite tame, while over here it was wild and full
of currents. They looked awed at the wild, brown water foaming
quickly past, carrying all manner of things, and the sound and
smell of it was like nothing Luna had ever experienced. She asked
Ivana why the water was brown, and was told that the riverbed
was mud and clay, and the turbulent water made it come to the
surface. Large, white pipes dipped on the sides of the river here
and there, and Luna was curious about them. Ivana said that they
were irrigation pipes; that they brought water to their fields, and
without the river there would be no point in growing tobacco,
because it needs a lot of water. Luna was amazed at the
complexities of farming, and wondered how many people worked
for Uncle Pas. Ivana said that he did everything mostly by himself,
but on planting and harvesting, the farmers all helped each other
with the work. She said that soon they would start the harvest,
and when they did, there would be banquets and parties after the
harvest in every farm they went. Luna's dreams came crashing
back, and she felt elated:
"I wonder if Aunt Esther will help me get a peasant blouse,
the kind that leaves one of your shoulders bare." She thought.
The sky was turning from red and orange to black, and the two
girls held hands while crashing through the brambles on the path.
They got home red cheeked and disheveled, and Aunt Esther,
after listening smiling to their adventure and chiding them for
getting too close to the river, told them to change into their
housedresses and come down to the evening meal:

"Changing again!" Smiled Luna, and she was almost happy. If only Mom, Dad and, yes, even Kyle, were here, she could almost be happy in Italy in the 1950's.

After a late supper of a thick wedge of vegetable omelet and a small piece of cheese, with a small slice of bread and some tomato slices, they visited the black hole and then went up to their rooms. They both carried with them a glass of spring water garnished with a slice of lemon left over from supper. On her bureau Luna found a cup containing a toothbrush and a small tube of toothpaste, next to a small pitcher of more fresh water. Next to it she found the large pitcher and bowl she had seen when she had first arrived, and it was full of lukewarm water, with a white towel folded on top. On top of the towel Luna found a small bar of yellow soap and a small square of linen. She stuck her head out the door and asked Ivana where she should throw the used water, and Ivana responded:

"Out the window!" At that, Luna brushed her teeth, did her ablutions, and wore one of the little cotton nightgowns from her suitcase. All of her used clothes were now on the floor, at the foot of the bed. She was sure that tomorrow Aunt Esther would take care of them for her, like her Mom always did. She was pleasantly exhausted, and slid gratefully under the blankets. The small wind-up clock on her bureau said it was nine o'clock.

River Liri waterfall.
Vintage Photograph

It seemed that Luna had just put her head down on her pillow when someone was shaking her awake:

"Wake up sleepy head, it's getting late."

"What time is it?" Mumbled Luna:

"It's already five o'clock, we have to hurry up."

"Five o'clock in the morning?" Luna said disbelieving, "I don't think I've ever got up at five in the morning in my entire life!" Ivana laughed:

"Well, you will from now on, believe me! Besides, if you sleep the day away, you'll miss all kinds of stuff. I for one can't wait to get up and get started." They got dressed (Luna was starting to run out of clothes).

"I hope Aunt Esther takes care of this mess fast." She thought. They went downstairs, and there was no one around:

"Where is everyone?" Asked Luna:

"Dad is working in the north field today, and Mom is washing clothes at the Pilone, our fresh water spring. Come on, we have work to do." Luna and Ivana quickly visited the black hole and Luna thought how they didn't really need a fancy bathroom, they never spent any time in there like at home, and they were always too busy running around somewhere. After the black hole they went in the kitchen to pick up earthenware jugs to get spring water for the day. Ivana explained how the water they pumped in the kitchen was not as pure as the spring water, and they did not use it for drinking, cooking or making coffee, that two jugs would be enough for the day. These jugs were rustic, made of pink, unfinished pottery; they were round and had a pot belly and two large handles, and rudimentary designs on the front. Ivana said that they were called cannatas, and that the water soaked right through the unfinished and unglazed surface and kept the contents fresh and cool all day. They turned left from the front door, and walked down to the drive going to the country road. They passed it, going down to a little knoll at the bottom of the hill. Spread out in front of her Luna saw an idyllic sight; to the left there was a long, rectangular pool of water, in two gradations, with a cement wall holding the water in, and on the right there was a very green, overhanging canopy of some flowering plant, held up by a pylon. Luna knew at once that pylon was pilone in Italian, hence the name for the spring. Under the plant a round font bubbled with spring water, the noise coming from it gentle and steady. From this the water was guided onto the pools, and at the end of the second one, Aunt Esther was kneading and swishing clothes in the water with leisurely motions. From there the water went into a bubbling brook, and Ivana said that that was the water that ran under the walnut trees. The girls greeted Aunt and then went to fill their jugs. While they were doing so, some young boy came down to the pilone with two large cows. His name was Remigio, and he was helping Great Uncle Biagio. Luna was introduced, then the cows drank their fill on the first gradation of the pool, and they left. Near the bubbling, round brook, Luna suddenly felt very thirsty, and told Ivana how they should have brought cups. Ivana laughingly said they didn't need them, and proceeded to pull a large, flat leaf from one of the aquatic plants growing between the rocks that formed the well from which the water sprang. She twisted the big leaf to form a cone, dipped it in the spring, and came up with a container full of the freshest water Luna had ever seen. She offered it to Luna, and Luna drank her fill. Then they dipped the jugs into the open well, and pulled them up full and dripping. Afterwards, they walked back home. Luna's jug was heavy, and she kept juggling it from one hand to the other, but Ivana seemed not to mind, so Luna did not complain, even though her dress was getting soaked on the side. When they got home, they put the jugs in their spot near the back door, and went back outside. Ivana asked Luna:

"What do you want for breakfast, curds and whey or bread and fresh farmer's cheese?" Luna had never had either one for breakfast, but considering that she did not know what curds and whey looked like, (she only ever heard of them when Little Miss Muffet was Sitting on her Tuffet) she opted for bread and farmers cheese:

"Bread and cheese it is, then!" Said Ivana. Luna followed Ivana to a large building in the back of the house. They pushed the large, heavy door and entered a long, semi-dark chamber. Inside it smelled almost like a zoo, and Luna saw various animals tethered in their open stalls. There were a couple of very large cows, a small animal that looked like a horse (Ivana said it was really a donkey), a real horse, and a smaller, tame-looking cow. Ivana picked up a small stool, pulled it next to the cow, grabbed a large bucket and put it next to her. She then went to a rough sink in the back of the barn and scrubbed her hands thoroughly. After that she sat down and grabbing the cows hanging, large udders, started to pull down rhythmically at the hanging things under them. Luna was horrified. She whispered:

"What are you doing?"

"I'm milking the cow of course. How do you think we're going to have cheese for breakfast?" After a surprisingly short time, the bucket was full of steaming, frothy milk. Luna thought to herself:

"I'm not having any of that stuff, that's for sure!" Ivana said:

"I'll teach you to do it, so we can take turns." Luna backed up slowly, unbelievingly. She was going to draw a line on touching the private parts of large animals with her hands, and that was that! It was amusing how the cow just kept on eating her cud while someone was pulling on her big 'things' hanging there, but Luna was not going to do it, no siree Bob, and no one was going to make her!

Soon, Luna found herself pulling and squeezing at the same time, and Ivana was cheering her on. Luna was milking a cow! When finally the white stuff started coming out and spraying in the bucket, Luna was so elated that she didn't even mind touching the cow's private parts. After all, if the cow didn't mind, why should she? She remembered what Myrna used to say when someone urged her to drink milk at school:

"What, you want me to drink a cow's bodily fluids? Not me, that's for sure!" And Luna was laughing to herself. It seemed that her real life was a million years ago; or maybe just sixty years from now. Suddenly very sad, Luna spilled some tears in her fresh, raw milk. When they had two buckets full, Ivana poured one of them in a large glass jug with a narrow neck, put a cork stopper on it, tied a piece of rope to the neck of the jug, and told Luna to wait for her. After a few minutes she came back, and at Luna's question she responded that she brought the jug to the Pilone and tied it to a nail in the wall of the well, letting the jug of milk hang in the cold, pure water so it could stay fresh all day, until her mom needed it for something. Then she took the second bucket, poured the milk in an oblong tin container, fed the cow some hay, and together they took the remaining milk back home. The tin container was trusted on top of the quasi-stove; it took two burners since it was so long, and two small fires started under it. After a few minutes, Ivana took some milk with a spoon, tested it, moved the tin to the next two burners and picked up a dried up piece of stuff from the hutch. It looked almost like beef jerky, and Ivana cut a small piece and threw it in the milk. Luna looked curiously at her, and Ivana said:

"Rennet! It's what turns milk into cheese by clotting it."

"What it's made of?" Asked Luna. Ivana said:

"You don't want to know. I'll tell you some other time, when you're more used to how we do things here." After mixing the milk a bit, she covered the tin with a cloth towel, and declared that they should go to their rooms to wash-up and get dressed for school. Luna had forgotten about school. She noticed on the big, wind-up kitchen clock that it was seven A.M.:

"What time are we going to school?" She asked Ivana:

"Nine o'clock!"

They brought with them some warm water from the kitchen in little cannatas, and went to their respective rooms. Luna washed up, wore the plaid skirt with a pink blouse that picked-up one of the colors of the plaid, her brown shoes, and fixed her hair nice, by teasing and fluffing, and pulling small, stray curls around her face. She thought that she truly looked nice for her first day in the new, strange school, in a new, strange place, with a new, strange teacher, in an old, strange time. She walked into the kitchen and found Ivana picking up a great lump from the tin, and putting it in a colander lined with some kind of loose cloth. Ivana said:

"Our cheese will be ready in about half an hour. Let's finish our chores, and then we'll eat." Luna couldn't believe that the milk she had squeezed out of the cow was already turning into cheese. She followed Ivana outside and they donned some big aprons, in whose pockets they put large handfuls of dried corn. They walked to the back of the house, and Luna saw a small wooden building surrounded by chicken wire. Ivana said that was the chicken coup. They opened a small gate in the wire fence, and walked inside. Lots of chickens came out of the small building and surrounded them. Some were roosters (Ivana explained that to Luna) and some were hens. Some were chicks and some were capons. The capons, Ivana explained, were young chickens which her mother had neutered in the spring. They were bigger and fatter than the other chickens, because all they were interested in was food. When they got neutered, after Aunt Esther was finished taking all of their little chicken beans out of their little bodies and sawed their skin back up, they had a large plate of chicken beans left and boy, were they delicious fried with onions! Luna hoped to God she would never have to see that, and eat parts of chickens that were still running around alive. Together they spread the feed on the ground before going back home. Ivana pulled the cloth out of the colander, tied it very tight and hung it on a hook over a basin. She religiously saved all of the yellow water which leaked out from the cheese, saying that her mother was going to make ricotta with it. They then went back to the barn, and fed the rest of the animals some hay. By then it was around eight o'clock, and Ivana said they were now going to eat breakfast.

They put out two large plates, took a loaf of bread out of Gargantua, sliced two nice slices out of it, replaced it, laid some forks and two glasses of milk, and sat down to eat. Ivana opened the cheesecloth in a large bowl, took two jelly-like slices of cheese, tied it back up tight, and hung it up over the bowl again. She plopped one slice in each plate and they dug in. By then, Luna was starving. She cut a small piece of cheese with her fork, put it in her mouth, and accompanied it with a small piece of bread. The cheese was soft, buttery and so tasty; it almost melted in her mouth. Together with the piece of bread it was so heavenly, so delicious, and just so GOOD, that Luna, who had never liked cheese before, ate the whole thing with pleasure. Imagine, the milk she had squeezed out of that cow had turned into delicious cheese, the best she ever had, in just two hours. She was starting to like making her own food, and she thought of her friends and how surprised they would be if they knew that Luna Blue was turning into a bona fide farm girl.

Pontecorvo Bridge, circa 1950's
Vintage Photographs

Ivana said:

"Let's go to school, then." Luna asked what they should take with them, and Ivana said: "Just our handkerchiefs." In fact Ivana had one in the pocket of her skirt. Luna looked in her handbag, and indeed she did have a handkerchief, but no pocket to put it in. Ivana said:

"Just put in your waistband and let's go." Luna didn't believe how easy this was. She remembered going to school so loaded with stuff, from notebooks to her unbelievably heavy school books, from every kind of pen and pencil to various other supplies that she never remembered ever using, that she felt like a mule. Not to mention the ever present fear of forgetting the cell phone or the (supposedly not allowed) IPod. That cell phone was so important in her life, that it was impossible to go a minute without it. And God forbid you lost the stupid thing (which happened to Luna more than once) It was screams and reiterations, and cancelled allowances to pay for a new one. Here a cell phone was not the all-important thing everyone thought it to be. In fact, Luna had not thought of her cell phone even once since coming here. She felt carefree and light, and skipped along the long driveway on their way to school. When they got to the road, they took a right, and walked along for some minutes, and then they turned into another driveway and after a few minutes a large house stood in front of them right in the center of a large clearing. In front of the house, a group of young people stood, milling around. They were of different ages, from children to teenagers. Ivana saluted everyone with confidence, and then she introduced Luna as her cousin from the North, who was going to spend three months with them. Everyone was interested, and Luna felt shy with everyone looking at her. She was hoping nobody decided to dislike her and start bullying her, like what happened to a lot of new kids at home. She also noticed that the girls were mostly dressed like Ivana, and their hair was mostly braided, making her look different. Luna knew how kids who were different were sometimes ostracized, and it was very difficult to feel part of the group. Some of the girls walked up to her while Ivana was talking to the mother of one of the younger children, and Luna involuntarily took up a defensive stance, ready to defend herself. But the girls smiled at her, and asked her how she fixed her hair like that. They were all amazed at how her hair stood up soft and curly, and wanted to know how she did it. Some of them speculated the maybe Luna had gotten a permanent at the new hairdresser in town, but Luna said she had seen the place on her way from the train station, but she didn't go in. She said:

"First you have to cut your hair, of course!" At that first they all laughed, and then they all sighted and said that if only their mothers were more modern and let them do it. Luna told them that long hair was wonderful, and that braids were very nice, if only they would change their style a bit. Everyone said:

"What can you do to braids? There's only one way of doing them." Luna said that where she came from braids were so appreciated, that even people who had short hair wanted to look like they had braids, so they attached fake ones to their hair. The girls were amazed and very pleased, and they wanted to know if she knew other ways of fixing them. Luna told them that she really didn't know much about hair, but she could help them to learn how to do French braids. She used to help Myrna with her French braids, and a small twinge hurt her, thinking of her friends so far away, in both time and space. Ivana was informed of this development, and she told everyone that she would ask her mother when they could get together. Although Luna was feeling very happy here, things big and small constantly reminded her that she did not in fact belong; she was from sixty years in the future, after all, and it would be impossible for her to forget everything she knew from her own time, ever. If she stayed here too long, she would just end up feeling sadder and lonelier as the memories piled up around her. She knew she would absolutely go home, to face her problems and be a normal and happy girl. And no matter how impossible those problems would seem, she knew that she would need to face them to have a future where she belonged. All of a sudden, Luna started feeling homesick for her time even more, and no matter how wonderful things were here, she just wanted to go HOME!! But she also knew that there were things to finish here first. And no matter how mad and upset she'd been before, she would face everything as best she could.

Maybe Uncle Pas could help her, or Balthazar would come back for her. How would Valeria have felt, being totally separated from anything she knew? True, she would have gone to the future, not the past, but Luna was starting to understand why Balthazar had chosen the way he did. Valeria would have been just as sad and lost as Luna was right now.

As everyone stood around outside, a door suddenly opened, and a woman walked out. Ivana murmured:

"The teacher!" Luna looked at the woman, not knowing what to expect. The teacher was a small woman probably in her late thirties; she wore her dark hair with a part on one side, and large waves that almost covered her eye, on the other side. The hair was collected at the base of her head in a stylish chignon. She wore make up, and a white, crepe shirt tucked into the waistband of a grey, straight skirt with a slit in the back. She looked attractive and genteel, if a touch faded and shabby, like her clothes were kept in immaculate condition, but were very old. On her feet she wore black pumps. As she moved among the people, Luna noticed that she was wearing nylons, but they had a seam in the back of her legs. Luna guessed that the teacher was a little old fashioned even for Italy in the 1950's. She was reminded of a movie her mother loved; 'The Great Gatsby'. Her mother had it permanently on her DVR, and it was not easy to ignore when she played it constantly (Mom had a thing for Robert Redford). Finally the teacher stopped in front of Luna, and Ivana moved right next to Luna in a protective gesture. The teacher extended her hand to Luna and when Luna took it hesitantly, the teacher shook it up and down, and said:

"Hallo', I'm to be your teacher during your stay with us, my name Is Gianna Longo, you may call me Mrs. Longo, or Teacher, as you please. You are a very pretty girl. Your Uncle said that you are from the North. We will talk some more later about where you come from. I myself came from the North of Italy, many years ago." Then turning to everyone: "Let's go inside, we have work to do." They all followed the teacher inside and walked right into a large room with lots of small tables and chairs. At one end of the room stood a large desk on top of a wooden platform, and behind the desk, a large blackboard hung on the wall. Luna stayed close to Ivana, but the teacher had other ideas. She pointed to a table and chair and told Luna to sit there. She then walked over and told Luna she had to talk to her later, to see where she belonged in the class. She then proceeded to pick up homework from everyone (it seemed that school had been already in session here for a few days) and handed out some work for everyone while she assessed the new girl. She sat across from Luna and started to ask her questions. Luna was at first scared, but she found that she knew the answers to what the teacher wanted to know. It was actually stuff she had really done in school. The teacher declared that she was surprised at Luna's knowledge, but actually she knew that schools were much more advanced in the North. The curriculum here was paced very slowly, and there was nothing that she could do about it, she had her orders and she had to follow them. After a while she gave Luna a book and she told her to start reading. She would later have to write an essay on it. The book was titled 'The Betrothed' by Alessandro Manzoni. Luna hated to read big books, and as far as big books went, this one took the cake. Luna found out, looking at it, that it was actually three volumes in one. It started placidly enough, talking about Lake Como, a country priest named Don Abbondio and two young people named Renzo and Lucia who were engaged and wanted to get married. But it soon became a sad and violent story about the rights of the lord over a poor country couple. And this was just the first ten pages. It was a relief when the teacher announced that it was time for a break, in case anyone needed to go outside. Luna was surprised to see that it was already eleven am, and that two hours had passed so fast. She went outside with Ivana and the other girls their age, and did not need to use the black hole, so they just stood there talking about their work. They told Luna that the teacher would take it easy on her, because she was new, but they had to work really hard to pass this class. One of the girls wanted to be a teacher when she grew up, because being a farm wife was just too hard. She said her mother worked from sunup to sundown, and she didn't want that life. Ivana said:

"My mother is a farm wife, and she loves it!"

"That's because your father is a nice guy." The girl responded: "Some husbands are not nice, and they make their wives work like mules. I will not let a man order me around; I'll be my own person and take care of myself." Ivana got very close to all of them, and whispered:

"I heard my mom and dad talk, and they were saying that the teacher's husband is a brute, and that he beats her!" Luna was horrified. One of the girls said:

"I think it's her fault, she's a teacher and she has her own money, why doesn't she leave him?" And another girl said:

"She stays with him because she loves the big brute. She told my mother that he beats her because he is too ignorant, and thinks that she looks down on him, because she is educated, but it's not true. She loves him, only he does not believe her." The girls turned to Ivana and said:

"Her husband is your uncle. Can't your father speak to him?" Ivana shook her head:

"He can't, he believes that you can't stick yourself between a man and his wife. Besides, once my mother saw the teacher with a black eye and wanted to tell him off about it and the teacher got mad at my mom and said that she had banged into a door and it was her own fault if she had a black eye." One of the girls said:

"If she leaves her husband, she will not have her own money, because they will fire her. She has to be above reproach to keep her job, and when people separate, it's always the woman's fault; they will call her ugly names, and decide that she's not fit to teach children. I, for one wouldn't be able to come to school, because my father would be afraid she's teaching me bad stuff." Luna was depressed, she liked the teacher, and she did not want to know this information:

"I guess life is not easy here." Thought Luna, and she felt bad, because, somehow she also knew that in Italy, in the 1950's there was no divorce, and women had no way to be free. She walked back into the classroom and decided to be kind to the teacher, if she could.

The teacher had some work for Luna to do, some writing and some math. She also had some questions and answer sheets for history and geography, but Luna didn't even attempt them, as she really felt inept at those two subjects, even thought, to her amazement, she had some knowledge about Italian history and geography floating around in her head (Balthazar, undoubtedly). The teacher determined that Luna was well advanced, and she just needed a bit more strength in her writing, because for some reason, she tended to invert her nouns and pronouns:

"It's almost as if you're writing in English." She had taken English in college, and felt almost as if Luna was acquainted with the language by the way she wrote. The teacher shook her head at her own foolishness. It was decided that Luna was going to read 'The Betrothed' in class every day and write an essay per week about her reading, and she would hand one in every Saturday morning. The rest of the time she would study history and geography. She was a little surprised at Luna for being so smart and advanced, but lacking in her history and geography. By then it was noon, and everyone was sent outside to have lunch. In the back of the house there was a large grapevine, and under it a long table with benches. Everyone sat at the table in small groups, and Luna sat with Ivana and the three girls their age. Their names were Ada, Concetta and Luana. Ada was short and plump, with long braids, Concetta was small like Luna but had blond hair in a ponytail, and Luana, tall and angular (she reminded Luna of Myrna) had two shorter braids the ends of which were tied to the beginning of the braids, like the handles of a cannata only with a ribbon on top of each handle. Luna was starving, but she didn't say anything. Ivana said:

"Are you ready for lunch?" Luna said:

"We don't have any food!"

"Yes we do, silly; I brought our lunch with us!" She opened a small bundle she had taken from home, and Luna was very surprised, because she thought Ivana was carrying books or other school stuff. In the bundle were two smaller packages. Ivana gave one to Luna and kept one for herself. They both opened their napkins on the table, and inside was a chunky piece of some kind of pie, and Ivana pulled two shiny apples and put one next to each piece of pie. Luna asked:

"What kind of pie is this?" Ivana said:

"Rustic pie. It's stuffed with hard boiled eggs, prosciutto ham, cheese and raw eggs to tie it all together. My mother baked it last night, after we went to bed, and packed it for us this morning, before she went to do the laundry." The other girls had similar things or sandwiches, and some kind of fruit. They all ate companionably, talking desultorily about this and that. Near the table was a small counter and on it was a large, sweating cannata with an assortment of cups next to it. Ivana got up, took two cups, washed them well with some of the water, and then filled them up and brought them to the table for the two of them. The rustic pie was out of this world, crunchy crust and tasty, soft interior. After she finished it, Luna was full and satisfied. She sipped some of the water and it was cool and fresh. They then picked up their apples and started to crunch them with gusto, while the juice from them was dribbling off their chins and they had to use their napkins to wipe it. Ivana looked at Luna and asked:

"When are you going to do your laundry?" Luna was startled:
"My laundry?"

"Yes, your clothes! You don't have almost anything left to wear." Luna stammered:

"But I thought that your mother was going to do it for me." Ivana was laughing so hard, she had to cover her mouth with her hand, because the other girls turned and wanted to know what was going on. Ivana said, still laughing:

"Luna is leaving all of her dirty clothes on the floor of her room, and she expects my mother to wash them for her." The other girls looked at Luna like she had two heads and Luana said:

"What makes you think that your aunt will do your laundry?" Luna started to get pissed at these girls:

"My mother does all my laundry, at home; I don't see why I shouldn't expect my aunt to do it here too." Ivana looked at Luna and saw that she was starting to get angry. She had fast learned to recognize the signs. She looked at Luna seriously and said:

"I've been doing my own laundry since I was twelve. I don't expect my mother to do my wash. She has enough work doing hers and my father's; on top of all the other things she has to do. I do mine twice a week, it's not so bad. Sometimes, in the winter, I'll do my laundry almost every day, so it doesn't accumulate, especially the heavy winter clothes. You're lucky that your mother does all of your laundry at home. Maybe she doesn't have that much to do, that's why she can." Luna looked at Ivana and said:

"I don't know how to do my laundry!"

"Don't worry, I'll teach you!" Said Ivana. Luna looked at the other girls:

"Do all of you do your own laundry?"

"Yes!" They answered in unison:

"I don't suppose that anyone has a washing machine at home?" Ivana said:

"I think that you're watching too many American movies. We don't have those fancy things over here." That led all of them to talking about the latest movie to come to the theater in Pontecorvo. Ivana said:

"I may be able to convince my papa' to take us. He knows how much Mama loves going to the movies. If only they played a good one soon!" All the girls were sighing:

"James Stewart! Humphrey Bogart, Rodolfo Valentino!" Ivana said:

"Right now they're playing 'The Bicycle Thief'; I don't want to see anything sad. The next one it's going to be 'Year Zero' That's sad too. I'm going to wait for an American movie. Maybe a Tarzan movie! American movies are always funny and romantic."

When they finished their lunch and went back to class, Luna couldn't help thinking how restricted the lives of these people were, and how much they had to work to be able to go on, yet they were always happy, and the smallest things were big treats to them:

"Maybe we have too much in the future." Thought Luna. The teacher gave Luna some more individual attention, and she said it was because she was assessing her, to decide what kind of program to put her in. After today, of course, she would again go back to dividing her attention evenly amongst the children and the different classes. Luna realized that the teacher worked very hard, with so many children of all the different classes. Finally, after a short recess at two p.m. to visit the black hole, it was three p.m. and school was over for the day. On the way home, Luna asked Ivana why the teacher wanted to have her essay delivered on Saturday, when there was no school. Ivana said:

"What do you mean that there is no school on Saturday?" Luna was puzzled for a moment, and then a suspicion nagged at her:

"You mean to tell me that you have school on Saturday, aren't you?"

"Of course we do, don't you?" Luna shook her head:

"No, we don't, I thought that no one had school on the weekend!"

"Boy," said Ivana, "you're so lucky and you don't even know it. You must come from a really wonderful place. Maybe someday I'll come to visit you." Luna almost choked on her spit. She was mad at having to go to school on the weekend, she was sad because Ivana could never visit her, and she wanted to go home to hug her family, yes, even Kyle, and to say she was sorry for all the nasty things she said to them, but she had a long wait, and she didn't even know for sure if she would really go back. She didn't trust that Balthazar no more. He had tricked her, she started to think. Things were not really turning out the way they were supposed to. Life here was not all dances and frolics, people here worked hard. Poor Uncle Pas had a big farm to take care of, all by himself, that's why they hadn't seen him since last night. Girls had to work here, they only had three dresses and two pairs of shoes each, they had to wash their own clothes, and they only ate food at mealtimes, never any goodies in between. And Luna suspected that her food tasted so good so far just because she was starved all the time. No candy bars, no chocolate, no chips, no soda, no donuts, never anything good, just like Aunt Palma said; just crappola regular food! Not even a McD's with shakes or Big Macs! Big Bummer! Also, there was no TV, and even if there were, no one would have the time to watch it, as they had to run around all day, get up at five a.m., do lots of chores and walk everywhere. There was no Saran wrap here, no paper plates, paper napkins, or plastic cups. No foil; they kept wrapping everything in a piece of cloth that, of course, had to be washed later. Ivana and the girls at school were right, she was lucky! By now Luna was in a frantic need to go back home. She was getting more worked up by the minute, and she almost felt like shouting:

"Balthazar! The past sucks! I want to go home!" And suddenly in her mind she heard Balthazar's falsely dulcet voice:

"Temper, temper Luna Blue! We haven't learned anything yet, have we?" Luna shook her fist at him, running to catch up to Ivana who was way ahead of her.

When they arrived home, Aunt Esther came out to meet them, and said:

"Luna, you have a visitor! She's in the good dining room, waiting for you." Anna! In all the to-do about everything, Luna had forgotten all about Anna. Luna almost felt that Anna was a connection to her old life; she was the first person Luna met in this time, and the first to like and help her. Luna ran into the good dining room and saw the old lady, resplendent in a large, embroidered red shawl, sitting at the table. She ran to her and fell into her open arms and started to cry. Anna hugged her and crooned to her:

"There, there! My goodness! What did they do to you! Come tell Anna all about it, I'll have a talk with these people if they hurt you." Luna sniffed loudly, and wiping her eyes, a little ashamed of herself, started to pour her heart out to the old lady:

"I have a small room under the eaves, and the only decoration in it is a picture of Saint Maria Goretti looking down her saintly nose at us regular girls, I found out I'll have to stay here three months, and I had to milk a cow, and make my own cheese for breakfast, and wash my own clothes, and I don't even want to tell you about the bathroom! And there is no tub; we have to wash with a small cloth, and I only have three going out outfits, and the Italian police are going to check my papers and make me go to school. And school is six days a week, instead of five, like at home." Luna took a deep breath, and continued: "And the teacher expects me to read an enormous book while I'm here, and I have to write all about it every week." Anna was holding in her hand a shot glass filled with some green liquid, and in front of her stood a bottle that said 'Cynar'. Luna knew somehow that it was the dreaded artichoke brandy Ivana was talking about. Anna said, swishing the green brandy from side to side:

"Worse thing I ever drank, bitter as all get up. But it did settle my stomach, though." Even though they never ate anything sinful, people around here didn't think about anything else but settling their stomach. They did it even before they ate anything, and they called it aperitif, and after they ate their proper meals, they called it digestive. Let's face it; they were strange in this place and time. Anna had pulled Luna on her ample lap, and Luna sat on it unashamedly, she needed the comfort. Thank God there was no one else in the room; they had given them some privacy. Anna was looking at Luna's small face still streaked with dry tears and shook her head:

"That Balthazar, I like to punch him in the nose! He should have known better than to drop you off in this place; it's too different than what you're used to." And while Luna looked at her, stunned, she continued: "Let me tell you a little story about your Gianna the Teacher." Luna kept looking at Anna with her jaw hanging:

"How do you know…….." But Anna shook her head warningly, and kept talking:

"Many years ago your uncle Pasquale went into the army, and was sent to Milano for two years. Over there he met Gianna the Teacher, and she fell in love with him. He never encouraged her, because he had a sweetheart at home which he loved very much. You guessed it! Your aunt Esther! When his stint was over, he came home to take his place in the community and get married. Gianna followed him home, she just showed up one day and declared that she had applied for, and just obtained a job teaching the children of these farms, because they were too far from town, and most of them had to be home-schooled. You can just imagine what they were being thought at home; nothing! So the authorities decided that was a great idea, and gave her the job. You must admit that she's very persistent and very smart. She's a good teacher, I'll give her that! She settled in the house she's in now, which is owned by your great uncle Biagio, and started the school with great success, while all along trying to get between your uncle Pasquale and Esther. But she didn't succeed, your uncle had loved Esther since they were children, and he was faithful to her. Even now they're sweethearts, and love each other to the exclusion of everyone else. Some people don't think it's even decent to be so in love with your wife so many years after you're married, but they don't care." Luna was fascinated. She had realized that about her Aunt and Uncle, and in fact she quite liked it. She forgot all about even Anna knowing who she was and where she came from; she blamed Balthazar for all of it. It seemed that on top of everything, he didn't even know how to keep his big trap shut. Anna went on:

"When your uncle married Esther, Gianna realized she had lost, and instead of going back home, she decided that she liked it here, she had a good, secure job, and she could be the belle of the ball with her Milano ways and her fancy clothes. She set her eyes on the son of her landlord, and one day, when Saverio went up there to get the rent, she had him find her in a veil dress, one you could see through, and Saverio being a big oaf of a country boy couldn't resist her and she had her way with him. He's quite handsome, you know! Of course, he thought that she was too good for him, and didn't want to be sorry later, so he stopped going up there for the rent, but when she told him that she was having his baby, he did the decent thing and married her. They have two children now, a boy and a girl, and could be happy. Sometimes they are, but Saverio drinks, and when he does, his devils come back, and he accuses her of not loving him, and beats her, out of pain. The funny part is, that she really does love him, now, but their lives are messed-up and there's nothing they can do about it." Luna's chest was so tight that she almost couldn't breathe, and she resolved even more than before, to be nice to the teacher. So much pain in this place! People took everything so seriously! She knew people at home who had done worse things than that, and no one cared, or even noticed. These people were too deep, and felt too deeply. She hung onto Anna like to a lifeline, and didn't know what she was going to do. Anna gently let her sit on one of the chairs and took her small hand in her own rough, warm ones:

"Don't worry, dear, this too shall pass, you know! Everything passes, and when's all done, you'll regret it if you haven't explored everything that comes your way. This may seem hard to you, but you'll look at it fondly when you're back home. And who knows, maybe you can come back sometimes, if you want to that is!"

"You always know what to say to make me feel better."

"I haven't raised nine children without learning a thing or two!" Said Anna: "And you'll get to meet them all, except for my little Franco, who died when he was five."

"I'm so sorry about little Franco," whispered Luna. Anna said:

"These things happen, God calls the little angels to Him, and we have to accept it. Not that I could ever forget him. Maybe I shouldn't say this, but he was my favorite, you know! I almost wanted to talk to Balthazar about going……" She shook her head: "No, What's done is done! Just try to learn from this, sweet girl." Then, brightening up: "I've decided to stay with my daughter for the time being, maybe I'll stay for three months, and maybe I'll even sell my small house and move here for good. She can use the help, and her Mario is a real good guy, and real nice to me. We're going to build a new barn soon, but first there'll be the burning, you'll like that!" Luna was listening wide eyed:

"Oh, Anna, I do love you! I'm feeling a lot better, and what's a burning, anyway?"

"The burning is when we get rid of the old barn. It's filled with varmints, rats and the like, and when you burn it, they all run to the fields and stay there. And when they run, we throw water on them, and that scares them into never coming back. Don't worry, we don't kill them, they're God's creatures too, although I don't know why God bothered to create them." By then, Luna was laughing, Anna was certainly not above criticizing anyone, even God. In a very nice manner, of course! While they were talking, Luna kept looking at a beautiful ornament propped right in the middle of the shiny dining room table, on top of a doily; it was a group of horses with their heads down, seemingly grazing, and just one horse with his head up, mane flowing, who looked into the distance as if guarding all the others. Luna said:

"What's that?" Anna looked at the horses and said:

"I think it's one of the carvings that your uncle Saverio does, you know, the teacher's husband. When he's in the mountain, watching his heard, he whittles all of these figurines, and then gives them away to his friends and relatives. They're not as perfect as the store bought ones, but some people seem to think they're very good." Luna was amazed; her uncle Saverio was an artist!   By then Aunt Esther came back into the room to invite Anna to dinner and Luna forgot about the carving. Aunt said that Mario had gone back home because he had something to finish before it got dark, and Uncle Pas was going to take her back whenever she was ready to go home. Anna said:

"I don't want to inconvenience anyone, it's only two miles back, and I can walk them in a jiffy." But Aunt Esther shook her head:

"It's no problem, he came home early today, and he's not going back to the fields until tomorrow. It's nice having him home early, and I thank you for that."

"Let me help with dinner, then." Said Anna, and with a pat to Luna's head, followed Aunt Esther to the kitchen. Luna ran out of the room, her heart once more light and happy, and went in search of Ivana. Ivana was doing her afternoon chores, and Luna helped her.

They sat down to dinner at five, and her Aunt Esther had really outdone herself for Luna's guest. They had a plate of antipasto with prosciutto, creamy goat cheese, olives, pickled vegetables and hard boiled eggs. After the antipasto there were bowls of hot chicken soup with some very, very small pasta in it, and little brown chunks of some kind of meat. Luna asked Ivana what those brown chunks were, and was told 'gizzards'. Luna did not look too closely at them, they were very good, whatever they were. After the soup they had the chicken Aunt Esther had made soup with, and it was so tender, it just fell off the bones. For a vegetable Aunt Esther had made stuffed artichokes, and Luna was staying away from the dreaded, bitter things, when she saw Ivana lift one out and put it in her plate:

"Are you going to eat one of those?" Asked Luna,

"Of course," said Ivana. "They're the best!"

"But you said the brandy was very bitter."

"The brandy is but not the artichokes themselves. You've never had one, have you!" At Luna's pained look, Ivana started to shake her head:

"I'm starting to think you come from the moon, instead of the North." And at Uncle Pas sudden burst of laughter, Luna smiled a conspiratorial smile at him and cheerfully watched Ivana show her how to properly eat a large, juicy, succulently stuffed artichoke. Anna frowned at them, but no one paid her any attention. For dessert they had some round cookies Anna brought. The cookies looked like small rings, no bigger than two or three inches across, and they were brown and crunchy, rustic looking, peppered with some kind of seeds:

"These used to be my husband's favorite," said Anna, "he used to pick the wild anise seeds when he took the sheep to pasture, dry them and bring them home to me, and I made him these wine biscuits, my own mother's recipe, so he could take them to the pasture the next time he went. They last forever, and they're grand when dunked in red wine." Ivana had to try it immediately, and she poured a small amount of red wine in her glass and in Luna's. They tried it, and it was true, they were wildly crunchy and sweet, and smelled of aromatic seeds:

"If you eat these with wine every day, you'll live to be a hundred." Said Anna: "My Domenico didn't make it to that, but he was almost ninety when he passed, I bet that if he didn't like his food so much and ate a little less he would've made it. He always said that I would be the death of him, with my good cooking, but he would certainly go with a smile on his face." Everyone enjoyed Anna's cookies, and Aunt Esther asked Anna for the recipe, because the beatific smile on Uncle Pas' face when he was eating the cookies made her want to give him as many as he wanted. Anna said that she would gladly give her the recipe, but there were tricks to it, and no one could make them as she did. She said that she would do something she had never done for anyone, she would come over and show her all her little tricks, and teach her how to do it. Aunt Esther was very grateful, and started making plans for the lesson. After Anna went out to have her cup of espresso with Uncle Pas and Aunt Esther, Ivana and Luna did the dishes, and for the occasion they also had a cup of espresso instead of the bitter chicory coffee. Out of habit, the girls loaded their espresso with sugar, and it was so sweet and good, that Luna was grateful that they had espresso in the future. When the adults came back inside, Anna said her farewells, promising to see them in a few days, at the barn burning, and Uncle Pas drove her home. Ivana told Luna that they should really go to the Pilone and wash their clothes, and so they did. Luna learned to wash her clothes, and it wasn't so bad, with Ivana splashing her, and them both playing the underwear game. They would let their underwear float on the water until it was almost in the stream going to the walnut trees, and then they would rescue it just before it got swept away. Ivana said:

"One day I was washing with Giustina, but she's not fast enough for this game, and her underwear and bra got washed away to the walnut trees. We ran all the way after them, but they got stuck on branches we couldn't reach, and we had to ask papa' to get them. Was she embarrassed! Good thing that papa' can keep his mouth shut, Giustina's father would have been really upset if he knew that a man had touched her unmentionables." Before they knew, the clothes were washed, and they took them home in leaky baskets. Luna's basket was much leakier than Ivana, as she hadn't mastered the art of squeezing her clothes very dry yet. By the time they got to the house, Luna's dress was all wet in the front, but she didn't care. They hung the wash with pins on the clothes lines in the back of the house, and went back inside to do their homework. Luna wrote part of her essay on the book she was reading, being very careful not to invert her nouns and pronouns, and read some pages on the partisans of the First World War. For geography she had to learn about the nineteen regions of Italy, and be able to name their capitals. She worked her way up to five of them. After the big meal they had, their late supper was very light; just one egg poached in tomato sauce, with a small slice of bread and a small potato salad just made with bits of boiled potatoes, oil and vinegar and sprinkled with a little parsley. Because of having a visitor and doing their laundry, it was quite late when the girls went to sleep, almost ten p.m., and they slept as soon as their heads hit the pillow.

Five o'clock came even sooner this morning, but it was actually six for Luna, as Ivana let her sleep an hour longer while she started on her chores. After Luna was up and dressed, they went to collect the fresh water from the Pilone, but while they were there, they did their small wash from yesterday's clothes, because Ivana said it was easier to wash a couple things every morning than to do the laundry all at once. Aunt Esther was already at the Pilone washing clothes, and Luna realized that this clothes washing was a constant, heavy burden for everyone. They got back home with their cannatas full of water and went back for their baskets; the baskets, of course, leaking all over their clothes again. It was short work putting the wash on the line, then they had to remove the wash from yesterday and get it ready to put away. They folded their under things, and ironed the rest. Getting ready to iron was quite a production. First of all, they were going to iron on the table, over a thin blanket folded and laid on the marble, secondly they had a strange iron with a lid, and under the lid there was an empty space you had to fill up with the lighted coal from the fornacella, the cooking barbeque stove. After the hot coals were in the iron, you had to wait a couple minutes for the whole thing to get hot, and then you held the iron by the handle with a pot holder, as the whole thing got hot; it was made of cast iron. You couldn't control the intensity of the heat, and you had to iron really fast, because the iron got cold after a few minutes, and you had to replace the coals. With Ivana's help, she finished ironing her clothes, put them on hangers and hung everything on a wooden bar in a corner of her room. The folded under things went in the bureau. Luna was exhausted! When she went downstairs, Ivana said that today they were going to have a quick breakfast, for lack of time. She took two large disks of some dry bread from Gargantua, like two brown rusks, and put them in two large plates. She then took a pitcher of spring water and poured some on the rusks, waited a couple minutes, and then poured all the water out. The rusks were softer, but still crackling, and she made a bowl of cut up red tomatoes, some oregano, salt, pepper and olive oil, and she poured half of this mixture over each dish. Luna said:

"That's what we'll eat for breakfast?"

"Yes," said Ivana, "when we don't have time to do anything we eat this, it's called friselle and we all love it, it's very good for you."

"Italian Fast Food!" Thought Luna, we'll see! The half crunchy, half soft brown bread was very pleasing, and the tomatoes and all the other toppings reminded Luna of bruschetta, and she was not that interested in food, anyways, she wanted to go back to school and see what was going on with everyone. Same as yesterday, everyone waited until the teacher came out and invited everyone inside. They all sat in the same seat, and Luna was happy not to be seating near anyone, because she didn't want people to see how she was butchering Italian history and geography in her reports. She read another chapter of the sad story of Renzo and Lucia, and was in a depressed mood when they went out for their break. She listened listlessly to the other girls without contributing anything. She perked up her ears a bit when Concetta started to whisper about a book her cousin had gotten from another cousin of theirs. It was supposedly a banned book, and it was very explicit about what women and men did.

Luna knew, of course, she had had a course on sexual education, but the way the girls were talking about it, this was simply horrendous, and they all shivered with delicious fear and horror about it. Concetta said that when they got together to do their hair, she was going to borrow it from her cousin and bring it; the name of the book was: 'Lady Chatterley's Lover'. Luna though she heard that title before, but said nothing. For their lunch Ivana produced hard boiled eggs, dry cheese and bread. Luna didn't care anymore, she was not going to complain, after all they were giving her their food and shelter for nothing, and she didn't have any rights here, as far as she knew. She all of a sudden realized that she had not bought anything since she got here, she had no money, and even if she did, there was no place to buy anything. A new feeling stole over her; she felt hopeless and tired. That night she ate whatever they put in front of her, thanked everybody and went to bed. It was only eight pm, and she slept a long time. Her dreams were not happy either; she dreamed that she was back home, but she had been told that there would be no more allowance, there were no more stores to visit, and she was going to wash her own clothes and make her own food from then on, in fact she would have to wash Kyle's clothes, and make his food also. She didn't even mind, because she was so sad and depressed, nothing mattered anymore. She woke up groggy and tired and listlessly went through the motions of washing, doing the chores and eating breakfast. She walked to school tiredly and barely heard Ivana's chatter about this and that. She woke up and started to take part when Ivana said that they were going to the barn burning this coming Sunday. Ivana said that Mario's father had sent a message around that they were to go to the burning, to dress up because there was no work to be done, and there would be a party after the burning, and at that time he would make a very important announcement. Luna started to come out of her inertia, because she would see Anna and a lot of other people. She also wanted to see how these parties went around here. She started to think about what she was going to wear, and got depressed all over again. What could she do with her meager wardrobe? Luna asked Ivana:

"What are you going to wear at the burning?"

"I'll wear a dress, one of my better ones, not my best thought." Luna didn't say anything. After they got home, changed, did the chores and sat down to eat, Luna and Ivana cleared the kitchen, did the dishes, had their coffee and dessert, and sat down to their homework as usual. Aunt Esther had disappeared right after dinner, with Uncle Pas, as usual. While they were working, Aunt Esther came in with a seamstress measuring tape and asked Luna to please stand up so she could take her measurements. Luna asked with sarcasm:

"What I'm to be measured for, my casket?" Aunt Esther looked at her levelly and said:

"No, my dear, I'm measuring you for a new dress to wear to the burning on Sunday!" Luna colored a little, ashamed of her outburst, (somehow, over here you could never voice your worst thoughts, because afterwards you were made to be ashamed of them) and meekly let Aunt do what she wanted. She was thinking how everything they needed had to be made by hand. She hoped Aunt Esther could sew:

"I hope they don't expect me to saw my own dress, or I'm in trouble." Thought Luna. After a while Aunt Esther came down with some pieces of material draped over her arm, and asked Luna to pick what she liked best. She had some soft brown cloth, some bright green knitted material, and a grey taffeta' dotted all over with small, cornflower blue flowers. Luna picked the grey taffeta', and was happy, because she loved the crisp, lustrous material dotted by flowers here and there. She asked Aunt Esther what was the dress going to look like, and Aunt said she was going to like it, and not to worry. Luna went to bed a little less depressed that night. The following day was Friday, and all was as usual, except that the girls talked about nothing but the barn burning. Even the teacher had been invited, and everyone thought that it was going to be more than a barn burning, that something was going to happen at that party, and everyone was curious and excited. Ivana said that on Saturday, after school was over, they would help Aunt Esther make something to bring to the party. Luna asked what, and Ivana said her mother had not decided yet. Uncle Pas was going to bring a large basket of fruit. They had the best fruit trees around, and their peaches were humongous and sweet, while their figs were so good, that everyone always said that they were full of honey. Also they had beautiful pomegranates, and concord grapes. Luna was getting used to eating fruit with every meal, and she especially loved the grapes. She had never had concord grapes before, and actually, they didn't eat much fruit at home, and whatever they ate was not as beautiful, fresh and unusual as what she ate over here. At home they always had apples or bananas, sometimes oranges, but Luna always preferred donuts or cookies to fruit. Here there was not much to choose from, it was either fruit or nothing, and Luna was now starting to look forward to it.

That day, at dinner, everyone had a plate of some yellow concoction, and there was a bowl of red sauce on the table, and a container of grated cheese. Luna asked Ivana:

"What is this stuff?" She answered:

"It's polenta, Girl from the Moon!" Luna was starting to get sick of Ivana making jokes about where she came from. She was just about to explode and tell her that she knew a lot of stuff more than her, and that she came from a much more advanced time and place. But she knew she couldn't; she didn't want to piss off stupid, old Balthazar. He was so cold and stern; he may leave her stuck in the eighteen century of 1950 forever. Besides, everyone would think she was crazy, and she didn't think Uncle Pas was going to help her, he wasn't supposed to talk about it either. She swallowed her anger and asked politely:

"What's in it?" Ivana said:

"Just salt, corn meal and water. You can eat it like this or you can put tomato sauce and grated cheese on it. I'm surprised you never had polenta, they say that up North people eat nothing but polenta; they're called Polentoni because of it." Luna looked at Aunt Esther and Uncle Pas and said:

"Do I have to eat this?" Aunt Esther said:

"No, dear, you don't have to eat anything you don't want. We don't believe in forcing anyone to do anything." Luna was relieved, and pushed the plate of yellow mush away from her. She waited a little while, and then asked:

"Where is my food, I'll get it myself." Aunt looked up from her plate and said pleasantly:

"Your food is in front of you. If you don't want to eat it it's your business, but that is all you get." Luna was stunned; she could not believe that they would be so mean to her. She felt a rage coming on, and she felt that she would explode if she didn't let it out. She yelled:

"I'm hungry and I want something else." No one even looked up from their plate of junk, only Ivana threw her a scared look and kept eating. Luna was not going to be ignored; she would not stand for that! She grabbed the plate of mush, and smashed it on the floor. Everyone kept on eating, except for Ivana who let out a surprised squeak and covered her mouth with her hand. Luna looked at Uncle Pas and saw that he was looking at her knowingly, and a little amused. Aunt Esther kept eating serenely. Luna thought:

"What must one do to get some reaction out of her?" Ivana in the meantime started to get up and get something to clean up the yellow mush that was now resting among the pieces of pottery. Uncle Pas said:

"No, Ivana, leave it!" At that Ivana sat back down, uncertainly. Luna's anger dissolved. She felt lost. What was this world she was in, that her rage didn't bother anyone, and even made them smile? Why didn't they scream and rage at her and her bad behavior, why didn't they punish her, call her names. She could cope with that, she was used to it, but this calm niceness threw her for a loop. She got up, went to get the broom, some rags, a dustpan and a bucket, and proceeded to clean the floor. When she was done, she sat back down on the table, and said:

"I have a wallet in my bag, if there is any money in it, I will pay for the dish." Uncle Pas said:

"Don't worry about the dish, it was an old thing, we have a lot of them." Everyone went back to eating, and Luna sat there, humiliated, while Ivana shot her furtive glances, her eyes moist. On the stove Luna saw the pan with the mush just seating there, and she asked to no one in particular:

"May I get some more food for myself?" Aunt Esther said:

"But of course, Luna, you're a growing girl, you have to eat." Luna took another dish from the hutch, spooned some yellow mush in it, and brought it to the table. She then picked up a large spoon from the saucer of tomato sauce, and spooned some on her polenta. She added some grated cheese, and started to eat small spoonfuls of her food. To her surprise, and shame, it was quite good, and she finished it without lifting her head up. Aunt Esther looked at her and said:

"Luna, dear, have you ever had lasagna?" Luna answered:

"Yes, my mom makes it on special occasions."

"Good," said Aunt Esther, "we'll make a very large lasagna to take to the barn burning, and you girls can help, tomorrow after school." Luna was a little relieved, and she felt so bad that she wanted to do something to make up for her outburst. She looked at Uncle Pas. He was smiling at her. He was just the most beautiful man Luna had ever seen, and she meant inside more than his looks, even thought she was starting to think that he was even more handsome than she thought at first. He seemed to know what she was feeling, and said:

"Never mind, Luna Marina Blue, it's all forgotten. Just go on with what you have to do, and think of the nice party we are going to on Sunday." Luna ran to him and unashamedly hugged him. He briefly held her to him, and quickly let her go. Uncle Pas smelled pleasantly of his fresh tobacco, clean soap, and earth. Luna knew she was going to remember that smell for the rest of her life.

After doing the dishes, having their coffee and dessert, and going outside to pick up their dry laundry, the girls sat down to do their homework. At one point Ivana raised her head from her work, and said:

"It was my fault you threw the dish, wasn't it? I know I make fun of you sometimes, but I don't mean anything by it. You know that I love you, don't you? I know that you're much smarter than I am, and that you come from a much more modern part of Italy than here. I just like to make jokes, and I only do it to people who like me. You still like me, don't you?" Luna just got up from her seat at the table and hugged her. They eventually had their late supper of a large platter of different kinds of cheeses, vegetable pickles, small (and delicious) potato croquettes and stuffed, fried zucchini flowers. Luna waited for everyone to fill their plates, and did the same. The bread was starting to be hard. Ivana said:

"When are you going to bake, Mom?"

"Tomorrow!" Answered Aunt Esther:

"Will you make sugar focaccia Mom?" Aunt Esther smiled and said:

"I certainly will! I have to make a lot of it, because this big baby next to me is going to eat the lion's share of it, and there won't be any left for you girls when you come home." And she sent an affectionate smile Uncle Pas' way:

"No one knows how to bake like you do, Estherina, and you know how much we appreciate it!" Ivana mouthed, for Luna's benefit:

"Estherina!" And rolled her eyes. They all laughed good naturatedly, and proceeded to clear the kitchen. Luna sank gratefully into bed that night, and while she was falling asleep a thought nagged at her:

"Why do I like these people so much? They're making me do things I don't want to do, all the while pretending that they don't. They're so cool in front of my rage, as if it didn't matter very much. They always end up getting their way no matter what I do!" A nasty thought floated around in her head, just before she fell into oblivion; she had heard that most victims of kidnapping eventually came to love and depend on their captors: "That must be it!" She thought: "The Stockholm syndrome!"

Junior High, Pontecorvo 1956.

High School, Pontecorvo 1959.

On Saturday morning, there was a lot of excitement running around. The girls couldn't do their chores fast enough to run to school and compare notes with the other girls. During the first break they found out that pretty much everyone had been invited to the barn burning. They talked about what they were going to wear, and Luna said she was going to have a taffeta' dress but she didn't know what it was going to look like, because Ivana's mother was still making it. They all agreed that it was going to be beautiful, because her aunt Esther was well known for her sewing skills. During lunch one of the girls was talking excitedly about a new movie coming to town soon. Her uncle worked in the projection room, and he said they ordered a new American movie. Some of the girls wanted to see cowboys' movies, and some wanted to see funny movies. Concetta said that she had seen a Shirley Temple movie and she had loved it:

"I especially liked it when she danced," said the girl, "especially the stair dance she did with that black guy, Mrs. Dugentle." Luna corrected offhandedly:

"Mr. Bojengles." No one paid her any attention, except for the teacher, who was standing near them to help the younger children sitting on the other side of the table. She threw Luna an assessing look, but didn't say anything. After school, they ran home as fast as they could, and they were not disappointed. The kitchen table was covered with the fruits of Aunt Esther's labors for that day: Large loaves of brown bread, white flat breads covered in glistening sugar, regular flat breads peppered with herbs, salt and pepper, fat brown breadsticks and small, round sweet breads were piled on the table. There were also some kinds of pies, apple by the smell, but instead of a crust, they were covered by dough lattice work and next to the pies were platters of cookies. After everything cooled off, it would go into Gargantua to be used all week. On a chair in the corner, laid a dress made of shiny taffeta' with cornflower-blue flowers. It had puffy sleeves, a round neckline, was gathered at the waist, and it flared out like a flower. Next to it laid a petticoat made of many layers of white materials. Luna was stunned. It looked like one of the dresses that Ella Enchanted wore in her fairytale world, and she only wished she had some black patent leather Baby Jane's shoes to wear with the dress. She had always liked dressing up in costumes, and this was better than any Halloween costume she ever had. Then she looked on the floor, and saw them; black patent leather Baby Jane's shoes. She looked in wonder at Aunt Esther, and she said:

"Your uncle went to town today, and he took one of your shoes with him for size to get these for you. The dress is not completely finished; we'll try it on after dinner." During dinner, while Aunt Esther and Ivana were busy with food Luna looked up at her uncle and asked:

"Are we going to wear old fashioned costumes to the barn burning, Uncle?"

"Are you talking about your dress?"

"Yes, uncle, no one wears dresses like that anymore. Don't get me wrong, I think it's beautiful, but it's very old fashioned."

"It's not old-fashioned in this time and day, Luna. If you like it, enjoy it, you will be in perfect harmony with all the other girls, you'll see." Luna looked into Uncle Pas' beautiful grey eyes, and said quietly:

"Thank you!" After everything was cleared out, they started to work on the Lasagna. Aunt Esther made sheets of dough for the lasagna, there was a great pan of tomato sauce bubbling on the fornacella, as they called the barbeque pits in the kitchen, and the girls were making very small meatballs to fry and then add to the sauce. Uncle had brought in a large pan of mozzarella he had made the day before, and a large pan of homemade ricotta. There was a container of grated hard cheese already on the table. Luna had never seen a sheet pan as big as the one Uncle took down from the wall, and after it was washed and rinsed, Aunt started to assemble the gigantic lasagna. First sauce went on the bottom, then the boiled sheets of pasta, then sauce with tiny meatballs, ricotta, mozzarella and grated cheese. On top of all that, Aunt sprinkled some chopped hard boiled eggs. The layers were repeated until everything was used up, and on top of the lasagna she sprinkled sauce, grated cheese and some mozzarella. This lasagna was so big and thick that it could choke a horse, thought Luna, but the horse would go with a smile on his face! It took both Uncle Pas and Aunt Esther to pick it up by the handles and carry it to the side, where the pan rested in a container full of cold water that came almost to the top of the pan. Aunt Esther stuck a few wooden dowels in it, and on top of these she draped a white cloth; she would be up very early to bake it. Luna realized that not having a refrigerator, everyone had to work very hard and be very careful to keep food fresh. The lack of Saran wrap and foil were also a big problem. While Aunt Esther and Uncle Pas caught a few minutes of privacy with their coffee and cookies, Luna and Ivana cleaned up the kitchen. Afterward Aunt Esther helped Luna try on her new dress, and it needed only a few small changes to fit perfectly. The petticoats kept the skirt full and bouncy, and Luna just felt like a little princess wearing it. After they decided how to finish Luna's dress, Aunt Esther put it back on top of the Singer sewing machine and they pulled out Ivana's. Ivana had a pretty buttercup yellow dress, kind of similar to Luna's, except that it had an inlaid strip of golden lace all around the hem. Aunt Esther made some hair ribbons with the left over material that she had saved, and added a row of tiny gold buttons from her neckline to her waist. Ivana looked very nice in the frilly dress and the ribbons braided into her hair, and Luna told her so. After they finished their homework and their chores, they had a light supper of whole, fried Italian peppers, some grilled pork liver sausage (Luna didn't dare question it, but she liked it in the end) a small salad and a piece of the famous sugared flat bread. Again the girls cleaned up, while Aunt Esther sat at the Singer and pedaled quietly to finish the dresses.

After everything was done, the girls had their Saturday night bath with Aunt Esther supervising. Uncle Pas took down the great copper tub hanging on the wall and placed it near the back door in the kitchen, then made himself scarce, while Aunt Esther heated up great quantities of water on all four burners of the fornacella. Luna went first, and a little shyly sat in the deep copper tub with water almost to her chin. She scrubbed herself, and then Aunt Esther helped her wash her hair. While Aunt Esther rubbed her scalp vigorously with shampoo, Luna thought about her mom, and while she had her head tilted back and her eyes closed so that Aunt Esther could rinse her hair with a pitcher of warm water, Luna missed her mom terribly, and she also knew that her mom would never wash her hair like this; at home you had to be independent, and not so close to one another. Luna shed a few, private tears while her eyes were closed, but no one seemed to notice. She cried for her mom, and for what her and her mom had missed. When she was done, Aunt Esther wrapped Luna in a warm, giant towel and she sat to wait for Ivana to have her turn. Then Aunt Esther called Uncle Pas from the barn, where he was tending to the animals, and he dumped the water outside by tilting the tub over the threshold. After that, it was Ivana's turn, and it went the same except for the hair, which took considerable extra time for being so long. After they were done, Uncle Pas came in and repeated the job of emptying the tub. They were finally done and went upstairs to their bedroom while Aunt Esther refilled the tub with hot water. Luna said:

"It's so much work for your mother and father to do this bathing thing. Now they have to do it again twice."

"No!" Said Ivana. "Only once, they wash up in the same water!" Luna said:

"Who's going to do your mother's hair?" Ivana answered:

"My father." That evening, Luna sank into bed exhausted, and fell asleep immediately:

"No insomnia here," she remembered thinking just before she slept. "There is so much to do that even if we had a TV and a phone, we wouldn't have time to use them." She did remember seeing Uncle Pas sitting in the good dining room listening to a large, antique radio they had, while the women cleaned up.

In the morning, Aunt Esther was busy with her own dress, baking the lasagna, and ironing Uncle Pas' good shirt and pants. Aunt had a simple, straight dress, like a shift, made of some satiny, blue material. The dress had two slits on the sides, at the waist level, and Aunt produced a beautiful, wide belt, made of copper with intricate designs on it, and she wore the belt, hooked in the back, on the inside of the dress, and only showing in the front, where it was wider with some inlaid blue stones. On anyone even slightly heavier this would have looked funny, but on Aunt's tall and willowy body it looked wonderful. Luna was amazed at how stylish and beautiful Aunt Esther looked in the plain dress, her only decoration the beautiful belt. Dressed like that, the coronet of braids on her head made her look almost regal. She wore pumps with a slight heel, and stuck a fancy comb in the back of her head just under the coronet. Uncle Pas looked very handsome and young in his good black pants and white shirt, with a very light grey jacket and his hair slicked back. The party started at noon, and they finally were on their way, after doing all the chores, securing the house and loading the lasagna, apple pies and humongous basket of fruit in the back of the truck. Luna was very happy and excited, and very proud of her 'family'. Aunt Esther said that they were to forgo church today, because there was no time to attend, but the following Sunday church would come first no matter what. Besides, Don Attilio, the local priest, would be at the party, and he would bless the burning, the food and the people.

Soon they arrived at their destination. The farm was a white, sprawling building, with outbuildings a distance from the house proper. It was a beautiful warm day, as it almost always was in this part of Italy, and the big yard was full of people sitting and walking. Everyone was dressed up in their good clothes, and talking and laughing together. There were long tables covered with all kinds of food, and drinks flowed everywhere. Luna was delighted, she knew a lot of the people already, and they waved at her calling her by name. There was Aunt Palma sitting on the place of honor, being the oldest person there, and she was enjoying a platter of delicacies like there was no tomorrow. Luna whispered to Ivana:

"I don't think that Aunt Palma is going to eat just beans today!" Ivana responded laughing:

"She never does, she just likes to say that! She loves good food!" Great Uncle Biagio was standing with the men, and so was his son, Uncle Luigi, Giustina's father. Mario was there, and Uncle Pas joined the men, while Aunt Esther went to the tables and deposited the fruit basket. Uncle Pas walked to the truck with Mario Merolli and they brought back the giant lasagna, and then went back for the pies. Luna and Ivana, splendid in their finery, looked around for the other girls. Ada, Concetta and Luana were there. Concetta was holding her little sister in her arms, her name was Teresa, and she was cute as a button. Ada was talking excitedly about some boy from Roma who was here for the weekend visiting his grandparents, and Luana did nothing but pirouettes showing off her beautiful, full, organza skirt. She couldn't wait to show that Pilone boy, Remigio, her dress. The skirt was a very light blue, but underneath, her petticoat was a darker blue, and the effect was wonderful. They all admired each other's clothes, and laughed joyfully trying to guess the surprise at the party. Luna looked around for Anna, and soon she saw the old lady making her way amongst the people looking right and left. When she saw Luna, she opened her arms to her, and Luna ran right into them. Anna was resplendent, dressed up in the local ancient costume. She was wearing her 'Anna' shoes, of course, but they were new and shiny. Anna had on a full, black skirt embroidered all over the hem, a dazzling white pleated shirt, and over it she had a black felt corset also decorated with fancy embroidery in all the colors of the rainbow. Luna had seen Anna with a kerchief on her head before, and she didn't even know if the old lady had hair. Now she knew Anna had hair. She had long braids on both sides of her head, and they were curled up and tied with hanging ribbons the same color of the embroidery. On her ears she was wearing great golden hoops, but what amazed Luna more than anything was Anna's other jewelry. She was wearing a very long, fancy gold chain twirled many times around her neck, in grading loops, and the whole thing was then picked up in the middle of Anna's chest and pinned up with a great, beautiful brooch. Anna saw Luna look at her, and twirled around for Luna's benefit, to show off her beautifully embroidered skirt. Luna laughed and hugged Anna, and the old lady held her off with her hands and looked her up and down:

"You look beautiful, my little Blue Moon. Do they have clothes like this where you come from?" Luna's eyes looked sad for a moment:

"No, we wear pants most of the time!" Anna pulled her to her bosom and held her for a long time:

"I'm sure you look great in pants. Remember what I told you, Luna Blue; live in the moment, enjoy what you can. Grab the gusto, pain will come of course, to all of us, but right now you're here with your family and your friends. You look beautiful; everyone likes you, and when you get the pain remember the good times and you will be stronger." Luna kissed Anna's cheek and the old lady pushed her away saying:

"Go, go! Go mingle with the other young people! I'll see you later." Luna ran off eagerly, and went to find everyone else. The Girls were talking to some other young people Luna did not know, the only ones she knew were Giustina and the newly arrived Remigio, and they were talking about school. Giustina went to school in town; her Aunt Nannina took her every day when she went to work, and some of the other kids went to another school closer to their farms. There was a boy about sixteen, who lived on a farm very near Pontecorvo, and thus went to school in town, who kept looking at Luna. He was olive skinned, with longish hair, and very dark eyes. He was tall and slim, and wore some very nice clothes almost like the grownups at the party. Luna kept looking at him too, and at one point he introduced himself:

"Hi, I'm Luca; I've never seen you at one of these parties before. You must be new in town!" Luna responded, self-consciously:

"I'm Luna. I'm here to stay at my uncle's for three months; I'm from up north!" They shifted their feet for a while, and then Luca asked Luna if they had parties like this where she came from:

"Good gracious, no! I've never been to one before; I love it very much." Luca said:

"After we eat, the music man is going to play the accordion, and everyone is going to dance. Will you dance with me once?" Luna motioned yes with her head, and ran off to find Ivana and the girls, to tell them about Luca. Right at this moment, she felt light as a feather and life was joy. All at once, loud talk subsided, and everyone stared at a truck that just drove up. Ivana said:

"The teacher is here." In fact a few moments later a couple started to walk towards them. The teacher was at the arm of a blond giant of a man, all dressed in black. He looked like Howard Keel in that old movie her mother loved so much; 'Seven brides for seven brothers'. She remembered having to watch it with her mother once because she wanted to know what happened in the end and her mother wouldn't tell her. One of the songs got so stuck in her head, that she was humming it to herself for days! Going courtin, Going courtin indeed! She watched the teacher approach on Howard Keel's arm, and felt a little sorry for her. She was wearing a tight, silvery dress that reached under the knees, and there were silver ruffles edged in white on her hem and neckline. Her hair was in her usual style; flat waves held back by a fancy comb. She was wearing make-up, and she held a large box in her hands. Her husband abruptly pulled away from her, and walked towards the men. The teacher was teetering on very high heels, and the farm ground made it very hard for her to walk normally. No one moved, watching her approach alone. From a distance she looked beautiful, if a little cheap, but up close she looked faded and a little sad. Luna suddenly stood and ran up to her to help with the box. Ivana followed her, and soon all the school children were grouped around the teacher. She said hallo' to all of them by name, and they guided her to the tables. Aunt Esther invited her to sit with the women, almost next to Aunt Palma in her place of honor. Gianna looked grateful, and smiled tentatively. Aunt Palma looked up from her food and exclaimed:

"Well, well! Here's the teacher, all dolled up as usual. Don't sweat it, honey, that big lug of yours doesn't deserve it. I had one of those, good looking as Lucifer, but nothing good in that beautiful head. When he pissed me off, I always used to put my hands on my hips, and told him off, may he rest in peace. I used to say 'I'm a beauty, I'm the belle. If you don't like me, someone else will!'" She laughed uproariously and then, pulling a chair next to her: "Sit, sit. Eat something! If you don't eat and don't drink, what strength can you have? I'll tell you more stories about that handsome bonehead I was married to." The teacher lightened up, and eagerly accepted a plate from one of Anna's daughters:

"The women are having their antipasto, before we have to serve the men!" She said, and everybody laughed loudly. Anna asked:

"Where are the children?" Gianna answered:

"I left them at home, I hired a girl from Pico to take care of them, they both came down with a cold, and I didn't want them to fuss and upset their father." Someone hollered:

"What's in the box, then? Is it a secret?" The teacher cut off the string by which she had carried it, and opened the box; inside were row upon row of very small pastries, and there were many layers of them. Everyone gasped:

"Those are beautiful cassatine! Where did you get them?"

"I made them." Said the teacher:

"You know how to make cassatine? Only Richetta from the pastry shop knows how to make them, and she would not show anyone. When she's making them, she closes all the doors and windows, and no one can even watch her. The problem is, she never makes enough of them, and if you ask for more, she tells you that they are very hard to make, and of course, she charges an arm and a leg for them. Why didn't you ever make them before?" They all said that same thing and the teacher blushed and told them:

"We don't get invited to too many parties, and I didn't know if people wanted my stuff." Anna, who was seating on the other side of Aunt Palma, said:

"I want your stuff!" Then reached over and took one, and she was going to pop it in her mouth, but the teacher said:

"Wait a minute, please!" She pulled out a large glass jar from her handbag, and twisted the cap open. With a small spoon from the table, she picked up a small maraschino cherry and plopped it on top of the pastry. Anna was then able to pop the pastry in her mouth and after chewing for a little while, rolled her eyes and said:

"Best cassatina I have ever had!" All the women took one, and Gianna the teacher was busily plopping cherries on top of the pastry, and the women said:

"It's going to be a while until we eat. Today we'll have cassatine for antipasto." They then took a shiny silvery tray, laid a white napkin on it, and piled the remaining pastry on the tray while putting cherries on them. When that was done, they all surrounded the teacher and said:

"What gives then, with the cassatine, are you going to tell us where you learned to make them?" Gianna was flushed and happy, obviously enjoying all the attention:

"When I was going to college, to support myself I worked in a pastry shop in Milano Center. It was the only job I could keep, as I spent all my days at school, and the job was at night. I used to get barely four hours of sleep at night, but it was a good job."

"Where was your family?" Asked the women:

"I didn't have a family; I was raised by nuns who found me on the doorstep." Answered Gianna. At their look of pity, she said: "The nuns were very good to me. I still correspond with Mother

Superior; she was the only mother I ever knew. She's very old, and the nuns are very poor, sometimes I wish I had more money, so that I could help them." There was a silence, and then Angelina, one of Anna's daughters said:

"How fortunate for us, that you had to work in a pastry shop in the center of Milano. Do you know how to make something else?"

"Pretty much everything you can buy in a fancy pastry shop; I worked there for four years." Everyone was talking at once, and they were asking Gianna to teach them how to make this and that. Luna had been standing behind Anna for a while to ask her where the 'black hole' was, because Ivana didn't know and Luna was ashamed of asking anyone else. At these questions, Luna pulled on Anna's skirt to get her attention, and said something quietly to the old lady. At the words, Anna held Luna to her bosom for a moment, and told her:

"I believe that no matter how you feel about where you come from, they make them smarter there. You came up with a wonderful idea, and I'm going to tell everyone it was your idea." Then she clapped her hands and when everyone was quiet she said: "My little Luna came up with the best idea; Gianna is a teacher. She knows how to teach people things. How about teaching a class on pastry making, and anyone who wants to learn, can attend to their heart's content?" Everyone was stunned by this simple, yet amazing idea. The teacher looked at Luna with something like wonder in her eyes. She whispered to herself:

"Where do you come from, little girl?"

At this point it was time to call the men to eat, and all the women got busy arranging the multitude of dishes that were on the tables. Amelia, Anna's daughter who was married to Mario, was directing the women and the beautiful food was being grouped according to what it was, while silverware and linen napkins were arranged neatly at the end of each table. There were large hams, containers of rosemary roast pork with roasted potatoes, platters of gnocchi (potato dumplings) covered in red sauce and grated cheese, homemade pasta, Aunt Esther's lasagna, stuffed and rolled up roast beef covered in gravy, sausages fried with red peppers, a large platter of Arancini, which were orange colored rice balls the size of small oranges, stuffed with meat, peas and cheese. Anna said that the wife of one of her sons made them, she was Sicilian and these little oranges were a specialty from Sicily. Anna said that her son imported the Sicilian when he went there as a soldier, and they did not like her at first, but after she started to cook, they ended up loving her; they needed new blood and new recipes, and the Arancini had become a favorite. These were on the table together with lots of other dishes. Then there were vegetables galore, and omelets, and big platters of mixed sliced boiled eggs, potatoes, tomatoes, red onions and cucumbers, the whole drizzled over with green olive oil. And there were flat breads and salads galore, all kinds of breads, rolls, and breadsticks were arranged together, and the dessert table was a sight to behold. The great platter of the elegant and exquisite cassatine was the piece the resistance. All the women worked busily, arranging everything beautifully, and the teacher went to the table full of watermelons and other fruit, to work on that, but Aunt Palma hollered:

"Sit yourself down, Gianna, you'll fall off your shoes and break your face, they don't need you!" The teacher walked back to her chair and sat down, mortified. Amelia looked at her pensively, and then she dropped what she was doing and went back into the house. A few minutes later, she walked up to the teacher and handed her a small pair of grey pumps rimmed in white, with just a small heel. The teacher looked up, surprised, and Amelia said:

"I had these for a couple of years. When we lived in Frosinone we used run up to Roma once a month. I saw them in a fancy shop, they were on sale. The man measured my feet and everything, and it is my size, but when I tried to wear them, some days later, they hurt so much I wanted to kill something. Mario looked at them and laughed his head off; the shoes were narrow. Can you see my big feet squeezed in those narrow things? I've kept them so long because I felt guilty about throwing them out, but I see that it was actually so that I can give them to you, so you can help us. It's not a hand-me-down thing; they are brand new and they'll fit you tiny feet just right." Gianna took the shoes, slipped her feet out of her stilettos, and tried them on. They fit. She stood up to walk, and almost fell over, she wasn't used to wearing shoes this low, but after a while she started to walk around and show off. The shoes were cute and they matched her outfit and it was heaven not to hurt every time you took a step. She turned to Aunt Palma and said:

"Look, Aunt Palma, no high heels! I can walk without falling and breaking my face!" Everyone laughed and the teacher went to the fruit table and started to arrange everything beautifully and smartly, for people to be able to serve themselves. She cut the watermelons in two lengthwise, emptied the two halves, cut the flesh in cubes, and filled them up again, adding strawberries, grapes, and large black and white mulberries. She put serving spoons in them, and the watermelons looked beautiful and elegant. The men and the young people were called to the tables, and everyone took plates and silverware and chose what they wanted to eat. Don Attilio put down the glass of wine he was drinking, ran to the center of the courtyard, his frock flying behind him, and hurriedly blessed, in one fell swoop, the food, the people, and the barn. He then went to the top of the line, plate in hand, and dove in. Everything was delicious, and everyone ate, drank and talked to their hearts content.

Luna and Ivana took a piece of their lasagna first; it was the bestest thing they had ever tasted, their meatballs tiny and tasty, and the cheese still hot and stringy, while little rivers of Aunt Esther's delicious red sauce ran off all over the noodles; for some strange reason, it reminded Luna of her mother's lasagna. Of course, her mother made small, square lasagnas and then cut them in four smaller squares, one for each one of them. This one was the biggest lasagna Luna had ever seen, and she and Ivana boasted to all their friends that they helped to make it, and everybody tried some. After at least a couple of hours, everyone was replete, the food was being put away, the tables moved out of the way, and the accordion man took his place to play, so that they could dance. Luna and Ivana had been laughing, running, talking and joking with all the other teenagers there. Luca had been near Luna a lot, and when the accordion man took his place, he went to remind her of their dance. At that point, Mario's father, a small, frail looking man, walked in the middle of the clearing helped by his wife, and cleared his throat to make an announcement. Everyone held his breath; here was the surprise everyone was waiting for! Here was the reason for the party!

Sure, they were going to burn the barn, later, but everyone knew you don't have this kind of a party for a barn burning. Tonio Merolli called his son Mario and daughter-in-law Amelia and said:

"As you can see, I'm not a healthy man, and working this farm is just too much for me. A few months ago I called Mario to come and help, and he and his family came very willingly; I am blessed to have good children. My two daughters, Martha and Mariella, are very happily married, and they gave me lovely grandchildren, but I'm too busy and tired to spend any time with them. Mario has given me lovely grandchildren, but I'm too busy and tired to spend time with them either, even thought we live in the same house. I have been thinking about all these things, life is short and it's about time I started to enjoy my family, so my wife and I had a talk, and decided to retire. But it's not fair for Mario to do all the work and keep this farm going, when in the end, after I'm gone, they have to sell it and split the money three ways." At this point there were reiterations from his daughters, and from Mario. They said they didn't expect anything; that he was going to live another hundred years, etc. Tonio smiled, and put his arm over Mario's shoulder. He then motioned for his daughters to join him. When they came up, he motioned for another man to come up. He was a well dressed older gentleman, and Tonio introduced him as his lawyer. He told him to do his thing, and the man stood next to them and produced some papers. He said that Tonio had liquidated some ancient coins he had which dated to ancient Roma, that he had found when he was a young man, digging in one of the fields to bury his beloved dog who had passed away of old age. He sold a large piece of land he owned in the next town, San Giovanni Incarico, which was left to him by his grandmother, the sharecropper who had worked it for twenty years had been more than happy to buy it for a lot less that it would have sold in the open market. After that, he sold all of his mother's and grandmother's gold, which was in very bad condition and too old for anybody modern to want to wear. He took half the amount that was owed to him for various services and favors, as long as he was paid in cash, and he threw in half of his lifetime savings, to accrue as much money as two thirds of what his farm was worth, according to what the appraisers had deemed. He was giving his daughters the equivalent in money as what they would get if the farm was sold and the money split three ways, and he was giving Mario his farm free and clear and enough money to repair and restore whatever had fallen into disrepair. If everyone agreed with this, the papers would be signed right then and there, witnesses all of their friends and neighbors. At this point everyone started to talk at once, Mario looked stunned, his wife and sisters were crying, and everybody was patting him on the back and shaking his hand. The women were hugging Mario's sisters, and Anna and her other children surrounded Amelia and held her in turn. No one seemed to be jealous, and everyone was happy about their neighbor's good luck.

With great ceremony the papers were laid out on one of the tables, and Martha and Mariella's husbands examined everything, and declared themselves overjoyed at Tonio's generosity, and that the money would come in handy now, while they were still young enough to enjoy it and while they were still raising their children. The handsome accordion man was given the signal, and he started to play ballads and snappy tunes, after a while he played some romantic music, and sang along, and couples started to dance. Everyone got up and danced, but the blond brute, Saverio never went near his wife. She moved her feet to the rhythm, and looked longingly at her husband, but he never even looked her way. Nannina, Giustina's aunt, walked by the teacher and patted her on the shoulder:

"Don't give that big oaf brother of mine the satisfaction of pining for him, dance with someone else." The teacher didn't say anything. At one point, Luna saw Aunt Esther lean over and talk to Uncle Pas, and he got up and went up to the teacher. He gave her a courtly bow, like they were in a grand ballroom, instead of the courtyard of a farm, and offered his hand. She put her hand in his, and got up to dance. While they were dancing, Luna walked to the back where some of the men were still drinking and talking, and introduced herself to her Uncle Saverio:

"Hi, I'm Luna Blue; I believe you're one of my uncles." The man looked down from his great height, and smiled. He was gorgeous, with blue eyes and a blond mustache, and rippling muscles all over:

"Hallo' there, little girl! I have seen you around my house during school sessions, anyways. Are you enjoying yourself?"

"A lot more than some other people!" Said Luna:

"What is that supposed to mean, little girl?"

"It means that my teacher is unhappy, you big oaf, because you never even went near her during this whole party."

"You have a mouth on you, don't you? No wonder they got rid of you and send you over here! She seems pretty happy to me from where I'm standing."

"She's not. She's been looking at you all day and she's only dancing with Uncle because she was embarrassed at sitting all alone." He squinted at her, and then said:

"Watch out, little girl! I can put you over my knee lickety-split, and you'll be sorry!"

"Uncle Pas wouldn't let you!"

"I can take him too!"

"You can't take everyone!" Uncle Saverio looked at her with a puzzled expression:

"You're different, somehow. None of those kids would have had the guts to stand up to me like you did, and frankly, my dear, I don't think they give a damn if their teacher is dancing or not." With that, he walked over to the people who were dancing, and cut in on Uncle Pas. He then took Gianna in his arms, and danced her away. She looked up at him with a tremulous smile, and gently laid her head on his chest while they were dancing to Santa Lucia. While Luna was watching, in awe, at the striking couple they made, the blond giant and the small dark woman, Luca walked up to her and stood waiting for the new music to begin. When Santa Lucia finished, the Accordionist stopped for a while, and then began a slow and haunting melody. Luna never heard it before, but it pulled on her heartstring. Someone said it was called 'Shining window' and it was a Neapolitan song about a lost love. Luca turned to her and extending his hand asked:

"My dance, Luna?" She nodded yes, and took his hand shyly. They joined the other couples and started dancing. Over here they danced differently than at home. Luna had taken dancing lessons at her high school, so it was easy for her to adapt and follow Luca. Ivana and the other girls were also dancing, and Concetta's little sister was sitting on Anna's lap. Luca smiled at her once in a while, but didn't say anything, and Luna didn't know what to say to this Italian boy. But she loved dancing with him, he was very light on his feet, was very formal, and kept a proper distance from her. When the dance was over, he bowed to her, and went back to join his friends. The girls got together and, giggling, talked about the boys they had danced with. Ada had danced with her boy from Roma, and she was practically swooning, and Luana had danced with Remigio. No one talked about haystacks and kisses, and Luna realized that they could do whatever they wanted, but always within sight of the adults. Luna actually quite liked it, she felt safe that way, when she knew Aunt Esther and Uncle Pas were watching out for them. After dancing for a long while, the signal was given for the burning. All the children got accounted for, then all the adults. Mario, his brothers-in-law, and a couple friends walked into the great, old barn and checked every corner to make sure it was indeed empty that not even a kitten was left inside. Then a few adults ran around with torches, and they set the barn on fire. At first nothing much happened. Then a few seconds later it went up with a gigantic roar. The old wood, well dry and seasoned, burned very fast and bright as everyone watched in awe. It was starting to be very late afternoon. As Luna stood there with her friends and family, the flames painted everyone and everything with orange, blue and crimson highlights. She suddenly thought about her parents and friends so far away into the future, and silent tears ran down her cheeks. Uncle Pas put his arm over her shoulder and hugged her to him for a few seconds. Where was her life, thought Luna, here or there? At this point she didn't know anymore, and so she buried her head into Uncle's side and sobbed quietly.

That night in bed, Luna dreamed that she was watching Emperor Nero burn Roma down to the ground. The entire city had been torched, going up in one giant fire. Huge flames of red, orange, blue, and every other color reached up to the sky, smoke blowing everywhere and blocking the night sky from view. People screamed and ran away as fast as they could, and the stench of burning wood was almost too much to bear. While the flames burned ferociously, Nero was seated high on a hill overlooking the burning city, and while he was plucking the strings of his lyre, he was murmuring to himself:

"Ho, what sweet sorrow!" With tears streaming down his cheeks, he began playing Santa Lucia. A large group of people were standing together a bit far off into the dark, while Luna was standing in the light of the fire, all by herself. As she watched helplessly, dry wood that had been set alight by Nero's 'men' burned too fast to be believed. How could Emperor Nero order the complete destruction of his capital city in this way? Did he not even care about the people who didn't escape? Luna thought. To her, Nero was obviously a complete madman who cared for no one and nothing but being completely evil! As Luna was thinking of giving Nero a piece of her 'mind', Balthazar suddenly came up behind her and put a hand on her shoulder.

"Emperor Nero must look like a complete monster to you, doesn't he?"

"YES HE DOES!" Luna screamed and cried. "Just look at him sitting there, playing and crying, while everyone down there gets killed and everything get destroyed!" As tears streamed from Luna's face, both from the smoke and from being angry at Nero, Balthazar told her:

"Luna, many things in life are not at all what they seem. For example, is it correct to stop a child from burning himself on a hot stove? You do have to yell at him, making him cry, but that's far better than letting him burn himself."

"I am fourteen, not a small child!" Luna said in anger. "Nero is destroying everything, and we can't stop him!"

"Luna," Balthazar said, "burning the entire city may look like the act of a maniacal madman, but believe me; Emperor Nero is in actuality quite sane here. You see, Luna, the city of Roma has stood almost untouched for centuries, if not longer. In that time, the entire city had become a cesspool of stagnation, dirt and filth. Rats and other vermin infested the sewers and nearly every building, including people's homes, and disease has killed more people over the centuries than the entire population right now. There was no possible way that things could stay the way they've been. Drastic action had to be taken. Tell me, Luna, what happens when you don't clean your room for a month?"

"It gets dirty and rumpled, and Ma yells at me to clean it up."

"And your clothes? What happens if your Ma never washes them?" Balthazar asked:

"They get dirty and smelly, and I get mad at Ma." Luna admitted:

"You see, Luna, everything needs to be cleaned and renewed. I'll admit his methods may seem maniacal and mean, but Nero has always done things in his own way! He may not have Blue Eyes, but he certainly did it His Way!"

"Why didn't he at least warn the people to leave first?" Luna asked:

"He almost certainly gave them plenty of warning, Luna. But few listened, and most of those refused to leave. Should Nero allow Roma to deteriorate further and further, as past Emperors have done, with the stench, vermin and disease epidemics getting worse by the year, or should he tear it down so it can be renewed and rebuilt? What would *YOU* do in his place?"

"I - I don't know!" Luna finally admitted, realizing the need to look at things and see other possibilities.   After a long pause, Balthazar turned back to Luna, speaking:

"Luna, I know the experiences you're going through right now are very painful, and you feel lost, like you don't belong in either place, yet you belong in both places."

"I just want to go home and be with my Real Life family! Yet I feel so close to my 'family' in Italy. Can't I have them both together? Maybe while in my home time?" Balthazar looked right into Luna's deep, dark eyes:

"Luna, this pain *will* pass for you, sooner than you think, and after it's done, you will be much, *much* happier for going through it. You will be renewed in every way, and you will learn and grow from this. About the city of Roma, visiting it in your own time will show you just how right Nero turned out to be, for it could never have become so beautiful otherwise. And as for being with both families you love simultaneously, well, Ms. Blue, that is much more possible than you could ever imagine. Trust me; you'll be very happy very soon!" And with that, Balthazar gave Luna a dimpled little smile, and then disappeared in a puff of smoke, his laugh lingering behind for a few moments.

L' OVAIOLA

Egg Vendor Up on the Mountain
Drawing by F. Palizzi

Morning came awfully fast, and last night's dream was still very much in Luna's head, as if she'd been there while ancient Roma burnt to the ground, making way for the beautiful city it would eventually become. As she remembered what Balthazar had told her about how old things must be taken down so the new can be created, Luna prepared herself for another day. After the chores were done, and before their breakfast, Ivana said that they were going in the back of the house to get snails. She said that it had rained during the night, and the snails were still out, so they had to hurry and pick them up, before they retreated into their abodes in the dirt. Luna just picked up a bucket, like Ivana, and they hurried outside. Sure enough, the stalks of the large weeds in the back were covered by snails. Ivana showed Luna how to get them by sliding them out from the bottom up, a large bunch at the time. After a while their hands were slimy, and the snails kept trying to escape by climbing the sides of the buckets. After the snails had laboriously climbed almost to the top, Ivana kept knocking them down; so did Luna. When the two buckets were almost full, Ivana said:

"We have enough! Let's go in." They went back into the kitchen, and Ivana put the snails in the large oval tub, sprinkled flour on them, and put the cover back on. On top of the cover she put two large, flat rocks she took out of the bottom of the hutch. While she was doing all of this, Luna looked puzzled:

"Why are you putting flour on them? And why the rocks?" She asked. Ivana said:

"When they eat the flour they purge and purify themselves, and the rocks are there so they cannot push on the cover and get out. Once, they got out and we found snails everywhere in the house for days." Still puzzled, Luna asked:

"But why are we doing all this to the snails? What are we going to do with them?" Ivana looked up and said, smiling:

"Why, we're going to eat them, of course!" At Luna's look of horror, Ivana laughed and laughed. School was not productive that day, as everyone was still excited and talking about the party. Even the teacher was in a dreamy mood, and didn't care if they worked or not. Luna was sick to her stomach, and not even their nice lunch of provolone cheese, fresh bread and a beautiful bunch of grapes could raise her mood. She kept thinking about those snails, and the nasty smell that came out of them, almost like wet dog, and she prepared to go without dinner. When time for dinner came, a large platter of steaming snails in pinkish sauce was put on the table. With it there was a large platter of potato salad, another platter of refried pasta, and a beautiful salad. Luna heaved a sigh of relief; there was enough food that if she didn't want the snails it didn't matter. The refried pasta was delicious. Usually Aunt would refry the leftover pasta from the day before. This was pasta from the party; Luna remembered seeing a large tub of it. Aunt would put the cold pasta in a large, hot frying pan with a few drops of olive oil, and she would fry it until the whole thing was golden brown and crunchy. Luna had some of everything, and she was pretty full, but when she saw the others eat the snails, she became pretty curious. They each had a large needle with which they pulled the snail out of the shell. The snail was long, and at the bottom of it, there was a brown piece hanging. Ivana saw Luna look at her, and said:

"Poop!" Then discarded the brown piece and put the rest in her mouth. The light sauce of the snails smelled wonderful, and after a few minutes Luna started to feel left out. She tentatively took one of the snails, stabbed it with the needle next to her plate, and pulled it out. She discarded the brown part, and gingerly took a small bite of the rest. It tasted almost like the conch salad they bought at the deli in the summer. Then it came to her; the Conch was nothing but a large sea snail! She had eaten snails of a kind before. She looked up and saw Uncle Pas look at her with a small smile:

"We have snails where I come from too. We also have very large snails that come from the sea, they're called Conch and we make salad with them." Uncle Pas replied:

"The place you come from sounds pretty wonderful." Luna said:

"It is, most of the time." After dinner, while uncle Pas and Aunt Esther were outside having their coffee, and the girls were cleaning up, a vehicle drove up. It was the Carabinieri, Italian gendarmes, and they had come to look at Luna's papers. Luna was impressed and scared by the two uniformed men. They were very tall, had a dark blue, formal uniform with gold braids, brass buttons with an insignia on them and medals and other stuff hanging on their chests. There were red stripes down the sides of their trousers, and they were heavily armed, with leather holsters and guns right outside their uniform. They had very fancy hats, and they wore dazzling white gloves; they were beautiful! They were also very formal and proper. Luna ran up and took the envelope right out of her handbag. She had checked it some days before, but she didn't understand any of the papers. She hoped everything was alright. But then she wasn't worried, Uncle Pas was there, and he would take care of everything. She handed the envelope to the two gendarmes, and they checked all the papers inside. They had a brief conversation with Uncle Pas, saluted everyone, and left. Luna heaved a sigh of relief. She went back upstairs, and put the envelope back in her bag. She handled her buttercup yellow bag for a while, and wondered when she would have the chance to use it. She put it back and went downstairs to do her homework. Now she knew why there was nothing in her room; she only slept in there. Because she always had so much to do, there was no time to spend in her room. She remembered what she did at home; spending so much time in her room all alone. True, she had a phone, a computer (and Facebook) and a TV, but she was still alone. It was much better to be with people, although Mom and Dad were so tired every evening that they just wanted to be by themselves as well. Things were very different here, and Luna didn't know yet if she liked it better here or at home. Couldn't her home be a little more like here, where people actually talked with each other face to face, at least some of the time? That way, she would feel far less lonely and abandoned. Why couldn't her parents pay more attention to her, like Aunt and Uncle did? At night over here it was very quiet, almost lonely, and sometimes Luna felt isolated, wishing for a little more noise. During the day she had no problems, but wondered what would happen when the bad weather came, and people couldn't walk outside so much. While they were sitting doing their homework, Luna asked Ivana what they did when the snow came. Ivana looked up amazed:

"We don't do anything! We don't get snow! I wish we did. It would be fun to play with snowballs, and make snowmen, but unfortunately we don't get any snow." Luna said:

"Ever?"

"Well," answered Ivana, "it snowed a couple of years ago, but by the time my mother made me wear coat, boots, mittens and shawl, when I went outside it was almost all melted. Do you get snow up north?" Luna looked at Ivana:

"We certainly do! But it's not all fun and games. It's very cold, and it's not easy to do anything. We have to shovel the front of the house otherwise we can't go out, and it's very dangerous to walk, especially when the snow turns to ice. We have to travel everywhere by car, but sometimes the cars get stuck because of the snow, and we have to dig them out. You're very lucky to have this nice weather here." Ivana was listening as if Luna was talking about the moon, and said:

"You must be very rich if you can travel everywhere by car, up north everyone must be so rich." Luna said:

"Not everyone, but a car is a necessity, and everyone has to have one. As soon as I turn sixteen I'm going to get a driver's license and get my own car." Ivana said with a sigh:

"I wish I lived where you do. I'm sure I'd like it, you have so much more there than we do here." Luna said:

"You have a beautiful home, lots of friends, and parents and family that loves you. Believe me; you have everything you could possibly need, and much more than we do up north." That night just before she went to sleep, Luna remembered thinking:

"I like it here, and I like the people, but that's only because I know I'm going to leave. If I had to stay here forever, I'd simply go crazy. But there are things here that I want. I wish my parents were more like Aunt Esther and Uncle Pas, I wish we had a lot of relatives to get together with, I wish everybody was calmer, and that they had more time, I wish people cared more for one another, and I wish I could like my teachers and my school like I do here." And then suddenly it came to Luna; she wanted this life, only she wanted it back home in Boston. But, as Rudyard Kipling said, in a ballad the English teacher back home read to them often:

"Oh East is East, and West is West, and never the twain shall meet." As she fell into oblivion, Luna thought:

"I can't even imagine how I remember that!"

Most of the week went by without anything notable happening. Luna was really into her book, by now, in fact she took the tome home almost every day to find out what happened. At this point in the story, Lucia had been kidnapped by Don Rodrigo, the bad guy, and taken to Milano. Renzo had traveled to Milano to try and find her, but found nothing but famine and disease. Milano was besieged by the plague. Luna had never heard of such disease, and could never imagine how poor and desperate people could be. She felt happy that she didn't live in the olden days, if she was ever to go back home! Oh Balthazar, what did you do to me! Like Anna had whispered to her at the party:

"Are you used to this time and place yet little Luna? Old Balthazar deserves to be smacked, crazy old wizard, always pissin and moanin about keeping everything a secret! The first time I saw that old coot, he was wearing a dress. Never trust a man in a dress!" Deep in their conversation, they never even noticed that Gianna the Teacher was passing behind them and heard what they were saying, and walked away with a frown. On Saturday evening the bathing ritual was repeated. At home, Luna hated to bathe; she liked very long showers that drove her dad crazy. Here the bathing was another way of getting close to each other, a way to help each other. Luna didn't miss having an indoor bathroom.

On Sunday, after breakfast, they dressed up to go to church. Aunt Esther was working on new blouses for them, and the next time they came to church, they would be wearing fancy blouses with a bit of lace on their collars. They drove way into the brush and up the mountain. The road was little more than a trail, and the truck had a hard time finding enough room to pass through. Luna asked Ivana what they would do if another vehicle came down the same trail, and Ivana said that there was another trail that went down. They were going to the Sanctuary of the martyrs S.S. Cosmo and Damiano, the healing saints, and it was only twenty minutes from the farm, in fact if you looked up the mountain right in front of the farm, you could see the white building half way up. Ivana told Luna that today, September 27, they were going to have the celebration of the saints, and it was magnificent, people came from all over for it, and there was to be a feast with stalls for shopping and all kinds of entertainments. Uncle Pas commented that some people liked to call the saints Cosma and Damiano, but since they were two guys after all, he had always called them Cosmo and Damiano, never mind what they were called where they came from.

When they arrived at the church, Uncle parked the truck on the dirt, some distance away, and they walked the rest of the way. There was a clearing right in front of the church, and there were lots of stalls. Aunt Esther said that it was market day usually on this Sunday; they had it once a month, but this was better than market day, much bigger and more populated, and they just happened to be here on the right Sunday. Luna and Ivana wanted to go investigate, but Aunt Esther said:

"After the mass." And so they went inside. A lot of people they knew were there. Anna waved them over and eagerly made room for them by pushing everyone else to the end of the pew. The church smelled of wax and incense, and the statues of the brother saints dominated everything. There were flowers and fine linens on the altar, and a sense of adoration and worship floated around everyone. You just wanted to be quiet and think. The entire mass was in Latin, not like at home, where mass was in English. Luna's family was catholic, but not practicing Catholics, she went to mass on occasion, when she stayed at her grandmother's (Grammeva always dragged her to church), or for funerals and weddings, and she felt really bored in church. Here it felt sacrosanct, somehow, and the respect everyone had for their church and their religion was palpable. Luna kept getting up and sitting down when everyone else did, and when they went up for communion, not knowing what to do, she stayed in her seat. Ivana had told her that here you couldn't go up for communion unless you had gone to confession first, and Luna was afraid of making a mistake. Father Attilio finally blessed everyone, and then stood near the front door to salute his parishioners and shake hands. Uncle Pas shook Father Attilio's hand and slipped him a note, so did most everyone. Luna told Ivana that where she came from, they passed a basket to people for their donations, but Ivana said that Father Attilio didn't want to put anyone on the spot, in case they didn't have any money, and if someone wanted to help their Sanctuary, then they would do it on their own. Finally they left the church.

After the dimness and holiness of the Sanctuary, they emerged into the bright sunlight, and the girls made fast tracks to the colorful stalls. At home, Luna was pretty bored by small stores that sold knick knacks and other small things, but she hadn't seen a store since she got here, and she eagerly wanted to do some shopping. She regretted not bringing her bag with the small wallet in it, but Uncle Pas told them they could spend a thousand liras each, and they were exhilarated, until Luna worked it to maybe about five dollars American money. She was crestfallen, until she saw the prices on things. Everything was from fifty liras to a hundred, and the most expensive things were two or three hundred liras. Then she remembered that this was after all the fifties, and things cost a lot less back then. In the stalls they had a great variety of things; fancy combs and hair ribbons, pins, bracelets, brooches, belts, shawls, socks, underwear, perfume, soft robes, cloth of course, purses, pots and pans, perfumed bath powder, beautiful sweaters, and then there were the stalls that sold candy, marzipan fruit, nougat, dried fruits and licorice. There was a fancy silk stall, there were stalls that sold home things, like tablecloths and doilies, and then there was cheese and olives, and sugar and flour. And of course there were numerous statues of the saints, holy water in small bottles, and prayer books. The Cannatari pottery makers had one of the biggest stalls in the market; they had so many kinds of cannatas that blew the mind. There were big ones and little ones, plain ones and fancy ones, rough every day ones and fancy decorating painted ones, tall ones and squat ones, and tiny toy ones for little girls. They also had other toys; rattles full of dried peas, painted doll's heads, hands and feet to be used for rag dolls, small whistles with a trapped dry pea inside that made a shrill sound and colorful little bells with flowers painted all over and great, red, tin clappers hanging inside. They had flower pots, platters, dishes and all kinds of brown earthenware pots to use for cooking spaghetti sauce. But what Luna liked the most were all kinds of chamber pots; they had small ones and big ones, short ones and tall ones, plain ones and fancy ones. Some were striped in all the colors of the rainbow, and some had beautiful designs on them. Luna laughed and even asked how much they cost, but Ivana said, seriously:

"Some people still use them, the elderly and the sick, and what would you do if you needed one in the middle of the night and outside it was raining or something?"   Luna was duly chastised, but she couldn't help being dazzled. Uncle Pas handed them the money, he gave each of them ten one hundred lira bills as big as handkerchiefs, and he took off with Aunt Esther. The girls examined everything minutely, not spending anything until they saw everything and were very sure about what they wanted. Ivana bought two beautiful combs with pearls, and a container of licorice sticks. After serious thought, because they cost three hundred liras each, she bought a beautiful red sweater and some red shoes to go with it. With the last of her money she bought a small shiny box for her father's cigarette papers and a small, round bottle of perfume for her mother. She was missing one hundred liras to complete her purchases, but since she had spent a lot of money in the same stall, she haggled until she obtained everything she wanted.

Luna hadn't thought about spending any of that money on anyone else but herself, but she found that she felt a certain pleasure in buying something for someone else. It was a first for Luna, and she gave a lot of thought to what to buy for whom. She bought an expensive double frame for Anna, to put her deceased husband and son's pictures in it, a new leather pouch for Uncle Pas' tobacco, (his old one was frayed and almost ready to fall apart) and some shiny golden hair ribbons for Aunt Esther. She was going to fix Aunt's hair in French braids, one day, and she meant to intertwine the ribbons with the dark braids. For herself she bought some nice, slim suede shoes in pale blue (blue suede shoes, of course!), a pair of combs with shiny little blue stones, some sweet smelling bath powder (it said Blue Fern on the blue container, and it smelled heavenly), and a soft azure sweater with flowers embroidered on the front. She was missing thirty liras to get the sweater, and she was going to put it back, because she didn't feel like haggling, but the vendor said it was enough and pulled the last of her money from her unresisting hands. She did not have any money left for candy, but she meant to sponge some off of Ivana on the way home. They held their bundles carefully while they looked for Uncle Pas and Aunt Esther. They found them in the fancy silk stall, and Uncle Pas was draping a beautiful, hand embroidered silk shawl over Aunt Esther shoulders. She demurred saying that it cost too much, but he said he wanted her to have it. Aunt Esther remarked that she didn't have too many places to wear it, and Uncle Pas said she could wear it to bed. Aunt Esther colored at that, but looked up to smile impishly at him, and accepted it. Luna had never seen Aunt Esther look impish, and she rolled her eyes, like Ivana was doing, but then they both burst out laughing and joined the two adults. Afterwards, while Aunt and Uncle socialized with the adults, and Ivana showed what she bought to Concetta who was there with her parents, Luna looked for Anna. She found her in the food stall, handling some small pieces of yellowish, brown cheese to the protests of the vendor:

"Some of these marzolline are so small you scrape the gook off of them and there's nothing left to eat!" She exclaimed. Luna had eaten the small pieces of cheese, the size of a cannoli, for supper a couple of nights before, and knew that despite the strong smell of dirty socks, they were so tasty she could become addicted to them, and she approved Anna's tactics. After the purchase was made, combined with haggling and denigrating remarks from Anna, Luna took her to the side, and gave her the bundle with the frame:

"Uncle Pas gave me some money," she told Anna, "and I wanted you to have something to put your husband and son's pictures in." Anna looked at her with tears in her eyes:

"You don't have anything of your own, you're so far from home, and you spend your little bit of money on me?" Luna hugged her, and said:

"Uncle gave me a thousand Liras, I bought a lot of stuff for me too, so don't worry about me."

"Your uncle always was a very generous man with his money. Of course it don't hurt when you're rich, naturally!" Luna blinked:

"My uncle is rich? I didn't know that!" Anna said:

"You won't think so, he doesn't advertise it, but he worked very hard all his life, and he's very comfortable indeed. They live comfortably, but not ostentatiously, and they quietly do a lot of good." Luna was surprised at this tidbit about her unassuming uncle. Anna loved the frame, she said she had two wooden frames for her dear departed, and they would love being together on earth like they were in heaven, and especially in a fancy store-bought shiny frame.

On the way back, Luna asked Ivana what kind of candy she'd bought and Ivana said:

"Licorice sticks." And she showed Luna a round cardboard container with a cover. She then opened it, and Luna was amazed to see that the container had nothing but little pieces of wooden branches in it. She said to Ivana:

"I think you got cheated, there's nothing but wood in your box." Ivana laughed:

"That's the candy, silly!" She then proceeded to put the end of one of the sticks in her mouth and started to chew and suck. After a while seeing Luna's stunned expression, she handed her one, and Luna hesitantly stuck it in her mouth. She started to chew and suck like she saw Ivana do, and to her surprise, a sweet, licorice flavored juice started filling her mouth. She realized that this was licorice's natural state, and she was amazed at how good it was compared to the kind she used to buy at home. Aunt Esther admonished them:

"Don't eat too much candy; you'll spoil your appetite for your Sunday dinner!"

After Sunday dinner, when all the work was done, they all put their purchases on the table to show each other what they had bought. Aunt showed her beautiful shawl, and some things she had bought for the house, and then kissed Uncle lightly on the mouth to thank him. He winked a little and said:

"Wait until Christmas! You'll want to thank me even more." Aunt Esther said:

"You think so, don't you?"

"Yes, I do!" Said Uncle Pas, and gave her an impudent grin, his teeth gleaming white in his dark face. Luna and Ivana walked around the table to Uncle Pas, and they both hugged him. Luna said:

"You're the most generous Uncle I have ever had. Thank you!" And she handed him her gift. He was surprised, and when Ivana handed hers, he took the old small box and pouch from his pocket, and made a big showing of throwing them out in the trash. After that, he put his papers in Ivana's box and his tobacco in Luna's pouch. To show how much he liked their gifts, he made himself a cigarette, while the girls looked on with pride, and then leaned back his chair to savor the tobacco. Ivana's mother declared the perfume her favorite, and proceeded to rub some on her wrists and ear lobes. Uncle Pas looked up at her with half closed lids, a twinkle in his eyes. Aunt loved Luna's ribbons, but she didn't know what she would do with them yet. Luna told her that she knew how to make a different kind of braid, and she would eventually show Aunt how to intertwine ribbons in the new kind of braids. Aunt was intrigued, and promised they would try it soon. Aunt Esther, ever frugal, had also bought some cloth to make Uncle some new shirts, and some pretty soft wool to make the girls new dresses for the winter.

That night Luna drifted off to sleep immediately, and dreamed she was in Pinocchio's Land of Toys. There were toys and cotton candy everywhere, there were candy apples and ice cream cones, chocolate bars and lollipops, marshmallows and chocolate fudge; there were soda fountains and chocolate milk fountains, both hot and cold. Luna was hungry and grabbed everything she could lay her hands on, but as soon as she touched anything, it turned into a stick of wood, and no matter how she chewed and sucked on it, it just tested like a piece of wood, even the soda. Eventually Luna realized that she was starving in this land of plenty, surrounded by more candy than she had ever seen in her life, by toys and music and merriment. All she really wanted was to be back home with Aunt and Uncle, and to have a nice plate of polenta in front of her, and a big glass of spring water with a twist of lemon.

On the Monday, it was back to normal, and it was almost a relief. Luna had never had so much excitement at home, where she was surrounded by such a myriad of things that she couldn't' even remember them all. It was almost like over here there was more flavor to life, feelings were stronger, things were appreciated more. Or maybe it was the closeness with the rest of the family. In their quiet, unassuming way, Uncle Pas and Aunt Esther were always there, helping and protecting the girls, and it was the sense of security they gave them that made the girls feel good about everything; they knew they were going to be told if they did wrong and they were going to be praised if they did good. They felt on solid ground this way. On Tuesday, Ivana told Luna on the way to school:

"Today is my birthday."

"Your Birthday?" Exclaimed   Luna: "No one said anything. How old are you?"

"I'm fourteen!" Said Ivana:

"When are you having your birthday party?" Asked Luna:

"I'm not having a birthday party!" Said Ivana. Luna was amazed:

"Why ever not!" She asked:

"Here no one has a birthday party, it's not the custom, but maybe my mother will make a cake." Luna started to think like Luna, and a small good (bad) idea started to germinate in her head. Maybe she should help Ivana to have some fun today; after all it was her birthday! And, of course, if Ivana had fun, so would Luna. She thought hard for a moment; here you couldn't go to the mall or anything, if you decided to play hooky, and she didn't want to go shopping anyways, but there should be something to do that was better than school! She asked Ivana:

"What would the teacher say if we don't show up for school?" Ivana answered her:

"She would think we were needed at home, and save us the work for another day." Luna said:

"How would you like, since it's your birthday, to play hooky today?" Ivana looked puzzled:

"What's playing hooky?"

"It's when you say you're going to school but you don't."

"Why would I want to do that?" Ivana was curious, and Luna told her that since it was her birthday, and it was a very important day, and since no one was doing anything for her, she should do something for herself and have a fun day. Ivana asked her if she had ever done it, and Luna said, truthfully, that she had done it many times and those were the best days she remembered. Luna didn't discuss the consequences, of course! Finally, Ivana was convinced, and they sat down on a large tree stump and decided what to do for fun. Ivana knew that the Russo boys were not in school today, as they were moving their distillating equipment to another barn, and they were needed at home, so they could go over to the Russo farm, and see what the boys were up to, and after that they could go visit Aunt Palma and have some of the cherry pies she always made on Tuesday. After that they could go to the river and maybe go in the water half-way up their tights. They would have to, scandalously, lift their dresses way up, of course, and maybe even show their panties! Luna thought that it would be fun to stand in the roiling water and even more fun to watch the Russo boys work. They were shy and never talked to them at school, but they were very handsome, and maybe they would talk to them away from school.

They hid their bundles in a secret place Ivana knew, and lightly skipped over to the nearby Russo farm. The place was already a hive of activity, and they found the boys behind their largest barn. Marco and Marcello were surprised to see them, and asked them what they were doing at the farm:

"We decided not to go to school, because today it's Ivana's birthday, and we're just hanging around having some fun." Luna told them. Marco and Marcello looked at them like they were Martians, and then asked:

"What are your parents going to say?" At that Ivana started to look uncertain, and Luna quickly spoke up:

"What they don't know won't hurt them." The boys started to look interested, and decided to join the fun, at least for a little while. They looked around to see if they were being observed, then quickly motioned for the girls to follow them and ran away from the farm, downhill. Luna and Ivana wanted to know where they were going, but they said:

"You'll see!" and kept running. At one point, the river came into view, and on the river there was a kind of houseboat attached to the shore by a long wooden pier. From the shore, the boys called:

"Fiorello!" A few times, and when there was no response, they said: "He's not there, let's go in." The girls followed them on the thin, wooden pier, and finally they pushed open the small door of the houseboat, and went in. The place was stacked with packages, boxes, rows of wrapped, round object that looked like nougat candy, colorful papers, and chainlike hanging paper sausages in all the colors of the rainbow, and frames made of steel that resembled men on bicycles, pinwheels, and fountains of cascading water:

"What is this place?" Asked Luna. The boys, as proud of the place as if they owned said:

"It's the firework shack. Fiorello is a friend of ours; he and his family own it."

"But why it's on the water?" Asked Luna. The boys looked at her like she was asking stupid questions, and Ivana said:

"She comes from the North. She usually doesn't know anything about what we do." And shrugged her shoulders. The boys took turns explaining the obvious to Luna:

"On this shack, they make fireworks, and once in a while, the whole shack explodes, fireworks are made of explosives after all. The law says that the shack has to be at some distance from everyone, and on the water, so that when it explodes it won't hurt anything or anyone." Luna remembered seeing fireworks at Disney, and on Fourth of July, and didn't know that behind the fun lay so much danger. She asked hesitantly;

"Does it explode very often?" Marco said:

"Every couple of years." Luna asked:

"What happens to the people inside?" Marcello said:

"Kaboom! They die!" Luna shivered, and Marco said:

"Don't worry about it, Fiorello has a lot of brothers; when one blows up, another takes his place!" Luna started to slowly back up, and they all followed her, laughing. They ran and gamboled like colts, and chased each other mercilessly. After a while, they stopped near a large, gnarled tree and picked up persimmons. The fruits were very ripe and juicy, and they ate them while the yellow juice ran down their chins. They wiped their faces with soft grass, and then lay down on the grassy knoll overlooking the river and stared at the clouds. They each tried to see what the clouds resembled. Luna saw wholly sheep everywhere, but Ivana saw unicorns and wholly mammoths. The boys could only see pirates on a ship, and cowboys running after their herds. In the end, they lay down exhausted and stared at the sky quietly. Suddenly, a faint voice was heard calling the boys' names, and they jumped up:

"They're looking for us. See you in school tomorrow! Good Bye!" And they ran away as fast as they could.   Luna and Ivana stayed a little longer, dreaming, and then they got up and decided that it was time for Aunt Palma's cherry pie.

The little munchkin of a woman received them joyously and they were soon sitting on the table in the tiny dining room, with a large piece of cherry pie in front of them. They chatted for a while, then Aunt Palma looked them square in the eyes, and asked:

"What are you girls doing out of school?" Ivana looked guilty, and blushed, but Luna explained that it was Ivana's birthday, and they thought that she deserved to have some fun, since no one had done anything for her. Aunt Palma looked as if she knew something, but then changed her mind and said:

"You girls better squeeze a lot of fun in today, because I think you'll need it." They didn't know what Aunt Palma meant, but she wouldn't say anymore. Aunt Palma then went to a drawer in the dining room, and pulled out a large piece of sparkling white lace. Ivana looked at it with awe. She whispered to Luna:

"That's the nicest piece of tombola lace I have ever seen!"

"What kind of lace?" Asked Luna. Ivana explained that in the olden days ladies wore pieces of that kind of intricate lace hanging at their waist when they wore the costume, and now you didn't see it anymore, because the tombola lace was a lost art. Almost no one knew how to do it, and it required a great amount of time and skill to use all of the little tomboline, as they were called, to make it. Anyone who had some of the lace sold it for a lot of money to city people who used it to make fancy things. In Luna's brain the translation said Bobbin Lace, and she knew that the art was not dead, it had been resurrected, and there were people doing it even in her day. Aunt Palma said:

"I do it when I feel like it. As a girl, my mother used to make me sit for hours at the tombola pillow, doing tombola lace, but now I just do it for pleasure. I have been making this for you, little Ivana, it took me six months, as my eyes are not that good. Wear it with your paisana costume, and remember me when you do." Ivana hugged the little woman, and told her that she couldn't take it with her just yet, but she would come back for it a little later. They both kissed the soft, paper thin skin of her cheeks, and left. On to the river!

The river was everything Luna remembered and more. The noise from it was deafening, and it carried a plethora of strange things from upriver. Luna was curious to know why further down, on the Russo farm, it was placid and pleasant while here it was wild and scary. Ivana told her that there was a waterfall just before the river reached their farm, that's why the water was so turbulent. By the time it reached the Russo farm it had calmed down and evened out. Also the bed of the river was not so deep near the Russo farm. Ivana thought that the river was much more exciting here, and so thought Luna. They took their shoes and socks off, lifted their dresses high and waded in. The water was warm, and sluiced around their legs like molasses. But the more they went in, the more it gripped them, until they felt like it had tentacles, and it was trying to suck them in. Ivana got scared and started to back up, but Luna was caught in the excitement and danger of it and kept going. Ivana started to scream for Luna to go back, and when Luna kept doggedly going, Ivana tried to run up to her and she was so scared that she slipped on some rocks and fell face down in the turbulent, yellow water. Luna screamed, and tried to go back and help her, but the water was too strong and wouldn't let her go. She was an especially strong swimmer; she was on the swimming team, so she just threw herself down and started to swim in the semi shallow water. She finally made it to Ivana who was still trashing and bobbing up and down. They hung onto each other, and made it to the dry land. Ivana cried noisily, with great gulps, and Luna comforted her. Ivana said:

"I thought that I was going to drown, I don't know how to swim."

"Then why did you come after me in the water?" Asked Luna. Ivana looked her in the eyes and said:

"I didn't want you to drown. I love you like a sister, and wanted to save you. Instead you saved me! Where did you learn to swim like that?" Luna answered carefully:

"I learned at school. I'm on the swimming team." Ivana seemed perplexed:

"I've never heard that people learned to swim in school, or that they had swimming teams."

"Well, they do in the North." Mumbled Luna. They got up, and holding each other, their wet clothes sticking to their bodies, gingerly walked home. When they reached the house, they realized that there was no way they could sneak in without being seen. Aunt Esther was at the front door, obviously waiting for them, and Uncle Pas came out of the barn as soon as they reached the house. Aunt Esther cried out, when she saw what they looked like, and without comment helped them to undress and bundled them up in large towels, while they heated lots of water for a bath. Uncle Pas looked at them seriously, and then said:

"Take a hot bath, eat some soup and then we'll talk." The girls just nodded, miserably. After everything was done, and they were sitting warm and cozy in the kitchen, next to a warm fire lighted in the fireplace so they could take the chill off, Uncle Pas pulled up a chair across from them and sat down. Aunt Esther was sitting next to him, her eyes red, like she'd been crying. Uncle Pas said:

"I know you girls didn't go to school, what I like to know is what you did do all day." Luna whispered:

"How did you know……" Uncle Pas replied:

"I went there this morning looking for you."

"Why?" Whispered the girls. Uncle looked at them:

"I went to pick both of you up to take you to town, for your birthday presents." At Luna's surprised exclamation, Uncle said:

"I know it's your birthday too, Luna Marina Blue. Tomorrow you'll be fourteen." Luna hung her head down, ashamed, and Ivana jumped up and exclaimed precipitately:

"I was all my fault. Luna went with me, but it was my idea, I just wanted to have fun on my birthd….." Luna stopped her, and hugged her:

"You don't have to protect me, Ivana. I will tell the truth. I talked Ivana into doing something called playing hooky. It's something kids do where I come from. Ivana never heard of it. It means we lie about going to school, and we go have fun instead. I wanted Ivana to have fun on her birthday, but more than that, I wanted to have fun myself. I used Ivana's birthday to get myself some fun." Aunt Esther looked at her sadly, and Uncle Pas asked:

"What did you girls do all day? I went looking for you but couldn't find you." Ivana started to talk, but Luna stopped her:

"We went to the Russo farm, because Marco and Marcello were home, and they took us to see the firework shack." At that Aunt Esther shivered and moaned, and then asked:

"That the boys touch you girls?

"No!" The girls answered in unison, kind of surprised. Then she continued:

"After the shack, we ran around on the grass, and when we were tired we lay down on the ground and tried to see what the clouds looked like. When Marco and Marcello were called home, we went to see aunt Palma, and she gave us cherry pie. We then went to the river and waded in. The river was turbulent, and Ivana wanted to leave, but I won't, and when she thought I was going to drown, she came in after me. It's my fault she fell in. After that we just came home." Ivana looked at Luna and said:

"You forgot something. When I fell in, I was going to drown, but Luna swam out to me and dragged me ashore. She saved my life." Aunt Esther was now sobbing and exclaiming:

"Oh my God, what could have happened to us today. We could have lost our little girls!" And she fell sobbing into Uncle Pas' arms. He held her arms and shook her:

"Calm down, Estherina. Remember when we were fifteen and decided to explore Mount Leuci? They found us after two days, and your mother was acting like you are now and had to be stopped from killing me? Remember what stopped her? I stood up to her and told her never to worry about you again, that I was going to marry you and protect you, and be your slave for the rest of my life." Aunt Esther looked up at him with adoration and said:

"And you did that! I remember like it was yesterday; you were wonderful! You laid down over me to keep me warm those two nights, and never touched me except to rub my arms and legs to keep them from freezing. If I could have fallen in love with you more than I already did, I would have! On my wedding day my mother told me I was lucky, and that you were a good man, not to mention rich and handsome as all get up!" They looked at each other with stars in their eyes, and held hands. Luna and Ivana rolled their eyes and exclaimed at the same time:

"Excuse me you two? Can you please stop that? We were talking about us and our transgressions, if we're not wrong!" At that they stopped looking at each other, and came back to earth:

"Yes," Uncle Pas said, "we have to decide on a punishment for you two." He then got up and motioned for them to follow him out of the room. The two girls got up shaking, like they were going to the guillotine, and followed him;

"Do you think he is going to spank us?" Asked Luna with trepidation. Ivana couldn't help giggling:

"I don't think so; he never spanked me in my entire life." They followed him into the good dining room, and lo and behold they saw something that left them speechless. Leaning against the chairs were two beautiful bikes; one red and the other one blue. Luna looked at Ivana and whispered:

"What are those?" Ivana whispered back:

"Bicycles, dunderhead! What did you think they were?"

"I know they're bicycles," answered Luna, "but what are they doing in your dining room?" Uncle Pas was looking at them seriously:

"Those are your birthday presents." Both girls looked back, mouth agape:

"We were bad, cutting school, and lying to you, and you would still give us a birthday present?" Luna asked. Ivana put her arm over her eyes and started to sob:

"And what about our punishment?" Uncle looked at them standing there miserably, one crying and one full of trepidation, and said:

"I think you've been punished enough. Besides there would not be a repeat of this playing hooky, will there?" They both fell over each other assuring Uncle and Ivana's tears slowly dried up. Luna had never been this close to a bike, but she'd seen them, of course. Some dorky kids at school rode bikes, and some fanatics who raced had them, but they were never a concern for Luna. Now she looked at the two simple bikes like they were a new invention. They were shiny, and they represented freedom from walking everywhere, although Luna didn't mind walking; what she minded was the time it took.

When they took the bikes to the front yard, Ivana got permission to ride, and she started to do so joyfully. Luna, who had picked the blue bike, had to confess that she didn't know how to ride. Uncle Pas understood, and started to help her learn. Luna was afraid to be on top of the bike alone, and kept begging

Uncle not to let go. After a while, she almost got the hang of it, and went alone for short stretches. Finally, Luna was able to ride, wobbling and moving the front wheel constantly, but Uncle Pas declared that to be a great achievement, and Luna kept going more securely, until she suddenly found her face in the dirt. She had fallen off her bike! She couldn't believe it! She jumped up, ashamed, but Aunt Esther, who had been watching from the front door, ran to her, checked her all up, declared her perfectly alright, and hugged her.   Uncle Pas declared the bike also perfectly alright, barring some small scratches he could touch up easily, and they all went in to dinner:

"There's nothing that a good plate of steaming tripe in tomato sauce couldn't cure!" Declared Uncle Pas with a sly smile directed her way. Luna rolled her eyes, and followed him inside. After the table was set, and the food platters put out, they all sat down. There was a minestrone soup, full of greens, vegetables and herbs, a bowl of boiled, sliced beets drizzled with oil and vinegar, and a tureen of tripe in red sauce. Luna had never eaten tripe before, of course, and she knew it was a cow's stomach lining after all, and she could have satiated herself with soup and beets, which she had learned to love, but by now she knew to try everything, just in case she missed something good. After the soup, she ladled a small amount of the fragrant red sauce in her plate, and she saw that the tripe was cut in small strips, and the pink sauce wrapped itself around the strips lovingly. Everyone was eating the tripe with golden chunks of bread, and she did the same. She put some small bits of tripe in her mouth, and bit into the golden bread she had dipped first in the sauce. It was not love at first sight with the tripe, but, little did she know, it was going to be one of her favorite foods ever for the rest of her life. She looked up into Uncle Pas' face and mouthed:

"Thank you!" And Uncle inclined his head in understanding. They talked about the day, and Luna expressed her sorrow for nearly getting the two of them drowned; she didn't know how dangerous the river could be. They talked about the firework shack, and Uncle told them that it was against the law for them to go on it, and the Russo boys should be cautioned. He wasn't going to talk to their parents, but he was going to intercept them on their way to school and have a talk with them. Ivana told them how Aunt Palma had made her a large piece of tombola lace, to the amazement of Aunt and Uncle; Aunt Palma never did stuff like that anymore at her age. Uncle Pas said that Aunt Palma knew that he was looking for them; he had stopped there first, as even he knew how good Aunt Palma's cherry pies were. She had given him one, and they would have it for dessert. The girls declined the pie, and somehow they knew that cherry pie was not going to be one of their favorite desserts from now on. After dinner, Aunt and Uncle retired to their bedroom, for a nap and to get over the emotional day they had, and they could be faintly heard whispering and laughing. At one point Uncle Pas came down to get some espresso and a plate of 'Ammonia' cookies, baking ammonia that is, and he was wearing his 'good' burgundy robe over his pajamas. Ivana and Luna hit each other with their elbow, and giggled. Uncle Pas said:

"What?" And the girls said:

"Nothing!" And then giggled hysterically. Uncle left carrying the plate of cookies in one hand and the coffee tray in the other, holding his nose up in the air with injured dignity. That night, after their evening meal, Aunt Esther put out a small cake with two birthday candles on, and they sang Happy Birthday and had a good time. Just before going to sleep, Luna thought to herself how different this birthday party had been compared to the ones at home, and especially compared to the one she had dreamed about, but for some reason, she felt that her birthday had been noticed here a lot more than it ever was at home, even without all the frills.

Going to school the following day was tough. The teacher didn't make any comment, neither did anyone else, but the Russo boys avoided looking in their direction, and the girls knew Uncle Pas must have had his talk with them. They hadn't taken their bikes to school, Luna was not a good bike rider yet, but they told their friends about the bikes, and everyone was duly impressed. Luna saw Uncle Saverio lurking around outside of the classroom at one point, but she had other things on her mind. She loved her bike, and she didn't know how she was ever going to take it home. Going home started to be a big worry, and she felt split in half most of the time. How was she going to leave Uncle Pas and Aunt Esther? And how was she not going to go back home to her parents and her real life? The trouble was that this was starting to feel like her real life, and home and her parents seemed farther away every day that she spent here. But really, what was she going to do here when she grew up? She knew she liked it with Aunt Esther and Uncle Pas, but she couldn't be a farm wife. She would have to go away to a big city to work. And if she had to go away, then she would go away home. Only, if she went away home, she would never see Ivana, Aunt Esther and Uncle Pas again. What to do? Life had all of a sudden become even more complicated than at home. She should have behaved, and maybe her parents would have loved her more, and she could just go to school, grow up and have a nice life, instead of wishing for impossible things. That her wishes had been fulfilled was even worse, because now she had a new set of problems, and they were a doozy. Her grandmother Eva had always told her:

"Be careful what you wish for, because you just may get it." She got it alright! Boy that she get it!

On the following Saturday, the girls came home with them. Ada, Concetta and Luana had received permission from their parents to stay overnight at Ivana's house, after arranging it with Uncle Pas and Aunt Esther, of course. It was the day to try new ways of fixing their hair, and after a large, nice supper of pasta and beans and fried chicken with red peppers, they all cleaned up and enjoyed real espresso with meringues. After that, Uncle Pas made himself scarce and all the girls had their hair washed, even Aunt Esther, and then tried new things. Luna showed them how to do French braids, and everyone was amazed at what you could do with long hair. Aunt Esther looked amazing with soft, side French braids tied together on the back of her head, over the loose hair on her back. Of course, if she was to wear French braids outside, the long hair in the back would have to be shortened, or arranged in some kind of coil. Luna told them about dreadlocks, and they couldn't believe it, so they tried it on Concetta, whose hair was shorter than anyone else, and then they laughed themselves silly, thinking how funny she looked. Luana said that she had gone to Roma with her mother the year before, they stayed at her Aunt and Uncle's apartment, and they took her and their kids to the movies to see 'The Little Rascals' and in it there was a little black kid, Bucket of Wheat, who wore his hair almost like that. Luna told them that in fact dreadlocks were at first an African custom, but that everybody liked them now and they could be stylish and sophisticated. They looked at her like she came from the Moon, and Luna asked Ivana to dreadlock her much shorter hair, and when that was done, everybody agreed that it could be a fun hairdo, but they wouldn't wear it outside. Finally it was time to go to bed, Uncle Pas had opened up three cots in Ivana's and Luna's bedrooms, and finally they were alone, and from Concetta's bag out came the coveted book 'Lady Chatterley's Lover'. They all perused the pages, marked with pen at the most 'horrendous' passages, and screamed and giggled at the 'dirty' things they read there. Luna didn't think the book was that dirty, and in fact it seemed quite romantic and a little naïve, especially the scene where the gamekeeper was trying to braid flowers in Lady Chatterley's 'down there' hair. Lady Chatterley's husband was a mean, handicapped man in a wheelchair, even though that didn't excuse Lady Chatterley for committing adultery. But of course in Luna's day everything erotic was out in the open, even a young girl like her had seen and heard everything. Luna thought that the way they acted in some of those x rated movies in her time, they made sex look and feel gross and disgusting. She had learned from Uncle Pas and Aunt Esther that it could be a beautiful, loving thing, and it should be kept private. But so far, she had decided that she didn't want any part of such things, even though some girls in her class back home were already doing it. Myrna had tried it, and she went through absolute Hell before finding out she wasn't pregnant. Luna knew some girls who had children, and they looked burdened and unhappy. Some of them dropped out of school and disappeared. Luna didn't feel it was anything she wanted to do, ever, but maybe when she was grownup, and she could find herself a nice, loving man like Uncle, she would probably change her mind. Right now, if anyone touched her, she would break their face. Kisses were fine, even romantic, but that was it. That night Luna had dreams of her Prince, her birthday party's Prince Charming, wanting to braid flowers in her hair, and she was getting ready to sucker punch him in the gut, when she realized that he wanted to braid flowers on her head hair, and she grandly let him, and when he was finished she had hundreds of tiny braids on her head, with dandelion flowers peeping out everywhere. The girls had stood by watching the whole time, sighing romantically, until the prince was finished, and then they all laughed their heads off, pointing at the mess that was her mangled hair.

The following day they got up and ran around collecting their clothes, running to the Black Hole, helping each other get dressed, and generally having a great, if noisy, time. Luna thought:

"This is almost comically like 'Seven brides for seven brothers', I hope that song doesn't start haunting my brain again." She then also realized that you could have hoards of fun even without TVs, computers, phones and other technical gadgets; all you needed were close friends, happy parents, and good food. Talking about food, they were all starving, and Aunt Esther's call to breakfast was very much welcome. When they came down, the lovely sight of a beautiful spread made all of them run smiling to the table. They had fresh milk, hot focaccia, a platter of prosciutto, very fresh ricotta, hard boiled eggs and a basket of figs still covered in dew. After all that, there were cornetti, a kind of croissant, and a large pot of real espresso. The girls dug in like starving sailors, and soon the table was covered only by crumbs. Luna couldn't stop wondering at the fact that people really ate over here, but she hadn't seen any overweight kids or young adults. The older people were sometimes a little chunkier than they should be, but no one was grossly obese, unlike home.

"It must be the country fresh air." Thought Luna. The girls were supposed to ride with them to church, where the parents would meet them and take them home after the services. It was fun riding with the girls on the back of the truck, even thought Uncle Pas made them all stay down and not move around too much, for fear they would fall off and get hurt. Their mouths could still be used, and the talk, laughter and shrieks accompanied them all the way to the sanctuary of the Saints Cosmo and Damiano. There was no market this time, but other friends were there and they all ran to the truck to help them down and get the details of the sleepover. When they got home that day, they were all exhausted, and after dinner, cleaning up and coffee, everyone went to take a nap. After their rest, the house was quiet and the girls did their homework, helped with some chores, and had their late supper. After cleaning up the supper dishes, they ironed their clothes and retired to their rooms. Luna read a bit of 'The Betrothed' but she couldn't get into it, and went to sleep. She slept like a log, and soon it was time to get up and start their regular day.

In school, everyone had heard about the sleepover, and the girls were still talking about it excitedly. They kept talking about the dreadlocks hairdo. Concetta said that she had her hair braided like that little black kid on the 'Little Rascals', Bucket of Wheat. Luna corrected smiling:

"Buckwheat". No one paid any attention to her except the teacher, who looked at Luna almost with fear. Besides that, the day went well, and on the way back they walked for a while with the Russo boys. They wanted to know if Uncle Pas was still mad at them, but the girls said he had never spoken of that incident again, so it was probably forgiven and forgotten. The boys felt better and ran off ahead to their farm. When they got home, Aunt Esther said that Uncle Gaetano was coming over for dinner, and that he had news. Ivana started jumping up and down for joy, and Luna asked, a little miffed because she didn't know this new person:

"Is everyone related over here? Everyone is either an uncle or a cousin, and there's always a new one popping out of the woodwork." Ivana laughed, out of sheer joy:

"Of course! We're all slightly related, one way or another. The first Sargento to settle in these parts had fifteen children, and even though they did not intermarry, they were mostly boys, making us all cousins, uncles and relations of some kind or other. Our ancestor was a stregone, a medicine man, and he practiced his craft deep in the mountains of Sicily. When he was accused of practicing witchcraft, he escaped with his wife and children, and settled over here. Right now Uncle Gaetano is coming, but remind me later, I'll show you something really interesting; it's a secret!" She whispered. Luna was listening to this tirade with her mouth hanging open; she didn't really expect an explanation to her question, and certainly not one that corroborated her words. A little while later, a distant rumble could be heard if you paid attention, and Ivana listened for a few seconds, and then ran outside, screaming:

"Uncle Gaetano is here, run Luna, we'll be the first to say Hello' to him." Luna ran out after Ivana and asked:

"How do you know he's coming?"

"The noise, of course! It's Uncle's motorcycle! He's got a Gilera Saturno eight bolt."

"Is that good?" Asked Luna:

"Of course!" Answered Ivana, "That's not just good, it's magnificent." Luna couldn't see all the excitement over a motorcycle, and asked, nonplussed:

"What's a Gilera Saturno eight bolt?"

"Only the best and most powerful motorcycle around! The police have it and the army too. This motorcycle is so powerful, people are afraid to ride it. It won races everywhere. You'll see! But Uncle Gaetano is not afraid of anything; he works at the gunpowder factory in Colleferro." Luna was overpowered by all of this information, and blinked thinking that this Uncle Gaetano must be one of Ivana's heroes:

"What's this gunpowder factory?"

"It's where they make explosives. If you think the fireworks houseboat was dangerous, think again. If the gunpowder factory explodes, it'll take half the town with it. There was a small explosion there some years ago, and it was lucky it was contained, only because Uncle Gaetano ran into the fire and severed the connection between a department and another by hand, otherwise it would have turned into a chain reaction and it would have killed a lot of people. He got some burns, but was smart enough to wet all of his clothes in the fountain before going in. They said he was a hero, and he can do no wrong in Colleferro." By now Luna was very impressed with this famous uncle, and was dying to meet him. The distant rumble was coming closer, and suddenly a black and silver streak came up from the driveway, and stopped in front of their door in a huge billow of dust. Luna was trembling with excitement, just like Ivana, and when the dust settled there it was! A huge black and silver machine and sitting atop it the most fiercely handsome man Luna had ever seen. He looked like a young Marlon Brando in 'The wild one' another of her mother's favorite movies, only Uncle Gaetano was slimmer, handsomer, more dashing and gallant. Nonchalantly, he lifted one of his legs over the motorcycle, and stood up. He wasn't overly big, he was wiry and almost slight, His body was powerful and lean and it conveyed leashed power. He sported a thin moustache on his dark face, and bestowed a dazzling wolfish smile on the two dumbstruck little girls:

"Well, well, well! Per la Madosca! So this is our own little Luna! And a beauty she is! Come to Uncle, little girl!" And he extended his arms to her. Luna walked shyly to him, expecting a hug, but Uncle Gaetano wrapped his powerful arms around her waist, and twirled her around and around. When he finally stopped and deposited an astounded and dizzy Luna on the ground, Ivana ran to him screaming:

"Me too, Uncle, me too!" And he did the same thing to Ivana. By now they had an audience, as Ivana's parents stood at the door looking on with a pleased expression. Uncle Gaetano shook Uncle Pas' hand, and hugged Aunt Esther, then walked in the house with a swagger. He was dressed all in black, and took off his black leather jacket as he walked in; strangely for the times, he was wearing a helmet which he deposited on the sideboard. Luna whispered to Ivana:

"He's wearing a bike riding helmet!"

"Of course! All professional riders do!" Responded Ivana. The table was set, and Uncle Pas and Uncle Gaetano sat quietly talking while the girls helped Aunt Esther bring the food to the table. There were platters of fried artichokes, zucchini and eggplants with slices of tomato mixed in, mixed fry Aunt Esther called it, some risotto Milanese, and slices of meatloaf with a round of hardboiled egg in every slice. The usual salad of mixed greens was fresh and crunchy, the bread was golden and crusty, and they all got busy doing justice to Aunt Esther's wonderful meal. After they ate, talking desultorily, the girls helped Aunt Esther clean up the table while the man brought each other up to date on their work. Finally, the coffee was served to everyone on the table, with dessert, which was a yellow, soft sponge cake oozing yellow cream. They each received a gooey slice in their plate, and then proceeded to drown it with sweet vermouth. Luna had never eaten anything better, and it wasn't even that sweet. After the dessert, they sat back replete, and Uncle Pas asked Uncle Gaetano:

"How are things going with that Mariuccia from Roccasecca?" Uncle Gaetano shook his head and said:

"Something is wrong with the girl; I stopped in front of her house on Sunday morning, beeped the horn, and instead of running out of the house and jumping on the bike, as always, she opened her bedroom window and threw an hardboiled egg at me." Everyone stared at him with their mouth open. Uncle Pas asked:

"What did you do?"

"I fixed her! I picked up the egg, took off the shell and popped in my mouth." And everyone asked:

"And what did she do?"

"She slammed the window shut, and after five minutes I figured she wasn't going to come out, and left." Everyone was trying to figure out what would make a girl act that way, when Uncle Pas said:

"Maybe it was because of what happened the Sunday before." Everyone stopped talking and looked at Uncle Gaetano, and Uncle Gaetano said, looking sheepish:

"You've heard about that?"

"Of course I have," said Uncle Pas, "everyone has! The question is did I hear the right story! You might as well come clean, Gaetano, so I can defend you when I hear people talk about it." Uncle Gaetano looked a little uncomfortable, but he started telling the story:

"I picked her up on Sunday morning, and took her to mass at Saints Cosmo and Damiano, I saw you there. That day was market day, and I bought her a few trinkets. After that, she said she was hungry, but she didn't want the food they sold in the stalls, so we drove to Pontecorvo; she wanted to have lunch at trattoria Primavera. Right after we drove over the bridge, I started to take the high road that would take us to Civita, the high part of town. I remember thinking how wonderfully light she was, almost as if she wasn't even there, and when I drove by Giovanni Papa's grocery, looked in the display window to see what a wonderful couple we made, and I realized I was on the motorcycle alone." Everyone was listening spellbound, and they all asked:

"What did you do then?" He smiled that wicked smile of his, his black eyes shining with mischief:

"I turned around and went back to the Pastine, the lower part of town. I drove along until I reached the bridge, and there I saw a group of people standing around something. I stopped the motorcycle, got off, and walked over. And there was Mariuccia, sitting on the ground crying. I started cooing to her, and wanted to help her up, but she picked up rocks and dirt from the ground and threw them at me. She had a cup of water in her hands and threw it at me; she dirtied my boots! At that, I decided that I had done enough and left." And everyone, trying to stifle their laughter, asked:

"What happened to Mariuccia?" Uncle said:

"I found out later that she spent a couple of hours in the Ruscito trattoria, near the bridge, crying, while a passerby who was going to Roccasecca brought word to her father and he came down to pick her up." Uncle Pas said:

"After all that, you were lucky she didn't throw a hand grenade at you. She seems to like throwing things at people, though. Be careful if you take up with her again!" At that point, everyone was talking and laughing all at once, and Uncle Gaetano said:

"I won't take up with her again, or anyone else, for that matter; I'm getting married!" Everyone stopped and gaped:

"What did you say?" Asked Uncle Pas:

"I'm getting married!" Repeated Uncle Gaetano. A profound silence followed his words. Then all at once everyone started to talk at the same time, and the questions followed one another like a shotgun round. Finally Uncle put up his hands to stop them and said:

"If you all stop asking questions, I'll tell you what happened." They all stopped talking and looked at him expectantly. He then collected his thoughts and started his tale: "I had been half in love with this girl, Vanna, from a farm near San Giovanni Incarico, when her mother decided to leave for America; she had sons there. I then stepped up my courtship, and asked her to marry me. Her mother said that Vanna was not ready to marry yet, but someone told me that she expected Vanna to make a better marriage in America, and was not pleased by my proposal. She kept us apart as much as she could, and I didn't know even when they were going to leave. One day, as I was going to leave for work, a kid from a nearby farm accosted me. He said that Vanna had sent him, and that they were going to leave for America that morning. I went crazy! Her mother, that foxy old bird, had put one over on me. I drove to their farm and saw the car leave their house. I stopped the motorcycle, ran after the car, opened the back door, and sat next to Vanna. Her mother was sitting up front, next to the driver, and couldn't do anything to stop me. I held Vanna, and she cried. Right at that moment I realized that it was going to be Vanna and no one else. I told her so, and she stopped crying. When we were almost to Aquino where they were going to take the train to Napoli, I made her promise me to write, and she said that she had loved me for a long time. They got on the train, and in Napoli they were going to stay in a hotel overnight and leave on a boat for America the following day. I took the bus to Pontecorvo, and got a friend of mine to take me to my motorcycle. After they left, I didn't hear from her for a long time; I thought she forgot me. But a year later she wrote and said her mother and brothers tried to get her married, but she still loved me and if I wanted her, she was ready. I wrote back and told her I still wanted her. She said it was hard to get used to a different country, and to learn the language, but now she was comfortable with her new home, and she could speak some English, so she was ready to settle down; my Vanna speaks another language!" He said with pride: "We have been writing for a year, and finally she said I should put my money where my mouth is, and set a date. So I have, and she will be coming to Pontecorvo to get married in the spring." At that, everyone started to talk at once, and there were hugs, and laughter and congratulations. Uncle Pas and Aunt Esther didn't know the girl, and they asked what she looked like. He said she was not a movie star, but she was strong and handsome, tall and slim, and she had eyes to die for. He said that if you looked in her eyes, you thought that she was the only woman on earth. Everyone was very happy for him; he said he'd never seen her throw a thing. Everyone laughed, and their thoughts turned to Mariuccia from Roccasecca; they were happy that Uncle Gaetano had found a stable and strong woman to love him.

Luna and Ivana had trouble settling down to their homework that night, and when Ivana asked Luna if she was going to come for the wedding, Luna ran upstairs and locked herself in her room. Her head was throbbing; she so wanted to be here for the wedding, but she also wanted to go home right away! She didn't know what to do, and she didn't know what to think. She had liked Uncle Gaetano so much; she thought that she was even a little bit in love with him. If she wanted to be realistic, the moment she got home, he would probably be gone, like most everyone else she was getting to know in this time. She cried and she asked old Balthazar why he did this to her. Why was she here getting to know and love all of these people when she was going to lose all of them? If Balthazar were here she would punch his wrinkled old face in, that's what she would do! And she started to sob so hard that she felt like she was going to die. No one cared or even knew about her sorrow, and she couldn't talk to anyone about it. She couldn't tell Uncle Pas or Anna that she was heartbroken because they would be dead when she got home:

"Balthazar, you old goat, I hate you!" She cried. All at once, a bright light took up most of the room, and out of that light stepped Balthazar. Luna didn't really think that he was listening to her when she called him names, and recoiled, because he was probably very mad at her, and he was going to do something very bad, like send her home right now, or leave her here forever. Either way, she was going to be very sorry, and she cried even louder when she saw him. Balthazar advanced towards her with a smile, extended his hand and caressed her hair, he then opened his arms and Luna, startled, walked into them. He held her gently for a few seconds and then murmured in her hair:

"Remember in your life, little Luna, to be careful what you ask for, because you may get it. Be very sure what you ask for because sometimes it's not what you want at all. Also remember that you are the captain of your ship, and the master of your fate; don't ask anyone to do for you, when you want something, do for yourself. The Powers That Be were very touched by your affection to these good people, and they sent me to comfort you. Their lives will go on as they should, and your life will go on as it should. You will have these memories in your heart, treasure them, as not everyone gets to know anything about the past; what you learn in the past will be your foundation, and it will help you build your future. You are one of the fortunate ones. Go back downstairs, Luna, and do your part here and now. Tranquility and joy comes from doing your duty and what is right. Everything else is out of your hands." He leaned down and deposited a light kiss on her forehead, and then he turned around and stepped into the light again. Next thing Luna knew, the room was back to normal, and she didn't know if Balthazar had really been there, or if it was just a dream. But all at once she felt fine, almost happy, and she was ready to face everything in her future. She went back downstairs, and at Ivana's curious looks, she smiled at her. Uncle Gaetano would be a very special person in her heart, and no one could take her memories of him from her.

"I hope I see him again before I have to go home." Thought Luna. That night she dreamed she was a waitress in a bar, wearing high heels and seamed stockings, and Marlon Brando walked in, but he looked like Uncle Gaetano, and she said:

"What do you want?" And he said:

"Wine!" And when she told him that he was supposed to ask for beer, he told her that where he came from they drank mostly wine. He then gave her something, and it turned out to be a hardboiled egg, but it was made of marble trimmed in gold: "Don't throw this at anyone," he cautioned: "This could kill someone dead!" And then he laughed and laughed that irreverent laugh of his, smiling at her the whole time. The next moment, he leaned over the counter and kissed her forehead whispering: "Remember me!" And then he was gone.

The next few days stretched evenly punctuated by their familiar, and comforting, routines and Luna was surprised to realize that she'd been here almost a month already. School was a lot of work, but Luna enjoyed doing what she was supposed to do, it made her feel right about herself, and of course, all the other kids struggled to do their best and Luna realized she couldn't minimize their efforts by doing nothing, just because she knew she was eventually going to leave. She wondered if all the stuff she was learning here would stay in her head. The teacher had been a little distant with Luna, but she was still kind and interested, and Luna put it down to all the work the teacher had to do. The neighboring women and the teacher were trying to come to an accord on the pastry classes, but Luna knew that eventually all the chinks would be worked out. Anna had taken to visiting every couple of days, and she was to be found installed in Aunt and Uncle's good dining room for their one on one talks. She had also become very fond of Aunt Esther, and admired her parsimonious qualities and skill in turning out a well kept house and delicious food on very little expenditure. Aunt Esther was loving and accommodating to everyone, and Anna was fond of saying that 'the gentler the tree, the more it bends'. Not to say that Aunt Esther was a sap! One day they all were at a neighbor's for a basket weaving party, when one of the other women, a curvaceous blonde, said that her husband couldn't stay away from her, she certainly didn't have any worries about him straying. Then again, she said, men loved soft and round women; the bean pole type wasn't very pleasing to a man, and at that she looked at Aunt Esther. Aunt Esther said, with a serene smile:

"It's kind of sad when a man loves his wife because of the way she looks; looks change, and in time a soft and round woman can become a lot more soft and a lot more round, too much to be attractive; where I come from some people would call that fat. If a man loves you for you and not just your body, the changes will not make any difference to him." Anna cackled in glee and said:

"I do love you so, Esther mine." And everybody had a good laugh at that.   Aunt was also very fond of Anna, as her own mother and father had moved to Roma upon retirement, and she didn't see them very often; Uncle Pas parents were both gone, and she looked to Anna as a substitute mother. The new barn at the Merolli farm had been built the week before, and even thought it hadn't been a party like the barn burning, it had been fun. There was food, laughter, friendship and dancing. The teacher was there and she brought some other lovely pastry that they all liked. There was talk of the pastry classes again. Aunt Palma had brought some of the new Nocello, the walnut husks elixir, and Luna thought that Ivana was right about it strangling you, but she still sipped some, and it really did settle her stomach. Marco and Marcello brought a big bag of some small firecrackers given to them by Fiorello, the firework guy, and they all had a try at shooting firecrackers in the sky. Luca was there, and Luna danced with him twice, under the watchful eyes of her aunt and uncle; he was a polite, mature boy, and looked at her with brown, soulful eyes. Luna enjoyed his company very much; during the second dance he tightened his arm a bit, and for a few seconds they were really close. There were plenty of people at these things and at church on Sunday, and Luna was getting to know almost everyone from the neighboring farms. Even thought they all lived their separate lives on their farms, when there was something going on, they all got together and had a lot more fun and companionship than they ever did at Luna's home, surrounded by neighbors as they were.

67. *Sposalizio di campagna.* Cartolina, bollo post. non leggibile ma precedente al 1927. Retro: "12507 Fot L. Macioce". E' probabile che la simpatica scenetta sia stata fotografata da un dipinto di cui si è persa memoria.

Pontecorvo, country wedding party. Picture taken circa 1927 of long lost painting.
Lorenzo Macioce

Things were rolling along pretty well until one Saturday, after Luna and Ivana had come from school. They were ready to almost sit down to dinner, when a truck stopped in front of the house, and then drove off after having deposited Anna and three of her daughters; Amelia, Angelina and Irma. Aunt Esther ran to the door, and Uncle Pas came down from the bedroom where he was changing out of his work clothes and stood in the hallway. The women swept in breathlessly, and Anna got out, before she collapsed on a kitchen chair:

"We got news!" Everyone was at that point gathered in front of the women, looking worried and expectant, but not saying anything. Anna got her wind back and exclaimed:

"The Fool's daughter is getting married!" Everyone looked shocked, and they exclaimed in unison:

"The Fool's daughter is getting married? Are you sure?"

"Yes indeedy I am, I just got it from the horse's mouth; The Fool himself told me. He's making his way down the main road, stopping at all the farms along the way to invite everyone to his daughter's wedding. I was coming back from Pontecorvo in the truck with Mario, and he hailed us. The way I figured, he will be here tomorrow morning, before church." Everyone was talking, they were talking over each other, and it sounded like the Tower of Babel. Luna had to shout to be heard over the din:

"Who is this Fool?" Everyone turned to her incredulously, and they said:

"Only the richest man in the entire region!" Luna took this in and asked:

"Have I met him?"

"Of course!" They all shouted: "At the barn burning!"

"There were so many people there! Which one was he?"

"The little old man wearing an old fashioned black wool cape, with black Cioci on his feet, and a wooden cane he uses to beat children and dogs with." Luna remembered him, and they said:

"His daughter was with him; a small replica of The Fool, only female. She looks like The Fool in drag." Ivana said:

"Actually, between her big clothes and her big hair, no one really knows what she looks like. She may even be cute under there!" Everyone laughed:

"Believe me, she's a dog! That's why we're so amazed that she's getting married. She's never gone out with anyone; maybe her father bought her a husband." Anna was clearly coming up with a plan, she looked wicked and foxy, and everyone stopped talking and looked at her:

"I'm thinking that this news deserves an enquiry. Enquiring people want to know and we're the only ones who can produce this information." They talked and conjured, until Irma said:

"From my bedroom window I can see the front door to their farm, with a binocular, of course. I can watch the house until I see The Fool and his daughter leave on business, and then someone can go talk to Mrs. Fool and find out everything." Anna looked up:

"I know I thought my children well! Well done, Irma! This is a job for Super Anna, and I'm going to do it! I'll go over there to visit, I'll tell I'm there to congratulate her on her daughter's good fortune and see what happens. I'm sure she has some complain about this; she complains about everything. When she complains, if you talk nice to Mrs. Fool, and seem concerned about her, first she cries and then she spills her guts; I'm sure that within the half hour I shall have picked up all the dirt on The Fool and his daughter." Everyone thought this to be a good plan, especially since it was Anna going into the lion's den and not one of them, and they all sat down to supper with the Sargentos, doing honor to Aunt's every day meal of potato stew with beef chunks and tomatoes, a vegetable omelet and a salad of yellow, red and green vinegar-cured peppers, julienned and drizzled with extra virgin olive oil; the whole accompanied by golden, fluffy cornmeal bread. After dinner, coffee and baked, yellow light-as-a- feather donuts, Uncle Pas ran them home. Anna was going to do the deed on Monday morning. The following day, as they were getting ready to go to church, they spotted a small, dark figure making its way up the major driveway. He wore a short, black cape, white shirt and black pants tucked in under his knees at the top of his leather Cioci, and he carried a wooden cane which he used to beat off the bramble and wild, thorny little roses that grew at the side of the road. A few minutes later, there was a knock on their front door, and they let the little old man inside. He was very old- fashioned, and very formal. From up-close you could see that his white shirt was adorned by countless small, vertical pleats, and on the front there were no buttons but it was laced up from his chest to his neck by laces resembling Anna's ancient costume. Luna suddenly realized that he was wearing the male version of Anna's clothes. In these parts the older folks still preferred to wear the costume, while the younger people tried to be more modern and up to date.   He bowed to everyone and after shaking hands with Uncle Pas, he said:

"I have come to invite you all to my daughter's wedding. As everyone knows, she's the apple of my eye, and I want to see her start her married life in the best way possible; I want all of her friends and neighbors to witness hers and her husband's happiness, and I want everyone to toast her new life."   Uncle Pas said:

"When is the wedding?"   The old man replied:

"I don't know yet, but a formal announcement will be forthcoming."   Uncle Pas promised:

"We will be honored to send your girl off with all our good wishes and felicitations. What kind of wedding is this going to be?"   The old man replied:

"The best kind there is, I am usually a very frugal man, but this calls for the best that I can afford, and you all know I can afford a lot. Be prepared for a formal affair."   After that, he said he was going to visit the other houses in the small hamlet, and briskly departed the premises. Luna was, somehow, impressed with the formal little man, and asked why they called him The Fool. Ivana shouted:

"Me, me, and ME!"   And at her parents' assent, told her the tale: "When the Fool was a child he was so poor, that he was rarely sent to school because he had to work the farm; he had been working since he was seven years old.

Every time he went to school, when the teacher asked him questions, he didn't know the answers, because he never learned anything by having to work so much.   When the other kids laughed, he got up and left. The teacher used to say to him:

"Don't be a fool, if you leave, you will never learn anything, and you will always be poor like you are now." But he never listened, and every time he got up and left, the teacher used to say:

"Look at The Fool go!" Every time he went to school, the other kids used to say:

"The Fool came back!" One day he had enough, he stood in front of the class, and he said:

"This Fool is never coming back to school! I don't need school, I have a brain, and I will use it, and you 'educated' people will come to The Fool's abode with your hat in your hands, and remember this; you have shown The Fool no mercy, and when the time comes The Fool will show you no mercy." He then worked like a man, and when he grew up he worked like a man possessed. Along the way he learned to read and write. When he turned twenty-five, he married a giant, ugly, rich girl. One day, not long after that, when he heard that one of his former classmates was in debt with the bank, and his farm was to be repossessed, he went to see him and offered his help. He would give the man enough money to pay off the bank, and all he required was the minimum payment of some interest month by month. At the end of one year, the balloon payment was due, and if the payment was not forthcoming, he would take possession of the farm. The former classmate decided that he would take the money, thus avoiding foreclosure; he then would sell his farm for much more than he owed The Fool, pay him back, and have plenty of money to set up somewhere else. The man thought to himself that he had a year to put this plan into action, and rested on his laurels, thinking to have made a great deal. He told his family:

"He was a fool when he was young, and he is a fool now." During this year, The Fool never bothered him, he sent someone to collect the interest, which was not much, and the classmate started to forget about his plans. It seemed that this was going to go on forever, The Fool being a fool even in business. Word of mouth spread how The Fool was helping his classmate for almost nothing, and people who were in debt decided to go to The Fool to borrow money, thinking to fleece him of his hard earned cash. On the day the year was up, The Fool showed up at his classmate's farm, papers in hand, and followed by a lawyer and two Carabinieri. The lawyer read a document giving possession of the farm to The Fool, and the Carabinieri after having called the farm family outside, proceeded to lock the farm. Anyone who went back inside would be arrested. The family couldn't believe that anyone could be so cruel, and they begged The Fool for a reprieve. He told them:

"You had a year to do something, you could come to me and I would have helped you set a repayment schedule, but you thought you could make a fool of The Fool, and you were wrong. You kept my money for a year for nothing, you told everyone that The Fool was still a fool; you looked to cheat me out of my hard-earned money. It was easy to do nothing and keep stealing from me, wasn't it? I am The Fool! But you forgot that The Fool shows no mercy." And from then on he was in the business of usury, and plenty of fools who thought that they could make a fool of The Fool, tried it, but they could never do it. He has three sons now, hulking Neanderthals who scare anyone into paying up or giving up their collateral, and he has a daughter who was home schooled by private tutors, she's an accountant and smart as a whip, or shall we say as a Fool. No one makes fun of The Fool anymore."

Luna had listened raptly to this story and even though The Fool was a very bad man, she rustled up some respect for him; after all, the people knew what he was about, and they still went to him to borrow money. The puzzle of the mystery-groom was gripping, and the anticipation of the largest wedding these parts had ever seen was growing by the minute.

Speculation ran rampant all weekend, and on Monday morning, after having gotten the signal, Anna went into the lion's den. Late afternoon, she left the Fool's farm, and went straight to Aunt Esther's, where her three daughters were waiting together with the teacher, Aunt Esther, and the girls. After school the girls and the teacher had run over to the Sargento farm to see what happened, and found everyone still waiting, and waiting, and waiting…………………………….

They had been waiting nervously for hours, and at one point Angelina wanted to mount a rescue party to get Anna back, but they all said Anna could hold her own, and not to panic; instead they all got busy making and frying dough knots. They made big sheets of lemony dough; they cut long strips with a pastry wheel, and twisted the strips into knots. The knots were dropped in hot frying oil and then popped out in seconds, and then they were piled on a platter, and sprinkled with granulated sugar. The afternoon was long, the ladies worried, and the pile of fried knots grew and grew. Finally, Amelia spotted Anna coming up the drive, and they all ran to meet her. Anna made a big show of containing herself until they got to the house, and then started speaking between mouthfuls of fried knots. She complained that she was offered only a cup of weak tea at the Fool's farm, and she was starving to death. She then proceeded with the story Mrs. Fool told her between bouts of crying, fist shaking and chest beating:

When they got invited to the barn burning, Mrs. Fool was not feeling well, and the three sons were out of town, so The Fool went alone with his daughter. When the accordion man, Rodolfo, started to play and sing, The Fool's daughter, Antonietta, kept looking at him through the hair that covered her face. At one point she pushed her hair aside, and her black, penetrating eyes followed his every move. The accordion man was tall, solid and handsome, with a wonderful head of black, shiny hair, a smiling countenance and brown, laughing eyes. Rodolfo felt like he was being watched, and looked around until he saw the small pile of black clothes on a chair at the end of the table. The girl looked like a bundle of old clothes and he felt sorry for her. Also, her black, feverish eyes intrigued him. At one point, Rodolfo called a friend of his who also played the accordion, and asked him to take over for a couple of songs. After the other guy started to play, he walked over to the girl and extended his hand to her. She hesitantly accepted his hand and got up; he circled her waist with his arm, after he found it in all the clothes, and guided her to the middle of the dancers. She danced with him without saying a word, and Rodolfo hooked one finger under her chin, made her look up at him, and asked her:

"Cat got you tongue?" At that she smiled, and Rodolfo was surprised to see her eyes shine while two small indentations appeared on her smooth, little dark cheeks. She had dimples! Rodolfo couldn't believe it! She was the least likely person he had ever seen who could have dimples. While they were dancing, she felt light as a feather, and her waist was really small. After the song was over, Rodolfo accompanied her back to her chair and bowed before her, and she looked up and said:

"Thank you!" When she did that, her hair hung over her shoulder for a split second, and Rodolfo saw her smooth neck; it looked like the neck of a swan, long and graceful, but then she looked down again, and Rodolfo didn't know if he had really seen anything, or it was only a false impression. Also, all through the dance she had smelled really good, like flowers or something, and Rodolfo couldn't get that scent out of his mind. When The Fool came back from a business discussion with a customer, he sat next to his daughter and saw her look at him:

"What?" He said. She took a little time to respond, and then she asked him:

"Papa', do you really want me to get married?" The Fool was a little surprised, but he told her:

"You know I do! That's why I took you to this party! You're going to be thirty on your next birthday, and I want to see you happily married, I'd like some grandchildren on my knees." Antonietta looked at her father with a little smirk on her face:

"My brother Romolo just had a baby, and my brothers Remo and Romano have children, why don't you dandle their children on your knee?" The Fool showed one of his rare smiles and said:

"Too big, all the babies are humongous, like your brothers used to be; if I dandle them on my knee, I'll need crutches for the rest of my life." Antonietta pat his knee:

"No need to worry, I think you have succeeded, I found someone I want to marry at this party, although I had seen him before." The Fool looked around at the group of men standing at the edge of the clearing, and said:

"Which one!" Antonietta pointed to the accordionist who was now playing and singing, and said:

"That one!" The Fool looked thunderous:

"Never! My daughter has to marry a man of consequence."

"No man of consequence would ever look at me twice!" Said the girl. And then, smiling: "You want me to be happy, don't you?"

"Is this joker going to make you happy?"

"Yes, I believe that he is!" The Fool looked pensive:

"Then we have to make him a man of consequence."

"If anyone can do it, you can Papa'!" Said Antonietta. When they got home, The Fool went to call on a man who owed him a great deal of money, and offered him a chance of dispatching half of his debt for services rendered. Carletto the Lawyer had a way to find out everything The Fool wanted to know, and he disposed of minions and associates who would do anything that was asked of them, for a fee of course! Antonietta told her mother she was going to get married, and she had picked out her groom already. She told her mother what happened. Her mother thought that the groom was very good looking, healthy and strong, always singing and playing, and very congenial, but he seemed to be a very poor provider, and looking at her daughter straight in the eyes she said:

"He'll marry you for your money!" Antonietta replied:

"So what! My money ought to be good for something. Once we're married, it'll be our money, and he'll be my husband forever! He'll make a kind husband." Antonietta's mother mumbled:

"That's what I thought when I got married, but kindness is not enough. Sometimes a body needs love and attention." To which Antonietta replied:

"I'll get that too, eventually!" A few days went by, and Antonietta never asked her father about Rodolfo, but she knew him, and she trusted him to do the best he could to make her happy. Some days later, The Fool got all dressed up, and went out. He came back a few hours later, and told Antonietta that she would get a visitor that very evening. Promptly at eight p.m. there was a knock at the door, and Rodolfo was there. The Fool bade him enter, and after a few formalities, he and his wife left the room. Antonietta sat with her small hands on her lap, and looked down. She had changed into a clean dress, and had combed her hair some, but that was all the concessions she made to her visitor. He cleared his throat a few times, and tried to start a conversation. Antonietta raised her head and looked him straight in the eyes:

"Have you come to ask me to marry you?" Rodolfo recoiled slightly, but then plunged ahead:

"Yes, I have permission to ask you from your father."

"I accept!" Antonietta said. Rodolfo looked surprised and said:

"But don't you want to know why I want to marry you?" Antonietta gave him a slight, serious smile:

"Because my father made you a very good offer to marry me?" Rodolfo had the grace to color slightly, and then said, a little angrily:

"I found you very interesting, and who knows what would have happened between us, if you and your father let it be." Antonietta replied, sadly:

"You wouldn't see me again for a long time, and by then my father would have chosen a husband for me, or you would have gotten married, and nothing would have ever happened between us." Rodolfo sit up straight and told her:

"What your father offered was good for my family, my parents, that is why I accepted." Antonietta looked at him:

"You are sacrificing yourself for your family?"

"I wouldn't call it exactly a sacrifice; I just think we could have had a courtship and maybe discover that we liked being together, who knows." Antonietta looked at him soberly:

"Let's promise each other here and now that if this marriage disgusts you, all you have to do is tell me to go back home to my father, and I will do so without complain. Whatever my father promised you will remain yours, and I will claim nothing that you are unwilling to give." Then she lifted a small hand, and they shook on it. Rodolfo sat next to her for a while, then lifted her small hand and played with it absently while he told her what had happened:

"I don't know how your father found out, but my father had been fired from his job. He worked at the sand and gravel pit, had been there many years, and recently due to a bad back, he slowed down a bit. My older brother worked there too, and whenever he could, he helped my father to give him a little reprieve. Someone told the owner, and they were watched, and this was considered cheating the owner, so they were both fired. My brother found another job with a trucking company, but my father is finished. The sand and gravel pit broke both his back and his spirit. Without a job he has to depend on his children, and he has turned into an old man overnight. He's only fifty-five-years old. Your father told me that if I marry you, he will purchase the sand and gravel pit and give it to us for a wedding gift. All of the papers will be ready to be signed on our wedding day." Antonietta threw her head back and laughed hard, like she never had done before. When she regained her senses she told him:

"Leave it to my father to do just the thing that would make you commit yourself to me." Rodolfo laughed too:

"The Fool is no fool!" Then covered his mouth with his hand: "Oops! I shouldn't have said that!"

"Oh, don't worry about it; he actually loves to be called that." Rodolfo told her:

"I never liked your father, but now I'm developing some kind of respect for my future father-in-law. But the sand and gravel pit is going to cost a fortune, and I didn't even know it was for sale."

"Don't worry about the money, what's it good for if no one uses it? Besides, he has lots more than that, I know, I keep his books!"

"You do?"

"Yes, I'm an accountant." Rodolfo stared at her with stupor:

"You're an accountant? But that's a man's job!"

"No it isn't! My brothers are all brawn and no brains, so my father had to rely on me; after all, who's going to take care of the family's finances if something happens to him? If he gets sick or even worse, no one is going to help us. My father never cheated anyone, but because he made a lot of money on the backs of the borrowers, and because he is not known for giving a break to people who don't keep their end of the bargain, people would like to see us go down the drain." Rodolfo looked at her with respect in his eyes, and then said:

"But how did he know the sand pit was for sale?"

"It wasn't," responded Antonietta, "he probably made them an offer they couldn't refuse." And they both burst out laughing together, and that is how The Fool found them when he came to tell them that time was up:

"So, what say you, young man, is there going to be a wedding?" And Rodolfo picked up Antonietta's hand and smiled at her:

"There certainly is, Sir, there certainly is!" The Fool accompanied the young man to his motorcycle, and saw him drive off. He then went back inside, called his wife and ordered:

"Arrange the best wedding these parts have ever seen, send all the bills to me, and let me know when it is going to be; we need to send formal invitations." After that he put his cape on his shoulders and left. The Fool's wife stood there with her mouth agape, and then she turned to Antonietta and said:

"I don't know anything about arranging weddings; you'll have to do it yourself." To which Antonietta replied:

"I'm the bride; I'm not supposed to arrange my own wedding. Besides, I don't know anything about weddings either; maybe you should call someone to help you, because I'm getting married soon no matter what the wedding looks like." She then proceeded to walk in her bedroom with her hair- covered nose up in the air. The Fool's wife gave in to desperation, and when Anna went to see her, sometime later, she was disheveled and angry and she poured out the whole story, begging Anna not to bandy this about, or there would be hell to pay, as the thing The Fool hated most in the world was airing the family's dirty laundry outside for all to see. Anna felt pretty bad for the woman, and promised to help somehow.

Everyone listened to this with their mouth hanging, and of course Anna delighted in the tale and their shock, but when it came to the end of it, everyone erupted into talk. What can we do, they said, it's none of our business, they said, a wedding is a lot of work, they said, and why should we help The Fool, they said, he never helps anyone; let him pay someone to do it. Times are tough, they said, our families need us, we have to try and make ends meet, and we have no time for a filthy rich Fool who wants to throw money around. Luna had sidled next to Anna and suddenly she said:

"Why don't you get that money for yourself, then?" Everyone stopped talking and turned to Luna, especially the teacher, and they said:

"How can we do that, silly girl?" Anna shushed them up and declared:

"Let's listen to my girl; I'm sure she will tell you, so far she's the one who came up with the best ideas." She then put her arm around Luna's waist and looked up at her. Luna felt a little uncomfortable with everyone looking at her expectantly, but plunged ahead:

"Why don't you hire yourselves as Wedding Consultants?" They all looked at her like she had two heads:

"What's a Wedding Consultant?"

"A Wedding Consultant is a person or persons who help arrange weddings for rich people who have money and want the best wedding, but don't know how to do it themselves, or are too busy or lazy to do it. They get paid a lot of money, but they have to make sure that everything comes off perfect and beautiful. They interview the bride, but especially the person who is paying for the wedding, to find out exactly what they expect, and then they get it done. They want to be paid some money upfront and the rest when the wedding is over, and of course all the bills go to the person who ordered the wedding. I know all this because the mother of one of my friends does it for a living." Anna held Luna tight and said:

"I knew my girl had a solution for this, she's the smartest one of us!" Luna blushed at this compliment, but she was also very, very pleased, and everyone around started again to talk and argue. We don't know how to do this, they said. We couldn't take on that big responsibility, they said. And how much money should we ask for, they said. While this was going on, Luna noted Ivana on the edge of the circle fidgeting and coloring, and convulsively trying to talk, but nothing came out. Luna looked at Ivana with a small daring smile, and motioned her closer, and Ivana suddenly blurted out:

"My mama can make the wedding gown!" They all turned to Ivana and stared. Anna extended her other arm and drew Ivana closer to her other side, and hugged her tight also:

"Another smart one! It's a sad day when we have to learn from our young ones, but there it is! Ivana has the right idea. We don't do everything together; we each do one thing, what we can do best, and then coordinate with each other." Aunt Esther stepped forward and said:

"I certainly can make the dress, but I can't decorate it properly, I'm a little weak in the embroidery department!" At that Irma said pensively:

"I'm very good at embroidery, and can decorate with seed pearls and sequins. I spent what seemed years at the nuns learning it, and didn't think I would ever use that knowledge at the farm, but maybe I can." Anna looked at Irma and told her:

"I'm sorry, baby, I shouldn't have left you there for that long; it was a year and a half. When your little brother Franco died, I couldn't take care of my children properly, and send them all away where they could be taken care of. I called all of you home as soon as I was able." Irma, Angelina and Amelia went to Anna and hugged her:

"Don't feel bad Ma, we were happy and treated well, you found good places for us; we love you, Ma!" And they went back to negotiate at the relieved sigh of Ivana and Luna, as they had got caught in the general hug, and couldn't breathe under all that tight love and affection. The teacher stepped forward and said, timidly:

"I can make the wedding cake and the pastry, with some help!" After that, the suggestions came out one after the other, and plans were made, and a name picked out for the enterprise, and so it came about that on the following Sunday, after church, when everyone was at home getting lunch ready, a small army of resolute women trailed by two girls, walked up to The Fool's farm and knocked at the front door. Luna was amazed by The Fool's farm; it did not look like all the other farms she had seen in the area. The entire house consisted of three long, low buildings, the front door being on the middle building, and the two side buildings sporting huge windows. They went from front to back, and with their round roofs that went all the way to the ground on the sides of the house, and the low, humongous windows in front and back, reminded Luna of the Quonset huts she had seen on Quonset Point in Rhode Island on a school outing. The roof was made of red, curved bricks, interlocked with one another, and the barn, a bit far off from the house, looked just like one of the house buildings. This farm was very strange, yet eerily familiar, and Luna's heart was beating fast when she looked around. When the front door opened, they saw that The Fool himself had come to welcome them, while his wife and daughter hovered in the back:

"Welcome ladies to my humble abode!" Said The Fool. And he held the door wide open for them all to come in. Luna and Ivana brought up the rear, and Luna was looking, puzzled, at the buildings. When they walked inside, after stepping into a large entrance they found themselves in a very large and long room. The first area was a formal dining room, then a kind of sitting room, and at the end a large kitchen. The floor plan was simple and almost wide open; there were just archways between the rooms. The wall at the end of the room was almost all taken up by a very large window, with a cast iron stove on one side, and a fireplace on the other, and everything was extremely light and bright. The archway at the entrance led to all of the rooms, and there were two doors on the wall of the dining room, one on one side and one on the other, and two doors on the kitchen walls, also on both sides of the room. Obviously these were doors that connected the central building to the side ones. But what astounded Luna was the fact that the ceilings were rounded, also like those of a Quonset hut, and ceilings and floors were covered in wood. Everything here in Italy was covered either in tiles, marble, stones or cement, they didn't seem to use wood like at home, but this farm was like an army barrack in which wood had been used as the primary ingredient; a very elegant army barrack indeed! Luna couldn't stop looking, and whispered to herself:

"This really is a Quonset hut!" At that The Fool, who was talking to the ladies, turned around and boomed:

"What did you say there, little girl?" Ivana grabbed Luna's arm and tried to shush her, but The Fool walked up to Luna and said: "What did you call my house, little girl?" Luna whispered:

"A Quonset hut, sir."

"What do you know of Quonset huts girl?" Luna was now getting scared, and everyone was looking at her with bug-out eyes, especially Gianna the teacher; Anna looked up as in prayer:

"I learned in……school that Quonset huts were invented by the Americans to build cheap, safe, efficient and comfortable housing for the military." The Fool laughed loudly, and hit the floor with his cane in his glee:

"This small girl is the first person who recognized my home for what it is. When I built this house, people said it was strange, they said it was ugly; they said 'The Fool built his family a fool house'. Brava my girl! Brava! I guess that wherever you come from they have very good schools, not like over here." And he looked straight at Gianna the teacher. She said defensively:

"I can only teach the kids what they want me to. If I go outside of the assigned curriculum, they'll fire me!" The Fool dismissed her with a wave of his cane, and then he turned to the group of women and told them:

"A friend of mine, a high official in the American army, suggested this design. Right after the war, when the government gave everyone the reconstruction rights and the miserly sum connected to it, I was looking for a better design than the usual farm. I wanted a house that would be warm in the winter and cool in the summer, not very expensive to build, spacious, very comfortable, and also attractive. This soldier, who was an architect, told me about these Quonset huts. The American army paid a lot of money for someone to come up with this design, and what's good for the Americans is good for me. My friend made me a design, an adaptation of a Quonset hut, and I have been happy about my house ever since." The women whispered to each other:

"He's talking about that man he hid on his broken down farm during the German occupation. I saw him come out sometimes, in the evening, big man; you could tell he was a soldier." The Fool walked back to the women, and made sure everyone had a seat at the table, then seated himself, and asked with an unctuous smile:

"No more digressions, what can we do for you, ladies? If it's money you want, you've come to the right place!" Anna bristled and blurted out:

"Yes, it's your money we want, you old goat, but not the way you think!"His smile disappeared immediately, and he asked coldly:

"State your business, Ladies!" Everyone was tongue tied, until Aunt Esther asked him about the wedding, and who was organizing it for his daughter. He told them that he expected his wife to take care of that, at which point said wife got up and ran out of the room. Antonietta had sat quietly the whole time, looking down at her hands, and slowly she looked up and got very interested in the proceedings. Anna took over and told The Fool that the group of women had decided to go into business, that they called themselves 'The Wedding Consultants' and arranged weddings for the most discriminating clients, because one person alone cannot take on such a thing as a huge, beautiful wedding, and they knew their business inside out. They would take care of everything, as close as possible to the client's desires, everything from wedding dress to decorations to food and drink, and special invitations. All they needed was to consult the client and they would get to work. The Fool looked very interested, and asked them their price, to which they replied that the price would be directly related to the kind of wedding desired. The Fool talked for a few minutes about what he wanted, and when he was done, the women turned to Antonietta and asked her if she had any preferences. She replied that she didn't care if she married in the barn as long as she got married, so they should just make her father happy. The women consulted with one another, and finally came up with a price. When he heard the amount, The Fool jumped up and said:

"Never! I'm The Fool, but I'm not a fool!" And they were arguing back and forth with The Fool repeating over and over:

"This is highway robbery. You ladies want to rob me of my hard-earned money!" When Luna whispered to Ivana:

"Do you people have portable cameras, here?" Ivana looked at her briefly and whispered back:

"Of course, but why are you asking me that silly question?"

"Do you have a place to buy film for the camera?"

"Yes, a drugstore!" Hissed Ivana!

"And do you have a place to develop this film? Is it expensive?"

"No, it's not that expensive!"

"Does Uncle Pas have a portable camera?" Asked Luna:

"Yes, we took pictures last year at the feast of S.S. Cosmo and Damiano. Why do you want to take pictures now, when we're having this big problem? Do you know that we would probably have to go home without this job? And no one else has the money to do a big wedding like this. Everyone was counting on that money already, they really could use it. My mom doesn't really need it, but she would love making her own money, and helping the others to do it." And she looked down almost ready to cry at their dashed dreams and failed efforts. Luna raised her hand to be noticed over the din, and Antonietta looked at her with curiosity. Then The Fool noticed her and boomed:

"What is it, girl? What do you want?" Luna whispered uncertainly:

"I would like to talk to you, sir!" He got up and said:

"Well, talk!"

"In private, please!" So he walked to the door, and stepped outside:

"Now, talk!" Luna collected her thoughts and told him:

"I'm from up North, and where I come from everyone uses a wedding consultant, or several if they want a big wedding; the mother of a girl who goes to school with me is a wedding consultant. It's big business." The Fool snorted:

"Get to the point, girl!" Luna dove right in:

"They offered you a great deal; they will make you a dream wedding. But after the wedding is over, people will forget about it, and anyone who wasn't invited will never know what you did. What they did not offer is a way to show everyone what you have done and how much you've spent, for years to come. You'll want to show your friends and family, and even your posterity, what you've done; maybe you want to show your enemies what you have done."

"Why would I want to show my enemies my pride and joy? You're daft, girl!"

"A famous philosopher said once 'Keep you friends close and your enemies closer'. If you show them what you can do, then they'll fear you." The Fool squinted out at her:

"Who are you, girl? You're definitely not from these parts. Tell me this thing that they have forgotten to include." Luna explained:

"It's a Wedding Album, sir. They would document everything they do, the shopping, the cooking, the decorating, the making of the wedding dress, the many women lined up to help and to cook, the flowers. Then they would document the arranging of the wedding, the wedding itself, from beginning to end, with pictures of all the guests and the sending off of the bride. Last, but not least, they would document the taking down of the feast, and the gift you would make of all of the leftovers to the poor of this place. This would be documented and kept to be passed down to your future generations. Of course they should make a copy of this wedding album, and any new client, only the rich of course, will have a chance to see what you did for your beloved daughter." The Fool looked at her for a moment, then, uncharacteristically, touched her hair and pivoted back inside of the house. He stood in front of the now terrified women, and said:

"The price is agreed on! Your fee plus all the bills sent to me; on one condition!" Everyone started to talk at once. Ivana looked at Luna with awe. Amelia croaked:

"What is this condition?" The Fool said:

"I want a photographic album that documents the making of this wedding. Hire a photographer at my expense; have him follow you around everywhere. When you shop, when you cook, when you bake, when you make the dress, the wedding, before and after, all the women you'll hire to do the cleaning and cooking, and my grand gesture when I donate the leftovers of this wedding to the poor. Of course, you will make two copies of this album, so you can have one to show every prospective rich customer what I have done for my little daughter! And remember, I want a real photographer! Only a professional, and not a silly amateur with a cheap little camera, will do." Everyone was stunned. They all looked from Luna to The Fool, and the teacher hid behind Anna with real fear etched on her face. Then Aunt Esther went up to The Fool, and shook his hand:

"Agreed! I speak for all of us when I say that you will not regret this. You will have our loyalty in everything connected to this occasion, and your daughter will be a bride no one will soon forget! We will draw a contract and will be able to tell you when the wedding is going to be ready by the end of this week." The Fool rubbed his hands together gleefully, and his wife, who was now all smiles, whispered something in his ear. The Fool slapped his thigh, and said jovially:

"To celebrate this auspicious occasion, where we all get what we want, we will break bread together; Ladies, you are all invited to lunch!" Everyone started to demur. We don't have time, they said. We have to go home and eat with our husbands, they said. We don't want to impose on your good wife, they said. But The Fool was adamant:

"We need this to cement our business, instead of shaking on it, we'll eat on it!" And then he commanded to his wife:

"Woman, bring me my cheese!" At those words, Mrs. Fool got up eagerly and went to the kitchen, while everyone cringed and looked a little ill. When Mrs. Fool came back carrying a stone crock, The Fool exclaimed:

"I don't usually share my good Pecorino Sardo cheese with anyone, it's very hard to get, and very expensive, but this little girlie here deserves it; would you like some of my soft, gooey and tasty cheese, girl?" Ivana grabbed Luna's arm and tried to say something, and everyone recoiled, but Luna had grown very fond of soft and gooey cheese, and didn't understand what the problem was. She pulled her arm out of Ivana's grasp and said:

"I would love to have some of your cheese sir." The Fool opened the crock, and pulled some white substance out with a wooden spoon. The whiff that reached Luna's nose said 'dirty socks' but she knew that sometimes the best of cheese didn't smell like a flower, that's for sure! The Fool plopped a small piece of the white stuff on a small plate and pushed it to Luna. While he proceeded to pick up a large piece for himself, and his wife was placing a large platter of brown holey bread on the table, Luna looked down into her plate. She wasn't sure; it must've been her mind playing tricks on her, because she thought that the cheese had moved. She was looking again at it, puzzled, when she thought that the cheese had moved again. The Fool said, waving his fork:

"The faster it moves, the better it is!" Then Luna really looked at her cheese, and she realized that there were white little things twisting and wiggling inside, and everywhere! Her eyes bugged out, and she asked in the silence:

"What are those live things?" The Fool said, his eyes twinkling:

"Maggots, my girl, big, fat, rich and tasty cheese maggots." For probably the first time in her entire life, Luna was speechless. She kept looking at the cheese with such a stunned expression, it was almost comical:

"What?" Said The Fool, thunderously, "You don't like my cheese?" Everyone gasped, and Luna could only stare speechless at the piece of cheese. A small giggle was heard, and then another, and finally Antonietta, under everyone's thunderstruck expression, couldn't hold it in anymore and started to laugh. The Fool looked from his daughter to Luna, and then he burst out laughing, and so did Mrs. Fool, and then everyone else. The Fool took Luna's plate and dumped the small piece of cheese on his own plate, then told his wife to get lunch for everyone else. While he started to eat chunks of the ghastly cheese, scooping up the straggly, whitish worms on his plate with a piece of the supple bread, Mrs. Fool brought up platters of sliced up calzone with many different fillings; ham and cheese, ricotta studded with dry sausage, Swiss chard studded with raisins and pine nuts, omelet with mozzarella and salami, soft potato filling with mozzarella and prosciutto etc. Everyone stopped looking at The Fool and his cheese, and started picking chosen morsels of different kinds to put on their plates. The only one who just stood there with a lost look on her face was Luna. Anna talked to The Fool's wife:

"Assunta, when did you bake?" Assunta answered:

"Yesterday! I bake on Saturday."

"Me too!" Said Aunt Esther. Assunta explained:

"Every time I bake, I make a lot of extra stuff; my boys drop in quite often, and they like my cooking. If there is a lot left over, before it goes bad, I send it over to them. Their wives are extremely thankful for that, between my kids and their children, there is never enough." Antonietta looked up and said:

"My brothers eat like cows. Actually they eat more than a cow; if the cows ate as much as my brothers we'd have to kill them and cook them. Too bad we can't kill my brothers and cook them!" Assunta said outraged:

"Don't talk like that about my boys! And you shut up!" To The Fool, who was laughing and hitting the table with the palm of his hand:

"My big boys have a heart of gold!" Said Assunta:

"And a head of wood and a stomach of lead!" Said Antonietta. Then, her eyes twinkling, she said: "Their kids are little vampires also, everything you put in front of them, they suck up, even Romolo's baby. Every time his mother breast feeds him, I check her out to see if she still has both of her boobs!" There was general laughter, over Assunta's protestations and warnings. Everyone was enjoying this banter in the sanctuary of The Fool's family, and they seemed more like regular people. No one knew why everyone didn't like them, maybe people just didn't know them very well or maybe because they were rich; but obviously they needed friends just like everyone else. All through this, Luna hadn't made a move, so Ivana took some calzone and put it in front of her. To drink there was a pitcher of fresh, frizzy new wine with cut up peaches and pears in it, and a pitcher of spring water with cut lemons in it; a big platter of fruit sat in the middle of the table. After everyone ate the delicious food, there was espresso and a deliciously heavy and crumbly yellow pound cake. Luna was coming back. Everything she ate, she perused very carefully, and slowly she enjoyed everything. After they ate, and the women helped Assunta clear up, Ivana asked shyly:

"What is the good smell that comes from the kitchen? I smell it on almost everything, and it's very enjoyable." Assunta said:

"These young girls have better senses than the adults. You please me greatly by asking that, girl. One of my greatest pride and joy is taking care of my home, and I'm very proud when people notice; the smell comes from sachets of bay leaves that I keep in everything in the kitchen. I have them in my cupboards, in my matarca, (They have a Gargantua too, thought Luna), in my sacks of flour and sugar, in my sacks of grains and in my reserve of pasta. Actually, in the flours and pastas I just throw the bay leaves in."

Everyone was very interested in this, and they asked why all the bay leaves. Assunta opened the door to the left of the kitchen, and showed them in a very large room full of shelves. There were boxes full of pasta, sacks of flours and grains on the floor under the shelves, sacks of potatoes and baskets of squash, sacks of sugar, baskets of dried apples, hams and sausages hanging from the ceilings, braids of onions, garlic and little red hot peppers, crocks of lard, gallons of oil, marmalades, honey and myriad other things; this was a very well stocked pantry! She told the women that when she was young she used to follow the housekeeper around, and watch how she did things. She loved that kind of work, and she wanted to see how her housekeeper managed everything.

Her family was very wealthy and they had servants and housekeepers. This particular housekeeper had practically raised

Assunta, as her parents were not very interested in her, only in her blue eyed and blonde haired baby sister. The woman taught Assunta everything about keeping a house, and all of the little tricks that helped to keep the house clean and healthy; bay leaves kept all kinds of varmints at bay, especially from the flours, breads, pastas, and grains and cured meats. Anna asked Assunta if she missed having all the servants and such. Assunta said that it was a relief to have her own comfy, private house, and to take care of it herself. She had never been one to primp and strut, like her sister, she was just too big and plain, she liked to feel needed. And boy! Did they need her! Her husband and daughter were always out doing business, and when they came home, the food, the clothes and everything else was always fresh and neat. If she wasn't there, they would starve to death in raggedy clothes and a trashy house. They didn't say much about it, but she knew they appreciated it. Antonietta got up, and in a very rare show of affection, put an arm over her mother's shoulder and told her:

"We know how hard you work for us, Ma. Without you we wouldn't be able to carry out business." The Fool looked at his daughter, his eyes mere slits, and she looked pointedly at him and then her mother. He cleared his throat, clearly embarrassed, and said:

"You have been a good wife and mother, Assunta; I have always been happy that I chose you." Assunta, who was obviously not used to compliments, even halfhearted ones, sobbed a little, and Anna held her for a few seconds, saying:

"You're a good woman; we should get together more often. Come to my daughter's farm to see me, sometimes." Then, to lighten up conversation, she asked what was in the rest of the house. Assunta threw open the door apposite the one for the pantry, and revealed a very large office with shelves and books galore, a large desk and some leather chairs. Assunta said that the two doors in the dining room were bedrooms, theirs and Antonietta's, with a couple of great walk-in closets. She said that the boys always had their bedroom in the barn, and it was still there for when they or their children visited. They thanked her, told her how much they enjoyed the wonderful food, and how happy they were that she was such a nice and friendly woman.

She teared up again, and everyone patted her on the back and invited her over, and Luna and Ivana offered to braid her hair in the new style French braids they knew how to do, and finally they were ready to go, with Anna saying that when all the contracts were done and signed, they would have to come back and have a talk with the bride. On the way back, everyone was talking excitedly about the job and what they were going to do first, and the co-op they had formed was the best ever, because they would all be able to use their individual talents, and the album of the whole thing from beginning to end was a stroke of genius. Anna said:

"As usual, my girl, little Luna, came through for us! And I must say, all of this genius must be catchy, because little Ivana was no slouch herself! Asking about the bay leaves was a wonderful way to make Assunta feel comfortable and get her to open up; looking inside those rooms was another boon, I was dying to see how that house was inside. It's true that it's strange looking from the outside, but the way it is comfy and easy to keep, it's really amazing." Then Anna said:

"Antonietta is going to say 'I do!'" And everyone laughed heartily. Then Amelia said:

"Rodolfo is going to say 'I do!'" And everyone laughed uproariously. Then they all said:

"They are both going to say 'I do!'" And they were all laughing so hard that they were practically rolling in the aisles. Luna was looking from one to the other bewildered:

"What are you all laughing about, are you going crazy or something?" Then Anna looked at the others and said:

"Should we educate this girl and tell her the Pontecorvo Creed?" They all screamed in unison:

"Yes! Yes! Yes!" And so Anna sat Luna down on a rock, and told her the Pontecorvo Creed:

"In Pontecorvo, when a girl turns thirteen, her mother sits her down and gives her 'The Talk'. And no, it's not about s-e-x; it's about her future:

"My girl," they say: "from now on you have a mission; your mission, should you decide to accept it, is to provide for your future. Your parents don't live forever; In the order of things, if things happen in the right order, you will outlive them. A woman cannot be alone, unless she is wealthy, and even then it's not pleasant to be a spinster. You need to be included and respected, and the only way for a woman to achieve this, is to find yourself your own little donkey; a little donkey who will escort you everywhere, and who will work and provide for you and your children for the rest of your life. Mind you, you have to pick well, otherwise that little donkey will ruin your life, and after you marry the right little donkey, you train him to the best of your ability, so he can serve you well and take care of you with pride; it's like winning the forever lottery." And then the mother goes on:

"Everyone knows this, except the men. When you are getting married and the priest asks you if you take this man to be your lawfully wedded husband, in good times and bad, in sickness and in health, to love him and honor him all the days of your life, what he's really asking you is if you take this man to be your lawfully wedded donkey, in good times and bad, in sickness and in health, to train and command all the days of your life." And then Anna said:

"Antonietta may have caught Rodolfo with her money, but after they say 'I do!' she'll have a good little donkey to take care of her needs and wants for the rest of her life; we all think she chose well, Rodolfo will make a wonderful, sweet and manageable little donkey!" When Anna finished talking, Luna was laughing too, almost falling off her rock, and promised everyone that she would abide by the Pontecorvo Creed when she grew up, no matter where she was.

When they got home, Uncle Pas offered a ride to the rest, who lived much farther, and much later it was Sunday dinner, and excited talk from Aunt Esther about their adventure and opportunity. Uncle Pas was all for it, he wanted Aunt Esther to have something of her own, and offered to take care of things in the house as much as he could, to help. Aunt Esther said:

"I knew I could count on you to be on my side!" And Uncle Pas replied:

"Just looking at you, all excited with rosy cheeks and sparkling eyes, makes it worthwhile. I never realized how beautiful you've become; you get more beautiful with the passing years." Aunt Esther said with a cheeky look:

"Let's take our coffee upstairs to talk about it, we can rest afterwards, I've had a long day." Uncle Pas smacked her bottom and said:

"Whatever you say, Estherina!"   Ivana and Luna giggled quietly, while mouthing 'Estherina' to each other, and then exploded in a fit of laughter they couldn't control. Uncle Pas picked up the espresso pot and put it on the coffee tray with cups, spoons, sugar bowl, and followed his wife upstairs with his nose in the air and a put upon air on his brow; but his eyes crinkled on the corners, like he was trying to suppress laughter.

The following day at school, it was all over the place how they had scored big by getting this job, and speculation about the biggest wedding they had ever seen was rampant. The teacher was excited and happy; everybody couldn't wait to see what the bride would look like.   In all of this, the teacher somehow managed not to talk or even look at Luna, and it was somehow strange. Ivana hadn't realized it yet, and neither had the other kids, but Luna caught strange looks from the teacher, who immediately turned away when she looked at her. At one point Luna raised her hand to go to the black hole, and after she came back, she saw the teacher's husband, Uncle Saverio, leaning on a tree, like he was waiting for her. He was in fact waiting, and said to her:

"Hallo', little girl, can I speak to you alone for a moment?" Puzzled, Luna said:

"Of course!" And Uncle Saverio leaned down and whispered to her:

"Come clean with your uncle, who are you really?"   Luna replied:

"I'm Luna Marina Blue, your niece!"

"No you're not! My wife thinks you're an alien from outer space. I think you're just a cute little impostor. Which are you? You better tell me the truth, Dear Niece, or I'll have to call the police to investigate you. Fake papers are easy to spot, and you can get into very big trouble!" Luna turned as white as paper, and whispered:

"I'll tell my teacher the truth, if she wants to hear it. But we're going to have to be alone to talk." Uncle Saverio pulled himself away from the tree he was leaning on, and looking at her directly, he said:

"Thank you! I'll arrange it." He swaggered away, and Luna went back to class, still shaken. Ivana whispered to her from her seat:

"What happened to you? You look as if you've seen a ghost."

"I don't feel very well!" Luna whispered back, and in fact her stomach hurt and her head ached. What was she going to do? She wasn't supposed to talk about home, but if Uncle Saverio got the police, they would find out she was a fraud, and that would ruin everything!

"Help me, Balthazar! I don't know what to do." Luna begged silently. Right then, a voice in her head said:

"Don't worry, Luna, help is on the way!" She sighed, relieved, and went back to work. After a while, Uncle Saverio stuck his head in the door, and signaled to the teacher. When she went to him, he whispered something in her ear, and the teacher followed him outside. About ten minutes later, the teacher came back, and she was as white as a sheet. She looked at Luna and had to wipe the perspiration off her forehead. Luna didn't know what happened, and all at once felt bad; she didn't want to be the cause of so much distress. A few minutes later, Anna also stuck her head in the door, and asked if she could talk to Luna. The teacher assented with a nod, and Luna ran outside and threw herself into Anna's arms:

"Shush, darling, everything's alright now. Don't you worry!" Luna asked her what happened, and Anna told her that Balthazar had appeared to her and told her that something unforeseen had happened. Apparently, the teacher had figured out on her own that something unusual was going on and had been making all kinds of assumptions, and she had to be stopped before she called all kinds of unwanted attention to Luna. He asked Anna to go talk to the teacher and tell her the truth, and explain to her that if she didn't keep quiet about this, Luna would get into very bad trouble. She was allowed to talk to her husband, but that was all. Too many people knew the truth already, so they had to be informed, or they would ask questions and ruin everything. Coming from Anna, the truth was much more acceptable to the teacher, but she wanted to talk to Luna herself. Anna looked in the room, and called the teacher outside. When the teacher returned, she looked at Luna with big eyes:

"Luna, are you really from the future? From about sixty years in the future?" Luna said:

"I'm not supposed to talk about it, but yes I am. It wasn't my doing, and I was sent here for punishment, because I was very discontented with my life and wanted to be anywhere but home."

"Are you ever going home, or are you going to stay here?" Looking down, Luna responded in a sad voice:

"Even though this was supposed to be a punishment, I love it here. But I have to go home to make up with my parents and little brother. I miss them too much. Now, whether I stay here or go home, I'll be homesick and miserable. I love everyone here, and I'm going to have to go away and never see anyone ever again. I can't let my parents suffer, I love them so much. This is entirely my fault, and I'm very sorry about this. If only I could have everyone here, as well as my family from home together, I would be happy!"

"Now that I know the truth," said the teacher, "I'll help you, if you'll let me!" Anna left with one last hug, and when Luna went back inside, Ivana whispered:

"What was that all about?"

"It was something about the wedding!" Luna whispered back:

"If you ask me, I'm starting to get sick and tired of the whole wedding thing!" Shot back Ivana, and Luna smiled. Ivana was a bit jealous of her, but there was no help for it; they would just have to make it up to her. A couple of days later, when Luna went to the Black Hole, she found Uncle Saverio waiting for her on the way back. He looked at her with something like respect, and said:

"So, tell me, Girl from the Future, what's it like where you come from?" Luna thought a little bit and said:

"Not much different from here honestly. Except for the technological advancements, people are still the same. Life is much harder and more competitive, and everyone is always running here and there. No one has any time for fun and laughter anymore, and romance is very hard to come by. People spend more time alone with their computers and televisions and telephones, and there isn't much fun in life." Uncle Saverio said:

"I've heard about those things, we already have them in the big cities, but I'm in no hurry to get into any of it."   Luna responded:

"You're smart.   When those things take over your life, they make it harder, not easier." Uncle Saverio said to her:

"Can you give me some advice?"   Luna looked at him seriously and said:

"You are lucky to be in the 1950's, this is a peaceful time.   You have a good life.   Just don't make it harder on yourselves by making your wife feel bad.   She loves you, and she would do anything to make you happy."

"What can she see in me?   I'm a brute while she's a beautiful, refined woman."

"She must see something she likes.   Besides I'm told that you're some kind of artist."

"You're talking about my carvings?"

"Yes, in my day almost no one does these things any more. You should make big, beautiful ones, and have my teacher help you to show them in a gallery or something.   When I go back I would love to see some of your work in museums or antique shops.   You're just as handsome and talented as she is, (don't get a big head now), and she adores you; you two can have a great life together.   More advice I can give you is to stop smoking.   In my day they found out that smoking takes years off of people's lives.   And   buy   some   stock   in   those   dreadful   computers, televisions, telephones and even cars, if you want to make some money.   I can't say anything else, because I don't know anymore." He smiled at her incredulously and said:

"So people have been talking about my silly little figurines?   I make those when I'm bored or upset; somehow carving makes me calm and happy, and I can think when I'm carving.   I truly hope they can bring happiness to others who see them.   Thank you for telling me, and thank you for all the other information.   I promise to remember everything you've said to me."   Uncle Saverio bent down, brushed a light kiss on her forehead, and left.   Luna walked back sadly; this was going to be harder then she thought.   The more she got to know these people, the more she knew she didn't want to leave them.   Yet she desperately wanted to go home and see her family.

Things settled into the usual routine, except for the wedding preparations. Luna and Ivana were a familiar sight zipping around on their bicycles, and the weather was still mellow and warm, even though it was already October. The upcoming wedding was all everybody could talk about and soon there was going to be another trip to the Fool's house to sign the contract and talk to the bride. It had been reported that the groom had been making daily trips to see his fiancée and he had been seen carrying flowers; he looked like a man in love. Ivana had started already talking about Christmas, and asked Luna to stay for it. Luna, who had been dying to go home, had a sudden desire to spend Christmas in this place, and waited for an opportunity to ask Balthazar if she could.

About a week after the first visit, the women and the girls went back to The Fool's house. The women stated that the wedding could be ready in all-of-its splendor by December. It could be done just before Christmas, or just after. The Fool decided that since Antonietta's birthday was on January six, the day of the Epiphany, and it was a Sunday, they would have it on Antonietta's birthday, and for an added occasion, La Befana would be at the wedding, and would hand out toys to any and all children who would come; the women should make sure they knew more or less how many children would come, so that there were enough toys to go around. Everyone was astounded, and they agreed that this was a touch of magic they would never have thought about. The Fool pranced around, proud of his idea, and thinking of all the people who would be talking about this, and how shocked they would be; and what an added attraction this would make to the wedding albums. He was going to talk to Carletto the lawyer and Ripetta the merchant, to see if they could recommend a place to purchase these great amounts of toys at a cut rate price. While everyone talked excitedly about it, and the women surrounded The Fool almost liking him a great deal, Anna signaled to Antonietta that she would like to talk to her. They went to Antonietta's room, a bright, beautiful and severely decorated room, and Anna sat on the bed with Antonietta. Antonietta's cat, a big beautiful animal with long orange fur, jumped on her lap. Anna asked the bride what kind of dress she wanted, and Antonietta, slowly caressing the cat's soft fur, said:

"I don't care what kind of dress I wear, you decide!" Anna picked up the girl's hand and said:

"Don't you want to impress your groom?" The bride said, a little sadly:

"He doesn't care what I look like, he only wants the gravel and sand pit my father is going to buy for us, he wants it for his family." Anna replied:

"I know the facts. But I've been told that he comes to see you almost every night and brings you flowers; they say that he looks like a man in love."

"In love with what I can provide for him!" Said Antonietta. Anna slapped her hand:

"What kind of girl are you? I thought you loved or at least liked the guy!" Antonietta looked down, embarrassed:

"I do like him more than anyone knows. I've been looking at him for a couple of years, that's why I don't want to hurt him; I told him that if he finds me repugnant, after the wedding I will go back home quietly, and he can keep whatever my father will give us." Anna was stunned:

"What did you say?"

"I said that if he doesn't want me, I'll go back to my father so he can be happy!"

"You fool girl! How happy do you think he would be after your father destroys him and his entire family? This wedding is your father's gift to you, even for a rich man like him this is a great expense, and he wants people to know how much he loves you. I don't know what my girl Luna told him, but she did her job too well, now he's like a runaway train, he comes up with idea after idea, and this wedding is becoming his masterpiece; if the groom sends you home afterwards, it would be the greatest slap in the face anybody has ever had. Your father is going to be a fury that no one could stop. If you truly care for Rodolfo, you better make this marriage last, you better show your father that it was all worth it, and most of all, that he gave his beloved daughter a great future. You better finish what you started, or a lot of people will get hurt, especially Rodolfo. Besides, if you leave him, he will have to be always alone, he can never marry again and have a family!" Antonietta looked stricken and just sat there looking at

Anna, while holding Arancio the cat to her bosom. Finally, she said:

"I didn't think of all these consequences, what am I going to do now?" Anna said briskly:

"You're going to make Rodolfo fall in love with you, and I'm going to help you!" Then Anna lifted some of Antonietta's straggly hair from her face, looked at her smiling and pronounced:

"Yes indeedy, we will make Rodolfo fall in love with you, that's for sure!" She took Antonietta's measurements and after that, she went back in the dining room and told everyone that the bride wanted a stunning wedding dress, and they would have to come up with some special design just for her. On the way back, the girls trailed the women quietly, and Luna touched Ivana's arm to get her attention, and asked her;

"What's La Befana?" Ivana looked at her strangely:

"You don't have La Befana up North?" Luna shook her head silently, and Ivana explained:

"This is an old lady, she rides a broom and she brings all the children toys on the day of the Epiphany, when they leave their stockings hanging on the fireplace the night before, she looks like a witch, but she's a good witch." Luna said:

"We have Santa Claus who does that! He does it on Christmas eve!" To which Ivana replied:

"You people up north are taking the American traditions, I saw 'Miracle on 34th street' at the movies, and they have a Santa Claus in America; I bet you even have a Christmas tree instead of a Nativity scene." Luna wanted to know all about the Nativity scene, and when Ivana told her, decided that maybe it would be wonderful to spend Christmas here, and the Epiphany; after all she couldn't miss the wedding, she was needed! She resolved to ask Balthazar about spending Christmas here In Italy in the year 1950. After a while, Ivana started to skip and sing-song a ditty about La Befana:

"La Befana comes at night, broken shoes, a broom astride, with her hat a-la-Romana, viva viva La Befana!" Luna linked arms with Ivana and together they started to skip along singing:

"La Befana comes at night, broken shoes, a broom astride, with her hat a-la-Romana, viva viva La Befana!" And all of a sudden the rest of the little group started to sing along. Gianna and Aunt Esther put Anna in the middle, linked arms and started to skip and dance while singing, and so did the three sisters, Irma, Amelia and Angelina. They all skipped along, singing and dancing; expressing their irrepressible joy at life. Luna was reminded of Dorothy from 'The Wizard of Oz', except that this was no yellow brick road, it was a lonely, unpaved and rocky country road but the women's joy turned it into a beautiful road to the future. A future full of happy possibilities, money to give their families everything they needed, promise of future friends and just joy in working together. Luna now had an overwhelming desire to be here for La Befana, and wondered if the old lady would bring something even for her; she was certainly going to hang her stocking the night before.

When they arrived at Aunt Esther's house, which was the closest to The Fool's farm, Uncle Pas drove everyone back home for their Sunday meal, and when he got back they had set the table and the steaming food was ready to be served. Aunt Esther had made the food before they went out, and Uncle Pas had watched it cook on the stove while they were away; he was even wearing an apron, and he looked really cute in it! They had the usual pasta (on Sunday it was always pasta of one kind or another) and to go with it they had rolls of very thin beef stuffed with parsley, garlic and salt and pepper. The rolls were pan-fried until brown, some white wine was added to the pot, with some chopped onion, and when the wine evaporated, tomatoes and grated carrot were added. It had been Uncle Pas' job to make sure these did not burn during the long process of slow cooking for at least three hours. With the pasta and the meat they had just a very large mixed salad, and instead of dessert, they ate big, crunchy wedges of white and tender fennel. Luna thought that yes! Life was good! After the chores and feeding the animals, it was back to homework and 'The Betrothed'. The people in the book were also like old friends to her, and she followed their antics with indulgence. That night they had an early supper of panzanella and some fruit and they went to bed early. Panzanella was one of Luna's favorite suppers, and it was so easy to make that sometimes the girls made it. It consisted of water with some extra virgin olive oil and a few cloves of garlic. When the water started to boil they put in it some precooked pastina, the very small kind, and some salt. After that they would gently break an egg for each person in it, and when the egg was poached, the panzanella was ready to eat. Sometimes instead of the pastina, they would put a handful of small pieces of dry, homemade bread in their plates, and the egg and soup would be deposited gently on top of it. The bread would saturate with the juice, but it would not get mushy, and the whole thing smelled wonderful. Luna was now paying a lot of attention to the food and how they made it, because she had decided not to go back to hamburgers and fries, at least not all the time, and she wanted to be able to make some of the things she had come to love.

On the Monday, they zipped to school on their bicycles and sat with the rest of the class while the teacher did her work. Lately the teacher seemed happier and looked younger and prettier; her husband often stuck his head in the classroom, and they looked at each other without saying anything. Ada, Concetta and Luana were whispering to Luna and Ivana how lately the teacher and her husband seemed like they couldn't take their eyes off of each other and they wondered what happened to those two. Concetta said to Ivana:

"They're acting almost like your parents! They're in looove!" And everyone laughed, but everyone was actually glad their teacher was so happy! There was something new in the classroom, and Luna spotted it almost right away; a beautiful eagle with wide spread wings stood on top of a shelf of books, it looked carved out of a solid piece of wood, and the wood rubbed until it looked almost like ivory:

"Uncle Saverio's carving!" Thought Luna, and smiled; he was indeed an artist. The Teacher saw Luna smile, and walked by her. Leaning down a bit she whispered:

"Thank you!" And walked away with a look of pride on her beautiful face. She had taken to wearing low heeled shoes and plain dresses, much like the kind other women wore to go to the store and such, and she looked younger and more comfortable. Her hair had been cut short, showing off her lovely features, and her makeup was toned down to just some lipstick and mascara. Luna and all the other girls liked their teacher's new image. Some days ago, in a rare moment of privacy, the teacher had asked Luna what the women were wearing in the distant future, and she had replied that no one wore fancy clothes and a lot of makeup or very high heels, unless they were going to a big, fancy party or they were in the entertainment business; no one had the time to waste on such fripperies. If anyone tried to be too different than anyone else, no one liked them. And besides, the women in the future preferred to show themselves like they really were, not covered up in stuff almost to disguise themselves. Luna told the teacher that there was a saying in her time:

"Less is more!" And she was happy to notice that the teacher was smart enough to understand and take the hint.

On the following Saturday, when the girls came home from school, Aunt Esther was already to go out to a neighboring farm to look at someone's wedding dress to get some ideas for Antonietta's dress. She was twisting her hands nervously because she was busy all morning baking, and there was nothing prepared for dinner. Uncle Pas had brought in a chicken, but she hadn't cooked it yet. Ivana was upset because she wanted to go and see the fancy wedding dress that the people had bought in Roma, but the chicken was on the table, still covered in feathers, and someone had to cook it. Luna stood tall, and said:

"Why don't you two go see the wedding dress, and I'll make chicken soup for dinner." Aunt Esther looked at her with hope, but said:

"I couldn't possibly leave you all alone to do this, it's not fair!" Luna smiled:

"I want to; I want to prove to everyone that I can do something useful! Please trust me!" Ivana said that she trusted Luna, and Aunt Esther was eventually convinced that it was not child labor to leave Luna all alone to cook the chicken. As soon as they left, Luna donned Aunt Esther large apron, picked up the chicken, and brought it near the fornacella, where a large pot of water was boiling gently. She got up on a chair, and did like she had seen her Aunt do so many times; she dunked the chicken in the boiling water a few times, then she brought it to the table and put it in a large bowl. Swiftly she pulled off all of the feathers and rinsed it in clean water. After that was done, she filled a large, clean pot halfway with spring water, added the chicken to the pot, and put in some celery, an onion, a few very ripe tomatoes and some salt. After that was done, and the pot was arranged nicely on the fornacella, she stoked a good fire under it, and cleaned up after herself. (Luna had certainly changed; before coming here, she would never have thought about doing something like this herself, let alone wanting to prove herself to anyone.) When the pot started to boil gently, Luna set the table and then sat, very satisfied with her work. She figured she had at least two hours before Aunt Esther and Ivana came back, and by then the soup would be ready to eat. After a few minutes, she started to smell something funny, and she looked over at the pot, worried. When she saw the chicken, she did a double take. It was floating on the water, almost coming out of the pan, and it looked like a giant soccer ball. Luna stared at it, bug-eyed, and afraid to go near it. Uncle Pas had just come in from the field, and looked at Luna, then at the chicken and said:

"Stand back, Luna, let me take that off the fire before it.............." But he couldn't finish his sentence, as with a popping noise, the chicken quite literally exploded, and brown stuff went all over the place, covering the backsplash of the fornacella and the floor. Luna stood there horrified, and Uncle Pas stared at the dirty wall and floor with dismay. Luna started crying, and babbled miserably:

"Aunt Esther and Ivana so wanted to see the wedding dress from Roma, at the farm up the street! I wanted to prove I can cook for the family, and said I'll cook the chicken. I don't know what I did wrong, I did it just like I saw Aunt Esther do it, I'm so, so sorry! I'm no good at anything, she trusted me to......." At that point she heard a funny noise, and she looked at Uncle Pas; he had his hand over his mouth, and it looked like he was trying not to cry. Luna was staring at him, when she realized that he was trying not to LAUGH! He was laughing! All at once, Uncle Pas let go, and laughed heartily. Luna looked at him bewildered for a few seconds, and then she too started to laugh. They laughed and laughed, until their sides hurt, and then Uncle Pas hugged her to him for a few seconds, and managed to say between bouts of laughter:

"The guts.......you didn't cut it open.......and take the guts and the gizzards out." Luna asked shrilly:

"The guts? I was supposed to pull out the guts and the gizzards? But Ivana always said that the little brown things in the soup were the guts and gizzards, and I thought I was supposed to leave them in!"

"No, sweetheart, you take them out, clean them, and chop them up before putting them back." Luna said, forlornly:

"Aunt Esther trusted me to cook this chicken, and I let her down!" Uncle Pas said:

"No, you didn't! Let's go, put wings on and clean up the wall and floor, I'll do the rest." While Luna frantically cleaned up, Uncle Pas took out the chicken shambles pot, buried the whole thing, washed the pot outside, got another chicken, quickly twisted its neck, brought it in, and then helped Luna finish cleaning up. The first pot of boiling water was still on the fire; they dunked the chicken, and frantically took off all of the feathers. Uncle then cut the chicken into small pieces and told Luna to get the great cast iron frying pan they kept hanging on the wall. He dumped the chicken in the pan, added some oil, and told Luna to watch it while it fried. He put some water in the cleaned pot from outside, with a little salt, and prepared some spaghetti next to it, ready to go. He chopped some garlic, put it in a small pan with some oil, and said they were going to have spaghetti with garlic and oil; the spaghetti would go in the water when everybody was ready to eat, it was a cardinal sin in this household to overcook pasta. While Luna watched the chicken, he came back with a basket of potatoes, and peeled and chopped them. After all of the golden brown chicken was taken off the frying pan and put in a platter to keep warm next to the fornacella, he dumped the potatoes in the oil, and Luna watched them, stirring and salting slightly, until they were reduced to moist and crunchy home fries. Right in the nick of time, as Aunt Esther and Ivana walked in the door while Luna was dishing them up with a large spoon. The spaghetti went in the boiling water, and a few minutes later, they all sat down to eat the fragrant food. Aunt Esther pronounced the food delicious, and pronounced herself very proud of Luna, although she was under the impression that Luna was going to make soup, and not fried chicken, which was much harder to do. Luna colored at that, and Uncle Pas said, nonchalantly:

"The fried chicken was my idea, I had a craving for it, and Luna was very amenable to it; she's a good girl." They exchanged a conspiratorial smile, and Ivana, who knew Luna quite well, knew right away that something was up, and resolved to get the truth out of Luna when they went to bed. Aunt Esther remarked that the kitchen looked unusually sparkling, and Uncle Pas said slyly that Luna had washed the wall behind the fornacella and the floor. Luna looked down modestly while Aunt Esther heaped praises on her. Ivana now really looked at Luna with suspicion; no one washed the wall and the floor unless they had to. Ivana could hardly contain herself while they did homework, chores, ironing and then had their late, light supper. As soon as they went upstairs to bed, she followed Luna to her room and sat on her bed:

"Now, what happened today?" Luna answered angelically:

"Nothing!"

"Don't give me that, something went on, and I'm not leaving until you tell me!" Luna kept preparing herself for bed, ignoring Ivana, but eventually, when she realized that Ivana wasn't going to leave if she didn't tell, she sat next to her and spilled her guts. Ivana sat staring at Luna with her mouth twitching, trying not to laugh. She hiccupped a few times, her eyes watered, and then eventually she had to giggle, and then laugh outright. At first Luna sat there offended, but after a while she started to giggle and then laugh, and the two girls held each other, and pounded each other's back when they were choking on their laughter. Uncle Pas stuck his head in the room and held his finger to his nose, admonishing them to be quiet, and whispered:

"You spilled the beans, didn't you?" And at Luna's assent, smiled and went away. Luna asked Ivana frantically:

"He's not going to tell Aunt Esther, is he? I don't want her to know how I let her down! She's so proud of me so far!"

"Don't worry, he saved me many times, and he never told. You're safe with him." With a sigh of relief, Luna started to lay out her clothes for Sunday mass, and Ivana helped her. That night, after falling asleep as soon as her head touched the pillow, Luna dreamed that she was trying to cut a chicken open to take out the guts and gizzards, but the chicken grew and grew, until it was ten times bigger than Luna and round as a ball, and then it was running after Luna to catch her and make her into soup; at least he doesn't have to dunk me in hot water and take my feathers off, thought Luna, because I don't have any. Eventually, Uncle Pas appeared brandishing a great cast iron frying pan, and hit the chicken over the head with it. While Luna escaped the chicken she could hear Ivana say:

"Don't you worry, you're safe with him!"

The night before, as Rodolfo approached his house in the dark, it was very late, a small figure detached itself from the wall and walked up to him. At first Rodolfo was startled, but then realized that it was his future father-in-law, and took off the accordion from his powerful shoulders; all accordion players had shoulders like quarterbacks. He invited him in the house, but The Fool said:

"What I have to say is for your ears only!" They walked away from the door, and The Fool asked Rodolfo why he was working so late. Rodolfo said:

"I'm trying to earn as much as I can, I have to come up with enough money for The Bride's Gold, and I don't want to embarrass Antonietta with something cheap."

"You'll never make enough for that by playing the accordion and singing." Said The Fool. Rodolfo said he knew, but he had no other way of getting the gold:

"My family has nothing, or they would've helped me. I so want to do Antonietta proud!"

"I know about your family," said The Fool, "and I want you to do Antonietta proud!"

"Please don't try to give me money," said Rodolfo, "I wouldn't take it! This is my responsibility!"

"I'm very pleased you feel that way," said The Fool. "I wouldn't try to give you money for The Bride's Gold, it wouldn't be proper; besides, if I did and Antonietta found out, she'd give it back and cancel the wedding." Rodolfo said:

"I have to do something, but I don't know what, yet!" The Fool smiled:

"I do!"

"What?" Said Rodolfo. The Fool squinted up at him in the dark:

"I've arranged credit for you at the best jewelers in town, I've guaranteed it. They'll let you pick anything you want, and if you don't pay, I will. I hope I don't have to."

"But where will I get the money to pay them?" Replied Rodolfo. The Fool shook his head as if to say that young people were dense these days:

"After your wedding, you'll be a rich man!"

"You mean Antonietta will be a rich woman!"

"No! No! She's already a rich woman; she has been investing for years! You both will be rich! But if it makes you feel better, you can use your share of the wedding money to pay for the gold."

"But the wedding money belongs to the bride!"

"Don't make me crazy, young man! Your situation is about to change, and you're not going to worry about chump change anymore!"

"You know," replied Rodolfo pensively, "I'm starting to find it a bit repulsive, the fact that we will get so much from you. I'm starting to want to marry Antonietta for other reasons."

"What you said couldn't please me more," said The Fool, "you're finding out what a pearl of a girl she is, aren't you?"

"Yes!" Said Rodolfo simply:

"Well, don't feel bad about the wedding gift I'll bestow on you two; after all, she's my only daughter, and what am I going to do with my money if I don't help my kids with it? You'll soon be one of them, you know! I've bought my sons large, prosperous farms, but neither you nor Antonietta are farmers, so a business is the best thing. She's an accountant, and the best business woman I have ever known; she'll teach you everything you need to know. Now, don't go get this gold alone, bring a woman with you, do right by Antonietta; she's small and delicate, keep that in mind. We'll have the presentation of The Bride's Gold in three weeks, at my house on Sunday. Be ready by then! Your entire family is invited, and some of our friends. My entire family will be there. Antonietta will give you the details." And with that, The Fool said 'Good Night' and slipped away in the dark. Rodolfo stared after the man he had always despised, and felt a small germ of affection starting to grow in him right together with the bit of respect that was already there.

The following day, after church, The Fool accosted Uncle Pas and invited him and his entire family to his house three weeks hence, on Sunday afternoon, after Sunday dinner, to witness the presentation of The Bride's Gold to Antonietta from her fiancé Rodolfo; there would be refreshments. Uncle Pas said he would be honored, and after thanking Uncle, The fool accosted the families of the other wedding consultants, and Aunt Palma, of course; she was the oldest person in the region, and it was proper form that she be present at all important functions, not to mention good luck. Aunt Esther started to talk excitedly about what they were going to wear, and Luna asked Ivana what a presentation of The Bride's Gold was. Ivana explained that when someone was going to marry, it was tradition that the groom presented the bride with gold, gold that she would wear for the rest of her life, and together with all future gold she would receive from her husband. In fact after they were married, husbands almost never gave their wives gold, unless they were rich, but at the time of the wedding, everyone tried to outdo each other with the gold, to show off to their bride's family and all their friends; it was the bride's best chance of getting some nice gold. Ivana said:

"Rodolfo doesn't have any money, I'm curious to see what he's going to give Antonietta." Uncle Pas turned to the two of them:

"He seems to hold her in high regard, from what I'm told; where there's a will there's a way!" Luna said:

"Couldn't The Fool give him the money to do this thing?" Ivana was scandalized:

"Of course not! If Rodolfo takes money from anyone to buy the gold, it would be most improper; it's his responsibility to buy it. He can borrow the money from his own family, and then pay it back, or he can buy the gold on credit and then pay it back later, but he cannot accept money from his bride's family for it. It's just not done!" Luna shook her head at this; so many rules to live by, over here, it was like a minefield if you arrived from another place, let alone another time! Luna wondered what these people would think if they saw how little of this happened in her own time. They would simply not believe it! As they were walking to the truck, Anna came running up to them all excited:

"I've heard about The Bride's Gold presentation! We're all invited. We must talk before we go to it. I've something to tell all of you girls that you don't know!"

"I can't wait until we get together," said Aunt Esther, "please tell me now!" Anna said:

"Alright, I'll give you the short version! But we still have to get together! Antonietta says that she loves Rodolfo, but he's only marrying her for the money, and after they're married, if he doesn't want her, she'll go home and let him keep everything. If he doesn't want her, she'll not have him. You know what this will do to everyone! There will be war, as The Fool will hurt anyone connected with this thing, we're going to be in the line of fire, there's going to be no wedding consultant business, we'll be a laughing stock from here to Roma. And frankly I don't want to see Rodolfo and his family go down, not to mention Assunta. Antonietta has agreed to let me help her win Rodolfo for herself, and I've got a pretty good idea on what to do, she's pretty under all that hair, but I need your help." Aunt Esther looked shaken:

"There's never a moment of peace when you deal with that family, is there? Arrange the meeting, I'll be there!" They went home quietly, the girls whispering to each other, and Aunt Esther and Uncle Pas discussing how you couldn't help feeling sorry for The Fool, so full of pride on his daughter's happy day, while the girl planned on destroying everyone with her stubborn pride. A lot of people had marriages of convenience, not everyone could marry for love, but they made the best of it, and in time love came to most everyone, after a lifetime spent together:

"Not everyone can be as lucky as we were!" Said Uncle Pas and Aunt Esther agreed:

"Not every girl can find a man as special as you, Pasquale!"

"No other man can find a woman like you, Estherina!" Aunt Esther put her head on Uncle Pas' shoulder, and he took one hand off the steering wheel to put it over Aunt Esther's shoulder, pulling her to him. The girls rolled their eyes and whispered:

"Here we go again!" And then, louder: "Lovey dovey is well and good, but when you're going to kill people to do it, it's not right; please put both of your hands on the steering wheel!" Aunt and Uncle started laughing, and while Aunt Esther straightened up, Uncle Pas put his hand back on the steering wheel. Sunday meal went a long way to reestablish a little jocularity, since the gnocchi potato dumplings were soft and fluffy, the sauce that covered them was red, tasty and sweet, and the goat cheese they grated over it was salty and sharp. The ragu' meat had cooked in the sauce for hours, and it was so tender that you would think it was a very expensive piece of beef meat, but it was chuck steak, and only the ministrations of Aunt Esther could make such delight out of it. The large, golden slices of bread made you want to dip it into the sauce, and the casserole of artichoke hearts stir fried in garlic and olive oil and then stewed was green, tender and sweet. After they had coffee all together, with small almond cookies and some dried figs, hope started flowing again. Suddenly, Luna saw an image that she knew since she was born, and exclaimed:

"I know what the wedding gown should look like! Ivana can draw much better than I can, before the meeting the two of us can have a picture of it!" Ivana and Aunt Esther looked at Luna enquiringly. Uncle Pas got up and went to take care of things in the barn:

"I'll leave you women to discuss fashion; I don't think that it's my forte, anyways." After Uncle left, Luna said hesitantly:

"There is a picture of my parents' wedding on the living room wall, at my house. My mother is petite, like Antonietta, and she's wearing a wedding dress that it's unlike any I've seen before. It's handmade, my great-grandmother made it for my grandmother, and she passed it down to her own daughter, my mother. My grandmother showed it to me many times, since I was little; It's a family heirloom, and very fragile, but my mother has it in storage, and supposedly I'm to wear it at my own wedding." Aunt Esther had tears in her eyes, and whispered:

"That's so beautiful! Somehow, this story about the wedding gown touches me deeply; I don't know why!" Ivana said excitedly:

"Tell me what it looks like, I'm dying to know!" And Luna tried to explain, but she didn't really have the words, so she took a piece of paper and tried to design it. Aunt Esther said:

"But, dear, the hem is uneven! Hems must be straight!"

"Not where I come from!" Said Luna. "It's the style, and it's very fashionable. I think that that style was invented in Paris or something. When you see it, you'll understand." It took Luna and Ivana all evening to come up with a design that did justice to Luna's memory of her mother's gown. When it was finished, they showed it to Aunt Esther, and she declared, with moist eyes, that it was the most beautiful thing she had ever seen, that she knew exactly what to do now, and the only problem was that after she was finished with it, she didn't know if she could give it up. She turned to Ivana and said:

"I will make you a wedding gown like this for your wedding, my beautiful child." She then turned to Luna and said:

"And I will make you one too, if you let me!" Luna looked at the beautiful, loving lady, and desperately wanted to wear a wedding gown made by her, but she knew it was impossible. She ran to her Aunt Esther and hugged her tight around the waist, like she never wanted to let her go:

"Thank you," she whispered, "I would love to wear a wedding gown made by you more than anything in the world!"

All of a sudden, a voice from deep inside told Luna that she WOULD, in fact, wear a wedding gown made by Aunt Esther! And it would be just as beautiful as she could ever imagine!

On the Monday, Anna sent word to the teacher that the meeting was at her daughter's farm tomorrow after dinner, the Merolli farm, to go there for dessert and coffee, and to tell the girls they were expected and so was Esther. At lunch time, the other girls were excitedly talking about the wedding, and what they were going to wear. Concetta tried to find out what Ivana and Luna had for the wedding, but they didn't know yet. Ivana whispered to Luna:

"If there even is a wedding!" Luana said that they were lucky to be invited to the presentation of The Bride's Gold, but it didn't matter; the presentation was really just for family and they were there in their capacity of Wedding Consultants. Everyone had been invited to the wedding and that was the best of all. Ada said that her mother was taking her to Frosinone, the Country-Seat of the region, to buy dresses and shoes for the two of them. There was a shoe store right at the entrance to the city that was called 'Centipede' and they had any kind of shoe imaginable, and there was a very large center with many stores and in one of them they sold ready-made dresses. Her mother was not a good seamstress, and they did not want to be embarrassed in front of the other ladies. Even her father, who was usually very stingy, had agreed that they needed good dresses and shoes. Luna and Ivana knew now that they had to put everything they had into this thing, because if the wedding was called off, the whole countryside would be disappointed. The following day, after dinner, everyone congregated at Amelia's house. Luna looked at the new barn as they approached, and remembered the night of the barn burning; it seemed a million years ago, but actually barely a month had passed since. She had never been inside the house, and was glad when Anna came to the door to welcome them into her daughter's house. She hugged Luna and Ivana, whispering:

"My wonderful girls!" And they all walked through an entrance, kind of like a mud room, where they hung their sweaters on hooks on the wall. Under the hooks, were chests that served as seats to take off muddy boots and the like, and then the cover opened up and the chests were lined with oilcloth, to stash the shoes in. As guests, they did not have to take their shoes off, but they rubbed them back and forth on a mat just outside the room. Luna realized why when they entered into Amelia's good parlor, and saw that there was a beautiful oriental rug on the floor, and beautiful couches and chairs were arranged around a beautiful and large coffee table; smaller tables were distributed around the room strategically, so that the people sitting in the chairs had a place to put their refreshments on. Everyone exclaimed at the beautiful sight, and Mario's mother, a small old lady with a beautiful head of curly white hair, who was sitting on the couch with Angelina and Irma, said proudly:

"My husband brought this furniture from Switzerland, where he went for work when we were young. He fell in love with the beautiful homes and furnishings there, and wanted to recreate at least one room; I've loved it myself all these years." Uncle Pas declared himself duly impressed by the beautiful room, and then went to join the men in the barn; Mario was showing everyone the new stalls they had just installed for the horses. He confided to Uncle Pas that this wedding thing came at just the right time; they were incurring so many expenses to fix the farm that there was never enough money. Uncle hoped the women were able to fix all the problems and pull off the wedding, because now so many people were beginning to count on it, for one reason or the other. A few minutes later, Gianna the teacher arrived, with Uncle Saverio. He joined the men in the barn, and Gianna seated herself next to Aunt Esther, and said happily:

"If this thing goes good, I'm going to send some of my share of the down payment to the nuns who raised me, they can really use the money, it will be a happy Christmas at the orphanage, and I'll use the rest to put a down payment on a new truck for my husband; he's been needing one for some time." Luna thought:

"So many plans, all dependent on this wedding! It had better go off perfectly!" At first Anna related the bad news about Antonietta being ready to cast everything to the wind, and then, at everyone's dismay and disappointment, she told them that there may be a way to fix things. Anna looked excited. She said:

"I think Rodolfo is already half in love with Antonietta. She's very deceiving, you know! She's a smart girl! And very attractive, if she just lets herself be attractive. I have an idea; you know how girls who do a striptease take off one piece of clothing at the time, to show their charms slowly?   When they do that, the men can't wait for the rest of it, they can't think of anything else; well, that's what we'll do with Antonietta." Everyone exclaimed:

"What? You want Antonietta to do a striptease? Her father will kill us. And by the way, how do you know about this, when did you see women stripping?" Anna cackled and said:

"Never you mind how I know! One day I'll tell you girls. What I meant is that we should show Antonietta to Rodolfo a little bit at the time. We will dress her to be very attractive, sexy even, by the presentation of the gold, but we will let her be covered by hair, as usual, until the wedding. The day of the wedding, we will unveil Antonietta in all her glory!"

"If there is glory to be unveiled!" Said everyone in unison:

"Oh, there is, there is!" Said Anna. At this point Aunt Esther looked around and said:

"My girls have something to show everyone!" Luna and Ivana got up took the big rolled up piece of soft cardboard they had been carrying, and unrolled it in front of everyone. They each held one side, and the women collectively let out a surprised gasp at what they saw; Ivana's effort had achieved a pinnacle even she didn't expect. The design of the wedding gown was beautiful and ethereal, the dress shimmering and elegant, and a design they had never seen before. The gown was made of heavy satin, with a scoop neck and long, slim sleeves. The front of the bodice was encrusted with seed pearls and shimmering glass beads in the palest ivory. The beadwork covered the entire front, encircled the tiny waist and ended in a point just under it. The dress itself flared at the hips, and floated in fluid waves to the floor. The crowning touch was the length. The dress was shorter in front, showing a well turned ankle and beautiful high heeled shoes, and it gradually fell to the floor in the back, producing a light train. On the head, the bride wore a coronet studded with seed pearls and glass beads to match the dress, and the face was absolutely devoid of hair, as the hair was all caught in the coronet, and piled stylishly high; she was wearing long, dangly earrings. An ethereal, almost invisible veil flowed from the top of the coronet to the floor, the same length of the dress and it rested lightly on the train. The effect was both regal, and beautifully elegant. Everyone was talking at once, and plump little Amelia was staring at it with awe. The teacher turned to Luna:

"Was this your idea? That's how all brides dress where you're coming from?"

"They do have beautiful wedding dresses where I come from, but this is my mother's wedding gown, and it's more than fifty years old, it's a family heirloom; my great-grandmother made it for my grandmother, and she passed it on to her daughter, my mother; I'm to wear it at my wedding!"

"So this dress could have been made in the nineteen hundreds, then?" Said Angelina:

"This one will be made now!" Said Aunt Esther and everyone sighted and said:

"If Rodolfo is not in love now, he will be in love when he sees Antonietta in this dress!" Anna looked at the dress, looked approvingly at the two girls, and then exclaimed briskly:

"We still have a long time between now and the wedding; we have to worry about more recent things."

"Like what?" Said everyone:

"Like the presentation of The Bride's Gold, that's what!" Everyone looked crestfallen at that reminder, but Anna had a resourceful smile on her face, and as she bend down and pulled a bundle from under her chair, everyone held their breath. Out of the brown paper package came a sweater top and a skirt. The gasps of pleasure were certainly not comparable to the ones uttered about the wedding dress, but they were enough to satisfy

Anna. She held up the top for everyone's perusal, and it was almost a piece of art. It was fashioned with the softest angora wool in a blue so pale that it was almost white. It had a beautiful oval neck, plain and sophisticated at the same time. The sleeves were slim and soft, and it gathered at the waist gently. Angora hair gently swayed as you moved it, giving the top hues of different blues; it was like air caressed and enveloped the whole garment. After the top, Anna pulled out a slim wool skirt, black, soft and slightly flared at the hips. After the skirt, she pulled out a pair of pumps with the slightest heel, in pale blue suede:

"We bought these at Centipede on the way out of Frosinone." She said. Everyone exclaimed at this show, and they touched the soft as butter shoes, the light as air skirt, and the cuddly top:

"Where did you get these clothes and where did you find the money for them?" Everyone asked, delighted:

"I went to The Fool yesterday and told him that for the presentation of The Bride's Gold, Antonietta had to be attired properly, that she needed to look better than she usually did, I told him she was pretty and we should show it off, and we should give the groom a small sample of what she was really like, since she didn't care to do so herself. Amazingly, he was totally receptive to this idea. He told me that she would not wear fancy clothes, she liked simple things, but there were all kinds of things you could do to dress up simple things. One of his son's drove us to Frosinone, to a big shopping center, and to a dress shop owned by a customer of The Fool. This woman was very grateful to him for advancing her the money to open the shop; she could never have done it otherwise. Obviously, he had given her very good terms, and she had already repaid him. I saw The Fool in a different light. The woman went on and on about how the banks had refused her credit because she was separated from her husband and had no collateral, but she said that The Fool asked to see some of the clothes she made herself, he asked her if she had a business plan, and when she showed it to him, he was very pleased and took a chance on her. The Fool said that he saw she had talent and would do well; besides, he could afford that small loss. Now she was doing very well, and she asked what she could do to be of service. When we told her that The Fool's daughter was to be married, and we needed an outfit for the presentation of The Bride's Gold, she assented knowingly; she had met Antonietta several times, and she said she knew exactly what was needed. She went in the back, and came out with these dream clothes. She said that they had been fashioned for a high society lady from Civitavecchia, who came to spend the holidays with her parents every year, this lady was petite like Antonietta, and she liked deceivably simple clothes, with beautiful design and precious materials. The Fool loved the clothes, and was willing to pay anything for them, but the woman said she had time to have another set made before her customer came for them, and she was charging so much, that she could easily effort to make a gift of them to her benefactor. Anna commented to The Fool:

"Now if we can only convince Antonietta to wear them!" The Fool replied:

"That, my dear woman is your job! That's what I'm paying you women for!"

"And so, here I am! Antonietta cannot object to this simple, wonderful outfit, and if she does, I'll remind her that she wants me to help her win Rodolfo for herself; that should do the trick!" Everyone was talking excitedly, this was a beautiful adventure, and everyone wanted to see Antonietta marry Rodolfo in the beautiful wedding gown. Aunt Esther was already talking about what kind of satin was needed for the wedding dress, and Irma was talking to the others about seed pearls, glass beads and sequins; sequins would not be appropriate, too garish, seed pearls and glass beads were indeed the right, classy choice. Angelina thought that Centipede in Frosinone would be the best store for the wedding shoes also, and Gianna said that they should send to Milano for the veil; her nuns would know what to pick. Amelia said that they could make the coronet out of very thin, flexible wood, cardboard wouldn't do for this special gown, and they could ask Uncle Saverio to do it, as he was known to do beautiful things with wood, and the teacher proudly said she would ask him. Irma said that she would embroider the cloth first, and then they would fit it to the coronet. So many ideas, so many joyful conjectures! Luna had never seen anyone get so much joy from a job in her life. At home, few ever wanted to do such a good job; they just went to work and came home, tired and grumpy, every day. The teacher sat next to Luna and whispered in her ear:

"I think it was you, Luna, who brought us good luck and this joy; we've never worked together like this before, and it's wonderful." Then there were refreshments, and the ladies partook with joy of the lovely tea' served in dainty china cups, the platters of Anna's wine cookies, and lovely anisette slices that were soft and light. The men, still hiding in the barn, had been given wine and a big plate of the wine cookies. There was some desultory talk about the entertainment for the wedding. The accordionist was going to be busy getting married, so they had to find somebody else. In fact there was a group of entertainers from San Giovanni Incarico who were very popular; it consisted of a guy who sang and played the guitar, and three women who played various instruments, a violin, an accordion and something else they couldn't remember. The man was funny, short, gold teeth in the front; he had red hair and wore a funny checkered suit with his black and white wingtip shoes. But they said that he sang beautifully, and was very entertaining. The women played beautifully to his funny repertoire, but they could also play beautiful romantic music, and even classic tunes. Irma said that her husband was going to San Giovanni Incarico the following week, and she would ask him to invite the group to come over and talk to them about the wedding. Angelina didn't think they were appropriate for an elegant wedding, and they should check also into classical music players. Amelia's mother-in-law suggested some dancers in the ancient local costumes, there were a lot of troupes who sang and danced to entertain the guests during dinner at weddings. Everyone suggested something, and their ideas merged nicely until the picture of a wonderful wedding was emerging. After the refreshments and the talks, everyone started to get ready to go home; everyone had chores that needed to be done before it got dark. On the way home, Aunt Esther and Uncle Pas were talking about going to Cassino to search for satin for the wedding dress, and Uncle Pas was saying that maybe it would be easy to drive to Pontecorvo and take a bus to the train, and go to Cassino on the train. Luna felt sheer terror about going on that train; after all that was the train Balthazar put her on, and she wasn't ready to go home yet. She touched Uncle Pas' shoulder and whispered:

"Please, Uncle, not that train!" He turned around, saw her face and understood completely:

"Don't worry, Luna, I've just decided to drive the truck there; we'll make a nice outing of it!" Luna relaxed, and sat back next to Ivana. She didn't want to think about going home. She desperately wanted to go home, but not quite yet, and she didn't want to think about losing Ivana. Of all the people she had come to love, Ivana was the one she didn't want to lose the most. For now she didn't have to think about it, she just wanted to go home, eat supper, do her homework and go to sleep. Tomorrow was another day! That night she dreamed that Balthazar came to see her, and he said she could take Ivana home with her. Oh joy, oh happiness! They could go home together and live together like now, be like sisters and go to the same school. She could envision herself showing off Ivana to her friends at school, and life would be just complete. Then in the middle of the joy of Ivana going with her, she saw Aunt Esther crying, and Uncle Pas comforting her:

"We're going to lose our little girls; we'll never know what will happen to them, we'll never see them again, we'll be dead and gone right after they leave and get to their place!" Cried Aunt Esther and Uncle Pas said:

"You'll still have me, Estherina; we'll still have each other!" But his voice was breaking and his eyes were suspiciously bright. Luna, heartbroken, started crying herself. She simply didn't know what to do. In her sleep she thought:

"What have I done? I'm causing the nicest people in the world a lot of pain; I wish I never started this, I wish I was a good girl when I had the chance. Please, please Balthazar, help me!" And from a great distance she heard Balthazar say:

"Don't you worry, my girl, everything will be alright, you'll see!" Luna was then filled with a feeling of calm and warmth, allowing her to sleep the rest of the night.

The next morning, news reached them that Anna had gone to see Antonietta and showed her the clothes they had bought in Frosinone, and Antonietta said she would wear them, and that was a big relief. Anna spent some time with Assunta, and they had lunch together, and Assunta asked Anna to go earlier on the presentation day, to help Antonietta look pretty, as Assunta had no idea about it at all. Anna loved being the center of attention and readily agreed. About a week later, the teacher was advised that the whole Sargento family would be away on the next Monday, to go to Cassino to buy the satin for the wedding dress. Mario, Amelia's husband said that he would drop by their farm to feed the animals, and Uncle Pas was relieved; Mario was a good man, and trustworthy. They asked Antonietta to go with them, but she said she didn't have time, and she didn't care if the dress was made of burlap, as long as she had something to wear for the wedding. The women had one more meeting about the wedding dress, and they all agreed that Irma should go, since she was to work on the dress and some satin didn't take embroidery and beadwork very well. Irma decided to take Anna, and at that point, the truck would have been too small for all of them. Anna said they should take the bus to Cassino instead, which was fine with everyone. Aunt Esther said that they should look for materials for their dresses, as well, and Luna and Ivana couldn't stand the suspension. Ivana said that they should dress up for the trip to Cassino, and Luna decided that it was time she used her beautiful, yellow bag. Aunt Esther talked about taking sandwiches and having a nice picnic in the park, but Uncle Pas nixed the idea:

"I'm taking my girls out and nothing but the best will do; we're going to a restaurant in Cassino. We'll go first class all the way." Luna and Ivana were delighted, but in the back of her mind the old Luna was thinking:

"A bus ride, some pieces of cloth and a diner meal! I don't call it going first class, that's for sure! We'll be a rag tag band of hicks straggling through town!" But the new Luna was very excited, and skipping around with Ivana, dreaming of walking down Cassino's Main Street dangling her lovely yellow handbag.

On Monday morning Mario drove them to Pontecorvo in the Balilla, the Model T lookalike, and they boarded the bus to Cassino bright and early; Mario would be back for them at six p.m., and if they were there sooner, Aunt Esther said that they could go visit the S. Bartholomew Cathedral at the top of the Civita Quarters. The big old bus rattled out of Pontecorvo by the same road they had taken when coming from the train, and this time Luna didn't feel lonely or scared, in fact she was fairly bouncing on her seat, just like Ivana. Irma, who recently moved to these parts to be near her sisters and brothers, had never been to Cassino, she just drove through it on her way to some other place, and was very curious. When they turned into the Via Casilina, from May Street that came all the way from Pontecorvo, she looked up at a mountain in the distance and asked what that was. Uncle Pas told them that that was Montecassino, and the large building on the top was the abbey built by S. Benedict of Norcia. It used to be a great and historic monastery, full of beautiful artifacts, paintings and statues. Before the war there was a funicular that brought people from Cassino to the Abbey in seven minutes, but the funicular and the Abbey had been destroyed during the Second World War. Fortunately, most of the artifacts and holy relics had been saved by the monks, who carried everything into the Abbey's basements, way into the bowels of the earth. The Abbey was such a gem and national treasure for the people of Italy that the Government was rebuilding it, but he doubted the funicular was ever going to be fixed; the only way to go up the mountain to see what was left of the Abbey was by car, on a treacherous mountain pass that was way too narrow for any bigger vehicle. Uncle said that up on the mountain, very near the Abbey, there were now large cemeteries of different nationalities for all the men who died up there during the occupation; people came from all over the world to find the grave of some loved one up there on Montecassino. Everyone was sad and quiet for a while, and Uncle talked about Cassino to cheer everyone up. He told them that there was a beautiful peace monument built in Cassino, to remind the future generations to beware of the evils of war. Cassino was ancient, and many martyr saints came out of there. In Roman times it was named Casinum, which meant 'ancient' in Latin, and it was a very rich city. The people of Cassino were very faithful to Roma, even thought Hannibal was idolized there during the Punic Wars. They say that S. Peter the Apostle passed through Cassino on his way to Roma, and he preached to them about Christianity. It was now a beautiful city full of stores, restaurants, parks, promenades, markets, artistic buildings and churches. By now, everyone was bouncing on their seats, eager to get there. They passed the entrance to Aquino, and Anna squeezed Luna's shoulder in solidity; they both remembered the last time they were there, and Luna looked up at Anna and whispered:

"Did that ticket man, Alfredo, get his blood sausage?" Anna replied, smiling:

"Of course he did! I made Mario bring me to his house in Roccasecca Scalo and delivered them to him myself! His wife was very happy and they invited us to supper. We had a great time; I always keep my promises! Besides, it's smart to make friends in high places." Finally, they arrived in Cassino. When they stepped off the bus, the place seemed so large, that the girls worried about going too far in case they couldn't find the bus to go back, but Uncle Pas told them not to worry, that he came to Cassino on and off, and knew his way around. It was about nine A.M. by the time they arrived, and the coffee shops were full of people having pastries and cappuccino. The aroma coming out of these places could have woken the dead, and everyone was salivating; they had had a quick breakfast of dry rusks and tomatoes before leaving, and were already hungry. Uncle Pas steered them to a very large, gleaming shop, found them all seats around a round table, and then asked what they would have liked with their espresso. Anna wanted a cannoli, Irma and Aunt Esther wanted a napoleon, and Luna and Ivana couldn't make up their mind. Uncle Pas told them to go to the case and take their time picking their poison, and the girls eagerly went up to the case to decide. After viewing everything, and Luna asking Ivana what everything was, Ivana picked a huge baba' au Rum, and Luna picked a large Napoleon. Uncle went to the cashier, and paid for their order, and then went to the pickup area and received a large tray with all their goodies. Luna and Ivana carried the napkins, forks and extra dessert plates. Their table was near the window, and from their seats they could see the fancy people strolling by, their espressos were huge, as Uncle had ordered doubles, their sugar was in light brown, friable cubes, and their pastries were just out of this world! Aunt Esther declared that someone had told her that Cassino was renowned for the quality of its pastries, and everyone agreed. Luna was amazed at the Napoleon she had been given; layer upon layer of crunchy, sweet, crumbly pastry divided from each other by soft, yellow, gooey cream and topped with white and dark chocolate swirls. Ivana's baba' looked just like a plain piece of dough, but when she bit into it, cream and rum gushed out of it, and Luna almost though she should have got a baba', but Ivana looked at her, and cutting a piece out of it, put it on one of the extra plates and handed to her. Luna did the same with her napoleon, and they happily tasted each other's goodies. With their espresso, they had received a small container of whipped cream, and Luna waited to see what everyone did with it before she touched it. They took a spoonful of the cream and floated it in their espresso. Luna did the same, and it was heavenly. This trip WAS first class, and Luna felt bad for a few seconds because she had doubted Uncle Pas; she should have believed him, he never lied. And they were not a rag tag band of hicks; Aunt Esther looked very classy and modern in her severe dark blue suit and white, silky shirt, with low heeled pumps and small handbag to match. Aunt Esther had a kind of special dignity about her, and so did Uncle Pas who looked young, handsome and prosperous. Irma looked great also, in her soft blue dress and nice, chunky sweater. Of course, Anna was wearing her costume, but there were a lot of older ladies wearing it, like a badge of honor, and Anna's was specially made, with beautiful embroidery and classic brocaded cloth. After everyone had finished their coffee and pastry, they just sat there for a while, enjoying each other's company and making plans for the day. This was one of Luna's favorite things, not just to eat and run, but to prolong the pleasure of the table by socializing with your family and companions after the meal was done. While the grownups enjoyed each other, Ivana motioned to Luna to get up and follow her:

"Where are we going?" Said Luna, afraid she was going to miss something:

"I have a surprise for you!" Stated Ivana. Luna followed her to a carved, fancy door that sported the sign 'WC' in gold letters, and lo and behold, it was a bathroom! Luna couldn't believe it. A real bathroom! It was a lot different than the ones she was used to, but it had a great toilet bowl, a large sink and another contraption that was between a sink and a toilet bowl. It was squat, and it seated on the floor. Luna asked:

"What is that thing?" Ivana stared at her:

"You never saw one of those?" Luna repeated embarrassed:

"I'm sorry; I guess they don't have those where I come from!"

"It's a bidet, silly!"

"What's a bidet, and what do you do with it?"

"It's for washing yourself."

"But it's so small, what can you wash with it?"

"Your bum, that's what! You sit in it, turn on the water, and it does the rest." Luna was fascinated with it; she walked up to it and turned on the water. It shot a stream forward, and Luna started laughing, so did Ivana, and then Ivana went out to wait for Luna to use the bathroom, and then it was Ivana's turn, and Luna waited outside. When Ivana came out, they walked back to the table arm in arm, and Luna said:

"What does 'WC' stands for?" Ivana explained:

"It stands for Water Closet; it's an English name." Luna happily sat back down, and in a little while, they all got up and left. Walking down the sidewalk of the main street, they enjoyed window shopping, and discussing the various styles and colors of the clothes displayed. There were so many wonderful stores, but the clothes stores were the best ones. Ivana and Luna walked ahead of the adults, and Luna proudly swung her bright little bag back and forth, for all to see. Ivana had a bag also, it was red patent leather, and it went very well with her red sweater and red shoes, the ones she bought up at the feast of Ss Cosmo and Damiano. Under the sweater she was wearing a white shirt and black skirt, and she looked very pretty and smart. Luna was wearing her blue sweater over a little plaid skirt and white shirt, but the plaid skirt had some yellow in it, and some black, so Luna's bag and her little black patent leather shoes completed her outfit very nicely. Luna's hair had grown almost to her shoulders by now, and she combed it back in a pony tail, like Concetta; she wondered what was going to happen to her hair when she went back. Even if it went back to being short, Luna wanted it to grow again so she could have braids like Ivana. As they walked, they heard someone hail them. Coming down the other way, they saw Nannina, Giustina and Aunt Palma. They waved at them, and then stopped to talk. After the salutations, Aunt Palma turned to the girls and said:

"So, you girls have been to that big pastry shop, have you?" And at their assent, she said: "I bet you've eaten one of those huge, fat, full of sugar pastries, haven't you?" The girls looked guilty and didn't know what to say. Giustina started to laugh, and Nannina said:

"Stop it, Aunt Palma, will you? Don't toy with those girls; you know very well that we went there before they did and ate some of those pastries ourselves. Why you yourself ate a sfogliatella pastry so big it could choke a horse." Aunt Palma looked sheepish:

"It doesn't matter what I eat, I'm old enough already. It's those girls I worry about." Uncle Pas said:

"Don't worry about the girls, Aunt Palma, we watch their diet very closely, and those treats are few and far between." And then he leaned way down and deposited a light kiss on her cheek. Nannina said that they were in town to start getting an idea about what to wear for the wedding, and Aunt Palma was looking for a new shawl and some regular shoes; it wouldn't do to wear Cioci at a fancy wedding! But of course, she would wear them if she couldn't find the right shoes! After a few more minutes, they all went their own way, with Aunt Palma wagging her finger and reminding Luna and Ivana of their tombola lesson the following Saturday after school. Irma said how lucky they were that Aunt Palma condescended to give them tombola lessons, almost no one knew how to do it anymore, and it was a shame to let a beautiful art like that die. Luna and Ivana had asked Aunt Palma to teach it to them when they went to retrieve Ivana's tombola lace, and aunt Palma gave Luna also a piece of lace, but it was one her own mother had made when she got married, and it was over one hundred years old. Luna was so entranced with the beautiful, yellowed piece of creation that she expressed the desire to learn how to make it. Aunt Palma was very pleased, and told them they could both learn, if they wanted, and to come back on Saturday, after school. They had been making a lot of progress, and the bobbins almost flew in their hands by now. After the others left, Aunt Esther directed them to a huge, fancy fabric store she knew about. When they walked into the fancy fabric store, Luna was amazed at how large and beautiful it was, and it also smelled really good. Uncle Pas said that he had business in town, and they set up a meeting place and time, and he left them. In the store there was any kind of fabric you could want, and Irma and Aunt

Esther went straight to the wedding isle. After a lot of discussions and many questions, they settled on something; white-bluish satin, soft, shiny and heavy. Irma then looked at their selection of glass beads and seed pearls, and some of the stuff was adequate, but they needed very special decorations, and eventually the owner brought out a catalogue; he said that the stuff in the catalogue was very expensive, and they did not stock it, so it must be specially ordered. They bought what they needed, ordered the most beautiful decorations of Venetian glass and seed pearls, and had everything put on The Fool's account. The next trip to Cassino would entail choosing the wedding party favors, but they needed all of the wedding consultants for that, since choosing the right favors and the best almond candy to stuff in them was a very important decision. They thought that the favors could be small sacks of netting material filled with the candy, and tied with a satin string. They were thinking of decorating the favors with a cluster of glass beads and seed pearls to match the dress, but they would have to include everyone in this decision. Next they started to look for materials for their dresses. There was a lot to think about; it would be colder by then, and they needed heavier cloth. Irma said that she would come back with her family to shop for all of their clothes, and Anna hadn't decided if she was going to wear her habitual costume or regular clothes.

After much choosing, Aunt Esther picked for herself soft, cream colored wool which she would make into a suit with a straight skirt and a three quarter length jacket, decorated with gold piping; she bought deep gold satin for the blouse to go with it. The girls were looking all around, not knowing what to get. Ivana was partial to bright colors, but she couldn't decide on anything until Aunt Esther showed her a roll of beautiful dark rose colored velvet. Ivana fell in love with it immediately, and had to have it. While they were discussing the velvet and what kind of dress they could make with it, Luna spotted something blue that seemed like it was calling to her; it was exactly the same velvet of the dress in her dream birthday. It was a beautiful, shimmering blue that seemed to glow with its own inner light, and it matched her eyes perfectly. Luna looked at the price and in the act of caressing it, put her hand down and sighed. She couldn't ask her Aunt and Uncle to spend so much money on her! Besides, maybe

Aunt Esther would be so busy that she wouldn't have time to make her a dress. She probably had time to make a dress for Ivana, but after all Ivana WAS her daughter. If she thought back, no one had said anything about making her a dress; she just assumed they would. She would just have to wear one of her old dresses, that's all! Luna just walked away with a hangdog expression, and feeling very sorry for herself; she didn't care what she wore to the wedding, anyways, because all she really wanted was the blue velvet. As she moved away, out of the corner of her eye she spotted Aunt Esther talking to the owner, and when he reached for the blue and the dark rose bundles of velvet and took them to the cutting table, she was rooted to the spot. Aunt Esther smiled at her and called her over, she said that she knew Luna wanted the blue velvet, and it was perfect for her, and to Luna's delight they started to discuss the style of her dress. Luna couldn't stop thinking how much she loved her Aunt Esther! After the material was all cut, they each carried their own bundle, and Luna couldn't express the feeling of joy handling the soft, sweet smelling piece of cloth gave her. Her and Ivana kept opening their bundles and comparing colors, and Anna who had watched the whole proceeding in silence when they were in the store, approached Luna while Ivana ran up ahead to walk with her mother and Irma, and asked her:

"That piece of cloth reminds you of something from home, doesn't it?" Luna treaded her arm through Anna's, leaned her head on her shoulder and said:

"Yes, I had a velvet dress this color in one of the special moments of my dream birthday. Prince Charming was there, and he almost kissed me, but my mother woke me up just as he was going to."

"Isn't it always like that? When something beautiful is going to happen, real life always intrudes. But the truth is that if you find your beautiful moments in real life, they last forever, while dreams go away and sometimes we don't even remember them. When I was young, I used to dream of a beautiful Gitano, a dark gypsy, all dressed in white, riding a black horse, who would come and take me away to exotic places, who would love me and make me Queen of the Gypsies; I so wanted a string of golden coins on my forehead and a dress like the Gipsy Carmen of the opera.

Instead I found my Domenico, he was riding a mule to market when we met, and he never wore anything white except his underwear, and he didn't make me Queen of the Gypsies, but he did make me queen of his heart and his home, and I soon forgot my gypsy because my real life was much better; I did buy myself a string of gold coins to wear on my forehead, though. One day when the Gypsies came to town, I went right in their encampment and bought it. When my Domenico and I were alone, I played dress up for him, and wore a gypsy outfit I had made; we had ourselves a wild time. So enjoy your blue velvet dress, and remember that real life is better and more marvelous than any dream you can have." Luna felt light as air, and skipped along next to Anna admiring the town and the people and the beautiful weather. At one point, they sat on a bench at the appointed place, and waited for Uncle Pas. A while later, when they spotted him coming their way in the sun, attractive in his good clothes, and his face smiling, they all felt happy and joyful. He took them to see some of the sites, including the beautiful peace monument, and they went into a few stores to buy some things for the house. Anna and Irma went their way and promised to meet at 1:00 P.M. at Mario's Restaurant. At 1:00, they walked into Mario's, and they saw Anna and her daughter already waiting for them at a really nice table right near the window, where they could see the people walk by, and enjoy the sun filtered by lovely, sheer curtains. The place was no diner, it was beautiful and spotless. The tables were decorated with centerpieces of fresh flowers, and baskets of fresh, golden rolls were waiting on the table. The snowy tablecloth was set with shiny silverware, and great pitchers of wine and spring water were already there. Uncle Pas ordered for all of them, and he asked for a bottle of gassosa. When the bottle came to the table, he opened it with a bottle opener, and the contents almost fizzled out of it, like champagne. Ivana eagerly held her glass forward, and so did Luna and when they had a glassful, they drank deeply. Luna was amazed by the drink, it was almost like ginger ale, but yellower, thicker and tastier, and very lemony; it was called gassosa because it had frizzy gas in it! Their meal, served by very formal waiters, was wonderful, and Uncle Pas was very gentlemanly and chivalrous to all the women. He was so handsome, young looking, carefree and pleasantly gallant during dinner that everyone wanted to talk to him. Aunt Esther, instead of being jealous, just ate quietly and looked on with gentle pride. Their meal was wonderful. They started with a large platter of sweet melon and long, thin slices of prosciutto ham, and a platter of freshly sliced buffalo mozzarella and creamy ricotta cheese together with fried zucchini flowers. Luna loved the yellow, crunchy zucchini flowers fried in batter, but was curious to know where they had got them; their zucchini plants at the farm were dead by now. Luna could have sworn to anybody that Uncle Pas had a sixth sense, because he was looking at her with his usual knowing little smile and said, offhand:

"The owners of the restaurant have big greenhouses at the edge of town; they can grow anything they want anytime of the year. Everything they serve, they pick fresh the same day." Luna looked up and mouthed:

"Thank you!" And uncle inclined his head in assent. After the antipasto platters, without hurry, they had wonderfully yellow, wide homemade egg noodles with red sauce and lots of Romano cheese and, strewn over the pasta, thin, green slices of zucchini fried quickly in olive oil. Luna couldn't believe how delicious this was; the zucchini went wonderfully with the pasta. After the pasta, they waited for a while, munching on the brown breadsticks, until the piece de resistance came out; a huge platter full of great, golden, crunchy fried calamari rings. Luna had squid at her Grammeva's house, and she liked it, but this was superlative. There were large slices of lemon with it, and they squeezed it on the calamari joyfully. After this repast, they could hardly touch the fruit platter that was served, but they welcomed their double espressos, and sat there sipping them and talking desultorily. All at once, the old Luna reared her ugly little head and made Luna say:

"How about the leftovers, are we going to have a doggy bag?" Everyone looked at her uncomprehending, and Luna explained with a smile: "It means you take home what is left of your food in a box, and just say it's for the dog." They all had a look of horror on their face, and Luna felt guilty for having put it there: "I was only joking." She said, and at Uncle's narrowed eyes look, she explained: "Where I come from, people hate to cook, and when they go to a restaurant if they have anything left, they take it home and eat it later." Aunt Esther digested all that and said:

"I feel very sorry for the people who have to take home their leftover restaurant food so that they could go without cooking. I personally would go without food if I had to embarrass myself that way, trying to take home a little bit of old stuff; over here they give that to the pigs, and if it's something really good, there are many poor people who can make use of it, the restaurants send over platters to the poor people regularly." Luna looked up at her Aunt and said:

"I don't think I would ever want to do that myself; taking home a little bit of leftover food from the restaurant is embarrassing. Living with you, I've learned that cooking is fun, and I like everything fresh like you make, and I'm very glad I'm learning to do it for myself. You're a great role model, thank you!" Her aunt and everybody smiled benevolently at her, and Ivana whispered:

"That was a nice save; you certainly came out of that one very well!" And Luna elbowed her, and Ivana elbowed her back, and they laughed and had their coffee. When they left the restaurant, after Luna and everyone else had made the acquaintance with the shiny WC, (here they also had a big bidet thing that Luna tried with glee) they walked slowly back to the bus. They had a lot of time before the bus left, so there was no hurry. On the way Uncle stopped at a bakery, went in alone and came out with two bundles wrapped in brown paper. He then stopped at a grocer, went in and came out with two smaller bundles wrapped in brown paper. When asked what was in them, he said:

"Never you mind, girls, I'll show you on the bus." He carried the bundles under his arm, and Luna and Ivana, who followed behind everyone, could have sworn that there was a heavenly smell coming out of those bundles. By the time they got on the bus, the sky started to get slightly purple, and Uncle said that it would be dark by the time they got home. Halfway to Pontecorvo, Uncle Pas pulled the two bundles from the overhead compartment and opened them. The big bundles held each a sliced loaf of American bread. American Bread? Luna was looking at it bug eyed and caught Uncle's little satisfied smile directed just at her. The smile said:

"I did this for you!" To the other people he explained that it was called 'bread in a box' as they baked it in a rectangular, tin box and it was American style bread; he ate it often when he was in Milano during his army days. At this Anna looked at Uncle Pas, looked at Luna and smiled approvingly:

"Let's see this American bread, then!" She said, and Uncle handed one loaf to Anna and one to Aunt Esther. He then opened the other bundles and revealed a package of exquisite, thinly sliced mortadella and two bottles of gassosa each with two glasses next to them; the glasses said Cassino and had a picture of the town on it, and Uncle told them it would be a nice reminder of their little trip. By now it had been a few hours since their meal, and a sandwich would be very welcome, not to mention the fact that when they arrived home there would be a lot to do, and it would be nice not to have to cook a late supper. Anna made two sandwiches with the square bread and the mortadella, and said that there would be enough left to make the kids one each when they got home. Store bought mortadella was always very welcomed by everyone, and the kids would think that the strange square bread would be awesome. Luna was delighted but also sad and uncertain; the mortadella reminded her of the day Balthazar put her on the train, and Anna shared her mortadella sandwich with her. She suddenly thought of home, and mom and dad, even Kyle, and she started to tremble. Anna looked up and understood everything. She got up and sat next to Luna. She put an arm around her shoulder and squeezed, and whispered to her:

"Remember, little one, live for the day, enjoy the moment, you'll go home soon enough!" Luna looked up at her with shiny eyes, and leaned on her shoulder. The others, except for Uncle Pas, didn't see anything, enthralled as they were with the strange, flat sandwiches. Anna said, colloquially: "The first time I met Luna, on the train, I gave her half of my mortadella sandwich." Uncle Pas understood, and nodded at her encouragingly. Luna felt lucky to have so many good people around her who loved and protected her. When Aunt Esther handed her the large, square sandwich, she accepted it gratefully, and bit into it with relish. They each had a sandwich with a nice glass full of gassosa, Ivana and Luna sharing one glass, and Uncle Pas and Aunt Esther also sharing the same glass. Uncle Pas had two sandwiches, on Aunt

Esther's insistence, and half of their mortadella and bread was left over so Aunt Esther handed it to Anna for the kids at home.

Aunt Esther was very interested in this bread in the box, and she didn't really want to make it a part of their daily meals, but she thought it would be fun to make when she had company, especially kids. Anna said she was going to write one of her daughters who lived near Roma, if they sold the tin, rectangular baking box anywhere it would be Roma, and she would ask her to buy one and bring it when she came down next, and try to get the recipe also. Uncle Pas said that they could probably get the recipe from Gianna the teacher, as she had worked in a bakery. Uncle finally pulled a few pomegranates from his bundles, and they spent the remainder of the trip trying to eat the sweet, red kernels without ingesting any of the yellow, bitter membrane inside the fruit. In Pontecorvo, they spotted Mario right away waiting for them in the same bar and coffee shop as the first day Luna arrived here, and soon they were on the way home, very happy to have had such a wonderful day, but even happier to go home. That night Luna dreamed that she was at her wonderful birthday party all over again, and she was trying not to hear anyone waking her up, she was wearing her beautiful velvet gown, and her hair was streaming glossily down her back. Ivana was there in her rose colored velvet gown, and Luna was pointing out to her the lovely Prince Charming, when a thump thumping noise claimed her attention, and when the prince was just about to kiss her, a no nonsense voice kept repeating:

"This is my daughter's wedding, little girl, no princely shenanigans shall be undertaken here. See here now, there's room for only one prince charming, and he belongs to my daughter!" And as Luna looked around, she found herself at a wedding, and her prince turned around and went to kiss Antonietta, who looked wonderful in her white dress, except that the prince couldn't find her mouth because of all the hair, so he finally gave up and left.

The following day, after school, they went with Anna to The Fool's house, and delivered the clothes to Antonietta, and waited for her to don everything to see if they fit. Anna and Antonietta went to Antonietta's room, and Anna helped her to wear the clothes. When they came out of the room, everyone gasped;

Antonietta looked like a different person in the plush top, the soft skirt and the delicate pumps. Her face was still covered by hair, but the rest of her was gorgeous. The words 'pocket Venus' came to mind, and Assunta wiped her eyes and said, putting a hand on her husband's arm:

"Oh Tarquinio, our daughter is beautiful!" Luna and Ivana mouthed 'Tarquinio' to each other, and then had to run outside because they didn't want to explode into laughter in front of everyone. Outside, they laughed so hard their sides started to hurt, until a brusque voice said:

"So, you girls find my name funny? I'll have you know, that two kings of Roma were named Tarquinio!" At that, Ivana tried in vain to hide behind Luna. Not an easy task given the fact that Ivana was much taller. Luna courageously confronted The Fool and said:

"I's a wonderful name, sir, but just a little tame for the likes of a man like you." He looked down at them with a frown, which eventually turned into a grin, and then unabashed laughter. He laughed and laughed, hitting the ground with his cane:

"I always wished my parents gave me a name with a little more grit to it." Then abruptly turned around, and went back inside saying: "Only the young have the guts to tell it like it is." They all went home leaving the clothes with Antonietta, and Anna admonished her:

"Don't touch those clothes whatever you do. I heard you say 'The skirt is too short!' I'll be here early on the day of the presentation, and if those clothes look different, I'll fix them up, and I'll make you wear your hair in a bun on the back of your head!" At Antonietta's horrified look, she smiled and patted the girl's shoulder. They skipped back home, and Anna helped Aunt Esther make a wonderful dinner of pasta and beans, everyone's favorite, tuna salad, and garlic bread. Luna loved the tuna salad; they cut crunchy lettuce in small pieces, added a can of tuna in olive oil and some black pitted olives, and mixed the whole thing with a touch of vinegar. Aunt Esther's garlic bread was golden and crunchy and it complemented the salad marvelously. For dessert they had some large, golden, fluffy cookies Anna had brought. Aunt Esther said with relish:

"Wedding cookies! I never saw them so soft and fluffy; they're as light as a feather. Is this a special recipe?"

"Yes," Anna replied, "it's my mother's recipe. She always added some baking powder besides the baking ammonia, she always used powder vanilla instead of liquid and she put a lot less flour in them than customary; don't tell anyone! She always baked them the day after she prepared them, letting the dough rest overnight, and she sprinkled granulated sugar on top to make them crunchy; they're the best dunked in espresso." Aunt Esther asked:

"Where do you get your powder vanilla?" Anna answered:

"I get mine at Nannina's grocery store across from Town Hall, she has a big turnaround, and her stuff is always fresh." At this point, they all tried dunking the wedding cookies in their coffee, and they all loved it. Aunt Esther said:

"These are definitely going to be part of the wedding menu." When Uncle Pas ran Anna home, Luna asked to go for the ride, and Anna held her on the front seat of the truck. At one point, she leaned over and whispered into Luna's ear:

"Is it true that where you come from everyone takes home their leftover food from the restaurant?" Luna answered:

"Yes! All the time!" Anna squeezed her shoulders and whispered back:

"You poor baby, you!" Uncle Pas, who must have had very good ears, laughed right out loud at that, and Luna first assumed an air of long suffering, and then smiled at him

On Saturday, right after school, Luna and Ivana went to Aunt Palma's for their tombola lesson, and she gave them their favorite after school snack, bread and sugar, to tide them over until dinner, before proceeding with the lesson as usual. Luna could never have imagined she could derive so much pleasure from making something with her own hands, let alone something as hard to make as this. But the bobbins flew in her hands, the lace grew, and she was planning on giving it to her mom at home, when a thought occurred to her:

"What if I have to leave everything behind when I go?" She felt her heart constrict at the thought of having nothing to remember this place by, but she resolved to go home and make more lace by herself, just as Aunt Palma had taught her. Even if she had to start all over again, she knew she would remember how it was done. She had learned from Anna that you can never give up; there is always something you can do, and eventually you achieve what you want by sheer determination. You never get what you're striving for by quitting!

"Better days will come! I'll make them come!" She thought. Her cooking was getting better and better, and the day of the bad chicken soup was becoming a distant memory. She felt some kind of power in knowing that she could make her favorite foods, without having to rely on anyone to do it for her. When she thought back on the days at home, when she sat down and waited for her mother to serve her, almost never getting what she wanted herself, she felt pretty bad about it. Not only did her mother have to decide what to make, she had to serve it, all the while listening to her constant complaints. How did her mother do it? Why didn't she say something? And a little voice in her head asked:

"Would you have listened? Would you have helped? Would you have cared?" And she had to admit to herself that, no, she would not have listened, she would not have helped, and she would certainly not have cared. She resolved that if she was lucky enough to go back, she would do things very different than before. She thought to herself:

"It is a far, far better thing that I will do in the future than I have ever done before!" Still, when she looked over at Aunt Palma and Ivana, her heart broke every time.

The Presentation of the Gold would occur in two days. Everyone who had been invited was already preparing the clothes to wear, and hoping it would be a good day. Anna would be there before everyone, and the outcome was in her hands; if Antonietta didn't make a good impression, the wedding was in jeopardy, and by now the whole neighborhood was depending on this wedding for one reason or the other. Everyone was also very curious about the Gold. Rodolfo had been pretty closemouthed about it, and everyone hoped he did himself proud otherwise Antonietta could take the whole thing the wrong way and cancel the wedding; one never knew with that girl. The Fool was seen walking into the office of a big lawyer in the region's capital of Frosinone, together with the owners of the sand and gravel pit;

they seemed in good terms, were laughing at something together and were slapping each other's backs. At home, Aunt Esther was getting ready to work on their clothes for the wedding. She said that once their clothes were out of the way, she could start working on the wedding dress with more peace of mind. The wedding dress would have to be finished, tried on Antonietta and adjusted, if needed, before Irma could start embroidering it. Irma was working on the coronet already, and the teacher was going to write the nuns about the veil soon; The Fool was not going to give them their advance payment until the Presentation of the Gold. If that went well, they would get their advance and proceed with the rest. The teacher was going to give her advance money to the nuns, for the orphanage, and Uncle Saverio decided that they would travel by train to Milano and deliver it; he wanted to see where Gianna came from, and who had raised her, since the nuns were the only family Gianna had ever known. He never expressed such desire before, and Gianna was overjoyed at his interest. She had decided to take some of the better pieces of her husband's carvings to show the owner of an art gallery in Milano, to see what he thought. This man had also grown up at the orphanage, and they knew each other since they were children; he would tell her the truth about her husband's work. When they left for Milano, they had nothing to worry about; Anna promised she was going to move into the house to take care of the children, and Nannina was going to take a few days off and take over the teaching. Luna was amazed at the way they all helped each other, at their kindness and good will. She never saw this at home, ever! Instead, everyone worried about lawsuits, liability, and insurance. Some of the women found out about Gianna's trip to the orphanage, and they were putting together a suitcase of scarves, hats, sweaters and socks for the children. Everyone was busy knitting, sewing, and even making beautiful felt dolls with some of those earthenware heads, hands and feet. They were even making felt wallets and handbags for the boys and girls. Uncle Saverio said that between the carvings and the presents they were going to be like two pack mules, but he didn't mind. Actually, it wasn't going to be so bad. The bus driver that would take them to Roma was a friend of Uncle Saverio, and he would make room on the bus for their luggage, and once they transferred everything to the direct train that would take them to Milano, they wouldn't have to do anything until they arrived. Once there, the Sisters would be waiting with a truck furnished by one of their grown children who was the proud owner of a small farm. Everything hinged on this wedding. After the wedding, if it indeed went off without problems, Gianna intended to use the rest of her money to buy her husband a car. If his carvings were as good as Gianna thought, he would be traveling everywhere, and it wouldn't do to show up in an old truck. Little did Antonietta know that her happiness was going to be like a stone thrown in the water, and the ripple effects would touch everyone in the vicinity, and even as far away as Milano. Even the neighboring children had a vested interest in this wedding; they heard that La Befana was going to be there, and they were dreaming of store bought toys and treats and even some wedding cake. Joyful times were coming for everyone, that's for sure!

Finally, the day arrived for the presentation. In church, everyone connected to the wedding was nervous and fidgety, and everyone else knew about it and it made everything much more difficult, as everyone was watching everyone. The only people who didn't seem bothered or worried, were Aunt Esther and Uncle Pas; it seemed that they were in a world of their own, and their smug little smiles seemed to say:

"I know something you don't know!" They almost reminded Luna of Kyle, when he had a particular juicy bit of knowledge he was going to spring on people in his own good time. When they got back home, while the girls took care of the animals, Aunt Esther set up their Sunday dinner. There was bucatini all'Amatriciana, which meant the red sauce would have juicy bits of prosciutto and pancetta in it, pot roast with soft, melting potatoes cooked in its juice and a platter of steaming, green, tasty broccoli rape. The bread was fresh and fantastic, and the dessert was more elegant than usual; small glass dishes were filled with twirled yellow and chocolate cream topped by a beautifully brown shortbread cookie. The girls became more suspicious as dinner went on, and finally Ivana threw her spoon down and jumped up from her chair:

"You two better say what's going on, this suspense is killing me! What's the matter? Is someone going to die or something?"

Luna looked from Ivana's angry face to Aunt Esther and Uncle Pas' beaming ones. She was scared, something had changed and she didn't know if she wanted anything to change. Uncle Pas helped Aunt Esther to sit down and said:

"We were going to wait until after dinner to tell you the news, but since you are so perspicacious, we will tell you now; Esther and I are going to have another child!" Luna and Ivana just stood there with their mouth open:

"Another child?" Luna replied:

"A baby brother or sister for Ivana." And turning to Ivana: "Ivana, dear, are you happy?" Ivana stood up so suddenly that her chair overturned:

"I don't want a baby brother or sister. Why did you have to go and ruin everything?" And with that she turned around and ran out of the room. Uncle Pas just stood there stunned, and Aunt Esther's eyes filled with tears. Luna jumped up and ran to her. She hugged her Aunt and exclaimed:

"That's wonderful news; I can't wait to see the new baby! Oh, I'm so happy for both of you! Don't mind Ivana, she'll come around! The moment she sees the new baby, she'll fall for it like a ton of bricks. She's just jealous that's all!" Aunt Esther and Uncle Pas looked relieved, and called Ivana back into the room. Uncle Pas held Ivana briefly, and then he went down on one knee and spoke gently to her:

"Ivana, you're our firstborn, our wonderful girl. No one will ever take your place in our hearts. We have enough room to love you and another child just as much. Don't ever doubt that you're first with us always and always will be." Luna, trying to help, added:

"You'll love the baby as soon as you see it; it's going to be wonderful!" Ivana turned to her angrily:

"What are you so happy about? You'll never even see this baby. Don't you know how to count? By the time it's born you will be home, far far away, and no one will even remember you were here!" Luna turned a deathly white, she looked at Uncle Pas, and he looked back at her with a stricken look. She had forgotten! She was not going to see this baby! By the time she got home this baby would be an old man or woman, and everyone would have indeed forgotten she had ever been here.

With a great sob she ran out of the room, and she could hear Uncle Pas talk to Ivana angrily. She had never heard Uncle Pas talk to Ivana like that. He said:

"How dare you hurt someone like that? All my life I tried to live a good life, to give you a good example, to spare people any hurt, and to hear my own little girl inflict pain on another so cruelly, invalidates everything I always stood for; go to Luna and apologize! Now!" As Luna lay on her bed crying, she felt a small hand touch her:

"Go away, you don't have to do anything; I'm glad I'm going away, I'm glad no one will remember me. I'm sick of all of this; I want to go home now!" Ivana held her tight, and cried hard:

"I'm so sorry, I'm so sorry. I didn't mean any of it, I just got scared, I don't want things to change, I don't want my parents to give someone else the love that belongs to me. I still don't want this baby, but I'm going to try to be brave. My parents don't deserve this, it's not them, it's me. Please forgive me, please don't cry! If you want me to, I'll go home with you wherever that may be, so we can be together forever." And then she sobbed harder, like her heart was breaking. Luna looked up and said:

"You can't come with me, I know this for sure." Ivana said resolutely:

"Oh yeah? You just try to stop me. Right this moment I swear to you that I will find you again wherever you may be, we will be together again, and this is a solemn promise; I don't know when or how, but we will find each other again." Luna hugged Ivana tightly and while silent tears rolled down her face, she realized more than ever that whatever you do in life has consequences. She would try to be good and fair in her life from now on, just like Uncle Pas, because the pain of these consequences was just too hard to bear. After some minutes, the girls went back downstairs holding hands, and Ivana hugged her parents and promised them that she would be the best big sister to her baby brother or sister that she could be. Uncle Pas hugged his little girl to him fiercely, and then kissed Luna on top of her hair, and said:

"Let's eat, we have a presentation to go to, and they can't start until everyone's there."

46. *Via S. Maria di Porta.* Cartolina, bollo post. 11/IV/1908. "CN - F. Macioce"; retro. "Cartolina Postale".

Pontecorvo, small street deep in the town, 1908.
(where weaver girl was singing)
F. Macioce

11:   Presentation of the Gold

In late afternoon, when they arrived at the Fool's farm, one of Antonietta's humongous brothers, Remo, directed them to the back of the farm. They walked around the house, and were amazed to find a beautiful, landscaped, large, round garden with a round patio in the center. There were chairs all around the perimeter of the garden, and the smell of the autumn flowers was intoxicating; there were chrysanthemums, perennial sunflowers, purple stonecrop, goldenrod, daffodils and late tulips; it was a beautiful setting. They took the next empty seats, but then Luna spotted Anna who beckoned to an empty seat next to her, and she ran over. Anna took one look at Luna and said:

"What happened? Did someone make you cry? And don't deny it, no one would know, but I do! Come to Anna and tell me everything!" Luna thought in passing how she was always telling her troubles to Anna, and Anna was the only one who always made her feel better; almost like a real grandmother, or even better as she was not this close to either one of her grandmothers. She whispered the whole story in Anna's ear, especially the part where she wouldn't be here for the baby's birth, and Anna held her and caressed her hair and said:

"Don't cry, sweetheart, you'll be here for everything you are supposed to be here for. I think that there was a reason you were sent to us, and I see it every day in all the things that wouldn't have happened without you. Take this wedding, without you we wouldn't be here to do this, and maybe the wedding wouldn't have happened. We're all going to benefit from this wedding. And let alone the fact that without you nothing would have happened, think of the children who will come from this wedding, when you go back home you will know that there is a whole generation of people just because of you. Maybe you'll get to travel back here and meet them, eh? Maybe Ivana's brother or sister will be here and you will meet this person, maybe Ivana will be here when you come back! Have you ever thought of that? Don't worry about her, just like you said, she's a little jealous, but she'll come around when the baby is here. And don't you worry about everyone forgetting you were ever here! That will never happen! You're just what this place needed, and you will be remembered always." Luna looked up into Anna's smiling, crinkled face and felt such love for the little old lady that she was exploding with joy just being with her. A few minutes later, Antonietta came out of the house accompanied by her mother. She looked trim and sophisticated in her simple but beautiful clothes, she had a perfect, svelte physique and she walked with lithe grace; all things that were hidden before under the bulky, graceless dresses and sweaters she wore. Her hair shined golden brown in the sun, but her face was still half covered by the sloppy hairdo she wore. Anna said:

"It took a solid hour to wash, dry and comb that hair a hundred times to make it so shiny."

"You could have combed it back a little more." Whispered Luna. And Anna smiled mysteriously and whispered back:

"All in good time, my dear, all in good time!"

The Fool was checking his pocket watch every few minutes, by now, and looking worried. Suddenly the noise of a truck was heard, and The Fool walked to the entrance of the garden to greet his guests. Soon, Rodolfo appeared, flanked by his mother and father. He walked straight and tall, and his parents stood proudly next to him. His mother was a small dark little lady, but his father was a tall, silver haired man, with muscled arms and chest, only a little stooped like his back was not whole. You could see where Rodolfo got his good looks! They were followed by Rodolfo's two brothers who were followed by their wives and children. A pretty large and close knit clan, as anyone could see. Rodolfo was greeted by The Fool with these words:

"Why are you visiting us this fine day, son?"

"I'm here to see my betrothed, and to pledge my love in front of her family and friends with a gift of gold befitting her beauty." The Fool stood aside and let them all pass. They found chairs and sat down, all but Rodolfo, who looked around for a bit until his eyes found Antonietta. He seemed speechless, and Antonietta directed a pixie smile at him, if he could only see it under all that hair! He was holding a large, flat velvet box, handed to him by one of his brothers, and he walked slowly under everyone's eyes until he reached Antonietta, kneeled down in front of her and handed her the box. She took it and said:

"What is this?"

"A token of my love for you, my dear bride." She snorted slightly, but she slowly opened the large box. A gasp escaped her lips when she saw what was in it. The people near her, who could see in the box also gasped, prompting a general run in her direction by the ones too far to see. In the box were various pieces of jewelry, but not gold as everyone expected; everything was plainly made of platinum. This was a metal rarely seen in these parts, as it was very, very expensive and then only mostly in rings, never in other kinds of jewelry. This box contained a chain necklace, a bracelet, earrings and two rings; one was an engagement ring, the other a wedding ring. Everything was dainty, graceful and beautiful. The chain was so fine as to resemble a spider web, and it held a pear drop shaped pendent all carved in filigree, with a beautiful diamond in the center. The bracelet and the earrings matched this piece, made of very fine chain and holding a pear shaped pendent. The dangling earrings were so fine, that it looked like the filigreed pendants with diamonds were hanging on thin air. The filigreed engagement ring had a pear shaped diamond held by four strong, shiny prongs, and the wedding ring was a simple band of platinum. Antonietta looked up at Rodolfo with awe:

"Are these real diamonds? Everyone usually gets brilliant stones." Rodolfo took her hand and said:

"These are for a lifetime, you deserve the real thing. The chains are very fine, but very strong, as strong as the metal they're made of, so you never have to worry about losing the diamonds; but even if you do, they are fully insured. When I saw this design, it reminded me of you; delicate as silk, strong as steel." The test was now, and Rodolfo wanted it over, so he put the box down on a small table next to Antonietta, picked up the chain and held in front of her. Slowly, without taking her eyes off of him, Antonietta raised her hands and lifted the hair off of her neck. Rodolfo gently put the chain around her neck and proceeded to fasten it. The gossamer chain was very pleasantly heavy, and the pendant rested in the small hollow on Antonietta's chest perfectly. Every time she breathed, the diamond winked amongst the soft yarn of her top; Antonietta looked down and raised her hand to touch it. Then, hesitantly, Rodolfo picked up the engagement ring. Antonietta first looked at him for long seconds, and then lifted her left hand and Rodolfo gently slipped it on her ring finger. It was done, his troth was completely accepted, there was no backing off, and the wedding would go on! Everyone clapped, and The Fool and his wife embraced in a rare show of emotion, then followed by their three sons and their wives and kids, walked up to Rodolfo and welcomed him into the family. Right after, Rodolfo's parents followed by their sons and their wives and children surrounded Antonietta and welcomed her to the family. Antonietta was clearly ill at ease with all the attention and Rodolfo took her hand and announced to everyone that he was taking his future bride for a walk. As they walked away towards the orchard behind the garden, Anna and Aunt Palma got up too. Anna whispered to Luna that it was customary for the oldest people in the group to follow the betrothed a few steps behind, to ensure privacy but also to ensure propriety:

"The proprieties must be observed!" She whispered. As she went, she took Luna to hold onto, and Aunt Palma beckoned to Ivana for the same reason. The couple walked on ahead, and Anna and Luna and Aunt Palma and Ivana made a little procession following them. Antonietta asked Rodolfo:

"This jewelry must have cost a fortune, where did you get the money for it? Did my father pay for it?" Rodolfo answered:

"No, I wouldn't have let him do that, but he did help me; he got me credit at the fancy jewelry in the Civita Quarters, and since I have been working nonstop, I used that money for a down payment. I intend to pay for this with my own money if it takes me the rest of my life to do it!" Antonietta looked up at him and in her very direct way asked:

"Why?"

"Because you'll be my wife and the jewelry you'll wear on your body will be from me alone. You're more beautiful than I thought possible, and I don't understand why you never let anybody see the real you."

"Because I don't care what people think, but I'm glad you don't think I'm hideous." Rodolfo laughed heartily, and Antonietta slipped her small hand around his powerful arm. Antonietta's little black skirt swayed gently with the movement of her hips, and the soft, low heeled pumps emphasized a well turned ankle and slim leg. The soft top hugged her tiny waist and well rounded form and Antonietta walked gracefully erect, hand in hand with her betrothed. The way they kept walking, they had got quite far from the garden, and the little procession following them was having a hard time keeping up, especially Anna and Aunt Palma, so they signaled the betrothed it was time to turn around. Anna said:

"My arthritis is acting up today, I'm creaking everywhere; how do you do it at your age, Aunt Palma?"

"I have my secret, my dear girl, and it serves me well!"

"Well, Aunt Palma, keep your secret to yourself, why don't you? You saw me hold my back when I got up, but you didn't say a word!"

"This is an ancient remedy, and sometimes people make fun of it, but it really works."   Luna and Ivana were now very interested in this exchange, and were following it with curiosity. Aunt Palma bent down towards Anna and whispered:

"Every night, just before I go to sleep, I eat nine white raisins soaked in gin. Not eight, not ten, NINE!" Anna, Luna and Ivana looked at Aunt Palma uncomprehending:

"Say what?" Exclaimed all three of them:

"What have raisins to do with this?" Exclaimed Anna:

"Everything," said Aunt Palma, "this is the remedy. It came highly recommended, there is some chemical interaction here, and it really works." Anna was pensive;

"Where did you find out about this?" Aunt Palma responded:

"I got this from my friend Sandra some time ago."

"Who is this Sandra, do I know her?"

"I don't know, she's the hatter's daughter, up in the Civita Quarters."

"You're talking about that handsome guy who married that big, blond, blue-eyed American Amazon?"

"Yes, I'm talking about his oldest daughter."

"Ho yeah, I have seen her, short women with a big mop of frizzy blond hair?"

"Yes, that's her! Took after her mother, only short, poor thing! She told me she found out about this ancient remedy from her sister, Adele. I don't suppose you know her?"

"No, I've never heard of her! Does she have a big mop of blond hair like her sister?"

"No, she's a hoity toity professor at that fancy school in town; no big mop of hair for her, she's an elegant brunette with long legs, took after her father." Anna said:

"If she took after her father she must be quite beautiful then!"

"She is! Sandra told me that her sister and her colleagues know everything about everything. You got a problem? You sic that bunch of cackling hens on it, and before you know it, they'll find you a solution; it must be all that education!" Anna asked:

"So, you eat nine gin soaked white raisins every night and that's supposed to help your arthritis?" Aunt Palma said:

"It certainly helped mine! You fill a glass jar with white raisins, not dark ones, cover them with gin, let them soak for three days, and then start your remedy. Every night eat nine of them, and within two weeks you'll feel the change. Just remember, only nine. We don't want a repeat of what happened to Stina Ciacia, now do we?"

"What happened to Stina Ciacia?" They all asked in unison:

"It was shameful really," answered Aunt Palma, "her sons came over one night and found her sitting at the kitchen table with a big bowl. In it she had a pound of white raisins and a quart of gin. She was eating with gusto, and when her kids tried to take it away from her she screamed and tried to hold on to it, and she mumbled something about killing her arthritis once and for all. It took all three of her sons to drag her off to bed and then she slept for two days, drunk. Shameful!" And then Aunt Palma mumbled to herself: "Although, it's strange but since then I've noticed she doesn't limp anymore, like she used to...........go figure!" As they walked back, Antonietta said, looking ahead:

"After we're married if I want to drive will you let me?" Rodolfo looked puzzled:

"Drive what?"

"A car, nincompoop!" Answered Antonietta. Rodolfo, still looking puzzled said:

"Why?" Antonietta responded impatiently:

"Why do you drive a car? To go places, of course!"

"But I will drive you anywhere you want to go."

"I know that, but I've wanted to be able to drive myself for ages and my father won't let me; he thinks no man would have me if they think I'm too forward." Rodolfo picked up her hand, turned to face her, and told her in no uncertain terms:

"You are free to do anything you want, except indecorous things naturally, I will never tell you what to do, or make you do anything you don't want to do. I thought you were afraid I wouldn't take you everywhere you desired, but it would be great if you want to drive yourself at times, it takes a lot of the burden off of me, and it lets you be free to go anywhere you want. You see women driving in those American movies, and if it's good enough for the American women, it's good enough for you! Just be careful and don't hurt yourself! Who's going to teach you to drive?" Antonietta said, with a dimpled smile:

"You are, of course!" Then she looked up at him again and said: "Can I take Arancio with me?" Rodolfo looked puzzled again:

"You want to take an orange with you? Why? I'll get you all the fruit you want!"

"I'm talking about my cat, Arancio, you double nincompoop!" Rodolfo laughed out loud and told her:

"Why are you asking my permission, Antonietta?" She said, seriously:

"Because I can't if you don't allow me to." Rodolfo stopped right in the middle of the dirt road, turned around to face her and exclaimed:

"Antonietta, you are a free woman, and after we're married you'll still be a free woman! Don't ask me again to give you permission to do what you want; unless you want to bring home another man, that I won't stand for!" He then grabbed her tiny hand with his strong, big one, and kept walking matching his long strides to Antonietta's dainty steps. Antonietta smiled to herself, and sighed happily.

When they arrived back to the garden, everyone was milling around, admiring Assunta's flowers and her skill as a gardener. Everyone was starting to realize, by now, that despite her looks and her gendarme figure, Assunta was a very accomplished and refined lady. While the betrothed took their walk, the tables had been set up, and a lovely spread of cakes, cookies, pies and pastry had been arranged on it. They also had bread donuts (some kind of Italian pretzels studded with anise seeds instead of salt) and fat bread. Luna had never seen fat bread; these little breads also looked like donuts, but they were brownish and were studded with brown bits. These had been added for the men, to have with their wine. From inside of the house, some women hired by Assunta for the day, came out with giant pots of espresso, and deposited them near the small cups, spoons and sugar containers. There was tea also and for the men, besides wine, a choice of strong alcoholic beverages or some more gentle cordials. Rodolfo sat next to Antonietta, and served her some sweets and some espresso and the same for himself:

"Aren't you going to get yourself something stronger?" Asked Antonietta. Rodolfo replied:

"I don't drink, I hope you don't mind. I drink a bit, socially, but nothing to speak of. I never liked alcohol; I just try not to be conspicuous about it." She looked up at him and whispered:

"Are you really this perfect as a husband, or are you putting me on?" Rodolfo looked wounded:

"With me what you see is what you get; I don't have to put you on. You have to accept me as I am; otherwise we wouldn't last long as a couple. Besides I thought that you knew everything about me, after all, your father had me investigated thoroughly." Antonietta snapped to attention:

"He did? I didn't know! He never told me. I'm going to have it out with him later; he had no right to question my choice of a husband!" Rodolfo whispered to her:

"Don't argue with him. When I have a daughter, I'm going to be even more careful about whom she associates with, let alone whom she marries!" At those words, Antonietta's visible eye glittered, and a pink color spread on her skin. Rodolfo picked up her hands and they silently held hands while looking at each other for a long time, unaware of everyone noticing this show of affection and looking puzzled:

"I thought this was an arranged marriage!" Snapped Nannina, who with her niece Giustina had accompanied Aunt Palma. Giustina said, pensively:

"They say men marry women who look like their mothers. Look at Rodolfo's mother; she's small and dark, just like Antonietta." Nannina said:

"Rodolfo's mother was a beautiful girl, before a life of sacrifice and deprivation, bestowed on her by the man she loved and married, took its toll. So far Antonietta hasn't been so shabby, what you uncovered is quite beautiful. But what about the rest of her! So far all we've seen under all that hair is one eye." Aunt Palma retorted:

"Maybe she's only got the one eye! Maybe she's a little cyclops, like in Jason and the Argonauts." Everyone couldn't stop at that, and their small circle started laughing uproariously, until they spotted The Fool looking at them intently. Then they stopped laughing and looked sheepish, although Aunt Palma couldn't help adding:

"I hope she doesn't send one of them lightening rays our way!" Nannina elbowed Aunt Palma:

"That was Zeus who did that!" There was another small sputtering of laughter, but the betrothed were unaware of it, and The Fool had walked over to the group of men congregated near the garden shed. Luna and Ivana hadn't said much during this time, but they had started to feel ashamed of their outbursts, earlier at home. At one point, they sat together and held hands. Both their eyes were moist, and they didn't notice the relieved and fragilely happy smile on Aunt Esther's face. Ivana had got up and made two plates for herself and Luna, and they were starting to get their appetite back. Luna picked up the brownish donut and bit into it. It was not sweet, but it was very good. It had an indefinable taste, something that reminded Luna of bacon, but juicier and tastier, and the bread with it was crunchy and soft at the same time. It was totally satisfying especially when you crunched one of the brown nuggets under your teeth. Luna turned to Ivana and asked:

"What's this?" Ivana answered:

"Pork fat bread!" An eerie feeling came over Luna. She thought this reminded her of something, but she couldn't grasp what. She asked Ivana why Aunt Esther never made fat bread, and Ivana told her that you only made that when you had fresh pork fat. She told Luna that The Fool had just butchered his pig, that's why they had the fat. She said that they were going to butcher theirs in the next few days, and Luna said, surprised:

"We don't have a pig except for Caramella. Is this the pig you're going to butcher?"

"Of course! You didn't think she was a pet, did you?"

"Yes, I thought she was a pet; we play with her every time we feed her. I don't know if I want to see this!" Ivana said, with a snicker:

"Why did you think we named her Caramella?"

"I don't know!"

"Because she's hard and sweet, like a piece of Caramella, hard candy!" Luna was flabbergasted:

"This is disgusting! You're like cannibals! I definitely do not want to see this!"

"If you don't want to see it, you're going to have to go and stay with Aunt Palma for three days. That's how long it takes to do everything, but you're going to miss the best part. We'll have blood sausages, with cinnamon and raisins, we'll have pork skins sausages with our pasta and beans, we'll make the lard with the pork fat, and the cracklings from rendering the fat we'll use for fat bread. My papa' loves the liver sausages fried with red peppers, and mama is partial to chopped pork meat with anise seeds. All of our friends will be over, their fathers are going to help papa' with the butchering, and their mothers are going to help with the preserving and cooking. Luana's mother knows how to make the best lemony little sweet breads, and Anna and her daughters will be over, you know what good cooks they are! There's going to be loads of food, we're going to play games, and mama is going to make Swiss chard pies, with raisins and pine nuts, and Papa' is going to grille small bundles of pork liver wrapped in their own membranes and stuffed with bay leaves. You, on the other hand, will be peaceful and quiet, Aunt Palma will make you do tombola lace most of the day, you'll help her cook your meals, she'll offer you a berry pie, and as soon as you say yes, you'll have to pick berries until your fingers bleed and roll pastry dough, and when the pie is finally done, all you want to do is run like hell away from it. And of course you'll have to enjoy elixir morning, noon and night. I should know! Last year my parents went to Roma to help Mama's parents with a project and I stayed at Aunt Palma's for a week!" All thoughts of poor Caramella forgotten, Luna kept munching on the fat bread, especially relishing the crackling juicy morsels, and suddenly said to Ivana:

"I'm not going anywhere; I'm staying for the butchering. You thought you could get rid of me and enjoy the whole thing yourself, but I'm not going anywhere!" And then the two girls embraced laughing under the pleased eyes of Uncle Pas and Aunt Esther, who were standing together, ready to soon say their goodbyes and go home. The Presentation had gone very, very well, and everyone went home happy; the wedding would go on as planned!

A couple of days went by without anything exceptional happening. There just was a poll of awkwardness and sadness over everything. What happened on Sunday had left a bitter taste in everyone's mouth, and they tried to go on as if nothing happened, but they couldn't. On Wednesday evening, Aunt Esther asked Luna and Ivana if they wanted to discuss their dresses for the wedding. Since they were going to follow the bride holding her flowers and corsage, they were allowed to wear a long dress if they chose, or they could also wear a regular length if they wanted. Luna looked up, eyes shining:

"Could I have a long dress? Puffed sleeves and pointed waist? A full skirt with lots of petticoats?" Aunt Esther smiled:

"You would like a Snow White dress?"

"Yes, Aunt, I would love a Snow White dress very much." Aunt Esther said:

"And you shall have it; I think the style will suit you wonderfully." She then turned to Ivana: "What would you like your dress to look like, my dear?" Ivana said, uncertainly:

"I have been thinking, I don't know if it would be alright, but I saw a dress in a book, Josephine was wearing it, you know, Napoleone Bonaparte's wife. It was called Empire waist, with frills on the neck, and a very high waist, with a long flowing overskirt open in the front over a slim skirt and little sleeves puffed on top and narrow the rest of the way. And she was wearing her hair up like a crown. If it's possible.....I know it's going to be a lot of work..." Aunt Esther walked to Ivana and held her in her arms for a few seconds, then, businesslike, she said:

"That is the perfect style for you. I was trying to come up with a special design; now I know what to do!" And all three of them talked animatedly about their dresses, smiling and flushed, and Uncle Pas, who heard the whole exchange from the dining room where he was listening to the radio, smiled also settling down on his chair with a sigh.

That evening, as Rodolfo dragged his accordion home, as exhausted as he could be, he saw a small figure detach himself from his house and walk towards him; he was used to meeting his future father-in-law this way. Rodolfo put his accordion down on his doorstep, and followed The Fool a few steps away from the house:

"My boy, you look all done in!"

"I am!" Said Rodolfo, sitting down under an old tree and flexing his arms. The Fool sat next to him, and asked him why he was working so hard:

"You know!" Exclaimed Rodolfo:

"I'm trying to make as much money as I can to pay for Antonietta's wedding jewelry, so she can wear it free and clear." The Fool laughed:

"My dear young man, at the rate you're going my daughter will be able to wear her jewelry free and clear when she's an old woman!"

"What can I do? Music is the only thing I know, and people think they can pay you with compliments and wonderful food, they don't understand that we're in it for the money; but cash is scarce these days, and the small amount they can pay is better than nothing." The Fool twirled the ends of his mustache in turn, and said, pensively:

"Not a very lucrative occupation, for all that you have to have musical knowledge, a good presence and endless congeniality to achieve it. After the wedding you will not have to play for ungrateful people anymore, but the family will totally enjoy your art; you'll be an artistic businessman, and you'll play your music only to enjoy yourself!" Rodolfo smiled in the dark:

"It almost seems too good to be true."

"It's not too good to be true." Said The Fool:

"Money will make it possible. Only money gives you the freedom to do as you please."

"I only wish it was my money and not Antonietta's doing this for me!"

"After the wedding it will be your money!" But Rodolfo was looking down at his clenched hands, dejectedly. The Fool looked at him, and almost against his own will, blurted out:

"Look, son, I'm going to tell you something, but never tell anyone else about it." Rodolfo looked up, surprised by the resolute tone of his voice: "When I was your age more or less, I had made myself some decent money, but nothing near what I wanted, nothing to really brag about. I was alone, my parents were both gone, my house was cold and dirty, and I was lonely. I was looking to get me a wife, a real wife. A woman who would take care of me and my home, who would give me children, not a flibbertigibbet who would worry only about the clothes on her back and her hair and nails; she would also have to have a large dowry, I was dead set on that. I had seen Assunta, and I had my eye on her for a while, she was not a model, but I was not averse to her looks. She was a solid, strong, clean and handsome woman, but her family thought her ugly, and was willing to pay big for someone to take her off their hands. I made friends with her housekeeper and found out everything about her; the more I found out, the more I liked her. Also I saw her look at me shyly, and knew she favored me. She cared for me from the first, and she has been the best wife and mother. On the day we were married, after the wedding breakfast her parents gave us, I took her to my cold and dirty house. She took her things from my truck and moved them into the bedroom. After she was done, we went to sleep, and when I woke up, she wasn't there in bed with me; I thought she had been horrified by me and my home and gone back to her parents. Instead, when I went downstairs, I found my kitchen to be spotless and nicer than I had ever seen it, and Assunta had made me the best breakfast I had ever had." Rodolfo asked:

"What did you do then?"

"I ate, of course, and then took her up to bed again!" The two men laughed uproariously and then The Fool said, seriously:

"I have never regretted marrying her. Yes, I married her for her money and yes I took it! But I did not squander her money, no I didn't! I worked very hard, and multiplied it many times over. I had fun doing it, it's a battle of wits with the world out there, always ready to take everything away from you and trample you.

Now our children can have good lives because of this money, including you and Antonietta. So, take her money, work hard, treat my daughter well, and give her the love she needs, if you can; it has all been worth it! I can tell you, young man; it feels good to know that your children will never feel the sting of poverty and the contempt of others, like you and I have!" Rodolfo turned to the older man and said:

"You know, you are not at all what people think of you. No one really knows you, you surprise me every time; you're actually a very nice, thoughtful man!" The Fool laughed out loud:

"Keep it under your hat, son, please! It's not good for business if people find out about my good side, no! It's not good for business at all!" And then becoming serious again: "I came to make you a proposition; hear me out. I have a customer of mine, a local boy who made good and now owns a radio station in Roma. I understand that he is looking for a replacement disc jockey for the station, because his current one is going away on his honeymoon for a month. Know that this is only a temporary job. It pays very well; I think you can practically pay off the darned platinum jewelry. When I said to do Antonietta proud, I didn't mean for you to spend a fortune."

"When I saw those pieces, I knew that Antonietta would shine in them, I just desperately wanted to see that jewelry on her, and nothing else mattered. I just don't want anyone to think I was bribing her to accept me by spending her own money on her."

"Believe me, son, she would've known, she's very astute, and you'd be wearing that jewelry yourself, right where the sun don't shine, if you know what I mean." Rodolfo was laughing so hard, tears were on the corners of his eyes: "Well, back to the business at hand. This job is temporary, like I said, and my client wants to audition you before he lets you have it, if he doesn't think you can do it, he will not hire you. But if he does, I'm risking a lot with this. You may be offered something permanent, and you may be tempted by some siren, in the radio station atmosphere in Roma; Antonietta would skin me alive if she knew. Can I trust you?" Rodolfo looked at him pensively:

"You know, it would give me some consequence to be accepted for my craft, if I'm hired, and I would love to be the big shot disc jockey for a while, but I don't want to live like that, always on the edge, always fighting other up and coming musicians, always having to prove myself! Even in this small sphere we are in, it's a fight to keep up; there's a guy from San Giovanni Incarico who's getting all the gigs because in the middle of the songs he dances up a storm, and he tells dirty jokes. I'll be damned if I'll get up in front of people and act like a dancing bear, or make off color remarks. To me my music is a serious thing! I want to have a home and a life, a quiet life with a woman, one that has to be, everyday more, like Antonietta.   There is something about that little girl that makes me feel like I'm finally home. Yes, I wouldn't give up life with her for anything! She and I will have a real home!"   The Fool smiled to himself, yes, Antonietta was right as ever; this young man was right for her, she'll be happy:

"Speaking of a home, the house that comes with the sand and gravel pit needs to be fixed and spruced up, before the wedding, but we'll talk about that after your job in Roma." Rodolfo stared at him:

"The sand and gravel pit comes with a house?"

"Of course, my boy, where did you think the owners stayed when they condescended to come and supervise once in a while? It's pretty nice, rich people's house you know, and my daughter will like it, but you and your brothers might want to go in a week before the wedding, take your mother and your sisters-in-law, I understand that there is everything you need in the house, and you will be getting a lot of wedding gifts, but the linens for the marriage bed are going to be provided by my wife, she insists on it. In fact you may want to take her too, she'll make the place a showplace; she's very talented that way." Rodolfo was staring at him in awe:

"We have a home? I was dreading taking Antonietta to live here in this house, but I didn't think I had a choice! I have never seen a house on the sand and gravel land." The Fool smiled:

"The house is about two miles away from the sand and gravel pit, on the other side of the hill. You didn't think that those great people from Roma would sleep in view of the pit, did you?" Rodolfo asked him, puzzled:

"How much land comes with the pit?" The Fool waived his question away:

"Oh, acres and acres, you'll find out! The whole hill behind it belongs, and the woods on the other side of it. You're going to need a watchman to patrol the property every day, at his discretion, and you need someone you can trust, I suggest your own father, but it's up to you. Walking is good for a bad back, I'm sure he's up to the job, give him an assistant, of course!" Rodolfo looked at him like he was crazy:

"Where will I find the money for all this?" The Fool laughed out loud:

"I can see that Antonietta has her work cut out for her, to teach you about business; the sand and gravel pit has a very large payroll, she's already taken it over, as the transaction with the owners is concluded. The watchman retired a few weeks ago, and the owners didn't bother with a replacement as they were leaving. The owners were relieved to get a buyer, one that paid well and in cash, they are also happily retired, and their manager, Attilio Turchetta, is conducting business as usual; it matters little to him who owns the place, he just conducts business the same as he always did. Have your father go to him for the job, there is no favoritism at play here, Attilio does the hiring unless forewarned about someone, and your father will get the job only if he's deemed able for it. Of course Antonietta will add him to the payroll as soon as she is told he's on." Rodolfo didn't know what to say, he was obviously overcome:

"My father would be destroyed if he didn't get this job, but he also doesn't want it if he cannot do it. You know the bad experience he had at the sand and gravel pit."

"He'll get the job, he's perfect for it, and Attilio knows who he is; don't you worry! Attilio wasn't the one who fired him; one of the other men at the pit reported him directly to the owners, to get him fired so he could get his job. The owners told Attilio to give this man an interview for the job, but after the interview, Attilio rejected him. He was not right for the job, and Attilio hates snitches, anyways. So, I'll make the arrangements with the radio station, and I'll let you know! In the meanwhile, forget those little jobs, give yourself some free time and go visit Antonietta a little more often, she's pretty miffed at you only going to see her once a week. Don't mention the job in Roma until you have won it. Good night!" And the little man disappeared in the dark with a wave. Rodolfo walked into the house in a daze; he was getting Antonietta, whom he now wanted more and more, and everything that went with her. His future father-in-law was right, he wasn't going to take the money for himself, he was going to work hard and multiply it for his children and their children. He envisioned a little girl with a great mop of curly hair all over her face and a sharp and sometimes sweet personality, and smiled to himself; he'll have sweet dreams tonight, and none of the anguish he had been experiencing thanks to his Fool future father-in-law.

The following Sunday, as Luna and Ivana were upstairs getting ready for church, all at once they heard a scream, it came from Uncle Pas and Aunt Esther's bedroom. They ran down to it and found Aunt Esther on the bed crying and shaking. Uncle Pas was already outside taking care of the animals before they left for church. The girls ran to Aunt Esther and held her and asked what was wrong. Aunt Esther looked up, her features distorted by anguish, and sobbed:

"I had a miscarriage, I lost my baby!" And then fell on the bed again, sobbing desperately. Luna was terrified, Aunt Esther, their rock, their steadying force, their anchor, was falling apart. Surely she could have another baby! Why the melodrama, why the misery. Luna just stood there not knowing what to do. She then turned to Ivana and was flabbergasted; Ivana stood there, white as a sheet, with tears running down her face:

"It's my fault, all my fault! I was selfish, I wished this baby gone, and now it's gone! My parents tried so hard to have another baby! The doctors said that my mama wasn't going to be able to conceive easily, and when she finally did, I ruined everything because I'm selfish, because I didn't want to share them with another child. I'm a horrible person, I'm the one who should have died, my parents are going to hate me and they'll be right!" And with those words, she turned and ran. Luna didn't know what to do, she wanted to follow Ivana, but she didn't want to leave the still sobbing Aunt Esther alone. As she was cradling her trembling aunt in her arms, she heard footsteps. Uncle Pas burst into the room:

"What's wrong? I saw Ivana run away and called, but she didn't answer me; what happened here?" Aunt Esther cried in anguish again, and lifted her arms to Uncle Pas. He went to her and sobbing she told him about losing her baby. He held her in his arms and crooned to her, but he was ashen, he looked almost like an old man. Luna, who never really took anything serious enough to cry, and was not really the crying type, felt wetness on her cheeks and a sob escaped her. It didn't matter to her if they had another baby or not, but they were obviously in a lot of pain, almost like a real baby had died. To her this had not been a real baby, just words, but to them it was obviously very real and they were mourning in each other's arms. Luna started trembling and in her mind she thought:

"Please Balthazar, please help them! You took me here and now look what happened. You have to do something! After all, it was you who said you knew everything there is to know; well, prove it!" In her mind she heard Balthazar's laugh, and then more seriously he said:

"I shouldn't do this, I most definitely should not do it, and The Powers That Be wouldn't like it you know!" And then, in a thin falsetto: " Que sera' sera', whatever will be will be, the future's not YOURS to see, que sera' sera'!" Luna snapped impatiently:

"Stop singing, Balthazar, and tell me what to do!"   Another laugh, and then:

"I wasn't going to get involved, but the pain I feel from your aunt and uncle is so strong that I'll jeopardize myself by revealing something." Luna touched Uncle Pas' shoulder to stay him, and motioned him to be quiet. Balthazar spoke to her, his voice getting more and more distant:

"This baby was not to be; he was already an angel, no one's fault, he's already taken his place where God wanted him. They are not to mourn but to rejoice; they have given God a new angel. In the fullness of time they will have twin boys. They will grow up to be strong, good men, just like their father." Balthazar's voice was getting dimmer and dimmer:

"When, Balthazar, when?" Asked Luna. The eerie sound of Balthazar's voice came over a great distance:

"Soon, soon, soon, soon........" Luna looked at Uncle Pas, who was looking at her with awe:

"I have talked to Balthazar......." Uncle Pas kept staring at her. Aunt Esther stopped crying and looked up:

"What's going on?" She asked with a teary voice. Uncle Pas looked at Luna and said:

"What did Balthazar say?" Aunt Esther said:

"Who's Balthazar?" Uncle Pas looked at her and said:

"It's best for you not to know, dear, believe me. But whatever Balthazar said to Luna, you can believe." He then turned to Luna and repeated: "What did Balthazar say?" Luna looked at them levelly:

"He said this baby was not to be, he was already an angel, no one's fault, and he's already taken his place where God wanted him. You are not to mourn, but to rejoice; you have given God a new angel. In the fullness of time you will have twin boys. They will grow up to be strong, good men, just like their father. He said it will be soon." Uncle Pas' eyes glowed like two stars, and he kissed Aunt Esther's forehead adoringly. Aunt Esther's eyes were now alert, and she looked from Uncle Pas to Luna:

"How can this be? And how can Luna talk to someone we can't see?" Uncle Pas responded:

"If Luna heard Balthazar's voice, you can believe it, my dear, it's true, and I can't tell you anymore, it's easier for you not to know. But believe it; our child is now an angel, and we will have twin boys who will grow up to be our pride and joy." Aunt Esther's tears had dried out, and she was now rosy and happy, cuddled in her husband's arms. She extended her arms to Luna and hugged her briefly:

"I knew there was something different about you! I don't know exactly what this is all about, but if my husband tells me it's better for me not to know, I believe him; maybe someday he will tell me. Just know that I still love you, Luna Marina Blue, whoever you are and wherever you come from, and I will pray to my little angel to help you be happy too. Please go look for Ivana and help her, dear Luna! You are the only one who can do it at this moment." With a jolt, Luna remembered Ivana and what she said, and was suddenly very scared for her, so she turned and ran quickly down and out of the house; she knew exactly where Ivana had gone.

Luna ran as fast as she could, and when she heard the sound of the river, she slowed down a bit and proceeded with caution. When she finally reached the river bank, she looked around wildly. Ivana was not in sight. Luna was starting to think she was wrong about Ivana being at the river, but suddenly she heard a muffled sound. She looked around again and then she spotted her; Ivana was crouched on the edge of the water with half of her body in the river, and the strong current was trying very hard to take her downriver. How Ivana was still there and not pulled off by the water was a mystery to Luna, and she had better get off soon, or the water would take her and then she'd be lost. She called her name very loud, and Ivana heard and said:

"Go away and let the river take me, it's taking an awful long time, but I'm too much of a coward to just jump in." Luna didn't know what to say to this, but after a while she yelled back:

"Go ahead and let the river take you, after all what do you care if your parents die of a broken heart, all you care about is yourself!" Ivana said angrily:

"It's not true; I want to do away with myself so that they can have another new baby without me hurting it."

"You not only are selfish and mean, but you also think of yourself as some kind of goddess, oh Ivana almighty."

"I hate you, Luna Marina! How can you say I think I'm a goddess, if I'm so disgusted with myself?" Luna hollered:

"Well, you think that just because you didn't want this baby, it immediately died. You cannot control anything like that; none of us mortals can. Only God can decide. For you to think you could do that, must mean you think you have the same power as God." Ivana looked up and stared at Luna:

"You don't think the baby died because I wished it to happen?"

"Of course not, no matter how you felt about the baby, he or she would have done just what he was supposed to do. Like I told you, in the scheme of things, what we want and what really happens doesn't depend on us or our whishes. Fate and the Gods do what they want and not what we want." Ivana kept looking at Luna with tears streaming down her cheeks:

"But I don't think I can go back after all this. My parents will probably be very happy not to see me anymore, and they're brokenhearted about the baby anyway and they don't need me to make things worse." Luna said:

"Your parents are very worried about you; they're scared for you, that's why they sent me to find you. If something happens to you they will die. You're their entire life, just like the new baby would have been if God didn't see fit to take him to Heaven and make an angel out of him." Ivana was going to say something, but all of a sudden she started to scream. She started to float away slowly and Luna didn't hesitate. She jumped in the water and grabbed what she could of Ivana and started to pull. Ivana was now trying to hang on to anything that she could, and she stopped the river by holding onto clumps of coarse grass and lichen that grew all over the riverbank. Luna knew that something or someone helped them, because they finally won against the current, and stumbled out of the water exhausted. While they were just lying there wet and dirty, they heard screams and running noises, and then suddenly Uncle Pas was there helping them up, picking up Ivana and carrying her home like a child, while Luna followed them sobbing. The new Luna's heart was breaking, but the old Luna inside of the new Luna was thinking:

"Thank God we're in the middle of the boondocks, In Boston there'd be cops and ambulances here already, and Aunt Esther and Uncle Pas would be terribly embarrassed. At least over here we get to suffer in peace." When they arrived home, Aunt Esther hugged Luna and whispered in her hair:

"Thank you, Sweet Girl! I think God send you to us. We are blessed to have you!" She then went to Ivana on the couch where her father had laid her, and kneeling in front of her held her and kissed her, and called her baby, and told her how much she loved her. Sometime later, the girls were both sitting on a chair in the kitchen, wrapped in a large, fluffy towel and warm, clean and cozy from their bath. After all that, Aunt Esther went upstairs to rest, as she was still weak from her miscarriage and Luna and Ivana went to their beds. They lay down together on Luna's bed, and went to sleep back to back curled up like two wet puppies. They woke up a couple hours later to the wonderful smell of food being cooked, and put on their fluffy warm robes over their nightgowns and went downstairs. While the three of them were resting, Uncle Pas had cooked dinner. Aunt Esther had a big pan of meatballs in red sauce already on the stove, so he cooked some ziti, ladled red sauce over them, added some pieces of mozzarella and grated romano cheese, bits of hardboiled eggs, and garnished the whole with meatballs, then put the pan in the Dutch oven, stuck it in coals in the fireplace and put coals on the cover. When they went down, the pan of pasta was gooey and crunchy brown, the meatballs had a delicious brown crust, and the simple salad that went with them was heavenly with Aunt Esther's yellow, crusty bread. Afterward, the girls begged Aunt Esther to stay put, and cleaned up everything. Eventually, they all sat at the table with their coffee and cookies, and just talked quietly of everyday things, enjoying just being together safe and well fed. The love everyone felt for each other was palpable, and slowly the nightmare started to recede and they started to make plans for the future. Through it all, Aunt Esther's eyes went to Luna once in a while, and she looked at her with awe and love all at the same time. Uncle Pas had looked like he aged overnight, but was starting to look like his usual self, and smiling he said:

"How would my three beautiful girls like a day on the town next Sunday? We could ask Anna to go with us. We could spend a day in Pontecorvo, taking in the sights, going to dinner, and then taking in a movie?" Luna and Ivana jumped up and hugged him screaming;

"Yes, please, please, please! What are we going to see?" Uncle Pas and Aunt Esther smiled at the girls' enthusiasm and power to regenerate so fast. Uncle Pas pulled a flier out of a drawer and opened it up on the table:

"I asked Giampiero, the film projectionist, when there would be a good American film playing. He's a great guy; he looked in his files and gave me this." It was a flier from the only movie house in Pontecorvo, The Supercinema, and it had a list of movies and when they would play; on the next Sunday, the movie playing was 'Bathing Beauty' with Esther Williams. Luna had heard that name, and she had seen parts of her movies as her mother liked to watch the retro TV channel and liked aquatic movies. Luna didn't like old movies as much at home, but here they were new, and she liked to watch Esther Williams swim. Her mother had sent away for a bathing suit once from Esther Williams, and she said it was the best bathing suit she had ever had. In her time, Esther Williams had a business and sold all kinds of things. Luna waited until Aunt Esther and Ivana were busy excitedly talking about the outing, and asked Uncle Pas under her breath:

"What language is the movie in?" Uncle Pas smiled, and said:

"It's dubbed in Italian; people cannot read the subtitles fast enough and some people cannot read at all. I picked it because you may want to see something of home. I hope you like it!" Luna looked at his dear, handsome face and said:

"I will like anything we all do together, Uncle. Thank you very much for thinking of me." After that, Aunt Esther and Uncle Pas retired upstairs, and Luna and Ivana felt the need to go out of the house. They got dressed and went visiting. Great Uncle Biagio and Great Aunt Marianna were their first stop. Dapper little Great Uncle Biagio kissed their cheeks and bowed to them and cute little Great Aunt Marianna guided them into the good dining room. They received some of the nice, soft, plump maritozzi buns Great Aunt Marianna was known for, a big glass of thick, rich milk and loads of love and sympathy. When they left, followed by thanks and requests for more visits, they went to see Aunt Nannina, Giustina and Uncle Luigi. Aunt Nannina was home alone, as Giustina and her father had gone visiting, and she was very happy to see them. She was wearing a cozy soft caftan in pale yellow that she had got in Florence, on one of the trips that she took with Giustina, and she showed them some black and white pictures of their trip. Aunt Nannina looked handsome and healthy, and she invited them into her personal parlor to have some American caramels she had bought in the Forcelle quarters in Naples. After asking about everyone, they talked about the following week, when Gianna the teacher was going to Milano, and Aunt Nannina was going to substitute at the school. Aunt Nannina didn't believe in the classics, she said that her students read a lot of the contemporary books, except for Sir Arthur Conan Doyle; Aunt Nannina loved Sherlock Holmes, and her students had read all the books in the series. Luna talked knowingly about the merits of Alessandro Manzoni, and Aunt Nannina said that although he was a great writer, the misery and suffering he talked about was enough to drive anybody to drink. Luna observed that she was halfway through one of his books, and she was not a lush yet. Everyone had a big laugh at that. Ivana was reading

'Misericordia' by Benito Perez Galdos and she was proudly talking about it. Aunt Nannina scoffed at that:

"What is it with Gianna? She likes misery and suffering? That story about the desperate streets of Madrid and the poor servant Benina who goes out to beg, so she can feed her selfish mistress Dona Paca is the saddest thing I have ever read; I especially disliked the scene where Benina finds a broken, dirty cauliflower on the ground, after the market stalls closed down, takes it home, cleans it, cooks it and serves it to her mistress and her son and daughter, and after enjoying it, Dona Paca calls Benina in and chides her because she likes her cauliflower in big pieces, not chopped. I like fun and joy in my books, at least a little mystery. My students won't have nightmares like I did when my teacher made me read that whole 'Misericordia'." Ivana protested that she was not having nightmares, but Aunt Nannina was adamant in her belief, and foisted a Sherlock Holmes novel into her unresisting hands. Ivana put the book in her pocket, and after kisses and requests of more visits, they walked to aunt Palma's house. Aunt Palma was waiting for them, and they stopped trying to find out how she always knew, and went into her welcoming little house. Their tombola lace instruments were set up in the little dining room, in a corner, but today was just visiting day, the tombola lace would have to wait until after school on the following day. Aunt Palma chided them about their caramel breath, and mumbled about unmarried ladies who had money to burn and bought themselves just about everything their little hearts desired:

"I never bought myself anything when I was young. My Alfredo was very strict, may God rest his soul, and he never even gave me enough money to buy household necessities. He always found the money to buy himself his drinks, though. I married him when I was sixteen, and I went without, a lot of times, I did! I thought we were poor and never complained. I used to thank God we didn't have any children, because I didn't want the poor mites to suffer. When I was almost thirty and my husband died, I found out that we were not poor, actually we were quite well set, but I never let myself go and spend more than was necessary; I kept up the regime! Of course, I had to buy myself some gold, just to let people know I wasn't destitute, and I had to do some traveling to see things I had dreamed about all my life." The girls looked at her big eyed:

"You did some traveling? Where did you go?" Aunt Palma gestured vaguely:

"You know! All the usual places: France, Spain, England, Germany etc." The girls were flabbergasted:

"You took the Grand Tour and you never talk about it, and neither does anyone else!"

"Of course they don't, they don't even know about it; they were not here when I did it! I was thirty years old, I went with a friend of mine and I didn't advertise it. I told everyone I was going to stay with my mother for three months, and instead I traveled." She then got a twinkle in her eyes and said:

"I have pictures!" The girls couldn't believe it:

"You have pictures? But it must have been so long ago; did they have pictures even then?"

"It was eighteen hundred and ninety, if you must know, and yes! They did have pictures, not small portable cameras like now, but you posed and they took your picture. You girls think that you are so modern in the 1950's, with your fast cars, your portable cameras and your telephones, but we did things too in the olden days; we were people too, and we did all kinds of things, and we had a lot of fun. Maybe even more fun than now, because we had more time in those days!" The girls said:

"Yeah, yeah, yeah!" Then downed their shot of bitter artichokes elixir without even feeling it, and clamored for the pictures. Aunt Palma went to a drawer in the hutch and pulled out from the bottom an old, yellowed album. She started to open it, and on the front page was the picture of a young couple; she was sitting in a chair and he was standing behind her; there was a large plant next to them. The petite young woman sitting down was wearing a beautiful dress with an embroidered yoke and flounces and frills, the high necked style suited her perfectly, and on top of her head she carried a glorious head of hair all riotous curls and ribbons. The blond young man standing behind her was wearing a white suit and he looked handsome and adoring, holding his panama in his hand. Ivana said:

"I thought your husband was dead when you traveled." Aunt Palma responded:

"He was!" The girls looked at tiny Aunt Palma with new eyes:
"Did your mother know?"

"Of course! She was the one to convince me. She said that I should get some gusto while I was young enough to do it, and it would be nice to have some wonderful adventures to look back on. 'Gather Ye Rosebuds While Ye May' she said; and I did."

There were more pictures of the two same young people in various settings and poses, on decks of boats, in front of the Eiffel Tower, at a bullfight in Spain, on a boat on the Rhine River..... All the pictures had a sepia tint and were in thick cardboard:

"I saw the Can-Can in Paris!" Aunt Palma said, and Luna asked, bewildered:

"What's a Can-Can?" Ivana explained, impatiently:

"It's a dirty French dance where the girls show you their underwear." Aunt Palma interjected, with a sly smile:

"That's where I got my other vice that no one knows about." The girls waited quietly for a while, and then they said:

"Well?" Aunt Palma said, coyly:

"Underwear!"

"Underwear?" They repeated uncomprehending. Aunt Palma responded:

"Yes, underwear! You know; mutandies!" The girls still didn't understand, so Aunt Palma showed them. She bent over slightly, lifted the back of her skirts, swayed them back and forth, and hummed the Can-Can tune; lo and behold, under her paisana costume she was wearing red silk underwear with ruffles, black ribbons and lace panels. Luna and Ivana had to hold each other up before they fainted with the shock, and after that, they laughed and laughed until their sides hurt. Aunt Palma joined their laughter, and after the merriment the girls said:

"Aunt Palma, you're wearing underwear like a call girl!" And Aunt Palma said that it gave her tremendous pleasure to know that no one knew her secret. She took them into her bedroom, and showed them drawer after drawer of beautiful, sexy and expensive underwear. She told them it was her beau's idea that under her demure clothing she wore sexy, call girl's underwear, after all who was ever going to see her underwear unless she got run over by a truck! She had delighted in that secret, and had kept it up all of her life, just like the regime her husband imparted; that was her homage to the two men in her life. She told them that she traveled to Roma every few months, on the train, and went to the red light district to buy her lingerie; she had friends there! The girls asked her if she was safe going to the red light district by herself and Aunt Palma said, blithely:

"Oh, I don't go by myself; I hire Armando to go with me."

"Who is Armando?" Asked the girls:

"He's a muscle man from the Centocelle Quarters, the girls in the red light district all love him; he shaves his head and looks quite fierce." And Aunt Palma told them anecdotes and stories that she had kept secrets of her heart for sixty years, while showing them her pictures, and she enjoyed the session just as much as the girls.

The girls enjoyed everything, and commented on how her friend must have spent a fortune for those kinds of travel that long ago. Aunt Palma said that she had paid for everything. The girls asked her why and she said:

"His harpy of a wife had all the money, she didn't give him anything. He told her he was going out of town to work, so on top of paying for everything, I gave him some money to show her when he got back."

"What happened to him?" Asked the girls. Aunt Palma looked sadly into the distance:

"I never saw him again after that, I was after all a respectable widow…..I heard he had died of Influenza about forty years ago." The girls were sad for a while, but after Aunt Palma swore them to secrecy she offered them a plate of little sweet ricotta turnovers and a small pitcher of fruited wine cooler, and they forgot all about Aunt Palma's long ago beau. On their way out Aunt Palma again wanted to make sure they would keep her secrets and the girls crossed their hearts and hoped to die, and then:

"Stick a needle in my eye!" They screamed, to Aunt Palma's clapping delight. On the way home they held hands and walked close to each other; it was quite dark by now, and they just wanted to get home. Once in a while they whispered to each other:

"Mutandies!" And giggled all the way home. It had been a long day. At home they declined any food, Aunt Esther commenting that they probably had been given chosen morsels wherever they went, which was the truth. Uncle Pas and Aunt Esther were settled down companionably for the evening; Aunt Esther was doing some mending, and Uncle Pas was sitting at the kitchen table grating stale bread into bread crumbs. On the following day, Aunt Esther was going to make her famous bread crumbs covered potato pie, and they all looked forward to it. The girls were very tired, so they just went up to bed. That night Luna dreamed that they were on the Eiffel Tower, and it was swaying in the wind but there was no way to get down unless you walked. She was afraid to walk down the small, see trough iron steps and just stood paralyzed with her back to the wall. Finally Ivana suggested they go down on their 'bum' with their eyes closed, and that's what they did. They were saved, but couldn't sit very well for days.

School was different on the following day; Aunt Nannina came to teach! Their teacher, her husband and all their luggage had been driven to the bus in Pontecorvo by Mario Merolli, and when he came to pick them up, he deposited Anna so she could look after the teacher and Uncle Saverio's children. They had a boy and a girl, both under ten, cute as buttons, and very vivacious; Anna had her work cut out for her. Aunt Nannina was a stickler for propriety, and she had told everyone that in class she was 'Teacher' or 'Miss Valenza', and no exceptions would be made for family. Luna and Ivana were glad, they did not want any extra attention from Miss Valenza, and they did not have to be loyal to the teacher when the other girls talked about her. Everyone thought that Miss Valenza was stuck up and pretentious, but her uppermost quality was that she was so boring that she reduced everyone to tears with her monologues; they nicknamed her Miss Vanilla. During the day, and during breaks, they saw Anna on and off, and Ivana and Luna received some supportive hugs throughout the day. Aunt Nannina was very smart and highly educated, but she didn't know anything about how to keep her students happy and engaged. But then, this was probably not one of her goals. That afternoon, when the girls rode their bikes home, they felt like escapees from Alcatraz. Freedom was sweet, and it went to their heads like sweet wine. They flew into Aunt Palma's little house, and they were so fidgety that it took them quite a while to settle down to their lace making. Aunt Palma didn't make any comments, until they were due for their break. After they stopped, she served them some food, and on the table appeared a bottle of gassosa:

"I keep this stuff for special occasions, and surviving Nannina's teaching for a long day is certainly something to celebrate." The gassosa was very cold for being in the root cellar, and the girls drank it joyfully. They rode their bikes home, and after their chores, ate their dinner and settled down to their homework. Ivana had a calendar in the hallway, and she marked another day off until 'movie day'. Aunt Esther spent every evening working on the wedding dress with much trepidation; Rodolfo was in Roma, working at the Roma radio station, and Antonietta was like a wild woman, angry and upset, rejecting anything that was shown to her. Just that morning she had refused to look at the list of sweets for the wedding:

"That good-for–nothing I'm supposed to marry is gallivanting in Roma. He's temporarily working on the big radio station. They say he's real good and maybe they'll offer him a full time job. He's a big shot now! Maybe he'll find someone better there, and we'll never see him again; I haven't seen him in two weeks. There probably won't be a wedding. Save all that work, you're probably doing it all for nothing!" The only one who could make Antonietta see reason was Anna, but she couldn't leave her duties at the teacher's house and was not there to help. The Fool was at the end of his rope, he didn't know what to make of all this; could he have made a mistake with Rodolfo? But then, if that's the way Rodolfo was, then it was better to know it now than after he was married to Antonietta. Then he remembered the way Rodolfo had spoken about Antonietta, and felt better, only to be assailed by doubts later. During that week, a letter came for Antonietta from Roma; it was from Rodolfo, and it was actually a fancy romantic card with hearts and flowers. In it Rodolfo had written:

"To My Love, with all my love. Wait for me, Antonietta, we will soon be happy. All I want is to be with you and I'm working so we can be happy! You'll find out when I come back. Love Always, your Rodolfo." Antonietta, who was always sarcastic and cold, snatched it when she was handed the card by her father, who intercepted the mailman, and ran to her room. She then carried the card around with her until it was nothing but a rag, suspiciously smeared and wrinkled, like someone cried over it. The Fool and his wife watched Antonietta sit at the window, waiting for who knows what, and whispered to each other. Assunta said:

"Our little girl is in love, I thought I would never see the day; I hope he's worth it, if she loses him she'll never trust anyone again." The Fool whispered back:

"I think he's worth it, I trust him. She'll be happy!" And while he was saying it, he couldn't help feeling a little shiver of fear run down his back. The classes at school became more and more tedious, with Aunt Nannina criticizing everything Gianna did, until Luana stood up and told Miss Valenza that they liked their teacher, and she was following a rigorous curriculum set for her by the school board. Everyone cheered and Miss Valenza snorted at that, but refrained from criticizing their teacher again. All the students were glad they didn't go to school in town, and were very happy that their teacher was going to be there on the following Monday. The little children were especially glad because they were afraid of Miss Valenza, and she didn't hug or comfort anyone even when they fell and got hurt. Slowly but surely, the next Sunday came and everyone was suddenly busy and harried. Mario was not available because he had to go to Pontecorvo to pick up Gianna the teacher and Uncle Saverio, so Uncle Pas asked Uncle Luigi if he could take care of the animals until they came back Sunday night, and he was glad to do it. They then dressed with care and went to church. Anna was still at the teacher's house, but Amelia was going over to care for the children until Mario came back with the parents. Before church, Uncle Pas picked up Amelia and dropped her off at the teacher's house, and came back with Anna. They all got in the truck, the grownups in the cab and the girls in the back, and went to church. It was a beautiful fall day, the sun was weaker than usual but golden, and the fruit was all ripe for the picking. In the coming weeks there would be parties galore, everyone having coordinated the times so everyone could help everyone pick their fruit.

Uncle Pas commented on how it was wonderful that they could have a full day all to themselves, to explore, to eat, to watch a wonderful American movie, and to generally enjoy each other's company at leisure. Somehow, everyone knew they had an outing planned, and asked questions and gave recommendations on what to do and see. Uncle Pas took everyone's suggestions gratefully, and smiled his thanks to everyone, but their plans were made and they were sticking to them. Anna suggested Trattoria Primavera for their dinner, and they all agreed. Anna whispered in Luna's ear:

"They have a real bathroom there!" Luna smiled thinking of the treat, and the old Luna peaked out for just a moment to whisper in the new Luna's ear:

"You've sunk pretty low, my dear girl, if you look forward to going to the bathroom!" But the new Luna squashed that thought and went bravely forward. When they arrived in Pontecorvo, Uncle Pas left the truck just after the bridge, in the Pastine Quarters, in front of the Ruscito trattoria, and they promised to keep an eye on it. They went inside the trattoria, and ordered maritozzi buns and a cup of espresso. The buns were huge and lovely, although not as light as Great Aunt Marianna's, and the coffee was dark and strong, made in the Napoli style. Luna was amazed when she saw the people turn the coffee pot upside down, but Ivana explained that they were using a Neapolitan coffee pot, the water was on the bottom and the coffee in the middle. The top was empty for the moment. When the water started to boil, they turned the coffee pot upside down so that the hot water flowed downwards, through the coffee and into the empty part, producing the most lovely and fragrant beverage. The old Luna said:

"Who cares!" But the new Luna was excited and wondered if back home they had stuff like that. While they were sitting at a square table near the glass window, Uncle Pas pointed to a spot on the other side of the street, and said, laughing:

"That's where your Uncle Gaetano dropped Mariuccia from Roccasecca off his bike!" They told the tale to Anna, who hadn't heard, and they all laughed hard. The hostess, Mrs. Ruscito, replied from the counter:

"Everything happens over here! Over the years, we've seen everything!" And they all laughed again. After they were done, Uncle Pas told them that they should take the shortcut to the upper town, and they took a small road to the left. The road was steep, and on top they found a fountain that bubbled and gurgled off a carved and decorated wall to the right. The girls wanted to drink, but Uncle Pas said that they shouldn't because that was soft water, and not drinkable. In fact, the fountain was called 'The Soft Water Fountain of St. Bartholomew' and the water came down from the top of the humongous rock on which the Cathedral of St. Bartholomew stood; it was not potable water. Besides, right after the war they had found the fountain buried and when they cleaned it out, there were dead bodies and skulls buried within. They all shuddered, and kept going. To the left, on the bottom of the little hill, there were huge apartment houses, and on the right they found the beginning of tiny stairs. This place was called 'The Little Stairs of St. Bartholomew', and the stairs were certainly small, but they went on and on, in a semicircular way. When they finally arrived at the top, they were surprised to be right in front of the St. Bartholomew Cathedral. There was a large, marble stairway, and on top, on the left, the front door of the Cathedral. Halfway through the stairs, on the landing, a huge statue of Pope Pius IX stood attached to the wall on the left; he had a great tiara, grand vestments, but unfortunately, part of his nose was missing since the war. At the top of the stairs, there was a large balcony with a marble parapet, and at the back, towards the Pastine Quarters, stood a huge, magnificent cross. If you walked around the cross, and looked down, you could see the whole of Pontecorvo, from the Pastine Quarters to the monastery of the Passionist monks on the road to Pico, to the left, and on the right you could see all the way to Mount Leuci; halfway up Mount Leuci, you could see the white of the sanctuary of Saints Cosmo and Damiano; the little road they traveled to go up there for mass and back was a snaking white line. Luna had never before been interested in sightseeing or great views from anywhere, but this was breathtaking, and considering that she knew practically every inch of the scenery they were looking at, she looked avidly at everything. Closer to them, if they looked down, they could see The Little Steps of St. Bartholomew winding their way up from the Pastine Quarters; there were so many of them, Luna didn't know how they had made it all the way up. She was amazed at Anna, who at her age and with her arthritis had kept up with everyone and even walked up ahead sometimes. Anna had seen her looks, and asked her quietly:

"Where you come from, do old people walk and stay active like we do here?" Luna had said, sincerely:

"I don't really know. You don't see too many old people around, unless you go to places that cater to them. I think young people feel that they don't want to drag old people around with them, I guess." Anna shook her head:

"Over here everyone feels that if you were smart enough and strong enough to get old, they can learn a lot from you, and they respect and admire old folks and want them along; it makes them feel secure. As far as agility goes, after a life of walking, running and climbing these old bones feel very comfortable with exercise. In this time and place, we old folks don't pamper ourselves. My mother always said that if you stop, you're lost!" In fact, Luna had realized, that having the oldest people in the community at anyone's affair, wedding, communion, christening, lent an air of acknowledgement and consequence to the proceedings; she kind of liked it. At home, older people usually kept to themselves and never had much interest. How sad Anna would be in her own time, she suddenly realized! After a while of staring at the cross and the panorama, Uncle Pas steered them to the front of the majestic cross and made them look up. And there it was the great, ancient tower everyone talked about: The Tower of Rodoaldo. It was rugged and tall. There was a very tall first floor, and then three stories with humongous open windows. At the very top floor, you could see the huge bell. In fact, The Tower of Rodoaldo was now a bell tower. Uncle Pas, very succinctly, told them the story of the tower. In 860, Rodoaldo, the Lombard Gastald of Aquino, built a fortress on an inaccessible spur, called 'Rocca Guglielma' overlooking the river Liri and the bridge that spanned it. From the fortress he intended to defend the village of Ponte Curvo from the Saracen intruders coming up the river. In the fortress castle there was a chapel dedicated to Saint Bartholomew. Hundreds of years later, on the ruins of the fortress was erected the Cathedral of Saint Bartholomew. The bell tower of the cathedral was a rebuilding of the ancient Tower of Rodoaldo. Over the years, two medieval quarters developed; Civita within the city walls, and Pastine between the city walls and the river. Through the wars, the tower stood while the Cathedral was destroyed and rebuilt. The last time this happened was during WWII, when the church was destroyed and the tower still stood. It was smack in the middle of the Cathedral, with the Church on the left and the rectory on the right. Uncle said that the humongous bell in the tower was called 'Susanna'. Into Luna's mind came the song Oh Susanna:

"Oh Susanna, Oh, don't you cry for me. I come from Alabama with a banjo on my knee."

"Darn," thought Luna, "now the song's going to be playing in my head all day long!" At that point, Uncle guided all of them to a smaller door to the left of the immense, ornate front door. The huge front door was inside of a gigantic marble portal, and the two bronze panels of the door each had a large bronze figure of a saint on it. In 1950 Italy, men had to take their hats off in church, and ladies couldn't go in unless their hair was covered. Luna and Ivana had small patches of lace given to them by Aunt Esther to cover their heads in church, and Aunt Esther produced a small hat with a bit of lace hanging in the front which she proceeded to perch on her head. On anyone else, that silly, small hat would have been a little ridiculous, but on Aunt Esther with her severe hairdo and patrician profile, it looked both chic and appropriate. Inside, it was dim at first and a smell of incense and flowers permeated their senses, but after everyone's eyes got used to the low light, a sense of calm and a feeling of perpetuity came over everyone like a mantle. The inside was grand, right in the center of the wall facing the people, high on the wall, there was a great, round leaded stained-glass window of many colors. There were many others on the side walls. There were the Stations of the Cross on the side walls of the immense room, and two long lines of special wooden benches were on both sides, leaving a long space in the middle. The huge, leaded glass windows projected a mystical light in many colors that fluctuated and covered everything, and small chapels were carved on the side walls here and there. The floor was covered in large, medieval stones salvaged from the original building, and they walked the long space between the front door and the altar stopping in front of the altar; it was beautiful and opulent, covered in costly embroidered cloths and full of flowers. In the center, way up high, stood the tabernacle, in which was enclosed the Holy Relic of San Bartholomew, all in a gold case that looked like the sun. They all crossed themselves, while kneeling down, and then went to the side and to some seats in the back. Luna noticed, passing all the seats, that everyone of them had a family's name engraved on it, and when they came to their seats, on the fancy carved bench it said 'Sargento Family'. Luna leaned to Ivana and said:

"Why is your family's name on the bench?"

"Papa' bought it for the church when they rebuilt it after the war. A lot of people did that, as you have seen."

When they came back out into the sunlight, they felt duly renewed and happy. Aunt Esther said:

"The Archpriest did a beautiful mass!"   And they all concurred. Uncle Pas said:

"His nephew, Don Giuseppe, finished up the service beautifully!"   And they all agreed.   Outside of the cathedral Cipriano the Sexton was standing to the side to salute the parishioners, and he had his wife Concetta and his four boys, Remigio, Fernando, Pasqualino and Peppinello lined up at his side. Uncle Pas shook his hand and slipped him a note, while Aunt Esther stopped to talk to his wife. She congratulated her on the beautiful sweaters the boys were wearing, and Concetta told her that she had unraveled some old sweaters that someone gave her and had used the yarn to make sweaters for the boys. Aunt Esther told her she was a gifted artisan, and the sweaters were just beautiful.   Concetta beamed, and Anna examined the sweaters herself, and declared them perfection.   She told Concetta that she had bought some yarn long ago, to knit for her grandchildren, but she didn't have any patience left, not to mention her poor eyesight. She asked Concetta if she had some free time, as she wanted to commission some sweaters. Concetta agreed happily, and Anna promised to come back the following Sunday to talk about it.   When they walked away Aunt Esther said:

"It's too bad they don't give the Sexton a small paycheck, they're raising those poor boys on nothing. It's a lot of work keeping this huge church clean, on top of all his other duties." Uncle Pas said he had given him a substantial gratuity:

"People help all they can, the church just gives the family free housing and they expect him to live off of the gratuities. Cipriano was telling me to thank Uncle Mimmo, Gaetano's father, for sending a large basket of food, even a small ham." Aunt Esther said:

"You have a nice family! But you're the nicest of all of them!"

"No dear, you're the nicest!" He replied. And they looked each other in the eyes. Ivana said:

"They're at it again!" Luna said:

"I know!" And they both rolled their eyes. Anna was mumbling distractedly to herself:

"Now to find out where they sell some yarn cheap!" And they walked down the cathedral steps into Piazza Del Duomo. It was almost lunch time, and Uncle Pas said that since they were going to have dinner in town, they should just get a light lunch, so they headed to a part of town called 'Porta Pia' to have something light. To Luna's delight, after they walked up to the Town Hall plaza, and then a long narrow street, they arrived at the place, and it was just where she had stopped the first day she came, when they met Mario Merolli to pick up Anna. Anna remembered also, because she squeezed Luna's arm and smiled at her. At the top of the road they headed to Rosina's bakery, and practically floated through the door on the marvelous scents coming out of it. Uncle Pas handed some money to Aunt Esther and told her to buy whatever they wanted, and left. At everyone's questioning looks, Aunt said that he had gone near there to Trattoria Primavera to pick a table and order their dinner, because they didn't have too much time between the dinner and the start of the movie, and they wanted to walk in before the movie started to secure some good seats. Aunt Esther confabulated with Anna and the girls, and they bought some juicy squares of tomato focaccia (just pizza without any cheese) and some small meat turnovers. After that, they walked next door to the fruit stand and bought a large bag of humongous loquats, all yellow and ripe. Further down, they went inside the Sports Bar and bought bottles of gassosa for everyone of them. When they walked back up towards Rosina's, Uncle Pas was walking towards them. He said that they were going to reserve a nice, large table near the front window for them, at five P.M. and he had already ordered their dinner and hoped they would like it. They wanted to be at the movie house before seven, and so they had just one and a half hour to eat. Regularly, Luna would have thought this an excessive amount of time to have a meal, but she had learned that here food was very important, and had to be savored, and at the same time eating together was a lovely rite also to be savored. (How different from home, where everyone ate quickly and ran, she thought!) Uncle steered them to the top of the street, and they walked into the 'Villetta'. This was a small garden in the middle of the town, with trees, flowers, little walks and benches to rest and enjoy watching a beautiful fountain and a sculpture of some kind of ornate nymph which stood in the center of the Villetta. They chose a nice, long bench in the back, with lots of privacy and a trash can right next to it. Aunt Esther divvied up the focaccia and the meat pies, with the largest share going, of course, to Uncle Pas. No one minded Uncle Pas getting more than anyone, he took real good care of them, and he was after all the man! They all ate slowly, taking small sips of their delicious gassosa. After the food was gone, they ate the wonderful fruit, and even thought Luna never had any of those loquats at home, she enjoyed them almost as much as the cheese-less pizza. After their meal, Anna said that she needed to go to the WC, and she wanted to explore a bit. The girls jumped up and down at this, they too needed the WC, and exploring sounded wonderful. Aunt Esther and Uncle Pas send them off with indulgent smiles, looking very happy to be left alone sitting very close to each other on the bench secluded in a wall of shrubberies and flowers. They went to the bottom of the road, then turned left and downwards, and after a while, on the left, there it was; the public bathroom. It looked almost like an octagonal pavilion, half of which was for the ladies, and the other half for the gentlemen. On the ladies side there was an elderly woman sitting down in the entrance. She had a small table in front of her, and on the table two small boxes. One was to put in the required payment to use the WC, very little, and one contained small tickets you could keep all day if you needed the restroom again. After they paid and received their tickets, the elderly woman handed them a small wad of toilet paper each. They walked into the spotless interior and each went to a door. Luna was never as excited to use a bathroom, so imagine her disappointment when she stepped into her cubbyhole and there was no toilet. She whispered loudly to Ivana in the next one:

"I don't have a toilet, just a hole in the floor! What am I going to do!" Ivana responded also in a loud whisper:

"Use your imagination, dunderhead!" Luna looked down at the hole and realized that there were marks, one on each side of the hole; the marks were foot prints, and next to the right one there was a small lever you could push down with your foot. She had to crouch down, and when she was finished she stepped on the lever and, lo and behold; she had flushed the toilet-less toilet! She went back out in the common area, and they all took turns washing their hands on the single sink there. On the wall hung a never ending rolled up cloth towel, and you just unrolled a clean spot and dried your hands and the used towel got rolled up on the other end. Luna thought that all of this was very ingenious and she liked it very much. They went back up to the main road and walked to the left some way until they reached a great, yellow building. This street was May Street, and Anna said that the yellow building was the fancy school in town, and that was where Aunt Nannina taught school. The girls were impressed by the beautiful building and the areas around it, but they both agreed that regarding Aunt Nannina:

"Better them than us!" On the way back, instead of going the same way, they turned left at the crossroad and then went up a series of small steps. Up there they found a whole new world; a small community of small houses, little stores, alleys and court yards. After walking through a myriad of small allies they saw a beautiful church tucked right in the center of them. Anna said that it was the church of San Marco. A group of people was standing around in front of it, and Anna found out that there was a wedding going on. They waited with everyone else, and after a while, the double doors opened and a couple stepped out followed by a lot of people. The bride was beautiful, blond with very short hair and large blue eyes. Luna thought:

"Lieutenant Tasha Yar, from Star Trek, TNG." Only, instead of the gold and black uniform, she was wearing a white and gold ethereal creation of yards and yards of white tulle and satin ribbons. The bride and groom were being pelted by very large grains of rice. Luna found out that it was very good luck for them, the more rice the better and Anna said the rice also meant fertility. Luna said:

"Oh my God! If this keeps up they'll have thousands and thousands of children!" Ivana elbowed her, and they all laughed and laughed. At one point, the bride had picked up her dress to exit more freely; Luna could not forget the bride's beautiful slender hand, her shining new ring on her ring finger, tiny, delicate blue veins showing through her pearly white, alabaster skin. The handsome groom could not take his dark eyes off of his new fair bride, and his large dark hand covered her pale one gently. Luna thought, in her head:

"I could just see Uncle Pas and Aunt Esther on their wedding day!" A consuming desire to grow up and have the same thing gripped Luna:

"I'm not going to ever get married, unless I find the same thing with a gentle, strong, wise man like Uncle Pas!" She thought. After witnessing this wonderful event, Anna and the girls kept walking, and from the San Marco church they came out onto a large balcony; on the bottom they could see Rosina's bakery and across the large street, the Villetta where Uncle Pas and aunt Esther waited. In a small alley, right near the church, they had come upon a small house with a very large window. They had looked inside, and there it was, a giant loom, and a girl seated in front of it was working the thread pushing some wooden shuttles back and forth. She was weaving some coarse red and white checkered cloth:

"That's one of the Colicci girls, they take turns; she's making tablecloth material." Whispered Anna. The girl was facing the window, she was beautiful! She had the darkest eyes, red cheeks and lips, and long, black hair streaming down her back. She busily weaved, looking up at people once in a while and smiling, and the whole while she was singing a sweet song. She sang about a rich young hunter who met the most beautiful peasant girl in the woods and stopped to talk to her. After they talked for a while, she fell asleep in his arms, and when she awoke she cried because she was now dishonored. But the hunter kissed her and said he wanted to marry her and take her home as his bride, for the happiness of his mom and dad. All Luna could think about was:

"Talk about multitasking! This weaver girl certainly knows a thing or two about that!" While they were going down the small stairs towards the bakery, Luna couldn't stop thinking about the young girl stuck in front of the loom, weaving and weaving for hours. More and more she was realizing how lucky she was to have been born when she was; the old Luna thought that if she had to work like that, she would have just died! Yet people did, and had done for so long! The new Luna thought:

"But she was singing, and she looked happy!" Luna was very confused, and followed the others quietly. Ivana said:

"Anna, how come you know so much about Pontecorvo when you just moved here!" Anna answered:

"Oh ye of little faith! You have to learn to trust your Anna; I know whence I'm coming from! Little do you know, I'm a Pontecorvo born and bred girl. My Domenico removed me to Caserta when we married, but I kept closely in touch with my birthplace and we moved back to the outskirts of Pontecorvo during the war; you can take the girl out of Pontecorvo, but you can't take Pontecorvo out of the girl!" When they approached the Villetta, they heard soft murmurings. As they approached the secluded bench, they could see through the brush and trees Aunt Esther seated primly on the bench, while Uncle Pas was down on his knee, holding her hand. Ivana whispered:

"Oh No! Not the Rubayat again! I can't stand it!" Anna and Luna asked:

"What's a Rubayat!"

"It's a book of poetry written by a Persian guy called Omar Khayyam; sometimes he reads to her from it." Ivana mimicked her father's voice:

"My love, my darling! All I need to be blissfully happy is a jug of wine, a loaf of bread and thou!" Anna and Luna thought that it was a lovely sentiment, and they didn't understand why Ivana didn't like it:

"Just wait and see," she said, "he never just stops there, he adds more and more to it. It's positively disgusting; I'm going to throw up!" But Anna whispered:

"Stop, I want to see this! It's not like we're eavesdropping, your mother's got her back to us, but your father saw us." In fact, there was a twinkle in Uncle Pas' eyes, and he was putting on a show for them. He looked up at prim and proper Aunt Esther and said:

"For my complete happiness, all I need, my love, is a jug of wine, a loaf of bread and…………..some pasta with some red sauce, and some grated cheese, and a couple of big meatballs, and some nice peppers and some tender green salad, and thou, of course, and…….." Aunt Esther's face crumbled, and she started to laugh while trying to swat his hand with her free hand. Uncle Pas pulled, and all at once Aunt Esther fell from the bench on top of Uncle Pas. Anna stepped through the trees fallowed by the girls and stood in front of them with her arms akimbo:

"Well, a fine example you give these two young girls here; we leave you alone for a couple of minutes and we find you in the middle of hanky panky!" Luna couldn't stand it anymore, she loved them so much! She took a flying leap and threw herself at them with open arms. They had just managed to get to their knees, and Luna knocked them down again. Not to be left out, Ivana ran and threw herself in the fray too. All four of them were nothing but a bunch of flaying arms and legs, and Anna shouted, holding her sides:

"Stop it, you crazy people; you're going to make me wet my pants!" All at once, they heard a shrill whistle. They all turned around and standing there was a tall, elegant, decorated and forbidding Carabiniere Marshall. Immediately they all jumped up, and stood there in a line, looking red and disheveled. The Carabiniere said:

"Well, what is this show of rambunctious behavior? You people are disturbing the peace!" Anna walked in front of the Carabiniere and looking up explained, while fixing the kerchief on her head:

"This is only a little family jocularity, Your Honor, Sir, Mr. Marshall! The children aren't doing anything wrong, they were just playing!" The Carabiniere Marshall looked at the messed up man, the blushing woman, the laughing old lady and the two disheveled young girls, and said:

"Well, carry on then. As you were civilians!" And then, a smile cracking his glacial expression:

"I have a family too. Maybe I'll just go home and create some family jocularity of my own!" And with that, he saluted smartly, turned around and left. They were all left staring after him, the women giggling a bit, and Uncle Pas looking endearingly embarrassed. It took some time to walk down to the public restrooms, tidy themselves up, take a leisurely stroll through town and salute some acquaintances who were passing by. Uncle Pas looked at his watch and said it was almost five P.M. and time for dinner.

On the way Anna asked:

"What are we having for dinner?" Uncle Pas said:

"I tried to order things we don't usually get at the farm, what's the use of going out to eat if we have to have the same old things?" They all prodded him with impatient looks:

"We're having linguine with red clam sauce, steamed mussels from Formia or Gaeta, and I left the choice of vegetables to them." Aunt Esther said:

"Steamed mussels are my favorite!" He responded:

"I know! That's why I ordered them! Good thing too! I had to do something to make it up to you after I pulled you off the bench and almost got us arrested for indecent behavior!"

"You can never be indecent, my darling; I think you're perfect!"

"No, you're perfect, my angel!" And they stopped in the middle of the sidewalk and stared at each other with love, their hands entwined:

"Pulleeezzzze!" They all shouted, "there is no time for that! We're hungry, and we don't want to throw up before we even get the food!" Uncle Pas and Aunt Esther smiled, absentmindedly, as they walked over to Trattoria Primavera, the girls rolling their eyes at them, and Anna looking wistful. They had a nice, round table near the large front window, and on the red checkered tablecloth there was already a large basket of soft bread rolls, a pitcher of lemonade with chunks of lemon floating in it, and another jug filled with red house wine. Uncle saw everyone look at the bread basket filled with rolls, and at the jug of wine, and made to go down on his knee again. Everyone started whispering, loudly:

"Don't you dare......We don't want to be kicked out of here, and have to leave all this nice food." They each had a nice soft roll with some lemonade, and soon large, steaming platters of linguine in red sauce, chuck full of clams, were put in front of them. They ate slowly, savoring the delicious concoction, and they all agreed that Primavera shouldn't be called a trattoria, it was a wonderful restaurant, and the service and food were superb. They enjoyed the linguine, and after the plates were taken away, they spent some time quietly talking about the day and what they found interesting. The 'Oh Susanna' song was rolling somewhere inside of Luna's brain, but she tried to keep it at bay. Sometime later a large bowl of wonderfully smelling mussels in some kind of juice came to the table, and they were given individual plates. The mussels were plump and tasty, much better than the ones Luna had eaten back home, and the juice was full of herbs and spices. They shamelessly finished the whole bowl, even dunking bread in the juice, and sat back replete. After some more time, they brought the vegetable. It was a magnificent platter of fresh shelled peas, steamed with baby onions, and decorated by a plethora of thin, pink slices of Prosciutto Di Parma ham. Their stomach readjusted itself, and they found more room.   Aunt Esther very graciously complimented the cook, and he came to their table to meet them. While Aunt Esther and Uncle Pas exchanged pleasantries with the man, Anna signaled to the girls to follow her. They walked to the back of Primavera, and went into a long corridor. They passed on one side the kitchens, on the other the pantries, some office, and they arrived into a beautiful courtyard filled with huge pots of lemons, figs, rosemary, laurel and loquats. On one side there was a garden of herbs galore, and on the other side there was a low, pretty building. They followed Anna inside, and there it was; the cutest, most colorful WC they had ever seen in any other place. It was spotlessly clean, and it did have real toilets in the stalls. There were only two, so the girls took turns, while leaving one for Anna all to herself. They went leisurely back to the table, where they found Aunt Esther happily clutching what looked like a hand written recipe.   Uncle Pas said that they should start slowly towards the Supercinema, and they all felt, now that they were replete and refreshed by their WC visit, joy and anticipation. Uncle said that they would have dessert after the movie, for the day's coronation, and everyone agreed, knowing that Uncle Pas would not disappoint them.

They walked into the Supercinema on May Street, almost across from the fancy school, and to the right there was the ticket booth. They were asked if they wanted the downstairs seats or the more expensive balcony seats. It was kind of early, so they had their choice of seats. They all agreed to sit on the balcony, front seats, and luckily there were five empty seats all in a row. They went up the curving marble stairs, and sat right in front of the huge screen. The projectionist, Giampiero, spotted them from the projection room and went down to say hallo'. He was a slim, good-looking young man with dark eyes and hair, and very nice and knowledgeable about movies. They talked for a while and got the skinny on 'Bathing beauty.' They all told him how lucky he was to be able to see all the movies for free, and he agreed smiling. After a few minutes, Giampiero looked at his watch and exclaimed:

"Well, time for me to go to work! It's a dirty job, but someone has to do it!" And he laughed good-naturedly.

While they excitedly talked about the movie, and took off their sweaters to get comfortable, a man walked up and down the rows of seats holding a basket full of small bags. Luna was very curious about what he was selling, but didn't say anything, because she didn't want anyone to think she was asking for something. But Uncle signaled the man to come, and bought a whole bunch of the small bags. He was given a brown paper bag and paid for the stuff (whatever it was). First he handed one little bag to Aunt Esther, and then to Anna, and finally it was the girls' turn. Luna eagerly looked in her bag, and a bit disappointedly saw that it was full of some kind of seeds. She asked Ivana:

"What are these?" Ivana didn't even remark on the fact that she didn't know what the seeds were; it was obviously a local thing:

"They're bruscolini, roasted and salted pumpkin seeds; they're the best, when you start eating them, you can't stop!"Luna doubted that very much, but she gingerly took a seed and put it in her mouth. It was pleasantly salty, but it was also tough to chew. Ivana turned around, saw what Luna was doing and started to laugh:

"You Dunderhead! You're not supposed to eat the shell!" And she proceeded to show Luna how you first crushed the seed sideways, and then you pulled off the inside with your tongue and spit the shell out. Luna got the hang of it almost right away, and joyfully started to enjoy the bruscolini; it was true that once you started to eat the bruscolini, you found it very hard to stop. When she had a handful of shells, she turned to Ivana and asked:

"Where do we put the shells?"

"Throw them on the floor!" Ivana answered. Luna looked down and saw that the floor was already covered, and she started to do the same without guilt; after all, she noticed that some of the people were throwing their shells off the balcony even, and surely on the heads of the people down there, and no one complained. Ivana saw her look down and told her that it was not unusual to see people walking around, after the movie, with pumpkin seeds in their hair; they laughed! The movie came on, and at first Luna didn't really get caught up in it, especially since the actors were moving their lips in English, but the words came out in Italian. But after a while she started to get involved in the plot, like everyone else, and the obviously American silly goings on started to pull on her heartstrings and made her want to cry right in the middle of laughing. She had never realized that Red Skelton was that cute and funny, and that Esther Williams was that beautiful and talented. When her mother watched those old movies, Luna had nothing but contempt for them, and she despised the way people looked and acted. Maybe, thought Luna, being in the past was affecting her, and she started to see things with old fashioned eyes:

"As soon as the wedding is over, I better go back home!" She thought with quiet desperation.

After the movie was over, they went out, everyone talking about the plot, the clothes and the swimming. Aunt Esther said that she would never doubt her man the way Esther Williams had, and none of the goings on had needed to happen if she had trusted her guy. Uncle Pas replied that if things had been that smooth, there would have been no movie! Even so, Aunt Esther was going to copy some of the dresses she saw, because they were really cute, toned down some, of course! Luna was the quietest of all, and Anna looked at her with sympathy. She held her gently by the arm and whispered:

"Homesick?"   Luna looked up at the dear old lady and whispered:

"It's not even like home, you know? It's very old fashioned and unreal, but it's still something that reminds me of home and family." Anna squeezed her arm gently:

"Enjoy your time here, you'll go back home for certain, and when you think back at this time and remember us, you'll be happy you were here and you'll wish you enjoyed it more." Luna leaned on Anna's shoulder and told her:

"I am so glad I have known you, Anna, you are so wonderful! Without you I don't think I'd have made it. I don't know how I will live without you!" Anna whispered back:

"I have been so happy that you came into my life! You made me young again, and you woke up this old heart to love again! After I lost my little Franco and then my Domenico, I didn't feel anything anymore. I feel alive again, and I will until God sees fit to reunite me with my child and husband. You have changed too, I saw a little girl flourish and change right in front of my eyes; you have matured and are ready to go through life aware of others and of yourself. There is only one life, and in life the only worthwhile thing is how you commune with other people. You can't take riches and things with you when you leave this earth, Dearest Luna, but your kindness towards others will bear fruit over and over, and your actions will influence generations!" Uncle Pas, who had slowed down a bit and joined them quietly, said:

"Well done, Anna! I couldn't have said what I was thinking in such a gentle and loving way. We were blessed when Luna came, because along with everything else, she brought us you!" He bent down and kissed both of their foreheads. He then walked up to his wife and daughter and exclaimed:

"Time for dessert, what do you say girls?" Everyone squealed in joy, and they followed the crowd to the Sport Bar, and sat at a nice round table outside. It was a little cool these days, but they were wearing warm sweaters, and looking up at the clear stars from their table was wonderful. It was after nine P.M., but the streets were jammed with people strolling, groups standing around talking, and families sitting outside eating delicious smelling things and drinking espresso. The town was alive and so were they.   Uncle ordered cappuccinos all around, and frozen cassata for everyone. The big, foam topped cups of cappuccino arrived first, and while they were sipping them, everyone received a plate with a large slice of the frozen cassata. It consisted of golden sponge cake laced with ice cream in many flavors, and perfumed with yellow Strega and green Chartreuse liqueurs. It was undeniably heavenly, and everyone ate it with relish, sipping cappuccino and then cleaning their palate with fresh and delicious spring water. They slowly walked back, and just before arriving at town hall, in the small street that went from the center of town to town hall, they heard music, clapping and laughter. Aunt Esther said:

"That would be Uncle Master playing for the people as he likes to do! Oh, he's playing the pansy song!" She started walking faster, and Uncle Pas wriggled his eyebrows. Ivana rolled her eyes. Luna asked Ivana who this was and Ivana told her it was the music teacher; he had a studio right on the street level, it was always open to everyone, and people loved to stop and watch him teach music to his students. On Sunday nights and holidays he loved to play the accordion and the violin and sing for people and generally clown around:

"The pansy song is a dirty little song but people ask for it all the time; my mother, who's as prim and proper as they come, loves it very much!" Aunt Esther put her fingers on her lips:

"Shush, dear, it's not a dirty little song; it's just a little salacious, but very romantic." And they all stood with the other people enjoying Uncle Master's antics.   Luna thought the little man looked like Groucho Marx, with his great mustache, long, center parted hair and a little black coat with tails. He was playing a funny little hexagonal accordion Ivana said was called a concertina, while wiggling his coat tails and rolling his eyes suggestively. He sang enthusiastically:

"What a beautiful pansy you have, what a beautiful pansy you got! Will you give it to me, will you give it to me, and will you give it to me right now! I have one on my lapel, and I'll wear them both together, your sweet pansy next to mine for the joy of our love!" And he did the two-step while leaning right and left and sparkling joy from every pore.   He was very funny and very talented, with his music, small dances, songs and jokes. They all clapped for him, and joined in to the popular tune, and some couples danced right in the middle of the street. When he was done, he bowed to everyone, and they all applauded and hollered:

"Viva Uncle Master, long life and happiness. We hope you will sing and dance for us forever!" And he smiled and made funny faces at them! Then he said:

"Time to go to sleep!" And closed his doors. After Uncle Master's show, they were all tired and droopy, and Uncle Pas said it was time to go home. As they walked away, everyone was commenting on the following day. It was Monday market day, and one of Uncle Master's best students would be there. Everyone was going to try to make it in front of Uncle Master's studio; Uncle Master's best student, Benito, would be there. He was an eerily beautiful young man, everyone thought he looked just like Rodolfo Valentino, and he even came from the same town, in the south of Italy. When Benito sang and played the guitar, all the young women sighted, but when he put his guitar down and danced Luigi Boccherini's Fandango to Uncle Master's violin music, they positively swooned helplessly. They said that Benito's usual attire was black, tight pants, white open-necked shirt and pointy shoes with a little heel. Uncle Master had various musical implements hanging on his walls, and Benito was known to pick up a little black sombrero with white pom-poms hanging around the brim, and some Spanish castanets, and use them like a professional. He was sultry and quite good, and everyone loved his performances. Luna and Ivana excitedly asked Uncle Pas if they could come some day to market Monday and see Benito, and Uncle Pas assented smiling. Like Uncle Master said, it was time to go home. They walked past the eerily quiet cathedral, and walked down the Little Steps of San Bartholomew, with other tired but happy people. The Soft Water of San Bartholomew made a pleasant splashing noise in the semidarkness and finally they were at the truck. Everything was dark and quiet, the truck stood alone in the proximity of the bridge, and Anna sat in the back with the girls, one on each side, her arms hugging them as they drove home. The Tower of Rodoaldo had reminded Luna of Susanna, and she unknowingly was humming the tune to herself, when Anna and Ivana joined in. Luna didn't know that they had translated the song to Italian, but was pleasantly surprised that it was so. After a while, Uncle Pas and Aunt Esther joined in too, and they all drove home in the dark happily singing together:

"Oh, Susanna, oh don't you cry for me, I come from Alabama with a banjo on my knee!"

The following day, when they arrived at school, it was business as usual, with Gianna the teacher coming out to get them, and presiding over the class. There was much to do, and the teacher had to read a synopsis of the work that was accomplished while she was away, so she told all the students to read for an hour, while she brought herself up to speed. The students were sincerely happy to have their teacher back, and didn't question anything she told them to do; they knew they were lucky. The teacher had brought everyone comics from Milano; the funny Sor Pampurio for the children, the Tex Willer ranger comics for the boys, and the Black Corsair comics for the girls. Luana said that she hadn't seen a new Black Corsair since the year before:

"He's sooo romantic!" She whispered, holding her magazine to her chest. They all started to read their comics and got so involved in them; you could have heard a pin drop. After school, on their way out, the teacher told Luna and Ivana:

"Please tell everyone we'll have a meeting of the Wedding Consultants tomorrow after school, here at my house, I have things to show them." Luna and Ivana pedaled home as fast as they dared to impart the news, and Aunt Esther could hardly wait to run over to Amelia's and tell her. By the following day, after school, all the ladies were there, and while the husbands got together near the barn, to see what Uncle Saverio had brought from Milano, the ladies and the two girls walked into the teacher's inner sanctum, her good parlor. The rest of the house was a regular farmhouse, but the good parlor was something else. She had maroon leather couches and chairs, mahogany tables and armoires, and crystal everywhere, mixed in with beautiful carved figures of animals, flowers, plants and people. Loads and loads of sheer, dark green draperies threw an eerie light over everything. Everyone was astonished at the lifelike and whimsical beauty of the carved figures, shimmering dreamily in the misty, filtered light as Gianna said proudly:

"My husband made all of these over the years; my friend who owns a gallery in Milano, told me that Saverio's work is museum quality, and he's one of the few new artists in this genre to emerge in a long time. He said that he would love to do a showing of his work, He thinks we will all get rich with this, but all we're looking for, really, is for Saverio to realize how gifted he is, because he still doesn't believe it." Everyone asked how she could put together a place like this, where had she got the idea, and Gianna answered:

"When I was a child, one of the nuns used to take me on her knees, and tell me stories of the books she read. She told me a story once of a girl who lived in the forest with an old man. Her name was Rima, and she sang like a bird. The forest was presented like a shadowy and sacred cathedral, full of misty lights and gentle shadows. The forest was drowsy and soothing, and you could feel the peace there. This was a book by William Henry Hudson, the book was called 'Green Mansions' and it became one of my favorites after I grew up, and the story is not quite as pleasant as my nun made it sound, but the picture she implanted in my mind stayed with me all my life, and as soon as I finally had a home of my own, I wanted to recreate that feeling of mystical and soothing ambience that I had craved since childhood. Saverio didn't feel exactly at ease in this room, he told me that to him it was almost spectral, but on the way to Milano, we had a lot of time to talk and I told him about my dreams; he now understands and we sit here peacefully together when we are free. Saverio's figures make it even more like my dreamy green mansion, and I will not sell them; he better make some more for the showing, because I'm not parting with these!" Aunt Palma went up to her and embraced her, and Anna caressed her hair. The other ladies said:

"It's wonderful how you recreated the shadowy and misty forest world you were talking about. Maybe when there are no weddings we can get jobs decorating for rich ladies who have dreams they like to see realized! You and Saverio really are a talented couple, but of course you need normal people like us to keep you anchored and to do the menial run around; can't live on dreams alone, you know!" Everyone clapped their hands at this, and soon the ladies were down to the wedding business.

The teacher brought out a box and gently opened it. She then pulled out a white, gauzy bundle. When she unrolled it, everyone gasped; it was a veil so fine and beautiful, that it looked like it was made with spider webs. Here and there were white dots that accentuated the fragility and beauty of the material, and the edge was a series of the dots just strung together. Everyone could picture the fragile veil fluctuating against the sturdy, heavy satin of the wedding dress. Gianna said that the nuns had owned the veil for the longest time; it was an ancient gift to the monastery by a lady from France, and it was the best preserved piece of Chantilly lace that anyone had ever seen. It was a rare piece, without any of the usual designs, just gossamer veil with dots here and there like they were suspended in thin air. The gift had been given in love, and they did not want to make a profit by selling it. The nuns wanted Antonietta to use it in good health, and to thank her for all of the wonderful things that had sprung from this wedding. It was time the veil came out of its almost refrigerated state and joined life. Everyone was amazed at the nuns' knowledge in preserving things in their coldest basement, hermetically sealed in the perfect environment, to make them last longer. Gianna then put away the fragile veil and handed it to Anna for safekeeping.

After the veil was safely out of the way, she brought out a large, flat box. She opened it and showed them many pairs of gloves in different colors. They were made of lambskin, soft as butter, and colored in the most beautiful colors. These were for the wedding consultants, and everyone was to pick the color that went with their wedding outfits. Gianna already knew more or less what everyone was going to wear, and there was the right color for everyone. They all were pleased and grateful for the wonderful gift, and caressed the soft, elegant gloves with careful fingers. Next, Gianna brought out a cookbook for Aunt Esther, a soft shawl for Anna, and a box of fancy chocolates for Aunt Palma. Irma, Amelia and Angelina each received a beautiful pin for the lapel of their jackets. Everyone protested that she had done too much, but Gianna said that she had received big discounts from everywhere she shopped, as the owners of some of the best shops in Milano were orphans from the convent, and she knew them; it appeared that the nuns had instilled some very useful ideas into their minds, as everyone that the nuns had raised, was a very important and prosperous member of the Milano society. She then walked up to Luna and Ivana, and handed them a shiny small box each. They demurred, saying that she had already given them the wonderful comics, but Gianna said that that was for her students, this present was for her friends.   Aunt Esther encouraged them to take the present, and they did, thanking their teacher with shy smiles. Into the fancy shiny box were two little, beautiful bottles of perfume, Luna had a lily of the valley scent, and Ivana had a scent of violets. The stopper was beautiful, made of ornate glass, and it was shaped to put a very small drop of perfume on the wrists or earlobes. The girls were thrilled. The pleasant, dreamy, welcoming room was tough to leave, but it was time to go, the men were probably starting to get hungry by now. Gianna had served everyone a delicious cup of tea, with some wonderful Amaretti cookies, and the women were not that hungry, but dinner had to be prepared. They hugged and thanked the teacher again, and she was happy and flushed by everyone's pleasure and by being part of this circle of friends.

The next couple of days were uneventful, Anna guarding the precious veil, but no one approaching Antonietta with news about the wedding. Until Rodolfo came back from Roma, they were not going to chance angering Antonietta and pushing her to cancel everything; they understood that she was scared.   Everyone worked diligently on the wedding, lining up people to do the cooking, deciding on the menu, picking the colors for decorations of the great wedding room, and of course, recording all of it in pictures by having the little photographer they hired follow them around to all of the important meetings. The problem was they did not know where the wedding was to be held, and when they tried to discuss this with The Fool, he adamantly refused to get involved:

"That's what I'm paying you ladies big bucks for!" He said. Aunt Esther was ruminating something in her head, but she hadn't talked about it to anyone yet, and she was waiting for an opportune moment to counsel herself with her husband. If he thought that it was a good idea, she would ask about the possibility of the place she was thinking of, and then bring it up to the Fool's attention. Everything in due time! First everyone was waiting to see what Rodolfo and Antonietta did at the end of the month, when Rodolfo returned; it was not too far away! If he returned, that is! Antonietta was a shadow of herself, and The Fool and Assunta carried on as usual, but with a sinking feeling of dread in their stomachs all the time. Aunt Esther and the other wedding consultants were worried sick over the dress size; if Antonietta lost too much weight the dress would not fit right, and no one was willing to go and take Antonietta's measurements again! But Aunt Esther was confident that as soon as Rodolfo came back, Antonietta would start eating robustly again, and she would quickly gain back the few pounds she lost.

On Sunday, after church and chores, as they were sitting down to eat Sunday dinner, they heard strange cries, and then a frantic knocking at the front door. They all stood back, while Uncle Pas opened the door. Ada stumbled in, sobbing, and throwing herself in Aunt Esther's arms:

"Please!" She cried: "Stop him, stop my father, please!" They were all flabbergasted, but Uncle Pas grabbed Ada by the upper arms, shook her gently and demanded:

"What's wrong! What's your father doing?" Ada looked up at him with teary eyes and whispered:

"He's hurting my mom, she's bleeding; I'm afraid!" Uncle Pas shook her again:

"But what happened, what started it!" Ada sobbed:

"The dog ate the Sunday roast and papa' was beating it, my mom tried to stop him and he turned on her instead." Uncle Pas stood there for a few seconds, bewildered, and then let go of Ada's arms and sprinted out of the house. Aunt Esther quickly looked around the kitchen to see if there was something going on, but all the pots were off the stove, and the fire had died down. She then pulled her shawl off the hook near the door, and sprinted after Uncle Pas; the girls ran after her:

"Pasquale, stop!" She screamed, and she tried to catch up with him. The girls ran too, terrified, Ada sobbing all the way. A few minutes ago they were all ready to sit down to their wonderful Sunday dinner of gnocchi potato dumplings and wonderfully thin and crunchy chicken cutlets, and now they were all running and screaming like the devil was after them. They ran down the drive to the main road, turned right, and then ran right up to the next drive. The whole thing took maybe fifteen minutes, but to them it seemed like hours.

When they got to Ada's house, Uncle Pas crashed in, and heard screams and whimpers, and then located Ada's mother scrunched up in a corner between the hutch and the wall, and Ada's father leaning over her with a fist lifted. Uncle Pas said:

"Arturo, what's going on here!" The heavyset, burly man looked up and said:

"It's none of your business, Pasquale, go home!" And then he proceeded to lift his fist again. Uncle Pas took in the scene, the dog lying down near the fireplace, the woman screaming, Ada crying like her heart would break, and said, his voice shaking:

"I'm making it my business, Arturo! Stop or you'll be sorry!" In answer the man landed a sharp blow to the woman's shoulder. With a roar, Uncle Pas grabbed the much bigger man in the back of his neck, pulled him off the woman and started to punch the living daylights out of him. The man was on his back trying to cover his face with his hands, and blows were raining on him nonstop. Ada screamed:

"Please, don't hurt my daddy, he didn't mean it, he just got mad!" But Uncle Pas was like a machine, just hitting and hitting the man; by now all the girls were crying. At one point, his raised fist was stopped by a vice-like steel grip. He looked up and saw that Aunt Esther was holding him. She commanded in a loud, firm voice:

"That's enough, Pasquale! Stop it now!" Uncle Pas did so, looked up at her, then down on his fists, and he seemed to wake up. He got up, put his head down on Aunt Esther shoulder and he seemed to shake, and if they didn't know any better they would've thought he was sobbing, but they knew better. Then, after he calmed down, he looked his wife in the eyes and said:

"I'm sorry Esther; I just saw red and couldn't stop myself. Thank you for reminding me I'm still a human being! I wouldn't want to be like this animal here. I'm so sorry you and the girls had to see me this way!" She caressed his hair, and held him. Uncle Pas turned to the man and said:

"Arturo, you're lucky my good woman stopped me, or I would've killed you. But if I hear that you're hurting your family again, I'll come back and finish the job!" The man looked up at Uncle Pas with his blood stained eyes, and told him:

"If you kill me they will put you away for a long time!"

"They don't arrest people for killing an animal, Arturo!" Responded Uncle Pas. Then he went to the hutch and helped the woman up. She just stood there, crying, and Aunt Esther went to her and held her. The three girls were holding each other, and they went to Ada's mother and Aunt Esther. Aunt Esther said:

"I am so sorry, Ernestina, I knew he was not a nice person, but I didn't know about this; why didn't you tell me?" Ada's mother looked up with a bruised and bleeding face and said:

"I was ashamed, Esther, so incredibly ashamed, and I didn't want anyone to know or talk about us; I still love him, and sometimes he is nice to me, and says he won't hurt me again. I'm so happy when he's like that! But then something stupid happens and he starts all over again. What am I to do? Who would help me? My brothers know how he is, but if I go to them, they'll kill him, and I don't want to put this on my family. I'm so sorry Ada bothered you, but this time it was worse than usual." Aunt Esther said:

"Ernestina, do you remember when we were young girls, you, me and Adriana? We made a pact to help each other when one of us was in trouble? You should have come to me! I'm always here for you!" Ernestina said, with a sob:

"We all have our own life, and no one can help us. We couldn't help Adriana!" Aunt Esther said, sternly:

"That was during the war, Ernestina; we couldn't have helped her even if we knew what was happening. The marauding soldiers raped and killed all over this countryside, and we were lucky our husbands hid us away so well that those soldiers didn't even know we were there." Ernestina said, with tears in her eyes:

"Arturo built a double wall and hid me and Ada in there, and when they came he didn't give us away even though they shot him in the head; he almost died of that wound." She turned to look at him with such longing and sorrow in her eyes that Arturo lifted up his hand as if to touch her; he was crying too. Aunt Esther said:

"You need some rest, and you need some medical attention. You and Ada are going home with us. Tomorrow is another day and we will decide what to do then." She put her shawl over Ernestina's shoulders, and guided her to the door, followed by the girls. On the way out, Uncle Pas bend down and picked up the dog, bloody and broken, but obviously still alive. Arturo wailed:

"Don't leave me alone, Ernestina, I'm sorry! I won't do it again! Please!" Ernestina sobbed on the way out, and Ada ran back to Arturo and threw her arms around his neck:

"Don't worry, daddy, I'll be back! I still love you; I just don't want you to be mean anymore!" Then she ran back to Luna and Ivana's arms and followed the grownups back home. Luna held Ada and sobbed out of fear and hurt. She was proud of Uncle Pas for being so strong and for helping the defenseless, but she preferred her sweet and funny uncle to this powerful and angry man. She felt really bad for Ada, and she was so glad her own father was so gentle and nice, if a little distant. The old Luna was thinking:

"I thought I was in the back of beyond, over here, but this is actually nothing but a hotbed of intrigue, just another Peyton Place!" When they arrived home, Aunt Esther took Ernestina and Ada to the guest room across from her bedroom, and brought them a pitcher of warm water, towels and clean nightgowns and robes. Luna and Ivana went to their rooms to wash and change too. While Aunt Esther helped Ernestina and Ada get cleaned and dressed, Uncle was working in the kitchen. He refried the cold potato dumplings in the great cast iron pan; he put the cold chicken cutlets in the Dutch oven, covered it, and put it in the fireplace to heat up. It was not exactly cold outside yet, but the fireplace made everything cozy and comfortable and it was usually used for cooking and keeping water warm. When Uncle had walked in, he had put the dog on the table, on top of a blanket, and had examined it, washing and taking care of the lesions and bruises. The dog had some broken bones, and Uncle Pas had put a splint or two on the poor animal, then fed it some warm broth and put it on a folded blanket in front of the fireplace. The poor dog felt he was in good hands, that he was safe, and had fallen into a deep slumber. When everyone was washed, changed and calmed down, they walked into the kitchen to the set table, food warming on the fornacella and the fireplace, and Uncle Pas in his shirtsleeves and apron busy fixing a beautiful salad and fruit bowl. He was back to his usual wonderful self, and Ernestina whispered to Aunt Esther:

"You're so lucky!" Aunt Esther responded, without conceit:

"I know! I thank God every day for my husband." The three girls had run to the dog, and petted him and loved him. After Uncle Pas said that he would probably be alright, Ada turned to Ivana and said:

"Do you want my dog?" Ivana was flabbergasted:

"I wouldn't dream of taking your dog! He's yours; he's part of your family." Ada said, crestfallen:

"He'll always be afraid now and my papa' will remember what happened because of the dog and he will be upset every time he sees him. I know you'll love him and take good care of him, and I can come and see Roffo every time I want; please take him, at least for a while?"Ivana looked at Uncle Pas pleadingly and he said:

"I wouldn't think of sending that poor animal back, if it's ok with your mom, and Ada and her mom." Both Ivana and Luna ran to Uncle Pas and hugged him:

"You're the best, always!" They both exclaimed in unison, and Uncle Pas raised his hand to caress their hair, but saw the scrapes on his knuckles, and put his hand down again. Aunt Esther went to him too and said:

"Our maid has just prepared our late dinner, let's eat and be happy as much as we can!" They dug into the golden potato dumplings, and then had the tasty chicken cutlets, and a big plate of tender salad, the whole accompanied by thick slices of brown bread spread with soft yellow butter. Everyone was seated and relaxed, getting new hope in their hearts, and a determination to make things better and be happy. After dinner, the girls made a big pot of espresso, and Aunt Esther put out a platter of golden pound cake to have with the beautiful platter of fruit Uncle Pas had provided. While the girls cleaned up, the grownups sat around the table leisurely talking about safe subjects like the crops and the next pig slaughter, which was going to be Uncle Pas and Aunt Esther's Caramella. Luna had long since stopped feeling bad about the pig, and now was actually looking forward to the slaughter. The old Luna said to herself:

"After all, at home we eat pork chops like nothing, and where do you think they come from? The same place, of course! We just never have to see it. At home, everything is store-bought, nice and clean." After everything was cleaned up, the three girls sat in a corner and did their homework, while Ernestina said she wanted to retire early and make plans. Uncle Pas and Aunt Esther were sitting together, talking quietly to each other, and Roffo was snoring gently near the dying fireplace. Peace was back, and it didn't take much, just the will to be generous to each other, to be gentle and helpful to our fellow human beings and our companions the animals, and in general to be tolerant and forgiving of each other's mistakes; it meant loving one another no matter what. After all, everyone makes mistakes, and stupid little things simply don't matter much to anyone. Life was much better for everyone that way. Anger and hurtfulness didn't accomplish anything, didn't make anyone happy, not even the perpetrators; it just made life miserable for everyone, if only the mean and angry people could see that! And it doesn't have to be physical either. Mean and humiliating words can hurt just as much and leave everyone just as wounded.

The following morning, very early, Ernestina and Ada left. They declined breakfast and were in a hurry to go home. Uncle Pas didn't feel comfortable letting them show up at the house alone, not knowing what they were going to find, and insisted on going with them. When they reached the front door, it opened immediately, even before they knocked. Arturo was at the door, clean shaven, dressed in clean clothes and looking anxious. He looked relieved, and thanked Uncle Pas for walking them home. Uncle Pas said:

"I'll be keeping my eyes on you, Arturo, remember what I said!" And then turning to Ernestina and Ada he repeated: "If something bad is going to happen, or if he does anything crazy, just walk out of the house as you are and come straight to my house. Esther and I will take care of you! You have a home away from home from now on. Remember what I said, Arturo!" He repeated forcefully. Arturo looked away in shame, mumbling something about taking care of his own family. When Uncle Pas walked away, he heard Arturo welcoming the women home and saying that he had prepared breakfast, just in case they came back. That day in school, Ada told them everything was alright, and begged them not to tell anyone about what happened. Luna and Ivana said that they wouldn't think of it, that her secret was safe with them. They hugged each other. School was back to normal, everyone was busy with their work, and the teacher was as happy to be back as the kids were to have her back. Anna had sent The Fool a message to go see her, whenever he could, that she had something to show him. An hour later The Fool was standing outside of the Merolli's front door banging on it with his cane. Anna came out and shushed him, as Mario's father was not feeling well, and he was trying to rest, and took him to her part of the house. She had the top floor of the house, the attic, and she had turned the two rooms into a very attractive space indeed. One was of course her bedroom; the other was a sprawling, low ceilinged sitting room. She had a comfy couch, chairs, a large chest of drawers, a great, walk-in closet as long as the room with a slanted ceiling and louvered doors, shelves on the wall, a sewing machine in a corner, and even a beautiful old gramophone. She gave The Fool a seat on her best chair, and went to get something. The Fool was looking with interest at the gramophone, and Anna coming back with a bundle said:

"You like my Victrola, I see!" The Fool intoned:

"His Master's voice!" And Anna laughed. Up close he was quite handsome for an old fool, Anna felt a little flirty, being all alone with him in her quarters and all:

"Well, let's get on with it!" Said The Fool loudly, banging his cane on the floor impatiently, and Anna thought he was just a bossy old man, and put the bundle down on a table near him. She opened the bundle and the lovely, fine lace came to light. She explained what it was, and The Fool touched the beautiful artifact with gentle hands. He could see his daughter adorned by the precious veil, and asked:

"Why did the nuns give this to Antonietta?" Anna answered:

"They couldn't profit by selling it; it's not in the nature of this gift, so they wanted someone to use it for what it was meant for. The teacher has told them about Antonietta, and everything that is going on over here. She donated her advance money to the nuns for the orphanage. Antonietta caused a lot of good with her wedding, and they wanted to wish her well and send her into married life with this priceless gift they're giving her. They have given exact instructions to the teacher to pass on to Antonietta on how to preserve it for the future. For generations all the brides descending from your daughter will be adorned by this veil, people will come from all over to see it brought out of hibernation once again every time. Antonietta has a veil more beautiful and priceless than any princess." The Fool was obviously touched. He looked at the precious, diaphanous thing and said:

"You know that my daughter is my pride and joy, I love my daughter more than anyone can know, and the blessing of these holy women means a lot to me. After I've recuperated from the wedding expenses, around spring, I'll hire a car and driver and have the teacher take me to this convent and orphanage; I'm sure there is something I can do to help." Anna brought her hands together as if in prayer and said:

"This wedding is a blessing, and Antonietta is surely going to be blessed in her married life"

"From your lips to God's ears!" Said The Fool. Then they had a nice little cup of espresso with some of Anna's round wine cookies, The Fool being in a wonderful mellow mood by now, and they talked about this and that leisurely, until he got up and took his leave. Anna noticed how well he wore his Cioci, not self conscious or anything but rather with an innate elegance, and he WAS handsome, and she lamented the fact that today's young men shunned the costume which made a man look like a real man should. The Fool walked briskly home, and pulled Assunta outside with the excuse of showing her something in the garden, out of hearing of the moping Antonietta, and sat her down to tell her about the veil. Assunta cried when she heard, and remarked that maybe they would be still alive to see a granddaughter married in the veil. The Fool assured her that she would be for sure, unless she got run over by a truck, because she was much younger than him. Assunta grabbed his hands and said:

"I hope you're here with me to see it, it wouldn't mean much without you!" The Fool looked at his faithful, handsome, strong bride and said:

"Assunta, have I been a good husband to you? Have you been happy? Your family entrusted you to me, I hope I carried out my duty well!" Assunta looked at the man who took care of her this many years and asked:

"Was it just duty, Tarquinio, and nothing else?" He looked at her pensively:

"You know that I married you for the money your father paid me, I never lied to you about that, but I knew you were going to please me, and in fact you did, very much so. I am not a romantic man, I never was, but I wouldn't have married anyone I was averse to. You worked hard to make my life comfortable, you gave me wonderful children, and yet I have to admit that to this day my greatest pleasure has been coming home to you after dealing with my work. I wouldn't enjoy making great deals and reaping benefits if I couldn't come home to you and tell you about it. And, yes! I have to admit it; I could not get into my cold bed at night without you in it. I look forward to being with you, and if this is not love, our kind of love, I don't know what is." Assunta leaned on his shoulder in an unfamiliar gesture and said softly:

"Sometimes in my life I have been so lonely, I didn't know how you felt about me; I have cared for you since the first day I met you!" The Fool, in an uncharacteristic gesture, gently caressed her hair:

"We're still here, together, our children are well, Antonietta is going to marry that nice young man, and maybe it is time that I told you how I feel about you; I have cared for you from the first too, and I'm only sorry that I was not sensitive enough to ever tell you. Everyone said that you were plain, even you, but to me you've always been just perfect. I thought you knew!" Antonietta was looking at them from the kitchen window to see what in the garden was taking so long, and she saw the most amazing thing she had ever seen in her life; her parents were kissing each other briefly. She fell on the chair stunned:

"I don't know what the world is coming to, but this I'm never going to forget!"

The following day, after dinner, there was a knock on the door. The Fool was taking a nap, and Assunta had walked over to Remo's house to deliver some cookies. Antonietta opened the door and Rodolfo's father was there. With a sinking feeling she invited him in. She expected bad news from Roma, and just stood there waiting. The man walked in, handsome but a little stooped and with a great head of grey hair. He smiled at her and asked:

"How are you, daughter? I hope you don't mind me calling you that, you'll soon be my daughter when you marry my boy." Antonietta wished she was as sure as he was, but inclined her head in assent and then asked anxiously:

"Is it the job? Is everything alright with it? Or is it news from Roma?" While they were talking, she had guided him to the dining room table and was pouring him a small shot of whiskey. Almost everyone loved a bit of whiskey, but it was very hard to come by, in that time and place, but The Fool had his sources, and his whiskey was reserved only for family. Rodolfo's father enjoyed the bit of drink, and then putting the shot glass down said:

"Both!" Antonietta sat down in front of him and looked expectantly, with her hands folded on her lap. Rodolfo's father said:

"The job is going great, I just love it, patrolling the property is an amazing way to make a living, and I found out just how great a property it is besides the pit, you own a great spot, you should be very proud of it." Antonietta said, absentmindedly:

"Rodolfo and I own it!" The man assented with his head, and said:

"I just love my job, but I don't want any favoritism, I want to earn my pay like everybody else." Antonietta's ears pricked up:

"Why, what happened?" The man explained:

"I just received my pay today, and there was more money in it, you should know, since you're the accountant for the company; I don't want more money if I haven't earned it!" Antonietta laughed:

"Weren't you listening when you got hired? After the first month, depending on your performance, you either get fired or get a raise!" The man exhaled, visibly relieved, and Antonietta said, impatiently:

"Now, what about Roma?" Rodolfo's father said:

"Oh, I had forgotten what I came for; yesterday we received a letter from Rodolfo, he says that he will be home next weekend, and to come over and tell you. He'll arrive home late morning on Sunday, and he will visit you on late afternoon of that same day. I brought you the letter he wrote, I'm sure he wouldn't mind if you read it." And as he spoke he pulled out a letter from his pocket. Antonietta fairly snatched it out of his hand, poured him another small shot of the golden liquor and saying:

"Excuse me!" Went into her bedroom. She sat on the bed and with trembling hands opened the missive. At the beginning of the letter Rodolfo asked about his family, and hoped his father liked his job, he told his mother that he was sick of restaurant food, and couldn't wait to come home to her wonderful home cooking, then he said:

"Tell Antonietta that I'll be back Sunday next, and after some time with the family and a much needed rest, I'll be visiting her at her home. I'll be there after dinner, after my mother's cooking and some rest will hopefully make me look human again. Life in Roma and especially at the radio station is brutal and I can't wait to be back home to our peaceful existence. I hope that Antonietta doesn't think I look like an old man now, and run screaming when she sees me. I have missed her more than I can say. The girls here are fake, forward and empty headed. I think Antonietta is smart and wonderful and worth hundreds of them (But don't tell her or she'll get a big head). Just joking!" Then he just asked about their health, told them what time to pick him up in Pontecorvo, at the bus depot, and that he had a ton of dirty laundry. Antonietta smiled then folded the letter and walked back into the dining room. Rodolfo's father was nursing his little shot of whiskey and looked up. Obviously reluctant Antonietta handed the letter back, but he said:

"No, no! We read it! Keep it, if you please, we would be honored!" Antonietta guiltily took it back quick before he changed his mind. They talked a few moments longer about the job. Rodolfo's father had some suggestions for a piece of land on a hill, he said it would be wonderful to cultivate, as it was sunny, had a stream, and looked to be very fertile. Antonietta said that it sounded like a great suggestion, but she only dealt with the accounting of the business, the other part would be Rodolfo's responsibility, and if he didn't think he should go into farming, then maybe he could let his family use the land rather than let it go to waste. The man left, and just before he stepped outside bent down and kissed her forehead saying:

"Good bye, daughter!" Antonietta ran back into her room and reread the entire letter, and held it to her bosom, and smiled through some very moist eyes. The Fool had heard the whole from his bedroom, and decided not to intervene, let Antonietta keep the secret if she wanted, so when he came out of the bedroom, sometime later, he didn't say anything. Antonietta told him her future father-in-law had been there, and she explained about the raise in pay. The Fool said that some people just didn't have the smarts that it takes to be on top of money, or they never learned how to do it. Antonietta told him, in passing, that Rodolfo had written his family that he'd be back on Sunday, and be there to see her after dinner. The Fool did not comment; it wouldn't do to let Antonietta know how happy he was at the news, she was so contrary these days, she would probably take it the wrong way.

The following Sunday came awfully soon, and there was just enough time to run up to church for the earliest mass, at six am, and come home and prepare for the slaughter. Luna didn't feel it at first, thinking of poor Caramella, but as time went on, she got caught up in the excitement. Anna and her daughters were first to arrive, and Luana's mother dropped off a big basket of little sweet breads covered in white, lemony, crackling sugar, as they had another engagement. They had no time to even think of food that morning, so everyone welcomed the sight. The girls made a big pot of espresso, and they all ate the tender, lemony, crunchy little breads. After that, it was all work. The barn had been turned into a work station from top to bottom. All the animals had been moved elsewhere, and they erected a large pit made of bricks right outside the door. On top of the bricks there was a giant griddle, and that is where all the food would be cooked. Of course, Aunt Esther's brick oven was right near there, and it was already going, wood burning in it slowly. Long tables and chairs were moved in, and pots and pans brought from the attic and the kitchen. There were boxes full of knives and great big scissors, and terracotta bowls and cannatas full of spring water were lined up on shelves. Luna looked askance at Caramella's pig pen, but she was conspicuous by her absence. She whispered anxiously to Ivana:

"Will Caramella cry a lot when they kill her?" Ivana looked at her like she had sprouted horns:

"You think that my father would hurt a poor animal like that?" Luna said, almost about to cry:

"I don't know! I've never been to one of these things!" Ivana said, mollified:

"They gave her a great big dose of poppies in her food this morning, she's asleep and dreaming, she'll never know what's going to happen; she's luckier than some people this way! My Papa' will do it quickly, don't you worry!" Luna was relieved, and stopped looking at the pig pen. She saw a group of men, Mario amongst them, go into the shed and didn't pay any attention to them. She realized later what happened in the shed, when butchered meat started coming from the shed to the barn. Remigio, the boy who helped Great Uncle Biagio, was there, and he managed to run up once in a while and spend some time with the giggling girls. Some young women from a nearby farm came, and Uncle Saverio came and said Gianna would be by later. The Fool dropped in and he was soon in his shirtsleeves working harder than anyone. He was in a wonderful mood, and said Assunta stayed home because later that day Rodolfo, who had come from Roma that morning, would be by to see Antonietta, and someone should be there. People asked, as everybody wondered, if there was still going to be a wedding and he smiled and nodded, and ran around doing this and that like a young man. At one point, a group of people came to the door of the barn; it was Ada and behind her were her parents, Arturo and Ernestina. Ada looked at Uncle Pas and said:

"We wanted to come and help! Is it alright?" Uncle Pas looked at her parents, standing there quietly, Arturo with his hat in his hands and looking down. Aunt Esther looked at Uncle Pas with trepidation, and he assented lightly with his head. Aunt Esther extended her arms to Ernestina and gave Arturo a hand:

"Come in, come in! There is a lot of work and the more the merrier. We have some lovely lemon rolls Luana's mother made. Sit down and have some with espresso before we start working." The continuously going coffee pot was put on a small table and some chairs pushed in front of it, and everyone stopped what they were doing and crowded around the table to talk to their neighbors.   It was not very often that Ernestina and Arturo showed up at these things, and they were all excited; Arturo was a bona fide butcher, he was a butcher in the army, and worked part time at the Pezzella butcher shop in town. This was going to be a feast, and the men were certainly going to watch Arturo to learn what they could. Ada looked for Luna and Ivana, and grabbing a fat lemon roll ran to them. They embraced and skipped away to talk excitedly about what was going to happen. Roffo the dog had been underfoot the whole time, running after chickens, begging for tidbits and generally frolicking around. After Ada and her family came, the dog had hidden in a corner outside the barn, trembling and whining. Before he sat down to eat, Arturo went outside to wash his hands. Roffo whined louder, then took a short run and threw himself at Arturo's legs. Arturo looked down and his eyes widened:

"Roffo, how are you, boy?" And he bent down to pat the dog on the back. Roffo whined and put his head down on Arturo's foot. Arturo went down on his knee, and held the dog's head to himself for a few seconds:

"I'm so sorry, boy! I don't know what came over me. I was sick. I still am, but I'm working on it! Soon, maybe soon you can come home again! Good dog! Good dog!" Roffo looked up, liquid brown eyes full of love, and then ran off again to try, in vain, to catch a large hen that was squawking and rasping in the courtyard. Arturo went back to the breakfast table, his heart feeling light as a feather and wondering why he never knew how his dog's love affected him.   After a while, a young man who was courting one of the girls from the nearby farm ran in, and was talking angrily to some of the men. Someone called Uncle Pas; they said he should hear this. The young man lived much farther down towards the town of San Giovanni Incarico, and told them that his neighbor Marcello was also butchering his pig this day, but he had started very early. Since a few hours now, his pig had been screaming, and when the young man went to investigate he was told that Marcello had heard that if you kill your pig slowly, the meat would be more tender and plentiful. The young man tried to argue about it, but he was shoved away and told:

"The pig is mine and I'll kill it as I please!" Marcello was a huge bully, and all the young man could do was leave. All the men were flabbergasted and angry, and Uncle Pas was looking red and angry. Aunt Esther took a step towards him and said:

"Let it go, Pasquale, there is nothing you can do!" Uncle Pas looked stubborn and said:

"I'm not letting it go, and there is something I can do." He bent down and picked up a long, sharp, lethal looking knife. Everyone gasped, and Aunt Esther said:

"What are you going to do Pasquale?" He responded:

"Don't worry, everyone, it'll be alright." Someone said:

"He's a crazy guy; if you fight with him you'll end up scorned and beat up!"

"I don't want to fight or argue with him, I just want to help the pig stop suffering." Aunt Esther looked frantic; she was hanging on Uncle Pas' sleeve and wouldn't let him go. Uncle Pas looked anguished, but he wanted to be free to go. Luna walked up to Aunt Esther and Uncle Pas and whispered:

"I learned something in school last year. A man named Abraham Lincoln said that to sin by silence when they should protest, makes cowards of men." Uncle Pas looked at her and said:

"Later I will ask you more about this Abraham Lincoln!" Then he asked the young man to drive him to Marcello's farm, and motioned Arturo to go with him. Aunt Esther was looking at her bewildered:

"Who are you, Luna? And how do you know such things?" She hugged Aunt Esther and whispered to her:

"I'm just a girl who loves you both, and I know that Uncle Pas is not a coward." Aunt Esther looked down at her and said:

"Thank you for making me understand; Pasquale would have stayed if I asked him to, in my fear, but he wouldn't have liked it." And with that she hugged her tight and she looked at the men as they left in a billow of smoke, with screeching tires. Everyone was worried, Aunt Esther more so than anyone, but she valiantly said:

"Pasquale knows what he's doing, and he has Arturo with him, everything will be alright." Ernestina looked proud and said:

"Arturo would do anything for Pasquale, they'll be fine." Everyone acted and looked nonchalant, but they were all worried, and there was a pall over the festivities. Now that Arturo was away, Aunt Esther pulled Ernestina to the side and asked her:

"How is it going, with Arturo?" Ernestina looked her straight in the eye:

"I won't lie to you, Esther, things could be better, sometimes he's almost ready to explode again, but he checks himself; he's trying real hard. I think that with our help he's going to change, a little bit at the time." Aunt Esther hugged her and said:

"If he does revert, come over and Pasquale will make sure he's not going to hurt you again!"

"I'm not going to call, unless something really bad happens. I know what you think of me, I'm just like Roffo, a faithful old dog with no pride and no self respect, but I love him, God help me, I love him!" Aunt Esther just held her for a while and caressed her hair.

After an excruciating hour, the truck was heard to come back. Everyone stood still, and Uncle Pas came in and threw the bloody knife in a large water bowl. Everyone gasped again, but Uncle Pas said:

"Pig blood." Everyone exhaled in relief, and then they all clustered around the young man, Uncle Pas and Arturo. The young man told everyone the story. The girls, who had waited, scared, at the end of the driveway, ran in and stood with everyone else to hear. When they arrived at Marcello's farm, the pig was still squealing in pain, and Uncle Pas ran into the shed followed by Arturo and the young man. Marcello wanted to know why they were there, and when he found out he told Uncle Pas the same thing he told the young man:

"The pig is mine, and I'll kill it as I please." A couple of women in the background recoiled at that and tried to hide. Without another word, Uncle Pas walked over to the pig, as he swiftly pulled out the knife from his waistband, and with one lightning movement slashed his throat. The animal fell silent, and Uncle Pas brandishing the knife said:

"Arturo here is a butcher and we came to help you butcher your pig; any objections?" Marcello backed away slowly, and shook his head. Uncle Pas handed the knife to Arturo, and with help from the young man Arturo proceeded to slash the pig in two, and then cut out the ham parts, and soon there was a bunch of well butchered pig on the table nearby. Uncle Pas saluted Marcello, who stood worriedly away from him, and said:

"Happy to be of service, Marcello. If I hear that you need me again, Arturo and I will be here lickety split, don't you worry!" And with that he tipped his cap at Marcello and the women and left, followed by the other two men. After they were finished telling the story, everyone shook the men's hands, and recounted the story to each other, adding small enrichments in the retelling. Ernestina proudly hung onto Arturo's arm, Ada ran to her father and hung on his other arm, and Arturo said:

"My women need me, I better wash my hands!" And to everyone's acclamations he swaggered over to a large bowl of water and a piece of soap, followed by his wife's and daughter's adoring looks. Uncle Pas, unseen, walked outside, and stood looking up at the sky. He was still heaving and upset, and Luna followed him and quietly said:

"Uncle Pas? Are you alright?" He turned to her and said:

"Yes, little ......niece, I'm fine! Don't worry about me!" Luna hugged him briefly and said:

"Uncle, I was so worried! I didn't want you to be hurt or to fight!" Uncle said:

"I didn't want to fight either, little one, but sometimes you have to. I've learned in life that in the long run it's always good to take the high road in all things human. Nonetheless, sometimes you have to defend yourself." Luna said, seriously:

"I'm glad you feel that way, and I'm also glad you can defend yourself when you have to. I'm glad you're a good person and always try to help others." Uncle Pas looked at her searchingly and said:

"Who is this man Abraham Lincoln?" Luna responded:

"A great American President; he's the one who abolished slavery in America." Uncle Pas murmured:

"I think I'm going to read up on this Abraham Lincoln; I'm sure I'm going to like him!" They went back inside and joined the merriment and the new Luna was happy, while the old Luna was thinking:

"I thought this place was quiet and dull, boring even, but at least I thought it was safe. Now it's turning out to be just like the Wild West, and you have to fight for what you want, and nothing seems really safe. I think going back home is going to be not so bad."

The work proceeded in great camaraderie, and Anna ran the whole operation with steely determination. All the women were busy at the tables cutting, chopping, seasoning and cooking. Sometimes late that afternoon, aunt Palma made an appearance. She examined the work in progress, deemed it adequate, then sat on a little table to the side and was served the best morsels of what had been made by the women so far. She motioned the three girls to join her, and they all partook of the feast while Aunt Palma supervised the proceedings. Ada snatched some goodies and ran out looking for Remigio; he should taste some of the stuff just like they were. Aunt Palma sat like a queen and she offered everyone first criticisms and reprimands, then encouragement; she was supremely happy. Everyone else was also ecstatic that Aunt Palma condescended to come over and direct the proceedings. The younger women gleaning nuggets of knowledge from her long life experiences, and her canny shortcuts, and Anna, who was otherwise the supreme commander over the younger women, was more than glad to relinquish the reins to the much older woman; it made her feel young to be supervised and reprimanded and she cheerfully acquiesced. From her vantage point, Aunt Palma was observing a chubby young woman with black hair and dark eyes who was oiling Aunt Esther's great cast iron frying pan. Someone said:

"Cook it fast, Candida, you know what they say; pork meat, warm up and eat!" She put the pan on the fire, and was just about to dump a large bowl of bits of pork meat into it, when Aunt Palma hollered:

"You there, Candida, stop that and come here." The girl dropped everything and ran over. The three girls, startled by Aunt Palma's hollering, stopped eating and watched curiously. Aunt Palma grabbed the girl by her hand and said:

"Listen to me, girl, 'cause I'm only going to say this once: First of all, if you don't cook the pork meat completely, you're gonna get sick, I've learned this in my long life, I don't know why it happens but it's true, secondly If you put the pork meat in the cold pan, by the time everything gets hot the pan will be full of water. Even if you let it all dry out on the fire, the meat is going to be dry and tasteless. You need to dump the meat in a very hot pan and quickly mix it well to sear it so that the juice stays inside. What did you put on the meat?" Candida explained, wide eyed:

"Oil and salt so far, I need to add anise seeds." Aunt Palma approved. Patting the girl's arm she said:

"Good girl, don't put anise seeds in it until the meat is almost ready, that way the seeds won't burn giving out a bitter taste. Come to me when you want to learn how to cook something and I'll teach you; you'll be a great cook eventually." Candida straightened up, tightened the strings of her apron and went back to the frying pan to do what Aunt Palma said. She decided right then and there to go see Aunt Palma regularly to learn how to cook and thus present her family the best food anyone had ever had. Aunt Palma was renowned for some of the things she made. After all, in her ninety years plus, she must have learned every trick in the book, and her tips would be invaluable. Candida found her calling, and she decided to be the best cook and housekeeper that she could be, and when it was universally known how good she was, with her modestly admitting that Aunt Palma taught her everything she knew, it shouldn't be too hard to snatch herself a fine, handsome husband. Smiling and humming under her breath, Candida did exactly as she was told, and everyone raved about the meat when they ate it. At the end of the day, all the tables were full of fragrant preserved pork; nothing went to waste, and Caramella really proved to be hard and sweet like her name said. There were great bowls of Italian sausage, great bowls of large soppressata (salami like sausage), bowls of pork skin sausage to be used with bean dishes, bowls of liver sausage to be eaten in the winter fried with vinegar peppers, and best of all, bowls of dripping hot blood sausage. This was to Luna the greatest revelation; the large sausages were made of pork blood mixed with cinnamon, sugar, pine nuts, raisins and bits of pork fat, cooked like pudding, and stuffed into large sausage casings. Then the sausages were boiled in water, and when they cooled, hung to dry. Some of it had been sliced and fried in hot oil, to be eaten today, and Luna had been given a morsel by Aunt Esther. It was the best thing she ever ate! There were prosciutto hams piled in wooden barrels and covered in salt, and bacon slabs rolled in salt and pepper to be hung to dry, and balloon like casings full of rendered pork fat, which was slowly turning white and becoming lard. The leftovers from the lard were the crunchy nuggets of pork fat, squeezed until all the fat was out and used to make big batches of fat bread, and of course the pork feet and ears together with the head; they would be used to make headcheese, which was no cheese at all, but delicious meat in gelatin. There was even a great bowl full of all the bones left over, which had been boiled in a great pan of water. Later all of the bits of meat would be picked off the bones and the following day there would be a savory and wonderful pork pie on the table. Everything had been cleaned out; Caramella was laid out on one of the huge tables, all fragrant and delicious, and the other tables were being prepared for the feast. Uncle Pas had grilled small bundles of pork liver wrapped in its own membrane, with bunches of fresh bay leaves inside, and Ernestina had made her famous Pasta and Beans with squares of pork rinds in the sauce. Red peppers cured in vinegar were sliced and fried mixed with liver sausage, great bowls of chopped pork meat fried with anise seeds were passed around and a great salad of the last of the yearly tomatoes mixed with cucumbers, boiled potatoes and onions were sprinkled with green and tick extra virgin olive oil. Loaves of brown, golden and flat bread were piled in the center of the tables, the result of Angelina's labors, and red wine, spring water with sliced lemons and fruited white wine were served in abundance. There was a platter of golden brown slices, dipped in egg, rolled in breadcrumbs and pan fried. Everyone was taking a small slice, carefully, and when the platter arrived at the girls, they each took a small slice; there was not so much of this, and everyone got a taste. Luna took a small slice, cut off a little piece with her fork and put it in her mouth. The food was white, creamy and delicious. Luna turned to Ivana and asked:

"What is this?" Ivana said:

"Caramella's brains!" Luna stopped chewing and stared at her. Ivana remarked: "You never had brains?" Luna shook her head silently. Ivana said: "They say that if you eat brains, you'll become really smart! That's why they made such small slices, so everyone can have some. If you don't want yours I'll take it!" At that, Luna went back to chewing and ate all the rest with relish.

The Fool, who had worked indefatigably, said:

"If I only had my walking cheese, this feast would be complete!" Everyone laughed at that, Luna cringed, and they all dug in with the joy of friends, good food, camaraderie, and a job well done. Uncle Saverio looked at Marcello and said:

"In two weeks it will be my turn to slaughter, I would be obliged if you can join us. You did a wonderful job here, and Gianna and I would love to have such professionally cut pork; the hams are just perfect, the bacon is thin and pink, and the casings came out unbroken. I understand that you don't usually join your neighbors for this, but I'm willing to pay you." Marcello proudly said:

"I know I speak for my family when I say we would be pleased to accept your hospitality, and there's no need to pay; friends help friends just for the pleasure of it." Uncle Saverio and Marcello shook hands, and Aunt Esther gently touched Ernestina's arm when she saw her surreptitiously wipe her eyes, and Ernestina smiled at her. Towards the end of the day, Gianna had made an appearance. She was finally able to leave the house as her mother-in-law, great Aunt Marianna, went to watch the children for a while. Everyone always made it a point not to bring small children to the pig slaughter, until they were old enough to understand the slaughter, and stay out of the way of knives and scissors. If the slaughter was at their house, they were sent to a relative for the day. Gianna had a surprise, a great big box full of their favorite cassatine for the grand finale, and big, fragrant coffee pots were being passed around together with Irma's yellow, cream filled cake. This was a feast in honor of Caramella; Caramella would be looking down from the rafters in the kitchen, while she provided for her family all winter long, and she would be remembered fondly by everyone.

Time was going by steadily, the wedding was not as distant as everyone had thought, and there was no appropriate venue for it yet. Aunt Esther had had a talk with Uncle Pas about it, and a meeting was arranged at Angelina's house. Angelina had lived in Roma with her husband for many years, but when first one sister and then another settled on a farm, in Pontecorvo, she decided to move there too. Now even her mother lived there! For one thing, it would be wonderful to be near family, but for another thing, living on a farm would give her and her family a little prosperity. Farm work was hard, but Angelina's husband was a small contractor, and jobs were few and far between, and they were hard put to make money from one job last until the next one, and life in Roma was not especially reasonable. Everything was more expensive than everywhere else, and the bigger paycheck did not compensate for the bigger living expenses. Her husband, Carlo, had to store his trucks and implements out of town, and a lot of times his things were stolen while he wasn't there. They had two children, a fifteen-year-old boy, Roberto, and a ten-year-old girl, Mariella. The children didn't like to be cooped up in the apartment, and there was no time to take them to the parks. Roberto was starting to get into trouble with some bad friends of his, and so eventually Carlo and Angelina decided to buy a farm in Pontecorvo; they had been happy ever since, and Roberto was working alongside his father every day. The farm was very old and abandoned when they bought it, and it had a huge mortgage, but it was Paradise to them, so when the wedding came about it was decided that the money was going to be put towards the mortgage, thus ensuring that the land was theirs and their children's after that.

Even if sometimes there was no money for groceries, on a farm you could rustle up something for supper no matter what! Right after they moved, Angelina had to make do with practically nothing, and her great culinary skills were what saved them from starvation. She could get a little bundle of beef bones at the butcher's for fifty liras and create a whole meal. A small scoop of flour and some water would make a nice bunch of homemade noodles, and the bones would make a tasty soup when boiled for a couple of hours in water, a tomato, a bit of celery and some onion skin; the onion would be saved for something else. The bones usually had a nice bunch of marrow in them, and this would be mashed in the soup. Sometimes Bernardo Pezzella, the butcher, would leave big chunks of meat hanging on the bones. He had a big family and he understood, and then the soup would have nice chunks of meat in it too, and that would be the best. At other times she would scour the farm for dandelions, which were delicious boiled and stir fried in a drop of oil with some garlic, or chopped in a pot of polenta, or added to a minestrone vegetable soup. Other times, if she was lucky, she would find wild asparagus or wild rapini. Bread was little more than bran stuck together with only a little flour, and there was very little meat, unless Carlo found a rabbit or a wild hen. Sometimes, they found eggs from the wild hens, and that was a veritable feast. Not too long after they moved to the farm, Carlo found an overgrown, abandoned potato field, and when he dug it out, he found potatoes still in the ground. They were small and a little ruined, but he managed to fill two large burlap bags. They ate like kings for weeks on those potatoes; she even made potato bread with them. Right next to the house, they found a field of wild Arugula, and she laughed when she remembered that in Roma she had to buy small bunches of it for a lot of money, and now they had as much as they wanted for free. Now she could serve her family big bowls of the spicy greens, drizzled with a few drops of oil and lots of vinegar, accompanied by big chunks of her brown bread. Her sisters helped whenever they could, and Carlo repaid them by doing construction on their farms whenever he could, but mostly everyone was strapped, the effects of the war still felt, even after these many years. But it was still easier to survive on a farm then it was in the postwar cities and towns.

After the first six months, of course, things got better. Carlo was still clearing fields to plant wheat, and he had managed to save most of the old, abandoned olive trees they found on the property. In a couple of years there would be plenty of flour and olive oil. Angelina planted a beautiful garden on a patch of land Carlo cleared out previously, right next to the house and with great exposure to full sunlight. She planted a lot of vegetables, right next to the beautiful arugula, and everything came up beautifully. She felt like the richest woman on earth when she could serve her family rich meals prepared with the fruits of her labors. In the fall, helped by her mother, she canned and dried so much stuff, that it was going to be a wonderful winter, snug in her home, and with all of God's gifts she had in her pantry. They were lucky, the farm had a beautiful orchard and trees of walnuts, figs, plums, apples, peaches and almonds; they never wanted for warm apple or peach pies, even in the winter, when she used her dried apples and peaches, fresh fruits and dried ones, and even beautiful prunes, when there was a need of them. After they moved into the farm, and they had nothing, her mother had given them two large crocks, one full of sugar and one full of salt; these were riches behind belief, as these items were very expensive and you could not make them yourself. And her sisters got together and gave them a milking cow, Carolina; Carolina had practically saved their lives. Now there was beautiful cheese in her pantry, fresh ricotta and curds and whey for breakfast, nice yellow pastry cream for dessert and clotted cream to enrich her pies and cakes; yes, you could live very well on a farm, even when there was no money coming in!

When they arrived at Angelina's farm, one day after school, everyone was seated in a comfortable, if a little shabby, parlor and the men were there too, as this meeting included them. Even Aunt Palma had been invited, for good luck and benediction; Aunt Nannina drove her over. Carlo and Roberto were still out on the farm, but they were expected soon. Everyone was curious, and Aunt Esther explained the decision since it was her idea, properly sanctioned by Uncle Pas:

"We need a place big enough to hold all of the people invited to this wedding, and also a kitchen nearby, as some of the food cannot be made beforehand, and we have to have the place for a few days to have time to decorate and to bring all of the tables and chairs etc. We also need it to be close by, since some of the people have no way to travel some distances. From the church to the reception, it's going to be a mad scramble, and it will not look graceful or aristocratic, putting a pall on all we're trying to do. We thought of the Hotel in town, but they want too much money, and they expect to furnish the food also, which wouldn't do, as they are not notorious for their food; a lot of people wouldn't like their fancy ladida' food, anyways, they want the food they're accustomed to." At this point, all the women broke into talk, and questions and suggestions were being bandied about, while the men waited quietly to know what their part in all of this would be. While they were talking, Carlo and Roberto walked in. Aunt Palma spotted them first, and whistled for all of them to stop talking. Luna had never met them, neither had Ivana. Luna looked at the short, muscled man with very black hair and blue cerulean eyes, and felt a shock go through her. He looked so familiar, more than familiar, that Luna blinked and tried to think where she must have seen him. He started talking, addressing everyone and thanking them for visiting his humble home, and all Luna could think was:

"I have heard this man tell children stories, I know him! But how could I? Maybe it's true, everyone has a doppelganger! Help me Balthazar! I'm so confused, and I feel like I'm drowning!" She looked at Ivana for comfort, but Ivana was staring at Roberto with her mouth open, almost drooling, like she had had a shock. No one was looking at the girls, except Anna, and she had a huge smile on her face, she looked almost like she was going to rub her hands together in glee. She cackled under her breath:

"Now I know that Fate cannot be stopped. Go to it, my girl, do your best, life awaits you!" At that very moment, Luna heard inside of her head:

"Just so, Luna, just so! Everyone has a doppelganger, or maybe something else!" And with this he was gone, leaving Luna to think how she could get hold of him and if he could be hurt, like a regular human being. Roberto was a young copy of his father, and very handsome. He looked older than Luna and Ivana, maybe sixteen or so. They had never seen him before, so he must be older than they were if he didn't have to go to school. Anna kept looking at Ivana and Roberto in turn, whispering to herself:

"Yes! Yes!" Nannina turned to her and said:

"What are you so exultant about, Anna?" Anna replied:

"That's for me to know and for you to find out!" Nannina sniffed:

"Oh, never mind! I'm sure that whatever it is it can't be anything that would interest me!" And she turned back to Aunt Palma. Luna pulled at Ivana's sleeve:

"What's the matter with you? What are you staring at?" Ivana said, without looking at her:

"Did you see him? Isn't he gorgeous? I think I'm in love!" Luna hadn't paid much attention to Roberto, but she looked at him. He was really a good looking boy, and he looked a lot like his father, but nothing to warrant Ivana's stupor. Every time there was a barn raising, a pig slaughter or something else, Angelina had attended with her mother and sisters. Carlo was new to these parts, and didn't really know anyone. He was also working day and night trying to make the farm profitable, as construction work over here was few and far between. There were bigger, better known companies around here, with more than one man and a boy to do the work, and word of mouth was their only advertisement; when you had no work, no one's mouth talked about you. This was the first time that Carlo and Roberto had met all of the neighbors.

After everyone was introduced, the discussion started again. Carlo was brought up to speed, and he was also very interested, the deposit money had already been fed to the voracious mortgage, and if all went well, the rest of the money would make it a manageable little tiger rather than the dragon it had been. Aunt Esther was getting lost in the morass of technical questions, and looked to Uncle Pas for help. He took over the explanations. The wedding would be attended by people close and far, there would be lots of cars and carts, to reach another place for the big celebration would require a fancy car for the bride and groom and family, there was a big expense already. As everyone knew, the Befana would come in and give the local children presents, but the local children were mostly poor, and their parents couldn't take them anywhere too far. The food would have to be shuffled from one place to another, and that would be expensive and disruptive. Having the wedding in town was not an option, because the locals who were not invited to the reception wanted to stand outside of the little SS Cosmo and Damiano's church to gaze at the bride and groom, and they shouldn't be deprived of it. Also, The Fool had said that the leftover food would be donated to any neighbors who wanted it, and in town no one would show up to take it, they would have too much pride for that; the people around here could certainly use it, though, and they would certainly take it! But there was nothing large enough and fancy enough in the vicinity that they could use for this reception. So, if Mohammed couldn't go to the mountain, the mountain would have to go to Mohammed! If they couldn't go to a beautiful, fancy, worthy-of this-wedding pavilion, the pavilion would have to go to them. Everyone erupted into exclamations, proclamations and questions. Uncle Pas was the man of the moment, and he was milking it just a little bit! They all screamed:

"Get on with it, Pasquale! Let's have it! What are you proposing?" Game over, Uncle Pas said succinctly:

"We'll build our own pavilion right in the back of the little church of SS Cosmo and Damiano. We will do the work ourselves for free. After the wedding the pavilion will be donated to the church to rent for occasions, and the suppliers will sell the materials for half the price if their name would be put on the dedication plaque. The name of the company, who does the work, will be on the plaque also, and that of all the men who worked with it. This is good advertisement and it will, hopefully, generate more work. There is a lot of reconstruction to be done yet, and there is work for everyone. I'm sure we can all use the extra money. The Fool will spend the same amount, more or less, for this pavilion than if he went to have the reception in town; he will donate the pavilion to the church in the name of the bride and groom, of course! I've talked to the Monsignor in charge of the church, and he told me that the little priests had been praying to God for some help, as times are tough and people can't give much, and they needed to make some extra revenue somehow; it seems that we're the answer to their prayers!" Everyone was stunned. Anna stood up, and as almost the oldest in the group, declared:

"God be praised, this wedding is the gift that keeps on giving, and the more everyone gives, the more they get!" After everyone was a little calmer, Carlo stood up and said:

"I would be honored if you let me be the contractor, in fact, the last job I did while in Roma, and the one that gave the money for a down payment on the farm, was one such pavilion." Everyone was very eager to know more, so he explained:

"It was a pavilion for some rich people who owned a villa on the Appian Way, far from Roma proper. They wanted to have guests all the time, but it made for a big mess in the house, and their servants were kept constantly busy, so they got the idea from an English friend of theirs. Since they were in a hurry to start, they couldn't wait for one of the big contractors, so they called me. In Roma, I had five men working for me, but when we bought the farm I had to let them go. This pavilion was rectangular, quite long, and could accommodate a great number of guests. They built bedrooms in the back for them, but we don't need those here. On one end of the pavilion was a fully finished kitchen, and on the other end, get this! There was a beautiful, finely appointed bathroom." Everyone gasped:

"A bathroom?" They said: "How can we put a bathroom up there when there is no plumbing?" Carlo laughed:

"Just like you would if you put a bathroom on your farm; with a cesspool, a large one!" They all broke into talk at the same time. This was getting bigger by the minute, would The Fool go for it?! Many people would want to have their wedding there, their christenings, their communions! The church stood to make some good money and would probably attract people from as far away as the Province of Frosinone. And it might come in handy to use the locals for all kinds of things; The Wedding Consultants would certainly come in handy! Luna was looking from one person to the other. These people's resourcefulness and willingness to get things done amazed her, their gusto for life was incredible, and Carlo was fast becoming her favorite person (After Uncle Pas, of course)! At home, there were too many worries about 'permission', 'lawsuits', and other excuses, so nothing ever got done outside of a courtroom. Unlike here, no one ever just went and did things themselves, and those who tried were looked down upon or got into trouble. Luna turned to Ivana to talk to her, but Ivana couldn't do anything; she just stared at Roberto, and stayed well away from him, almost as if she was afraid. Everyone was so full of hope and joy (another change from home), that they sent Mario to get The Fool, because no one was willing to wait any time at all to find out if he would go for it.

Angelina, helped by Anna and her little daughter Mariella, started to set up cups and saucers for the coffee, and platters to serve some of Anna's brown anise cookies and various cakes and biscotti brought by the other women. Gianna had brought a big box of cannoli; they looked scrumptious, and were everyone's favorite, after the cassatine. Everyone was amazed at how she made so many so fast. Gianna said that she had made the shells the day before, this very morning she had made some fresh ricotta, and just before she came, she added sugar, bits of chocolate and candied fruit to the ricotta and then spooned it quickly into the shells. Everyone said that after the wedding craziness was over, they should really get together and talk about the pastry classes. Angelina had baked some juicy, golden apple and peach pies, they also were delicious, Gianna asked what she put in her peach pies that looked like the peaches were covered in custard. Angelina said she would give her the recipe later. There were tubs of clotted cream to put on pies and to dump in the espresso. For the men, who didn't really go for the sweets much (except for Uncle Pas) she had made Swiss chard pies. Before they started on the sweets, Luna was handed a golden brown fat little pie, in the shape of a turnover, studded with anise seeds and stuffed with Swiss chard, raisins and pine nuts, the whole flavored by a touch of olive oil and sea salt. Luna couldn't believe how everything went so well together, and looked to Ivana to see if she was eating hers:

"Are you going to eat that?" She asked, but Ivana, without even looking at her, got up and went to offer it to Roberto shyly. Roberto, who had wolfed down two of them already, lifted his hand and took it, saying:

"What about you? Aren't you hungry?" Ivana shook her head:

"No, I'm going to have some cake."

"You're the Sargentos' daughter, aren't you? What's you name." Ivana whispered shyly:

"Ivana!" Roberto said:

"Nice name! Thanks for the pie!" And walked away towards the guys, while swallowing the pie in two bites. Ivana stood there looking at him walk away with (what looked like to Luna) a stupid smile on her face. She didn't know what came over Ivana, and she didn't care for it, but there was nothing she could do, so she went in search of coffee and cake. Her eyes kept going back to Carlo, and she drank in everything he was saying. Eventually, The Fool came back with Mario, and he listened to the plan with a serious expression. Anna felt she should say something, and looking around she said:

"This place we are going to build needs a name, and I think it should be called the Lucci Pavilion, since it's being built for Antonietta Lucci's wedding, and it will be donated to the church by Tarquinio Lucci. And it's a nice, short, catchy name for people to remember. Generations of Lucci's descendents will be christened, have first communions and get married in this pavilion. Antonietta is getting married in January; maybe next year there will be the first Christening of a Lucci child being celebrated in this place!" The fool looked at her with squinted eyes that said:

"I know what you're doing!" And then he thought of Assunta going over and decorating the place like she only knew how, and Antonietta dancing with her Rodolfo in front of everyone, and his competitors and enemies having to think of him every time they came to church and saw the pavilion. He wouldn't save any money going somewhere else, and he might as well be hanged for a sheep as for a lamb. The silence was getting a little too loud, and everyone was starting to sweat, and then The Fool smiled:

"Let's do it!" He barked, thumping his cane on the floor. Everyone jumped up and shook The Fool's hand, and right that very moment they all started to make plans and give suggestions, one better than the other, and those pies, cookies, cakes and cannoli were devoured with endless cups of coffee and cappuccino. During all this, Uncle Saverio swaggered forward, his thumbs hooked on each side of his belt, and said boldly:

"After the war, when people needed things built fast, I was part of a team that went around building stuff, like stables, barns, rooms etc. in one day; I was one of the fastest ones and a cracker jack at woodwork. I bet that no one can compete with me when it comes time to work on this pavilion." And while saying that, he flexed his muscles and looked wolfish. The fool looked up and down at the big man and said:

"I may be old and wrinkled, big guy, but I think I can best you!" Uncle Saverio's blue eyes crinkled at the corners, and his mustache lifted up showing dazzlingly white teeth:

"You're on, old man, and may the best man win!" And they shook hands to the whoops and hollers of everyone else. Gianna threw her arms around her man and kissed him. Luna was caught in the excitement too, and Ivana, who finally seemed more like herself, grabbed her and they danced around the grownups, soon joined by the women, who pulled the man to their feet and made them dance to the sounds coming from Angelina's radio, which she had just turned on to a musical program called 'Dance with us'. The old, ramshackle farm was hopping with joy, and everyone thought how lucky they were to have their friends, their homes, their children and a very bright future up ahead. Aunt

Palma was clapping her hands joyfully, and even the Fool was dancing, having put his cane down and extended a hand to Anna, who was thinking that he WAS a very handsome man indeed, wiry and strong too; life was good!

A couple of days later, Luna saw something she was not meant to see; she and Ivana were supposed to go straight to Aunt Palma's after school, but Aunt Palma had her heart set on hearing some more of the perils of Renzo and Lucia, and Luna hadn't brought The Betrothed to school with her that day, so while Ivana peddled on to Aunt Palma's house, Luna stopped at the house to get the book. She crashed happily in the kitchen, but there was no one there. She went upstairs to get the book from her room, and the house was empty and silent. At first she got scared, thinking something had happened, but then she heard murmurs outside, and from the kitchen window she spotted Uncle Pas and Aunt Esther sitting under their favorite fig tree. While she was looking, Uncle Pas got up and kneeled in front of Aunt Esther. While looking up into her eyes, he started to undo the small buttons on the front of her dress. Luna knew they didn't know they were being watched and she should leave, but she couldn't help herself; she was rooted to the spot. Half way down to her waist, Uncle Pas gently opened up the top of her dress, thus exposing a blindingly white cotton bra. He then proceeded to religiously lay his head on her bosom, closing his eyes. Aunt Esther lifted her hand and caressed his hair gently. Uncle Pas looked up at her, then straightened up taking her up with him, and they walked to the house. He had an arm over her shoulder, and she was cuddled up to him, one arm on his waist, and the other holding her dress closed. They walked into the house and up the stairs, never noticing Luna frozen at the kitchen window, with silent tears running down her face. She knew deep in her heart that what she had witnessed was true and sacred love between a man and a woman, and she wowed that she was never going to let anyone touch her unless they had that kind of love between them. She had never known that such love really existed, and now that she had found it, she was not going to be happy with anything less.

45. *Villino Porta Pia*. Cartolina. bollo post. 2/VIII/1915. "Riprod. vietata L. Macioce"; retro: "Cartolina Postale / Società Edit. Cartoline - Torino-Milano".

Garden with fountain, Pontecorvo 1915. This is where Uncle Pas
pulled Aunt Esther off the bench.
Lorenzo Macioce

12:   A Trip to Town

It was December! It was getting cold, and Aunt Esther declared that Luna needed a coat, so an outing was planned to go to Pontecorvo to shop for material at Ernesto Lena's dry goods store, and since they were there, they would go to Signora Bruno's shoe store and buy everyone new shoes for the impending wedding. Anna found out about it, and decided to go with them to buy herself shoes too; they would have to be special, to go with her brand new and fancy paisana costume. She was thinking to get a kind of baby Jane's for grownups, in black patent leather, with ribbons on top to hold them together in a nice bow; Signora Bruno would know what she needed, they were friends since the war, and Anna trusted her. A date was set, and Uncle talked to the teacher about the girls being out of school on that day. Also Anna needed to get some yarn for the sweaters she wanted to commission from Concetta Cipriano to give her grandchildren for the Epiphany; she would have to give Concetta enough time to knit them. Someone had told her that there was a yarn sale at the Ripetta shop, across from the bus depot, and she intended to go there while everyone was at Ernesto Lena's dry goods store, since they were only a few minutes from each other. This was not going to be a fun and games outing, just a quick business trip into town, but everyone was looking forward to it, and Luna was trying to decide what color cloth she was going to pick for her coat, to go along with her bright handbag. Light blue was out of the question, it would get dirty too fast, but then again she was only going to wear it for a month or so, after which she was going to leave for home, so it didn't really matter. Luna switched from a happy mood to being depressed and sullen, and Uncle Pas and Anna could guess why. Sometimes, Ivana tried to cheer her up by telling her that if her parents wouldn't let her come back in the summer, she would go see her herself. This gave Luna feelings of anger and helplessness, and she went from day to day as best as she could.

The day of the trip came on the following Saturday, and they set out bright and early. As usual, Anna sat in the back with the girls, and Uncle Pas and Aunt Esther had the cab to themselves. Anna said:

"I saw The Dress at Irma's house. You did a wonderful job, Esther! It's the loveliest thing I ever saw. You're not just a seamstress, you're an artist! Irma is going to start embroidering on Sunday, after mass. She's going to pray for inspiration, and then she's just going to dive in." Aunt Esther replied:

"I'm going to start the girls' dresses on Sunday! I meant to make the dresses first, but I didn't have the chance. It will be a weight off my mind when I'm finished; I want my girls to be beautiful! Afterwards I'm going to make my suit and Pasquale's shirt for his new suit. I know we have more than a month, but the last week is going to be dedicated to the wedding, and the week before that we have the pavilion raising. I hope it comes off alright, since it was my idea in the first place!"

"It was a wonderful idea!" Uncle Pas said, adding: "You are so smart; I'm the luckiest of man to have you for my own."

"No, no, Dear, I'm the lucky one!" But no one protested these declarations of love; they were used to it by now, and quickly swept them under the rug. This time they did not leave the truck near the bridge, but instead drove all the way to Town Hall, and left the truck at the piazza there. They took the shortcut to the center of town by crossing the Santo Stefano section, walking by the San Paolo church and coming out right in back of the Villetta with the fountain. While they crossed the Santo Stefano section, Ivana started to jump an imaginary hopscotch while intoning a nursery rhyme:

In the back of Santo Stefano there was a little spring.
I went to wash my hands and I lost my three gold rings.
I Looked and Looked again but they were not to be found.
Instead I found three fat fish and I took them to the Priest.
The Priest had gone to church, but the spinsters were at home.
Angelina and Lucrezia said the fish will make a feast.
They were making a small omelet and they gave me a little taste.
I didn't really like it much but I ate it quite in haste.
They gave me another mouthful but I threw it under the bench.
The bench was really deep and the wolf slept underneath.
The wolf was really old and didn't know how to change the

sheet.
The old hen out on the street was reciting the holy script.
The old mouse from up the wall was out draining his toilet bowl.

Luna was looking at Ivana flabbergasted:

"What are you doing?" She said. Ivana laughed:

"I'm playing the Pontecorvo hopscotch. Want to join me?"

"I don't know the words!" Said Luna. Ivana said:

"Repeat after me, you'll soon learn it." And they shot up ahead jumping and singing, Luna's bright, yellow-colored handbag swinging wildly on her arm. They were soon singing together, and Anna said:

"I used to play hopscotch to that nursery rhyme when I was a child!" Aunt Esther said:

"Me too, but I never knew what those words meant."

"Me neither," said Anna, "but I'm sure they knew what they meant a very long time ago, when they made it up. Now nobody knows; it must have been political." And at that Aunt Esther went to Anna and arm in arm, they started to jump hopscotch too, while intoning the rhymes together. Uncle Pas followed them laughing his heart out, and when they stopped, a bunch of little old ladies sitting on their stoop clapped their hands:

"Good show! That was wonderful! I wish I could do it myself!" Another old lady said:

"Want to try it, Maddalena?"

"And why not, Ernestina! We're still alive! Let's live a little!" And various little old ladies and some young ones got up and started to hopscotch in front of their houses, to whoops and laughter from other bystanders. Uncle Pas said, while grabbing Aunt Esther by the waist:

"See what you girls started?" To which a rosy and girlish Aunt Esther and a slightly heaving Anna replied:

"Hey, we're the movers and the shakers, you know!" To which Uncle Pas proceeded to swat Aunt Esther's bum lightly as she ran ahead of him to follow Anna, who was trying to catch up with the girls. In the middle of Santo Stefano, still ravaged by the war, with half the buildings still in rubble, and small dirt streets in front of the people's homes, everyone was having a great time! Laughter could be heard from the piazza, and hearts were joyful and full of life and hope. This is so different from home, Luna thought sadly. In her time, NO ONE talked or started dancing with anyone off the street, unless they were in a musical. Instead, 'don't talk to strangers' was the rule. But then again, 2012 was a much more dangerous time than 1950 Italy in this small, lovely place where nice people lived.

After they came out into the Villetta, they followed the road to the crosswalk and kept going until they reached a side street that would take them to the hospital. Right at the corner of May street and the hospital road, there was a large, beautiful store with a large sign that advertised all kinds of wonderful stuff inside, and it said in smaller captions 'Ernesto Lena, proprietor'. Mr. Ernesto Lena himself, a prosperous looking, jolly little man, was seated on a comfortable chair right in front of his establishment. When they reached the storefront, he got up from his chair and extended his hand to Uncle Pas as he exclaimed:

"Good day, Sargento, how is it going!" To which Uncle Pas replied, shaking his hand:

"Everything's fine, just fine. Meet my wife, daughter and niece. We're here to buy some cloth for winter clothing." Ernesto Lena beamed:

"I have just the right stuff. A new shipment came in yesterday, and you'll want to buy it all!"

"I just bet!" Replied Uncle Pas with a smile. As they walked in, they saw shelf upon shelf of beautiful bolts of material spread out in a panorama before them. Luna never even gave a thought to simple cloth before, and making your own clothes just wasn't done at home, let alone that it would have sunk her mother into despair. But now, every time she looked at a piece of cloth, she viewed it like a blank canvas, ready for the artist to make something beautiful. The heavy feel and fresh, heady smell of new material was new and exciting to her, especially that of wool, which just pulled at her. In unison the three of them walked to the shelves of new wool cloth, while Uncle Pas stood, talking to the little man. Anna had taken off for the Ripetta store, and Luna was missing her already. She wanted her friend to help her choose a great bolt of material for her coat, but Aunt Esther and

Ivana were there and they were already busily touching and rubbing soft, warm cloth between their hands. A good ten minutes later, Luna had chosen, with Aunt Esther's nudging, a bolt of azure, thick, soft wool, a little darker than normal blue, but not as dark as navy. Aunt Esther draped some of the wool on Luna's body, and Ivana stood back to judge how it looked, saying it looked just perfect on her. Putting the bolt aside, they went to find some wool to make Ivana a jacket. As usual, Ivana picked a rosy color, this time darker, almost red. But as Aunt Esther had said, in the winter, colors needed to be darker, because it was very difficult to wash and dry everything, especially coats and jackets, and after washing, the wool would never be as soft as when it was new.

They left Ernesto Lena's store, and walked to the Ripetta shop, where they found Anna arguing with the proprietor about the price of the wool yarn:

"They told me that there was a yarn sale here," she told them as soon as they walked in, "but all they've got here is highway robbery!" Uncle Pas intervened and talked to Ripetta, while Aunt Esther complimented Anna on her choice of yarn. She told Anna that this yarn was much better quality than some she had seen in the stalls on market day, and it would make soft, beautiful sweaters that her grandchildren would enjoy wearing:

"Usually wool sweaters are scratchy and itchy, and kids hate them. But these will be elegant, beautiful and soft. Still, the yarn in the stalls WAS less expensive, and you should really decide what you want to do." By now Anna wanted the soft, beautifully colored yarn desperately, but didn't want Ripetta to know. She said:

"I'll go up fifty liras, only because I want to drop it at the sexton's house on our way out of town, otherwise I would go get the one at the market on Monday. I'm a poor widow, you know! I can't go for these fancy things when I have to give up my food to buy them." Everyone knew that Anna didn't have to give up anything, she was actually well set, but Ripetta didn't know, and since Anna was buying quite a few skeins of yarn, and Uncle Pas told Ripetta that after those sweaters were made, they would advertise to all and sundry where the yarn came from, he relented and gave Anna the wool at her price. Everyone was happy! The girls were bored at Ripetta's and wanted to leave, Aunt Esther was very anxious to go home and examine the beautiful wool cloth and start making plans for its use and Uncle Pas had work to get done this day. Besides, they still had to go to Signora Bruno for the shoes. Uncle Pas told Ripetta that the sexton's wife, Concetta, was a gifted artisan, and if he could convince her to knit sweaters for his shop, he could practically double his money, since the yarn was much cheaper to him. The dapper little man in a fancy suit started seeing Lira signs, and then and there resolved to talk to the sexton after church on the following day.

When they arrived at the sexton's house, it was lunch time, and they took some cheese, olives, bread, focaccia and meat pies that they bought at Nannina's grocery shop across from town hall. They knocked at the door of the little two-storied square dwelling attached to the left of the stairs that went up to the cathedral, and when one of the children came to the door, they told him who they were. There was some confusion inside, but a minute later, Cipriano the Sexton came to the door and invited them in. The first floor consisted of only one room, and so did the upstairs. There was one single fornacella and a small fireplace up against the wall on one side, and some utensils were hanging on the blackened wall on the other side. A wooden table stood in the middle of the room surrounded by small chairs, and on the back wall, a small ladder was propped up for them to go to the second floor; underneath the ladder stood a sewing machine. Concetta was flushed and excited, and she showed them to their kitchen table. The table was set with a patched but scrupulously clean cloth, and some mismatched dishes were already on the table. They were invited to share their meal, and at first they refused, of course! Everyone knew that etiquette dictated that you always refused the first invite, you also demurred the second time they invited you, but the third time you relented and sat down to the meal. So as the invitation became more vigorous, they finally acquiesced and sat down. The children had been moved to the top of Concetta's Singer sewing machine, closed for the moment, and more dishes were set.

Concetta had made a large pot of vegetable soup, and she put big chunks of heavy, dark bread on the table. Uncle Pas said that they were planning on eating their lunch on the bench up near the giant cross in front of the church, but since they were invited to eat comfortably inside, they would share their food with them as their hosts were doing. He went to the truck and retrieved their supplies, and soon the little room was full of convivial discourse and joyful laughter. The Sexton brought out a flask of red wine someone had given him, and everyone did the Chianti justice, even the children, when a little bit was poured into their water. The girls soon got up from the table and were talking to the boys. Remigio was about their age, and they were curious to know all about his school. He told them that he frequented the school up the street, between the cathedral and the town Hall; he said that it was a very good school and all of the neighborhood children went there and that Saturday was only half day, so they had come home from school just in time for lunch. He offered the girls a look at the books they used at the school, and they followed him up to the second floor by climbing the wooden ladder. The second floor consisted of a room as big as the kitchen, and all around the room were five alcoves, four small ones and one big one. These alcoves were defined by sheets used as bed hangings, for privacy, and behind the sheets were the beds. There was a small window, and under the window stood a small desk and chair. That was where Remigio's books were; he said he did his homework there. The books were the same as the girls', and Luna realized that there really was not much choice in those days, in fact due to the war, they were lucky to have books at all. They rejoined the adults, and ate their lunch. The soup Concetta had made was green, thick and savory. Aunt Esther, always on the lookout for a good recipe, asked Concetta what was in the soup, that it tasted so good. Concetta told her that she had picked lots of fresh dandelion greens behind the cathedral, also adding carrots, green beans, bits of cauliflower, onions, chunks of potatoes, some celery and any bits of leftover vegetables she could rustle up from the vendors at the end of market day. She said that The Signora from the big house across the street, the hatter's wife, had given her a big piece of bacon and she had cut some of it in tiny pieces, had fried it with finely chopped cloves of garlic and had thrown it in with the vegetables. She added coyly that she had another little secret to her soup, but she was willing to share it with them; she mixed into the soup two large potatoes boiled and *mashed*. Aunt Esther was surprised at that, and questioned Concetta about the technique. Concetta said:

"When you have a family to feed and not too many ingredients, you sharpen your intuition, and come up with new answers, to give them pleasant fare without all the expense. Also, you must have some bitter dandelions, that's what gives the soup its tangy flavor. "   Aunt Esther commented that she was truly a magician, and her family was lucky to have her. The Sexton put an arm over her shoulders and said:

"I don't know what she ever saw in me, but I thank God every day for my Concetta!" Uncle Pas said:

"I know where you come from, I thank God every day for my Esther, but I know what she saw in me: Where else could she find a man as handsome, cultured, congenial, generous and gallant, not to mention smart and fun loving as I am, may I ask you?" At that Aunt Esther added:

"And may I say modest and unassuming!" And Uncle Pas tried to grab her, but Aunt Esther retaliated, and they had a quick wrestling match to everyone's delighted laughter. Luna was smiling at her family's antics and all at once a memory flickered in her mind:

"Robbie, the grass is so perfect; I can't find a dandelion anywhere." And a gentle voice she knew so well replied:

"Isn't it nice, my dear?"

"No, it's not! I needed dandelions for my soup!" Luna shook her head, dazed:

"Where did that come from?" But things were happening, and the fleeting memory was soon forgotten.

Finally, Anna produced the yarn, and she and Concetta discussed styles and sizes for the sweaters. Uncle Pas warned Concetta about Ripetta asking her to do some work for the store. He told her to charge him what the work was worth; taking into account how much time it took to actually do the work, not to work for nothing, because Ripetta was going to sell the stuff she made for very good money. Aunt Esther had some suggestions of her own. In Cassino she had seen young women wear furry angora caplet hats, like they wore in the American movies. They were gorgeous, looked like snowballs in pastel colors with the girls' hair spilling out of them, and they would be easy and fast to make. Some of them looked like baby bonnets. A small angora strap held them in place, and they could be decorated on both sides with felt flowers, like the ones on Luna's brightly colored handbag. Everyone admired those flowers, as Luna proudly displayed her bag, and Concetta's eyes shined at the new ideas that came to her. Aunt Esther turned around slightly and extracted a small amount of bills from her bosom. The only one who could see was Uncle Pas, and his eyes twinkled at her, and he laughed right out at her warning expression. She handed Concetta the money and said:

"Now that I think about it, I would dearly love to have my girls wear a hat like that, a light blue one for Luna and a white one for Ivana. No rush, they'll need them for Christmas. If you would do me this great favor, buy the yarn yourself, as we don't have time to go back to Ripetta, and please keep the change; if it's not enough for payment please give me a bill later. We have just enough time to go to Signora Bruno and buy the shoes and then we must go home." Concetta was grateful and overjoyed, but you could see that she was distracted, already planning what to do and how to do it; this Christmas was going to be the best they had ever had! She'd buy her kids new shoes and coats, and they could have some calamari on Christmas Eve and a stuffed chicken on Christmas day; heck! She was going to get herself a store bought red nightgown with lace and see her husband's eyes pop in shock on Christmas Eve. Yes, Life was good, and her ship might have just come in!

Around two o' clock, they left the Sexton's house and backtracked up the street to City Hall piazza, where they once again left the truck. This time they walked to the right of City Hall and at the end of the small street, right across, stood Signora Bruno's great palazzo, and on the street level was the shoe store. There were no signs, but you could see through the great glass doors rows and rows of shoes and boxes galore. They pushed the door, and a bell jingled. A few seconds after they were there, a door in the back opened, and Signora Bruno walked in. She was a portly lady with grey hair, refined and aristocratic, and she was wearing a somber, but obviously expensive grey suit; she wore lots of heavy gold on her ears, neck and hands. She welcomed them to her store, and asked how she could be of service. She then spotted Anna, and she fairly flew to her, her arms open:

"Anna, Anna I haven't seen you in ages; how are you?"

"I'm fine, Marisa, just fine! And how is Raffaele, is he here?"

"Yes, he's upstairs. I'll call him down to say hello'. He'll be so happy to see you! You're his adoptive grandma, you know that." She went to a door and disappeared for a few minutes, and then she came back followed by a handsome young man in comfy clothes and slippers. She told Uncle Pas to please browse to their heart's content, and Anna went to them and they were talking and hugging in a corner. Luna whispered to Ivana:

"Who are these people?" Sounding a little bit jealous of Anna's attachment to them. Ivana whispered:

"Anna took care of them during the war. Just before the war, Signora Bruno was coming home one day with her teenage son and saw her husband being taken away by police, and as he passed by he mouthed to her: 'Run!' And she did. After hours, exhausted and hungry, they gave up and knocked on the first cottage they saw on the outskirts of town; it was Anna's house, she took them in and took care of them until the war ended and the persecutions stopped."

"Why were they being persecuted?" Asked Luna with a frown. Ivana said simply:

"They're Jewish!" At that Luna understood, and she was not jealous any more of Anna's attention to them, she just felt privileged to be loved by a person like her. Signora Bruno, Anna and young Raffaele joined everyone, introductions were made and everyone was invited up to the house for coffee and dessert after their business was concluded.   When Anna told Signora Bruno what she wanted, she smiled, and went to the back of the store. She came out holding the most beautiful pair of shoes Anna had ever seen; they were black patent leather, had nice strong soles, they were very open on top, and two shiny strings of satin held them to the foot snuggly and forming a lovely bow on top of the foot. At the top of the shoes were a string of small pink satin roses all around the opening, and the shoes were wide and rounded in the front to accommodate the foot comfortably. Anna took them from Signora Bruno reverently while whispering:

"How did you know?" Signora Bruno laughed:

"I was expecting you! The wedding legends are all over town, and I knew that you may want fancy shoes with probably a wonderful new costume; do I know my Anna or not?" Anna ran to her and hugged her:

"Oh Marisa, you and Raffaele are the most wonderful friends a person could ever have!" Signora Bruno held her and whispered:

"You saved our lives, Anna!" And when Anna asked about the price of the wonderful shoes Signora Bruno laughed: "As if I would ever let you pay for anything in the store!" Anna tried the shoes on, and they fit her wonderfully. She walked around showing off, and then Signora Bruno's son, Raffaele, helped her tie the Cioci back on. Luna and Ivana wanted the same thing for their shoes, but Signora Bruno said that she had commissioned Anna's shoes especially, and there were none like them anywhere, but she showed the girls other styles, after asking what kind of dresses they were wearing. At this Aunt Esther launched into a description of the dresses, and out came the most beautiful shoes they could imagine. Luna had little pumps with tiny heels, in powder blue, with a small bunch of flowers on top, and Ivana had dark pink satin shoes which buttoned down on the side with three large shiny buttons. The girls were hugging their shoe boxes, thinking how pretty they would look with their dresses, while Aunt Esther bought herself some gold colored, plain and stylish pumps with a small heel and Uncle Pas got some black, pointed and slim shoes to go with his suit. Everyone was very happy with their purchases, and Signora Bruno insisted on giving all the shoes at cost. Anna whispered to Aunt Esther:

"She must really like you and Pasquale, she's usually not this generous, she's a very good business woman and gives people the best price already."

"It's because of you; your generosity to them begets their generosity to others. You are truly a wonderful person, Anna, and I'm glad my girl Luna brought you to us!" They left their shoes on the counter, and followed Signora Bruno upstairs for coffee and dessert.

They climbed a great marble staircase, and went through a humongous carved door into a large entrance and then passed a salon with satin couches and ornate chairs. There were golden tables everywhere and a large chandelier hung in the middle of the room. A plush cream carpet covered almost the whole marble floor, and from an archway, they could see a formal dining room with large, inlaid furniture. There were large paintings hanging on the walls, and an air of opulence rested on everything. Signora Bruno walked through the entrance, and guiding Anna and the rest said:

"You're family, and your friends are part of you, so we can sit in the kitchen, if you don't mind." Everybody agreed, relieved, they did not want to sit in those rooms, afraid of dropping coffee or something. When they walked into the large, sunny kitchen complete with appliances that almost looked modern to Luna, they saw a girl in a frilly apron working near the stove. Signora Bruno said:

"You can go, Maria, we'll take care of things." The girl assented, and left quietly, while Anna whispered to Aunt Esther:

"The maid!" Everyone felt a little self-conscious at first, but when Anna and Aunt Esther went to help Signora Bruno, and young Raffaele started to talk to Uncle Pas about the reconstruction rights that people had lost after the war for lack of funds to start building, they all felt better, not so intimidated; people are people whatever they might own, thought Luna, and the only thing everyone really wanted was friendship and a good life; they found just such fun, friendliness and congeniality in the humble home of the sexton that they found here in this rich palazzo. The women soon had a large coffee pot on the table, espresso cups, spoons and sugar, and a large platter of pastry. Signora Bruno said that while they were buying shoes, young Raffaele had sent Maria the maid to Richetta's pastry shop down the street, a bit farther down than Uncle Master's music studio, and told her to get some of everything. The pastry was truly magnificent, and they all did justice to it. Young Raffaele was going to be a lawyer, like his father had been, and he said he would work for people's rights, because when they took your rights away they took your life away; they should know! It was a very pleasant visit, and Signora Bruno told them that she and her son had been invited to the wedding, as she often did business with The Fool, and she looked forward to spending a lot of time with them on that day. At one point, Anna whispered something to Signora Bruno and she assented, smiling. Anna called Aunt Esther and the girls over, and they followed Signora Bruno out to the marble steps. Signora Bruno told them to go upstairs to the door right in front of them, and they followed Anna there. When they opened the door, the most beautiful, plush and large bathroom that Luna had seen in the 1950's was in front of them. It was all marble tiles, a large tub with fat golden feet stood on one side of the room, and of course a toilet and bidet were there, and you could see a shower behind a glass door. Everything was white and fat white and gold towels were hanging and piled everywhere. The sink was also carved out of living marble, and the faucets were gold colored.   They took turns using the beautiful toilet, and had fun flushing with the string hanging right on top of it, under the tank of water. Anna said that the Brunos were able to get back all their property and money that they had lost before the war, but unfortunately no one ever found out what happened to Signora Bruno's husband.   Aunt Esther commented that no amount of money could ever begin to repay a loss that great. They were all sad about that, and Aunt Esther went to Uncle Pas and squeezed his arm with tenderness. After a few more minutes, Anna commented:

"As much as I love being with my dear friends, we got things to do, and we're burning daylight!" And with smiles and thanks, they picked up their things and left after hugs and salutations, hugging the boxes with their beautiful shoes in them. Aunt Esther told Signora Bruno that she didn't think they could have found shoes this nice and appropriate even if they went to the great shoe emporium in Frosinone, the Centipede, and Signora Bruno said that the Centipede was certainly a great place to buy shoes, but they did not offer the personal attention which she lavished on her customers; she knew that a pair of shoes was very important to people, especially in this economy, and she made sure that everyone left her establishment very happy with their purchase. Luna didn't remember a time when she had enjoyed simply buying a pair of shoes! Any time she had done so before, it was all 'find what you want out of a huge pile and hope they fit.' No matter what you bought at home, there was nothing ever 'personal' about it. These wonderful people would weep at the stores at home.

Time was going by fast, they had the tobacco harvest on the following weekend, and there was as usual a lot of food, company and merriment, but Luna felt sad, because she knew that these people had no idea how dangerous tobacco was. Everyone there was working closely with the tobacco; the men picked the leaves from the stalks, small leaves from small plants to make cigarettes, and large leaves from the larger plants to make cigars. The leaves were put in large panniers that the women put on top of their heads and carried to a large room/barn next to the house. In that room men and women were stringing the leaves on strong twine, and then these strings were hung on different sides of the room; one side for the small leaves, the other for the large leaves. Everyone's hands were black with the tobacco juice that came out of the leaves, and people didn't mind. In fact, they loved the scent and often brought their hands to their face and inhaled deeply. Everyone was there, Luna and Ivana's friends and their parents, some of the neighboring boys, Aunt Palma was presiding over the tables leaden with food, and Anna was doing her bidding happily. Aunt Esther had cooked for days and Anna's daughters had brought more stuff.   Everyone was happy and enjoying the festivities and good friendship. Aunt Palma's voice could be heard above everyone's, screeching and commanding. As Gianna made an appearance with a large tray of cookies, Aunt Palma's commanding gestures had her running to her, and Aunt Palma said:

"What happened to you, Gianna? No more high heels, no more fancy clothes, no more wavy hair? Has that man of yours forbidden you to doll yourself up?" To which Gianna replied smiling:

"No, Aunt Palma, I just found out something; did you know that less is more?" And she looked at Luna and winked. The teacher seemed more relaxed near Luna and accepted her presence easily these days:

"Less dolling up, more comfort and joy, and that man of mine likes me just fine this way!"

"I bet!" Exclaimed Aunt Palma: "The less you do for yourself, the more you do for him!" Aunt Nannina, who was standing right next to Aunt Palma, vigorously agreed with her. At that, Uncle Saverio, who just happened to be nearby, went up to Gianna, took her in his arms and bent her over backwards with a long kiss. Everybody within distance whistled and whopped, and straightening up, Uncle Saverio swaggered to Aunt Palma and bent her over his arm also and kissed her forehead reverently. Then he flashed that wolfish smile at her, wiggled his eyebrows flirtatiously and swaggered away. Little Aunt Palma just stood there with a foolish smile on her face and then turning to Gianna said:

"He is certainly worth it, he reminds me of a friend of mine from a long time ago, he was a blond too!" And everybody applauded laughing. Ivana and Luna winked at each other and mouthed:

"Mutandies!" And they both burst out laughing. But underneath all the jocularity, Luna was very sad. She found out later that every night for a week Uncle Pas was going to sleep in the same room with the tobacco, to keep a fire going to smoke it and help it dry up. When the tobacco was crackling and dry, they would tie it into small bales and take it to a central place in town, called the Agrarian Syndicate, where it would be tallied and then sent to the Tobacco Warehouse to be made into cigars and cigarettes. This place was very large, and a lot of people worked there. This business in Italy was ruled by the government, as it was the business of salt, as funny as that may seem. This branch of government was called 'The Salt and Tobacco Monopoly' and they were very strict with lots of rules and regulations. She had found out that salt was very scarce, after the war, and it was very important to everyone and very expensive; one more thing to think about. She didn't know what to do, but resolved to talk to Uncle Pas alone as soon as she could. He knew where she came from, and maybe he would believe her and have an idea how to help!

Later, they had supper, after which everybody helped with the cleanup before leaving. When it was time to go to sleep, Uncle Pas said Good Night to everyone in the family, and left the house with a blanket rolled out under his arm. Aunt Esther went to bed almost immediately, as she was extremely tired, and so did Luna and Ivana. Luna couldn't sleep, and after about half hour, sneaked out of the house quietly, and went to the tobacco room. The door of this outside room was open for ventilation, and inside

Luna could see Uncle Pas trying to get comfortable on his pallet before he went to sleep. She thought of all the bad things he was going to breathe in during this night and the following ones, and how sick he could get because of it, and eventually even die of it, and she laid her head on the door's frame and started quietly to sob. After about a minute, she felt a gentle touch and raised her head. She met Uncle's concerned look, and she threw herself into his arms crying. Uncle Pas let her cry for a while, then raised her face with his hand and asked:

"What is it, Luna? Can you tell me?" She said, tears running down her cheeks:

"I don't know if you're going to believe me!" Her Uncle caressed her face and whispered:

"Try me, Luna. We will see." She hiccupped and then said:

"Where I come from tobacco is considered very dangerous. It makes people very sick. Almost anyone who handles tobacco, and those who smoke it, get very sick. People get all kinds of diseases, especially cancer. In almost every restaurant, office, school or other public place smoking is banned. The American Surgeon General has made the manufacturers put it right on every package of cigarettes; it says that tobacco kills, and anyone smoking it should know. In fact, even if you don't smoke, but are next to others who do, you could also get sick; it's called second hand smoke." Uncle Pas looked down at her small, earnest face and whispered:

"You mean like Esther and Ivana?" Luna assented while she was still hanging on his jacket. Uncle Pas picked up two small chairs and guided her to one, while sitting on the other:

"You're sure about this?" He asked her suddenly. Luna said:

"I would've never ruined things for you this way, if I was not very sure." Uncle Pas looked pensive, and then mumbled almost to himself:

"A lot of the women who work at the Tobacco Warehouse, where they sort the tobacco to prepare it to manufacture various products, have come down with all kinds of cancers, but mostly breast cancer; no one ever suspected it was the tobacco, they just thought it was the stress of their jobs." Luna was looking up at him with suspense. He looked down and said:

"I'll think about it, Luna. And you can believe I'll do what's best for my family. This time around I have to go on with the work, too much has been invested into it, but I'm going to think about what you told me, never fear; I consider myself lucky to have this small window into the future, and I'll fix it as best as I can. Go to sleep, little niece. You helped me see a little more of the future, and for that I thank you; it's not all rosy, is it?" Luna stated:

"Uncle, the future is beautiful in its own way, but it's also very dangerous because of all the new inventions and all the things people do that are not safe. It's much safer here, although not as safe as I thought. But you're still lucky to be in this wonderful, safe, happy place and time. I just wish things at home weren't so 'stressful' and 'depressing'." Thinking more and more about the differences between here and home, Luna quietly went back to her room and got into bed. That night Luna dreamed she had gone back home, and neither cigarettes nor other tobacco things existed. She asked someone where had all the cigarettes gone, but was told:

"What are cigarettes?" And then some old person said:

"They were made of tobacco, and people smoked them in their mouth!" To which everyone said:

"How disgusting! But why are they gone then?" And the old person said:

"The legend says that an intrepid, far seeing little girl warned everyone a long, long time ago that tobacco was deadly, and as the word spread and people became aware of the danger, everyone got rid of their tobacco farms. Everywhere, it became illegal, and tobacco was eradicated from the face of the earth. She saved millions of lives with that knowledge, because tobacco really was a deadly poison and it really killed." Everyone shouted:

"Thank God for that little girl, whoever she was!" And Luna smiled with pleasure in her sleep.

As time went by, everyone was getting increasingly nervous; the wedding was getting closer and every person connected to it was frantic. Antonietta walked around in a daze, with all of her gold on her all the time, and didn't answer any of the questions about her preferences, she just said:

"I don't care, do whatever you want!" The Fool didn't answer any of their questions either, he just said:

"That's what I'm paying you women for!" Assunta looked at everyone helplessly, twisting her hands and Rodolfo said:

"I'll marry Antonietta on the street if I have to; she's mine!" And walked away smiling. Everyone was floundering, they secretly started thinking that they had taken on too much, and there was no clear concept of who should do what when. They knew that they could do it; the trouble was in how to put it all together so that their concerted efforts would look effortless. The men were gearing up to build the pavilion, but they had a chief to hold them together: Carlo! He was truly magnificent, not only he was a wonderful builder, but he had a knack of getting the most out of people while he promoted cooperation and team spirit. The women secretly thought that someone should be in charge to pull everyone and everything together, but they all were afraid to take on the responsibility. Aunt Esther was a little depressed, and Uncle Pas was all tied up with the tobacco and didn't have the time to talk to her and cheer her up. One late afternoon, while they were just sitting down to dinner, they heard a truck drive up, and then someone was beating at their door frantically. Uncle Pas opened the door and into the house spilled Anna; she was not wearing her usual kerchief and her hair was standing up, her Cioci were laced all wrong, and she was still wearing the apron she usually cooked in. Everyone stared at her, terrified, while Amelia, Angelina and Irma filed quietly into the house. Mario stood just inside the door, looking worried. Everyone grabbed Anna, sat her down on a chair and then demanded to know what had happened. She caught her breath and then said:

"Mario just came from town; he had a letter for us. It was just addressed 'To The Wedding Consultants' and the mailman was awfully glad to unload it on him, as he didn't know exactly who The Wedding Consultants were and it also saved him a long ride on his bicycle. Since we were some of them wedding consultants, we opened it. Guess what!" Everyone shouted:

"What!" And Anna, regarding everyone with superiority said:

"We have Toscana, Lilliana and Inessa for the wedding!" Everyone repeated in stupor:

"Toscana, Lilliana and Inessa?" And Anna said, in unison with her daughters:

"Yes, Toscana, Lilliana and Inessa!" Everyone said:

"No, I don't believe it!" And Anna and her daughters repeated:

"Believe it, it's true!" They all said:

"Who is going to pay them? The Fool is overextended as it is; besides, he's going to say 'That's what I pay you women for!' and he'd be right." Anna said:

"They are going to work for free!" Everyone repeated:

"For free?"

"Yes, for free!" Luna had been looking from one to the other perplexed and nervous. Finally she couldn't hold it in anymore and shouted:

"Who are these people?" Ivana turned to her and said superciliously, arms akimbo, tapping her foot and with raised eyebrows:

"Only the best pastry chef, decorator and party planner in the whole region, that's who!" Anna said:

"They said that having heard about the wedding, they have a burning desire to be part of it, and it would mean also recognition and advertisement for them, and they are prepared to do the best job for us; they didn't know that there was anyone rich enough in Pontecorvo to throw this kind of shindig, and it would be fun to help put it together. They want to meet us at the hotel in town on Sunday next, in the afternoon."

So it was that on Sunday next, after church, the men drove them into town and they all went to the hotel and were ushered into a quiet meeting room and served with tea and fancy cookies, compliments of Lilliana, Toscana and Inessa. You can take just so long to have a cup of tea and some cookies. After a while Amelia, Angelina and Irma were fidgeting, Gianna was patting her hair over and over nervously and Anna and Aunt Esther were whispering quietly to each other. Luna and Ivana were almost getting bored, and were overeating, two cookies at the time (they were real good cookies!). Suddenly there was a noise outside, and the door was opened by a hotel employee and in stepped two women. One of them, a lush matron with brown eyes and hair, soft comfy clothes, an easy manner and a beautiful smile introduced herself as Toscana; she had a gentle demeanor and seemed very pleasant. The second one, a lovely brunette with flashing black eyes, stylish black clothes, high heels and longish black hair introduced herself as Lilliana; she was all fire and energy and had an imperious manner about her. There were introductions all around, and they all started talking about the wedding and their ideas for it, but Luna and Ivana were very curious about Inessa, and why she wasn't there yet.

At one point, everyone heard a distant tic-tac sound, it came closer and closer, and finally stopped near their door. Then the door flew open and there she was! At first, they thought that she was very tall, but then everyone realized that she was a petite girl on top of the highest, reddest shoes anyone had ever seen. She was wearing a red silk dress; it enveloped her body like a fluted champagne glass full of red wine, only soft and clingy. On one of her shoulders she was wearing a black, fringed silk scarf that hung down and swayed as she moved; it was pinned to her shoulder by a large cameo brooch, it was straight and narrow, and ethereal in its transparency; if they didn't know better, they would think that the scarf was just a fringe hanging midair. She looked around curiously, her long black hair flowing down her back, her large brown eyes shining, and then said:

"Hi, I'm Inessa!" Then she gave everyone an impish smile, and her face lit up like a candle; she had one single dimple! At first everyone was just overwhelmed, and then they all started to talk at once, and introductions were made and finally Inessa seated herself on one of the chairs and everyone clustered around her. Discussions of the wedding started up again, and Toscana and Lilliana had wonderful ideas, which coupled with the wonderful ideas of the original Wedding Consultants, bespoke of a wedding to remember. At one point Inessa asked:

"What are you going to do for the favors?" Everyone looked surprised:

"What favors?" Inessa raised her eyebrows like she was talking to children and exclaimed:

"I'm talking party favors, people! Wedding party favors!" Everyone exhaled:

"We were thinking the usual little sack made of net, filled with Jordan almond candy, tied with a ribbon and a small flower stuck in it." Inessa flipped her ebony hair over her shoulders and exclaimed:

"I will not allow anything 'usual' in the planning of this wedding." And when everyone looked at her expectantly, she said:

"I will look at everything you have prepared, the dress, the veil, the decorations, the bride and groom, and then I will decide." Everyone said:

"The bride and groom?" And Lilliana confirmed:

"Yes, the bride and groom are most important; the wedding has to reflect their personality, to a point." Luna and Ivana burst out together:

"Just put red hearts everywhere, 'cause they're in looove!" Toscana remarked with a dreamy smile:

"How romantic! We should make the cake in the shape of a heart!" Lilliana said:

"I thought the bride's father bought the groom for his daughter with his money!" Inessa turned towards the two girls and said:

"And what have we here? Laurel and Hardy?" To which the girls stepped forward, giggling and lightly elbowing each other, and introduced themselves. She looked them up and down with laughing eyes, and said:

"We will hear more of your ideas later, when we see for ourselves what this bride and groom are about." Everyone started to tell the story of Antonietta and Rodolfo, and the three newcomers got very interested in what was going on, especially when they found out that a special pavilion was going to be built on purpose for the reception. They also were enthralled by the fact that the bride was so shy that the groom had never really seen her face completely, and she was to be unveiled, so to speak, on her wedding day. The three experts said that they would return one week before the wedding, on December thirty-first, and start pulling together all of the Wedding Consultant's accomplishments. In the meantime, they would take a trip down on the day the pavilion was to be built, because no one wanted to miss this building frenzy, and the challenge between The Fool and his stalwart opponent; they said that they would bring some refreshments. Inessa said that she would make a decision for the wedding party favors on the day of the pavilion raising. Goodbyes were said, and everyone went their own way, with everyone taken by these three wonderful people, with Inessa being the most complex of them all; she had a look of childlike wonder in her big, brown eyes, an impish smile on her full red lips, the body of a model, and an inner core of pure steel. Her perfume stayed with everyone long after she had left. Anna said as how the wedding kept enriching their lives everyday more, and that Antonietta kept going blithely about without even realizing what hullabaloo she had caused. They went home, each preoccupied with all of the details to yet be ironed out, and expecting the photographer to pop up at any minute as he had been doing lately. Judging by the amount of pictures he was taking, Quagliozzi was going to hand The Fool about three hundred of the darned albums.

It was definitely chilly lately, but considering that it was already the first week of December, no one was going to complain.   Luna felt very lucky to have the soft, warm blue coat Aunt Esther had made for her, in a considerably short period of time, and Ivana was waiting for her dark rose jacket over the coming weekend.   They pedaled their bikes to school and everywhere else, and they were busy and excited. Luna thought life was good, here, and for now postponed thinking that she was going to have to leave soon. She took one day at a time, and decided to let the future take care of itself. She was surrounded by lovely people who cared for her, and exciting things were happening every day; no sense worrying about the things that she couldn't change. She was making great progress in school, and she was just about to finish reading her great novel by Alessandro Manzoni, 'The Betrothed'. She was already starting to pick her next reading project, even though she knew in the back of her mind that she would have to leave soon; they did have books at home too, and she would read when she got back. But going back was receding in her mind, and she could almost think that it was relegated in the very distant future, and that suited her just fine.

51. *Mercato*. Cartolina, bollo post. 29/IX/1936. Retro: "Prop. ris. Ed. G. Quagliozzi - Libreria e Cartoleria / EIS".

Pontecorvo, market day 1936.
G. Quagliozzi

The adults were more and more preoccupied with the wedding preparations, and the girls spent a lot of time with little Aunt Palma and even Aunt Nannina, who was a sort of Aunt Palma's escort. One day, on a Sunday, when they met Aunt Palma outside of the church, she told them that Aunt Nannina was taking her to the market in a tiny, neighboring town, Pico. She asked them if they wanted to go, and when the girls obtained permission, they all piled up into Aunt Nannina's small car, Aunt Palma and Aunt Nannina in front and Giustina, Ivana and Luna squeezed in the back, and took off. The place was only about half hour away, and Aunt Nannina said it was so small; that if you didn't keep your eyes open you just might miss it and never know you were there. They had to climb a steep hill to get to it, and they could see it in the distance; a mix of great white houses grouped around a humongous castle with a huge clock tower and a large church whose steeple was higher than anything else in the town. When they arrived in Pico, they entered the small, ancient town by a great stone arch that dated to many centuries back. As soon as they entered the arch, they saw a small piazza enclosed by great, big ancient stone houses all attached and forming a large circle. There were coffee shops, small stores that sold everything from food to shoes and clothes, and small restaurants. There were people everywhere, the place was festive, and music could be heard. Right in the center of the piazza there were multicolored stalls, and the three girls made for the stalls immediately. Near the stalls were people hawking anything and everything, and the girls were impressed by the man holding a box with a large, open drawer; on his shoulder he had a large, multicolored parrot. According to Ivana, for ten liras the man would let the parrot choose your fortune. This was a slip of paper that told you your future, your lucky numbers and your horoscope. Giustina bought one, and the man spoke to the parrot pointing to her. The parrot flew to Giustina's shoulder, beaked her hair a bit, then flew to the drawer, picked up a slip of paper among all of the many stacked neatly inside, and threw it at Giustina. She caught it and started to avidly read it, while Ivana and Luna jostled to be next in line and get their fortune. They each got one and they too started to avidly read it. Giustina boasted that her fortune told her she was going to meet a tall, dark and handsome man soon, and he would be the love of her life. Luna was told that a great journey was imminent in her life and her life would change drastically afterwards. Kind of shook up, Luna turned to Ivana to see what her fortune was, and she saw Ivana rip and mesh hers under her feet and stomp away angrily. She ran after her to find out what happened, but Ivana wouldn't stop. When she finally caught up with her, on a side street, Luna demanded to know what the fortune said, and Ivana suddenly threw herself at Luna and started to cry:

"Tell me you're never going to leave me; I demand that you stay with me forever! You made me love you and now you want to go!"Luna had a feeling of dread in her stomach, and asked Ivana what her fortune said. Ivana replied:

"It said that a dear friend and sister of mine will go away forever in a place I can never reach her. Please, Luna tell me it isn't true! Please don't go!" And as Ivana held her tightly around her neck, Luna looked terrified at the little man with the parrot, but he looked at the two girls impassively, and walked away. Luna held Ivana in her arms and told her:

"I don't want to go, but I have to go sometime; I miss my parents and my brother. But I will never forget you, you're my bestest friend and sister, and no one will ever take your place. I'll think of you every day and I'll be thankful that you were in my life. I'll never forget you!" They stood in each other's arms for a few seconds, and then Ivana looked up; she looked into Luna's eyes and said:

"I won't lose you, you know! I won't let it happen! Wherever you go, I will find you, I don't care when, just remember what I'm saying to you! I will search for you and I will find you no matter how long it takes me. I will not let you go!" Now it was Luna's turn to cry, and she did so loudly. Finally they turned around and walked back to the market. Aunt Nannina and Aunt Palma were there, and the stalls cheered the girls up. Giustina was nowhere to be found:

"Probably just looking for her tall, dark and handsome guy!" Whispered Ivana and the girls started to laugh tentatively. They walked amongst the stalls, and bought themselves a few necessities with the money Uncle Pas slipped to them before they left, and then Ivana triumphantly called Luna over and showed her what she had bought. It was a beautiful box that contained a shiny, large filigree heart in two pieces; it was made of silver and there were two little silver chains, one for each part. It was called a friendship heart, and they were each supposed to wear one because that insured that they would always be reunited when they were separated. Ivana had spent a lot of money on it, and Luna held her part reverently in the palm of her hand. She felt reassured, like somehow the heart was really going to work, and she felt happy all at once. Ivana felt the same way, and the two girls walked around the little market smiling and skipping. They wore their chains, and fingered the heart half as if to make sure it was where it was supposed to be. All at once they heard a commotion, and realized that Aunt Palma and Aunt Nannina were right in the middle of it. Then the people parted and Aunt Nannina marched away, her nose up in the air. Aunt Palma was standing next to a big, burly man with a handlebar moustache and a small beard. He wore the traditional costume and big Cioci on his feet. His pleated shirt was dazzlingly white, some laces open on top to show a large gold medal hanging on a thick gold chain and winking amidst the curly hair of his chest. On top of his shirt he wore a black felt vest embroidered in vivid colors and sported black trousers that were gathered at his knees; he had a colored, fringed sash around his waist and flying on his side. He wore the costume defiantly, like a proud badge of honor, and he certainly looked muscular and attractive in it. The girls ran after Aunt Nannina, and if they didn't know better, they would have thought that she was about to cry. They asked Aunt Nannina what happened, and she said:

"The great unwashed are a nuisance to say the least!" And walked away. They ran after her and asked her again what happened. She turned around and declared, like a Monty comic strip character:

"We will not spend time fraternizing with the Hoy Polloy and their desperate ambitions to consort with their betters!" And walked away again, leaving the girls staring after her with their mouths agape. Aunt Palma and Giustina came over, and the girls asked them what happened. Aunt Palma said that Aunt Nannina's old boyfriend from when she was a teenager had asked her out, and Aunt Nannina had politely refused, but when he had insisted, she had got furious and slapped him down, to which he had laughed uproariously and made fun of her. Aunt Palma said:

"She'll cry herself to sleep, tonight." The girls asked, with big eyes:

"Why, she loves him?" To which Aunt Palma replied:

"Maybe!" And the two girls said:

"So, why doesn't she go out with him and see?" And Aunt Palma said, sadly:

"She can't, she has to uphold her position!" Ivana seemed to understand, but Luna was nonplussed:

"What is wrong with him, then?"

"He's a farmer, albeit a rich one, and he wears the traditional costume; it's beneath her to step out with him. The only thing they could do is carry on a secret affair, but he'll have none of it, he wants to marry her, he's been after her for years!" Luna felt sad and sorry that two people could be kept apart by these silly social rules, each carrying on a solitary life. In this respect, she was glad she lived in modern day America, where you could marry anyone and do anything you wanted, as long as you didn't commit a crime. Giustina, still daydreaming and enamored of her slip of fortune paper, said:

"We're supposed to meet at that small trattoria in front of the market, the one with the yellow owning, to have a late lunch." They walked back to the piazza, and saw that the vendors were dismantling their stalls, the market was over, and everyone either was going home or taking refuge in the various trattorias, coffee shops or restaurants. Aunt Nannina was already sitting at a nice little table inside, and didn't look sad or upset. They all took their places, and aunt Palma ordered food for everyone:

"My treat," she said, "I used to come here often when I was younger. The food in Pico is just wonderful; I was always pleased with it. We'll have some bucatini all'Amatriciana, some breaded chicken cutlets and a platter of Pico's different kinds of olives and cheeses; you'll be amazed at what they make over here, and what they grow." Large slices of golden yellow semolina bread were served with a big Chianti flask of wine. Aunt Nannina said:

"Water for me, I'm driving." And Aunt Palma replied:

"We'll do justice to it, and take the rest home." While they waited for their food, they looked outside at the stragglers still left in the piazza, and saw Aunt Nannina's 'boyfriend' joking and laughing with some friends; he kept looking at them through the trattoria's window. Aunt Palma commented:

"Ferdinando's a strapping young man, isn't he, and quite hot!" Aunt Nannina said sourly:

"He's not a young man; he's fifty if he's a day!" And she looked longingly at him. Aunt Palma replied:

"He's a young man to me! It gives me the chills just looking at him! I wonder what he's like in bed!" Aunt Nannina got all red in the face and said angrily:

"Aunt Palma, please refrain from such vulgar admiration of the man's attributes. A woman like me can never find such a man attractive, let alone 'hot' as you put it!" To which Aunt Palma replied, cackling:

"I guess him and his vulgar attributes would be a mighty handful in a woman's bed!"

"Be quiet, aunt Palma, there are children present!" Aunt Palma looked penitent, but a slight smile hovered over her wrinkled little lips. At that moment their food arrived; they each received a full plate of delicious looking bucatini in a juicy red sauce, covered in grated cheese, and with bits of bacon and dry sausage mixed in. They ate in silence for a while, and then Aunt Palma said, pensively:

"How can anyone even think to mangle a good plate of bucatini all'Amatriciana!" The girls stopped eating and perked their ears; when Aunt Palma said something like that, offhandedly, there usually was a story behind it, and a juicy one at that. Everyone waited with suspense, and when Aunt Palma knew she had their attention, she started:

"It's that Stina Ciacia, again! She invited her sons and their wives for dinner, and when they asked what she was going to make, she replied 'some Amatriciana'. Her kids were happy, 'cause who doesn't like a good plate of bucatini all'Amatriciana? When they showed up and got all ready to eat their favorite, she served the food but guess what?" Everyone exclaimed:

"What? What did she do?" When the suspense was high enough, Aunt Palma said:

"She served everybody a plate of penne all'Amatriciana." Everyone was flabbergasted:

"Penne all'Amatriciana?"

"Yes, penne all'Amatriciana!"   Even the server at the trattoria, who was just putting down a platter of mixed cheese and olives and a platter of chicken cutlets on their table, exclaimed:

"Penne all'Amatriciana?"   Aunt Palma inclined her head sadly:

"Yes, penne all'Amatriciana!"   Aunt Nannina expressed everyone's question when she said:

"What did her family say?"

"Her sons were pretty upset, expecting a good plate of bucatini like they were, but her daughters-in-law were positively scandalized." Everyone shook their heads, including the owner of the trattoria, who had joined their group, and Aunt Palma said:

"Thank God her poor husband is dead, or he would be so humiliated by all the things she's doing of lately.   Everyone cautions her about her transgressions, but she keeps right on doing what she wants. And yet, she was a model wife when her husband was alive." Giustina said:

"I heard that he used to beat her!" Aunt Palma replied:

"She never complained of anything when he was alive, that's probably a story she put out to get people's sympathy and attention." Aunt Nannina said:

"Maybe she never said anything because she was afraid of him, and now she's just asserting her independence!" Everyone was quiet for a while, and Aunt Nannina, a look of stubborn resolution hardening her face, mumbled almost to herself:

"Maybe it is a good thing for a woman to be alone! No man is worth a wasted life." After the meal, not willing to leave the now peaceful Pico, their little group followed aunt Palma around town to see the sights. Pico was ancient, and when Aunt Palma took them to the street closest to the edge of town, it felt like they had gone back in time. At one side of the silent and still street were great stone houses, some with a riot of winter flowers spilling out of the windows and some with closed shutters and balconies. On the other side of the street was a great white wall, which surrounded the entire town. Over the wall you could see the tops of majestic trees, also ancient, as they swayed gently in the late afternoon breeze. They found themselves whispering, and it felt like they were walking inside a great cathedral.   Finally, they burst into the small piazza again, and there was no one left, except the street cleaners who were sweeping the piazza and Ferdinando, who was sitting on a chair in front of the café, looking all at once deflated and lonely. As they walked by him to the car, Aunt Palma said:

"Good bye Ferdinando, see you soon!"   And Ferdinando, smiling sadly replied:

"Can I come visit you, then, Aunt Palma?"

"Any time you want, big boy! Any time you want!" He got up almost cheerfully, and stretching his arms said:

"I'll come over Sunday next, around what time?"   Aunt Palma responded, with a smirk:

"Come for Sunday dinner, around two or three in the afternoon!" Aunt Nannina turned on her, angry:

"I thought you had asked me to Sunday dinner at two or three in the afternoon!" Aunt Palma waved her away blithely:

"My table can accommodate more than two people, Nannina. And it's my house, so I can invite anyone I want!"   Ferdinando's booming laughter followed them as Aunt Nannina sat mutinously in the driver's seat of her little car.   The sky was getting purple and Mount Leuci was getting lost in the mist as they made their way slowly and safely towards home.

The big day was almost here! In two days they were going to raise the wedding pavilion. Carlo and his boy had been working frantically on the foundations, as they were supposed to cure before they built on top of them. Luna had gone over with Ivana and Uncle Pas one day, to check on the progress, and she was surprised to see a great rectangle where the pavilion would be. It was made of cement, on the ground, and sticking out of the cement were long, thick steel rods.   Ivana told her that the cement went a long way down, and that Carlo had used his construction machinery to dig the big hole, and then filled it with cement. There were wooden cases holding the cement together. As far as Luna could see, there was going to be no basement. Ivana was watching Roberto with feverish intensity, while Luna could not take her eyes off of Carlo, she didn't even know why. On the site there was a mountain of squarish stones, in all different shapes and sizes, all of a yellowish color and quite shiny and porous inside. Luna asked Ivana where the wood was, and Ivana pointed farther off to a considerable pile of wooden planks. Luna was perplexed:

"That's all of it?" And Ivana said, impatiently:

"How much wood do you think they need?" Luna looked at Ivana, surprised:

"A lot, enough to build the whole pavilion!" Ivana stopped looking at Roberto and looked at Luna curiously:

"You sound like you thought that the pavilion would be made of just wood!" And Luna replied:

"It's not made of wood?"

"No, Dunderhead! It's going to be made of stones, like everything else around here!" Luna was flabbergasted by her blunder. She knew every building around was made of stones, except for the barns. She'd forgotten about this already! Some barns, like the one they burned, were made of wood and some, like the new Merolli barn, were made of cement bricks; she saw them build it! She asked Ivana what they were going to do with the wood, if the pavilion was built of stones. Ivana said:

"You don't know much about building, do you?" And as Luna shook her head, she explained, patiently: "The wood is used to construct the windows and doors. They also use wood for the roof frame, and they install beautiful wood rafters on the ceiling to make the room attractive and to have something to hang things on." Luna was amazed at how differently they made houses over here, and at how strong and secure they were. Before coming here, she'd never seen anything built differently than at home. Uncle Pas, who had listened to the two girls talk quite interestedly, asked Luna, privately:

"Do they really make houses and buildings entirely from wood where you come from?" Luna whispered:

"Yes, regular sized houses and even great big ones for rich people. But I think they use steel beams or something to hold them up, if the buildings are really large. I don't really know much about buildings!" Uncle Pas shook his head, amazed, and said:

"I am discovering a lot of things I didn't know since your arrival, Little Luna, and I'm going to read up about these wood houses; the world is an amazing place and if you can't go there to see all of these marvels for yourself, it's just as exciting to read about them." Luna leaned a little into Uncle Pas' side and thought to herself how amazing and adaptable her wonderful Uncle was. If he couldn't do something one way, he always found other ways to get it done, and he was like a sponge, ready to accept and learn new things about this world right from his little farm, in the middle of nowhere. Luna also started to understand the power of books, and how important they were to someone thirsty for knowledge. How she was going to live without her Uncle, and this world she was discovering, she didn't know! All of a sudden, she thought:

"Why had I never gone to the Internet to learn new things myself? Uncle Pas would take to the Internet in no time, and love every second of it!"

The big day was almost here. Carlo called a meeting of The Wedding Consultants, where he showed up with an elderly gentleman in a suit. He said that the gentleman was a retired architect from Roma, he had worked with him before, and since this building was so important, he had decided to call in Mr. Arcibaldo, who found the whole idea very exciting and would work for free if he was given room and board, and if his name would go on the plaque of dedication; everyone thought privately that this plaque would soon be as big as the pavilion itself, but thought this was a great idea all the same! Carlo had given Mr. Arcibaldo his best room, and set him up with a large desk created with two by fours and a large plank, everything he would need for this project, as well as a comfortable cot and chair for his private use. He was a very nice, youthful old man, and said that getting this excited at his age over a nonpaying job was truly amazing to him, but he was enjoying himself nonetheless. They all pored over tentative plans and each gave his or her idea, until everyone was satisfied, and the pavilion was shaping up wonderfully. It would be a rectangular, single story building, with a large, heavy door at each end, a line of beautiful, large windows on each side, and some skylights on the cathedral ceiling, between the rafters. The skylights had been Luna's idea, and Ivana suggested they get

Marcello the painter to paint beautiful designs on them. This idea was a tremendous surprise to everyone, they would have never thought of it. Mr. Arcibaldo was so excited by this forward thinking that he felt a new lease on life, and thought that maybe he would go back to work once back in Roma. The designs on the skylights would be a close replica of the leaded windows in the little church, and this idea was also original enough to excite the old architect.

But there were other, more mundane, but equally exciting, considerations to take into account, as well. Outside of the large back door, there would be a wonderfully large kitchen, and near it a finely appointed bathroom. The pavilion would have long lines of tables on both sides, and a beautiful long stage in the middle, only halfway down the length of the building, to leave a large space for dancing. On the center stage the wedding cake would be the centerpiece, and the rest of the food would be displayed next to artistic pieces provided by talented individuals in the neighborhood. Luna and Ivana knew that Uncle Saverio had been working on a large carving of the bride and groom, and the only thing missing from the bridal couple was the golden patina brought on by continuous rubbing. Their statue would certainly be the centerpiece, right next to the cake. Under each window would be a window box, like the ones used on the outside of houses, but these would be on the inside so that streams of flowers could be displayed for every occasion, and other decorations would be hung from the rafters. The floor would be made from white, nonslip tiles, and the walls would be covered by groups of tiles that would have large designs on them, which Carlo would be going to Sorrento to pick up. They had already decided on a theme, which would be Vivaldi's Four Seasons. A letter had been written to the tile painters, and they were already hard at work. News of the wedding was spreading fast.

53. *Scorcio sul mercato*. Cartolina (senza ulteriori indicazioni).

Pontecorvo, scene of market day.
Unknown

The big day was here! Bright and early, they all piled up in the truck, on a Saturday morning, two weeks before Christmas, and they were on their way! When they arrived at the site, it was already a hive of activity; farther back from the construction site, long tables had been set up under large tents, chairs were lined up next to the tables, covered containers were lined up on the tables, and Uncle Pas and Aunt Esther added their containers of food. There was a humongous salad of potatoes, tomatoes, cucumbers and onions, a great platter of chicken cutlets fried in batter, sausages fried with red peppers, rice timbale covered in red sauce, tiny meatballs and mozzarella cheese, and an enormous potato pie studded with specks of salami, parsley, mozzarella and grated cheese, and covered by golden breadcrumbs. Aunt Esther and Uncle Pas had been up late the night before, cooking. The girls were running around lifting cloth covers and pot covers to see what else was underneath, and the offerings were so wonderful that they could hardly wait to sample everything. Don Attilio and the other priests had brought out a large, dusty cask of their best red wine, and the men could hardly wait to sample that! Everyone was there, The Fool came followed by Rodolfo, and Rodolfo was, of course followed by Antonietta, and Antonietta was followed by her mother and Rodolfo's mother, and they were followed by Antonietta's brawny brothers and their wives and kids. Rodolfo's father was already there, and you could see by the light shining in his eyes when he spotted Antonietta, that he already loved her like a daughter.   To everyone's surprise, Antonietta, who was a little cold and shy with everyone else, hugged him warmly. Mario Merolli and his family showed up the next moment and Anna of course! Nannina and Giustina came after that, followed by Aunt Palma, who pushed them aside and ran ahead to take command of the food preparations. Next to arrive was the teacher, Gianna, carrying big boxes that everyone knew were most likely her delicious pastries, and Uncle Saverio, who had a box with a few bottles in it (everyone knew there was cordial and liquors in there and they all hankered for the end of the day, when coffee and anisette time came). Aunt Palma commanded Nannina to go back to the car and bring her bundles, and everyone knew they could eat to their heart's content because there would be bottles of Aunt Palma's elixir to settle their stomachs. Gianna had brought a great box of cornetti (a kind of Italian croissants) and another big box of maritozzi. Even Great Aunt Marianna, who was there with sharp little Great Uncle Biagio had to admit that as good as she was with maritozzi, her daughter-in-law's were masterpieces. Gianna had also brought some of her strawberry marmalade in a big covered jar, and everyone was salivating at the thought of eating cornetti and maritozzi for breakfast, stuffed with Gianna's red and sweet marmalade. There were fire pits on the outside of the clearing, and huge espresso pots were already going. Everyone had contributed their best, but the coffee, expensive as it was, was just abundant and wonderful. The aroma of espresso was intoxicating, and a little figure detached itself from behind the coffee pit and came forward smiling. She had the one dimple, streaming hair down her back, and she was all in black, with a tight knit sweater and loose lady trousers. Over her shoulders she was wearing a beautiful black woolen shawl, and on her feet she had some dainty leather boots. It was kind of cold, given that it was almost Christmas, and everyone was wearing winter clothing, but they were all mesmerized by Inessa and her stylish attire. Don Attilio had objected to the trousers at first, but after he saw how tireless Inessa was and how she herself dug the pit and set up the coffee, and looking at the big container of ground coffee beans and the huge bowl of sweet and expensive sugar, and noticing how she could work like a man, but could be also very modest because of the trousers, he accepted the strong, beautiful girl, and when he sat down to gobble a cornetto stuffed with marmalade together with a large cup of fragrant sweet espresso, he somehow felt even some fatherly love towards Inessa. Lilliana arrived carrying a large pannier filled with all kinds of soft oil Panini, and a big box of cold cuts; prosciutto, salame, soppressata, capocollo and large pieces of creamy gorgonzola cheese. She was wearing a red shirt, and black culottes, and on her feet she wore a pair of the cutest ankle boots, which over here were called Polacchine. On top of her clothes she wore a short, soft darker red woolen jacket, and she looked just like a little kid who skipped school for the day. Her jacket was in the new redingote style, flared in the back, and Aunt Esther was filing all of this information about modern clothes in the back of her mind; after the wedding she would have to do some serious sewing for herself and the girls, maybe even some lose trousers the girls could wear if they went out of town.   Meanwhile, Lilliana smiled warmly and was very congenial to everyone and a crowd surged forward to meet her, the smell of the creamy gorgonzola and sweet prosciutto attracting everyone in sight, and soon golden Panini stuffed with all of the expensive goodies Lilliana brought, were flying everywhere in people's hands.   Luna and Ivana were the first to follow her like puppies, and they got the first Panini in their hands after Lilliana found a spot on one of the tables and set up quickly.   By now, Don Attilio was used to women wearing modern clothing, and he didn't really care if Lilliana was wearing culottes, as long as she put an extra piece of prosciutto on his panino.   Toscana, in soft, thick blue woolen sweater, straight black, slim skirt and comfy wellingtons, was preceded by her husband, a handsome slim guy, who was carrying her offerings. Since she was originally from a more southern part of Italy than everyone, except the Sicilian, she had made specialties from her hometown; there were large mouth jars of dried tomatoes, mixed with garlic cloves, parsley, and tiny hot peppers, all steeped in fragrant olive oil. She had jars filled with pickled eggplant, in slices so thin you could see through them, also covered in fragrant olive oil, garlic, parsley and tiny hot peppers.   She was holding a box filled with sheets of focaccia at least two inches thick and covered with golden onions caramelized with olive oil slowly and gently in a deep pot and garnished with large, black olives and specks of tomatoes.   Everyone had to have a taste of the focaccia, before they were finally ready to put all the fun down and start working. Anna had laid checkered tablecloths on the tables, and big baskets of silverware were placed strategically everywhere.   The food flew and disappeared like snow in the sun.

By now, Aunt Esther didn't care about the food anymore; let someone else worry about that! There were enough women to do it! Anna was marching around giving orders and reporting to Aunt Palma, and the other women diligently carried out their orders no matter how strange or arduous. But everything was working out well, and out of chaos came a perfectly organized outfit. Aunt Esther knew everything was in good hands, and all she cared about was the pavilion, after all it was her idea and she wanted it to be perfect.   Angelina, Irma and Amelia worked hard cataloging everything and putting the same foods together, so later everyone could have an informed choice on what they wanted to eat; it wouldn't do to waste food if someone saw something they liked better than what was on their plate, and got rid of it to get the better morsel.   Ernestina, Ada and Arturo showed up late, because Arturo drove to Pontecorvo first to borrow a stone mason hammer from a friend of his; there were so many people working that there were not enough tools for everyone. Uncle Saverio swaggered over to The Fool and held out his hand. Everyone knew about the challenge and was electrified. The first one who was too exhausted to work would concede to the other gentleman. They shook hands and smiled crookedly at each other.   Everyone whooped and hollered, ready for the contest to begin!

Armed with a stone ax The Fool approached the giant pile of rocks, picked one up and started to cut and shape it with deft, quick, powerful blows. Everyone was flabbergasted at the little old man's energy and knowledge.   Assunta, proudly, told everyone:

"Tarquinio was a stone mason part time, when we married. Don't let his size fool you, that little man packs a big punch, I should know! I've seen him do things that would have scared a bigger man." The rocks were porous, true, so that the wall would breathe and dry fast, but they were heavy still, and they needed to be shaped so that they could be staggered and fit to each other to make the wall straight and strong. When the Fool's rock was ready, Uncle Saverio reached down, lifted the large rock over his powerful shoulder and, laughing heartily, brought it up to the foundation and plunked it down on the soft mound of mortar that Mario had just slathered on top of the foundation.   Everyone cheered:

"One down and untold hundreds more to go!"   And so on it went.   Arturo, strong as an ox because of his job at the slaughterhouse, attacked the stones like the Man of Steel himself. As Ernestina and Ada basked in the reflected glory, Aunt Esther gently hugged them to show her appreciation.   Stone after stone was carried to the foundations on the shoulders of the men, plunked down on the mortar that was constantly being replenished, and then positioned with sharp taps from rubber mallets and hit hard until completely buried in the mortar. Uncle Pas worked at shaping the stones for a while, and when there were enough for everyone to carry to the foundation, he himself picked them up, one by one and agilely climbed the ladder to plunk them down in front of the Inside Man; this was the guy on top of the ladder on the other side of the wall, inside the structure, who thumped the stones into place. This construction very much interested Luna. Not only had she never seen an actual building going up right in front of her, she could also appreciate how strong and safe it would be when finished. No fire would burn these houses the way it did the wooden ones so easily at home! During all this, Ivana told her that if this building had more than one story, they would use a machine called a Lewis to lift stones and dangle them on the wall before plunking them down, but with a one-story building, the men were able to carry the rocks up the ladder and build much faster themselves. Remigio, Roberto and the Russo boys were in charge of the mortar, and they worked very hard mixing it constantly in a big pit dug into the ground, Once in a while some of the men took over from them so they could rest, but the boys were strong and agile, and they put in as much work as any of the others. When they first arrived at the site, the huge hole in the ground gave out fumes, with a strong smell of lime. Luna leaned in to look down at the milky white substance bubbling below, when she suddenly felt someone pull at her strong enough to knock her backwards. She turned around to see who it was, and seeing that it was Ivana, she asked, heaving:

"What are you doing?"

"I'm saving your life, Girl from the Moon, what did you think I was doing?"

"Saving my life?" Asked Luna perplexed:

"Don't you know what that stuff is? It's unslaked lime, and if you fall in you'll be a skeleton in no time at all!" Luna stared at her best friend, asking:

"So what's unslaked lime, and what it's made of?"

"It's liquid lime. They make it by burning limestone in a lime kiln, and when they add water and cement, it makes a very strong mortar to keep the rocks together forever, almost!" Luna was amazed; it took a lot to make these wonderful stone buildings, and she loved being a part of it all. But she was glad Ivana was there to look after her; she didn't want to be a skeleton and this was clearly one of the cases where ignorance could be fatal.

There was a group, to which Rodolfo and his father belonged, who were working with the wood. They were shaving and sawing the long pieces and rubbing them with fine sandpaper to bring out the golden hue of the beautiful oak. Mr. Arcibaldo had set up a humongous trestle table, on which a great print of the building was displayed in detail, and the men referred to him once in a while, to place the wood in the strategic, special places where there would be a door or a window. The lintels of heavy timber and the door and window frames were beautiful and massive, and the wood shined subtly in the December sun. It was agreed that today they would establish the frame of the whole building, and in the following days, as many men as possible would work at refinishing everything else. They had twenty-five days to build the whole thing, and by golly they would get it done on time! The inside of the pavilion had to be complete and dry enough so that the women could work on the decorations and other preparations. The Sorrento people, who by now knew everything about the wedding, said that they would come down for three days and install their wall tiles themselves; the floor had better be dry enough to walk on by then! So everyone gave one hundred percent and worked very, very hard. But the hardest worker of them all was Quagliozzi the photographer; he was everywhere, toting his heavy camera and shouting:

"Stand still!" And: "Don't move or look away!" And: "Flex your muscles!" But when he started to yell: "Pick up that rock from the mortar and drop it again!" Or: "Come down from the ladder and climb it again with the rock on the other shoulder!" Everyone started to ignore him, so he had to switch to taking candid shots. The Fool worked methodically on the rocks, and when there was a large pile of them, he would pick up one at the time in his old, muscled arms and climb the ladder to plop it up on the mortar himself. Uncle Saverio, on the other hand, ran back and forth, up and down the ladder furiously and mostly worked like a devil while throwing heated looks at The Fool over his shoulder. The Fool looked back, inclined his head slightly and smiled. At midday, they all stopped for a lunch break and some rest. Lunch was set up on one of the smaller tables, and soon there was nothing left of the food. They were saving the 'big gun' dishes for dinner, after the day was done, but for now they finished Lilliana's cold cuts and Panini, Toscana's pickled vegetables and focaccia, a huge, rustic pizza pie stuffed with salami, hard boiled eggs, mozzarella, and fresh eggs to tie the whole together, brought by Anna. There were also mountains of meat-stuffed rice balls brought by one of Anna's daughters-in-law, the Sicilian. There were piles of Angelina's Swiss chard pies; she thanked God for Carlo who covered the tender Swiss chard with hay earlier in the season, or the occasional early morning frost would have ruined the beautiful tender leaves for sure. Amelia and Anna brought a large basket of Anna's wine biscuits, which everyone couldn't wait to munch on; after all you never knew if these old wives tales were real or not, the promise that you would live to be a hundred if you ate the biscuits dunked in wine was very attractive indeed. The men sampled the cask of the priests' wine, and what good wine it was! And the women and children enjoyed big pitchers of lemonade. Everyone sat on the ground, satisfied, and after a while the chatter stopped to let the men catch forty winks. Even thought it was December, to Luna it felt more like an autumn day at home. Everyone was pleasantly drowsy, and after an hour's rest, they all woke up to the wonderful smell of fresh espresso. Inessa was indefatigable, great cups of coffee were passed around, and soon the men finished waking up and the site was a hive of activity as work started up once again.

During this time, Luna sought out Anna and asked her why everyone took such a long lunch break, not to mention a rest afterwards, totally unheard of at home! Anna responded

"My Dear Luna, you think this is too long to stop work? How much time do people take at home?"

"Half an hour most of the time, although the 'big bosses' can take all they want. Many people simply have too much to do and not enough time to do it, so they don't take any lunch breaks at all. And no one ever rests. They just eat and go right back to work."

"Really?" Anna asked, not believing. Luna responded:

"It happens all the time. People are given more and more work to do, and less and less time to do it, so they work harder and also stay later in the day"

"What happens if you simply cannot work that hard?" Anna asked.

"It depends. Many times, those workers get fired and replaced by cheaper, faster people who simply work without asking questions." Luna finally admitted in a sad tone. Anna spoke softly and very sadly, with complete understanding,

"My God, Child! I've been talking to you for a while, and truly, it seems like no one cares for anyone where you're from, do they?"

"No, mostly they don't, Anna. No one is important to the huge companies, or to anyone else, anymore. There are constant news stories about some big company firing thousands of people at a time, with no second thought whatsoever! And these people simply have nowhere to go afterwards. Some of them do stupid things." Anna continued:

"What's wrong with people at home, Luna? What is happening there to cause all of this?! Is everyone simply going crazy?"

"I don't know, Anna! I really don't. But I can tell you that dad's never home when I come from school. He often comes home after I go to bed, so I never get to see him, and the few times I do, he's always angry at me! And so is Mom!" Anna then said:

"Luna, I've watched you very carefully ever since you came here on that train, and what I see is a girl who's never been truly cared for, guided or appreciated. It seems like no one has time for their families. Also it seems that no one has any faith left either. People cannot live without a strong center, Luna, no matter how many new-fangled 'computers', or whatever else, there may be at home." Luna couldn't believe how well Anna simply said everything she herself thought and felt. How was this possible?! Suddenly, Luna needed to be held really bad, and Anna, ever understanding, hugged her tightly as she cried softly:

"Yet you love your family, don't you, Luna? You just didn't realize it before because of the anger and bad feelings." Luna looked up and nodded, and said with a small voice:

"I don't want you to think that everything is bad where I come from, Anna, some people are nice, and they try very hard, it's just that sometimes, no one understand them; I know that I sometimes blame my parents and teachers for things gone bad, but I now realize that they have their own problems, but if we all try, things can get better. I now understand that sometimes when things went bad for me it was entirely my fault."

"To make things better it has to be a concerted effort, Luna, people should be willing to work together and help one another. Don't expect people to be nice to you right off the bat, you try and be nice first, and they will respond." Luna whispered:

"You are so right, and so wise, Anna!" And Anna hugged Luna and then continued:

"Luna, we will talk more of this later. But for now, be patient. You WILL go back home, and you WILL be much better off with the life lessons you've learned while here. Have faith, Luna. It will all work out in the end." Luna hugged Anna back, saying:

"Thank you so much Anna! I Love You!"

Towards the end of the day, as night was falling, Uncle Saverio, who had done the work of ten men, like a giant tree felled by one too many blows, lay down on the ground and looking over at The Fool, said:

"You win, Old Man, I can't go on any more!" The Fool put down his stone axe, sat next to him, put his head down on his knees and said:

"Let's call it even, Young Man. I'm pretty exhausted myself! You could have easily won, you know, if you'd only paced yourself a little more carefully. Ha! The exuberance and haste of youth! I knew it would get the best of you, and I was planning on it. You're much stronger than I am, Young Man, just not disciplined enough to make the most of your strength. Like a fire that flares brightly, only to burn itself out quickly, you went too fast for too long. I took a slower, but steady, pace and outlasted you as a result. I should know: I did the same thing when I was young. Everyone does. All you've got to do is be mindful of what you're doing, and you will outlast others, especially when they do the same thing." Uncle Saverio lifted his head long enough to say, smiling:

"You're a tough old bird, I must say! I didn't figure on you lasting the whole day like this. You surprised the heck out of me!" The Fool looked at the young man lying down on the grass and said:

"Mind over Matter, my boy. Mind over Matter!" Uncle Saverio extended his hand and they shook on that, and he said:

"One of these days I'll come over to see you. I'd like to know more about this 'Mind over Matter' thing." Everyone roared with laughter, and then they tiredly put their tools down, after which the site was then cleaned and prepared for the next day. Anna went up to Assunta and said to her:

"You have a real man there, my girl!" And Assunta whispered back, her eyes moist:

"I know, I know! I feel lucky every day, and to think that I hadn't even realized what a treasure I had until we started talking to each other about our feelings and that was only recently! We had some worries about our daughter, and that opened up the gates. Now we talk every night before we go to sleep, and we have found a new beginning in each other's arms, and in our old age too!" Anna shook her head:

"I have seen people go through life without ever telling each other how they feel; it's a tragedy, really! Communication is what we all need every day. But I'll tell you, Assunta, that if he wasn't already married I would have set my sites on that man. You're lucky and you know it!" And they embraced. Assunta whispered in Anna's ear:

"He never told me how he felt because he assumed that I already knew, and I never told him how I felt because I was afraid of rejection, so we just stayed away from each other." And a tear streaked down her cheek. Anna whispered back:

"But now you both know, and there's no reason to cry."

"I'm crying for all of the time we lost!" Then she turned towards her Tarquinio and her plain face took on a luminescence, a peaceful look of inner beauty as she enveloped her lifelong companion in a cocoon of private love.

They had already decided on the crew for each of the following days, and things were being planned so that the building would be finished and furnished for the wedding day. Torches were lit all around the site, because by now dark was encroaching, and everyone ate the beautiful food that was waiting for them, drank the wine and talked about the important points of the day. Gianna was glued to Uncle Saverio's side, and kept massaging his sore arms, and he leaned down often to deposit a light thank you kiss on the top of her head. Uncle Pas brought Aunt Esther inside of the pavilion and showed her things she couldn't see while they were working, and Aunt Esther's eyes shined when she saw how well some of her ideas were working; she knew that her Pasquale had fought for her and applied everything she had thought of for the sake of the pavilion, but even more to please her. Everyone was satisfied with each other's work, and the building was starting to look great indeed. Later, dessert was served, along with lots of espresso from Inessa and liqueur from Uncle Saverio's stash. Everyone was happy and calm, and no one was in need of Aunt Palma's stomach settling elixir, but they didn't dare say no anyway; she was watching everyone with gimlet eyes, and God help the person who scorned her offering. Ernestina was sitting next to Arturo, drinking in his words and looking adoringly up at him, and he caressed her shoulder once in a while, and Anna was seating with Luna, Ivana and Ada, swapping pastry and running up for more coffee every other minute:

"I'll be up all night!" Whispered Anna with a yawn. After the food and talk, while Anna dozed off, the girls quietly got up and walked inside of the pavilion. There was no roof yet, and no floor either, but it was humongous. It had a clean new smell of lime and wet rocks, and it had an eco. (Luna had almost never heard an echo inside a building before, and the newness of it all was quite surprising to her as well.) They could imagine it full of people, laughter, with music and flowers; a cathedral and a joyful place all at once. Luna thought:

"Life is good. Over here, everyone loves life and makes things happen. Why can't it be like this at home?" To which a voice resonated in her head:

"You can make it so if that's your desire, Young Luna. Every one of us can change the world for the better, if we really want to! Remember Emperor Nero's lesson of growth and renewal? Each and every one of us can change for the better! Sometimes it takes great effort, but as long as you follow your heart, it will always be worth it in the end!"   She hadn't heard from old Balthazar in a while and it made her feel secure to know that he was still there, keeping an eye on her.   It also made her sad, because she knew the day was coming when she would have to say 'good bye' to everyone and everything and go back to where she came from.   But she also knew it was absolutely impossible NOT to go back.   She had her family to make up with, and her future that would unfold in front of her:

"Parting is Such Sweet Sorrow." Balthazar whispered to her once again.   On the way home, Luna and Ivana cuddled in the rear of the truck, lulled by the quiet voices of Aunt Esther and Uncle Pas, as they talked about the past few days and life in general. Aunt Esther was deeply satisfied but drained and Uncle Pas was just about as exhausted as he could ever be, but they were happy and fulfilled, and so were the girls.

58. *Istituto Magistrale.* Cartolina, bollo post. 30/XII/1932. Retro: "Cartolina Postale / 121998 Commissionario A. Carbone / Riproduzione vietata".

Pontecorvo's fancy school on May Street, 1932.
Commissioned by A. Carbone

The next few days were busy and hectic. Everyone worked nonstop on the wedding arrangements, and Quagliozzi the photographer had become a permanent fixture of their lives. Two days before Christmas, everyone stopped working, everything was mostly done, and they prepared for the Blessed Holiday. Luna realized that Christmas in 1950's Italy was mostly a religious holiday with lots of traditions, and those traditions were mostly about church, food, and, especially, family and friends.   No running around to 'Shop 'Till You Drop', no lists of what to get for whom, no desperation about how much money to spend.   No worries about re-gifting' either. Luna KNEW what Anna would make of everyone maxing out their 'credit cards' every year, only to desperately try to pay them off after. The farm was happy and everyone was joyous about just being alive and celebrating. The more intimate people were making gifts for each other, and there was a feeling of Christmas in the air. Anna was baking baskets of her anise seed cookies for everyone, and she also made Neapolitan nougat candy, which was made of sugar and almonds, cooked together until the sugar was golden brown and the almonds nicely roasted. When barely cool, they were shaped into sticks as big as a small sausage. The sticks of nougat were dried and then wrapped in colored tissue paper fringed at the ends, and the ends twisted together, to form beautiful, delicious and sweet smelling treats.   Aunt Esther was making strufoli; a sweet comprised of hundreds of tiny bits of dough, fried golden brown and then rolled in melted honey and sugar. She would shape it like a large donut and then sprinkle tiny slices of orange and lemon peels on it, with tiny colorful nonpareils. When the strufoli donut cooled down, it was sweet and crunchy, orangey and lemony at the same time, and festive enough to please everyone. Aunt Palma, helped by Nannina and Giustina, was making mountains of mostaccioli, stubby sweets, diamond shaped, stuffed with dough made of cinnamon, cloves, nutmeg and chocolate, and covered by a shiny crust of darkest chocolate which hid a thin layer of apricot marmalade. The recipe came from Napoli, and these sweets were throwbacks from the days when Napoli first hired Saracen mercenaries to fight its wars.

These mostaccioli were everyone's favorite, but very hard to make, and exhausting to prepare before being properly cured. Gianna the teacher was making everyone a Panettone. This was the very best favorite for Christmas Eve, and New Year's Eve as well. The only thing was that no one knew how to make a real Panettone. They were only sold in stores already packaged, and were very expensive. But with her background in pastry making, Gianna knew the secret, and she was giving one to each family in the surrounding area. Angelina, Irma and Amelia were helping her, and getting lessons in Panettone making at the same time. There were scores of very fine parchment paper sheets around, and after the Panettones were cooled, the women would wrap the wonderful, tall, fragrant sweet breads bursting with raisins and candied fruits in this parchment paper and decorate them with ribbons and holly. During all this, Luna and Ivana were racing their bikes everywhere, to enjoy and participate in the preparations, and to snitch a taste here and there. Luna remembered all the times she'd seen Italian delicacies like these in all the stores at home, especially around the Holidays. Yet if her Mom bought anything whatsoever, it was a tiny Panettone, small and stale, which she often gave away. From time to time, her Grandma tried introducing her and her parents to food and traditions from the Old Country, but none of them had any time to appreciate her. Perhaps Grandma could help Luna remember her time here after all. Aunt Esther had said that the girls should prepare their own specialty, so they got together with Ada, Concetta and Luana at Luana's house, and made some Christmas ricotta turnovers under the guidance of Luana's mother. Luana's Mom was short, chubby and sweet, and she showed the girls how to make the pastry, while her father, lean and tall, gave them gassosa and pomegranates to eat. Luna had never had this fruit at home, even though she had often seen them in the supermarket. She didn't like them at first, because no matter how she tried, she always ate some of the membrane between the kernels, and it was very bitter, but now that she'd learned how to eat the fruit correctly, she loved it. Luana's mom told them they could eat some of the little turnovers, which tasted wonderful. They made half of them in sweet, white ricotta, and the other half in rich chocolate ricotta. The recipes were actually quite simple here, with very few ingredients, and Luna tried to remember how to make everything that she loved (which was basically everything). She didn't want to think about it, but she knew that when she left here, she couldn't take anything with her, only what was in her head. These days, thoughts of home made her sick to her stomach. She missed her parents and family so very much, yet she didn't want to leave this wonderful place and time, not to mention everyone she loved here, behind.

"If only I could have Ivana with me," she thought, "I would be happy to go home; being able to talk to her about everyone would make it so much better!" But then she remembered that taking Ivana away from her parents and family would break their hearts, and she felt unhappy and confused all over again; she could never hurt her beloved aunt and uncle. What could she do and how could she do it? A voice in her head said:

"You'll find a way, Luna, you'll find a way! And don't worry about losing Ivana. Just wait and see!"

"Oh shut up, Balthazar, I'm getting sick of you!" Ivana looked up and said:

"What did you say?" Luna replied with a smile:

"I said that if I drink any more Gassosa I'll get sick all over you!" Ivana looked at her, and slowly moved a little bit away, almost on the other side of the table, and Luna laughed right out at her, joined by the other girls, who had followed the later part of the conversation. That's what was so good here, everything was joyful and happy. No matter how bad things got, people always found something to laugh about and Luna had learned that laughing together was truly always the best medicine. As the girls worked side by side, they talked about la Befana and what they could hope to get from her. Luna was right in the middle of it, and when her turn came to say what she was hoping for, she said:

"I want to be able to go home and stay here all at the same time, that's what I want!" Luana looked up at Luna and said:

"She's la Befana, not a magician! You can only be in one place at once, just in case you don't know; the trick is to bring all of the people you love together in the same place." At that, Luna looked ready to cry, but she felt a small hand touch her arm, and as she turned around, she met Ivana's beautiful, smiling face. While she was looking at Luna, Ivana raised her hand and touched the shiny chain she wore around her neck, which she pulled out from inside her blouse. As Ivana's hand closed tightly over the small half of the silver heart, Luna reached up and did the same to her half. A great peace came over her, and she even smiled at Ivana a little conspiratorial smile, feeling in her heart that things would work out and she would be happy in the end, come hell or high water.

There was also the house to decorate for Christmas, and the girls helped Aunt Esther to iron the dazzlingly white tablecloths and napkins for the Christmas dinner, and to wash and dry the best dishes from the hutch, as well as the crystal goblets and silver bell that was to be used on Christmas day. After the housework was finished, they started on the Nativity scene for the Christmas village. Luna had only ever seen one, at Grammeva's house, but nothing elaborate like the ones here. In the early morning, Uncle Pas had escorted the girls in search of green, moist moss. They had found great expanses of it attached to the ground, near the roots of the ancient trees on the river, and they filled their baskets. At the same time they pulled very small branches from the bottom of the trees, and gently laid them on top of the moss. Then Uncle had brought down a large box of figurines from the eaves, and Aunt Esther supplied a large round mirror which was going to be the lake. The girls went out and picked up a basket of minuscule rocks, which would be used as gravel for the roads. The last time she was at the Pezzella butcher shop in town, Aunt Esther had asked the owner for some extra sheets of brown paper for their Christmas village, and he was very happy to oblige. Uncle Pas had constructed some wooden frames for them, and Luna was very anxious to see what they were for, and how everything would come out. There was no Christmas tree, but Luna didn't feel the need for one, after all if there were no presents, what would the tree be for? Uncle set up some trestles, where he laid a large plank of wood, and pushed everything against the wall near the fireplace, so that everyone could see the village from anywhere in the kitchen. Uncle had given them a small electric cord with a small light bulb at the end, which was to be placed inside the manger to light up the scene. The plug was right behind the table, just as they needed it.

First thing, Uncle Pas covered the whole table with a large, green blanket, and set the wooden frames all around the perimeter of the set, and then he told the girls to go to it, and call him if they needed help. Luna was all excited, as Ivana took great sheets of brown butcher paper and dipped them in a bowl of water. When the paper was soaked and soft, she directed Luna to watch what she did, and do some herself. Luna was amazed, realizing that what Ivana was doing was nothing but papier mache', and she was creating mountains and scenery with wet paper draped over the wood frames. Luna started to do some herself, and they wildly created nooks and crannies and mountain peaks. Under everything, they shaped a large cave, which would be the setting for the manger. In the very back of the cave, they made a round hole in the wet paper, where the light would go. When they finished, they called Uncle Pas, who sprayed their creation with green, gold and brown paint. After that, they had the wonderful dinner Aunt Esther had prepared, and as soon as the dishes were done, they went back to their work. Amazingly, the paper was already looking like mountains and caves, and they proudly looked at their creation. Everything was dry, so it was time to fill in the rest. After much discussion, they found a spot for the lake, quite far from the manger. Next was the placement of the moss. They laid it everywhere to cover and unify the setting. The network of roads was agreed upon, and the pebbles were laid to shape them. The last things were the small branches, which were the trees of the village; they were placed everywhere and looked like real trees, lacey, feathery and soft, pushed inside the moss and into the still somewhat wet paper of the mountains. Next they gently covered the mountain tops with some light, shredded white mattress wool, to simulate snow. Luna had the honor of crawling under the table and inserting the light bulb in the back of the cave. When the right spot was found, they plugged it in and watched as the whole little cave was flooded with light. They unplugged it for the time being, and the box with the figurines was pulled out. For these important decisions, the whole family gathered around the scene. First, of course, was the manger, with little Baby Jesus in his bed made of hay. He was of course the central figure. At the left side of Jesus the Virgin Mary was kneeling with her hands extended as if she was just going to pick up her baby and hold him. On the right side, S. Joseph was a little stooped, leaning on his cane and looking at the Baby Jesus with wonder. Behind this group, a cow and a donkey were lying down on each side of the cave, and in front of Little Jesus and his parents, right outside of the cave, were the Three Wise Men: Caspar, Balthasar and Melchior. Each of them was holding a beautiful golden vessel which contained their gift to the Baby Jesus: Myrrh, Frankincense and Gold. Behind The Three Wise Men stood their servants, holding the reins of three camels covered in golden fringed blankets. On the road winding its way to the entrance of the cave, were various figures that were obviously going to visit the Baby Jesus: a shepherd carrying a baby lamb on its shoulders, women with large panniers filled with goodies, children with bunches of flowers in their hands and elderly people walking with canes and whittled branches. Further up in the mountain, shepherds and shepherdesses sat on rocks watching their sheep, while down on the lake, adults and children were skating, unaware of what was happening up in the mountain. Small houses were situated in nooks and crannies around the scene with dogs barking in front of them, and on the front of the cave a beautiful angel was suspended midair, sounding his trumpet to gather one and all to the little newborn Jesus.

Luna and Ivana stood at a little distance to take in the whole thing, and to admire their handiwork; the scene was beautiful and serene, and Luna almost felt tears in her eyes. Uncle Pas and Aunt Esther stood behind the two girls and held them with love.

"You girls did a wonderful job," said Uncle Pas admiringly, "you two are quite the artists, I've never seen a more beautiful and appropriate setting for the crèche. The village and mountains convey feelings of sacred reverence and joy for everyone. We will keep the Christmas village until after the Epiphany!" At that, Luna's eyes moistened again, and exchanging a sad look with Ivana, the two girls held each other and Luna whispered:

"I'm glad I won't be here when you take it down." Ivana didn't say anything; she just picked up the little piece of heart on the chain around her neck and rubbed it with her thumb and forefinger. Luna smiled through her tears and repeated the gesture with her chain.

"Together. We'll always be together no matter where we are!" They softly promised each other. As the girls started feeling tired, they reflected on their day. It had been full and joyous, and they had gotten a whole lot done! When they went to bed, Luna and Ivana felt relaxed and serene, as if God was taking good care of them. That night, Luna dreamed that she was walking on the very gravel road they had made earlier, going to see the Baby Jesus, and she was carrying a very heavy bundle. She wore a peasant girl's costume: a long black skirt, a white shirt tucked in at the waist, and a blue shawl over her hair. On her feet she wore wooden clogs, the kind that women wore back then. Once in a while, she would put her bundle down to rest before picking it up again and continuing slowly toward the cave. Once again, the mountains looked exactly like the ones they had created. The three wise men moved aside to let her pass and one of them smiled at her. When his twinkling blue eyes reminded her of someone she knew, she stopped short:

"Balthazar?" She whispered, and then she shook her head: "No! It can't be! I must be dreaming!" She looked back to see if it really was him under that red beard of his, but The Virgin Mary was holding her hands to her, and she stopped looking at Balthasar, one of the wise men. She put the bundle down in front of Mary, and unwrapped it. Inside of the cloth, to her surprise, was a small, white and gleaming new microwave. She looked up shyly into the limpid eyes of The Virgin Mary and whispered:

"To warm up the Baby Jesus' bottle." The Virgin Mary smiled at her and said:

"Thank you, Sweetheart! It is a wonderful gift, and we'll keep it to remind us of the sweet girl who gave it to us. But we really have no need of this apparatus, since the animals in the manger keep the milk warm with their breath." At that Luna looked around and realized that they were in a cave, and there were no electrical outlets anywhere, although in the back of the cave a light shined brightly. She felt foolish and her eyes moistened, but Mary extended her white, beautiful hand towards her and smiled:

"Don't feel bad, My Wonderful Girl, for we appreciated your gift and thank you very much. Don't feel bad, Dear!" And she caressed Luna's hair with a touch as light as a feather. The Virgin

Mary was so sweet and loving that by now Luna's tears was rolling down her cheeks. Mary leaned down and whispered in her ear:

"Everything will be alright, Dearest Luna. You'll see! Go home in peace, sweet girl, and spread your love to all those around you! Be safe and be happy, for you have been wonderful and kind to us!" And then she deposited the light, sweet whisper of a kiss on Luna's forehead. Before Luna left the cave, she kneeled in front of the manger and timidly stole a look at the Baby Jesus. He was just a cherubic regular baby, no halo or anything, but his eyes were old, like he knew everything, as if he'd already suffered. He suddenly looked straight into her eyes, and smiled beautifully, which lighted everything in a golden, shining light. Luna slept after that, and smiled in her sleep, while dreams of home and love kept revolving in her head. She did now believe that her life would indeed be great, no matter what seemed to happen next!

Small country church, Photograph 1950's.

When morning came, the girls were up bright and early. It was Christmas Eve, and there were so many things to be done! They put the finishing touches to the presents of cookies and other homemade things they were going to give to their friends, and then they jumped in the truck with Uncle Pas as he went to town to pick up his order of squid and octopus from the fishmonger. On this day, they were going to have their fish supper, and squid was a must, and octopus salad was also very nice. They had eels, which Uncle Pas caught in the river with his eel trap, and on the way back they stopped at Anna's to deliver some large, fat eels for the Merolli's fish supper. Anna insisted on them spending a little time at the house, where she served them dry figs stuffed with walnut meats and they examined the Merolli's Christmas village. It was very nice, one of the best they'd seen, except for theirs. Both Luna and Ivana had to modestly admit that theirs was just the very best there was; Uncle Pas agreed. They left promising to see each other at midnight mass, up on the mountain, and they had just enough time to take care of the animals before the great fish supper got underway. As they finished their chores, Ivana looked up the road and started to jump up and down:

"The Zampognari are here! The Zampognari are here!" Luna didn't know what the Zampognari were, but didn't want Ivana to say: 'Girl from the moon!' Again, so she shut up to wait and see what would happen next. Coming from the street on the driveway, Luna saw two men and a boy. They were wearing ancient costumes, and carried some instruments. The boy had a kind of round oboe, and the men were holding something clearly made from some kind of animal hide. It was in fact the whole skin of an animal, maybe a small sheep, with a bunch of wooden pipes with holes sticking out of the neck hole; a long flute stuck out of the hole in one of the front legs; all the pipes were attached securely to the animal skin by thin leather strips tied around the skin very tightly. The newcomers walked up to the front door, took their hats off to salute, put them on again and started to play. The men played the wooden pipes with their fingers and blew into the single pipe, while the boy played a tinny part on his

oboe like instrument, which Ivana said was called a ciaramella.
Aunt Esther, Uncle Pas and Ivana started to sing, and Luna
thought with surprise:

"Italian bag pipers!" And she started to sing along herself.
This was a lovely, sweet Christmas song, and Luna, not knowing
how, knew it was called 'You come down from the stars'. It was
dedicated to little Baby Jesus, and went like this:

"You come from the stars, o blessed God, and you paid a
great price for having loved us!" After this first Christmas song,
the group played a few more, until the boy said, plaintively:

"Dad, my tooth is frozen, it hurts!" At that, Aunt Esther
rushed forward:

"My poor boy! Come in all of you, please! Come and eat
something warm!" She ushered them into the kitchen and set
three plates on the table. She gave the men and the boy small,
wet towels to wipe their hands, and then she presented them
with bowls of warm vegetable soup she had bubbling on the
fornacella for just that purpose. She pushed a plate of cheese at
them, and chunks of golden bread. They ate with relish, warming
up nicely, and one of the men said, looking at the boy:

"Your tooth isn't frozen in front of you food, is it boy?" The
boy looked up with a prankish smile:

"The food is warm, Papa'." They all had a good laugh, and
before they left, Aunt Esther gave them a small basket filled with
eggs, and Uncle Pas slipped the men a note. They said:

"See you next year!" And walked away tipping their hats and
smiling, as they made their way to the other houses. After they
went, the great fish fry got underway, and everybody was by now
famished and anticipating all of the delicious goodies they knew
were coming. The first thing was the octopus, which had to be
cleaned and boiled, and when it was soft and pink, they slid all of
the little sucker things from the tentacles, and emptied the ink
sack. Then everything was cut into small pieces and celery, oil,
lemon, salt and pepper were added, to make a lovely salad. The
octopus salad was put out in the cold air to cool off, and the rest
of the food was prepared. They had red Italian peppers that had
been kept in vinegar for weeks, and they stuffed them with a
mixture of bread, raisins and pine nuts; the mixture had been
fried in honey beforehand. The stuffed peppers, juicy and shiny,

were put in the cast-iron frying pan and settled on the perimeter of the fireplace, to gently become crispy and golden on the outside. The squid was cut into lovely rings, similar to onion rings, and then coated in flour. Aunt Esther made a scrumptious spaghetti sauce, to which she added tuna, capers and a touch of anchovies, and Uncle Pas made a wonderful platter of pickled vegetables. He had little hot peppers, as well as pickled slices of cucumber, carrots, beets, and cauliflower florets. He added olives to this, and everything looked so good, the girls could hardly wait to start in on the antipasto. At last it was time to set the table, while the spaghetti was put in the boiling water. Golden loaves of bread came out of Gargantua, and a beautiful platter of fruit and cheese was set in the middle of the table. After they ate a small plate of the savory spaghetti, Aunt Esther and Uncle Pas set a large, deep pan on the fire and poured in a large amount of olive oil. The girls were not allowed to help with the fish, because the hot oil could splatter easily, burning them very badly. Working as a perfect team, Aunt Esther and Uncle Pas first fried the golden squid rings, and then the cleaned and chopped sections of the eels. When everything was beautifully golden brown, Aunt Esther arranged the food on large platters, while Uncle Pas carried the pan full of boiling oil outside, and disposed of the dangerously hot liquid in a hole he had previously dug in the ground. The peppers were on the table, so was the fish, covered in lemon slices and still smoking hot, while the octopus salad in vinaigrette stood next to it, cool and crisp. They had little piles of pickled vegetables, large piles of fish, and all the lemons they could ever want; it was a veritable feast. Ivana said:

"You don't have to eat the fried eel, if there's a lot of it left, Mama puts it in vinegar and we eat it after Christmas!" Luna said:

"Why don't you leave yours then 'cause I'm eating all of mine!" Luna would have never tried it before, but the crispy sections were delicious, the meat white and tasty, and the loads of lemon squished on them made everything finger-licking good. She had eaten eels before, but they were grilled, and though they were also good, she preferred those that were fried. At home she remembered her mother having severe conniptions every time someone talked about frying anything, but over here no one worried about it. And honestly, she didn't see too many fat people around, so she concluded that frying stuff was not so bad, and it was tasty, too! The stuffed peppers were a Christmas specialty, which Luna had never tried before, but even thought she was by now stuffed and satisfied, she tried one. The pepper, vinegary and crunchy on the outside and soft and sweet on the inside, was out of this world, and when Ivana said they would eat them cold all week, just cold, Luna was very happy! After they finished eating, they were all laying on their chairs in satisfied stupor, and it took a lot of effort to rouse themselves to clean up and put everything away. Movement woke them up, and after everything was done, it was time for dessert and coffee. Aunt Esther had made white nougat candy with egg whites, sugar and almonds, which she cut in thick squares. It was awesome, and the espresso complemented this candy extremely well. It had taken aunt Esther a long time to perfect her nougat recipe, as the first years she tried, it just lay there for days as a liquid mess, and Uncle Pas had taken to eat it with a spoon, but her humiliation at that failure had disappeared, and her nougat was talked about in the vicinity, since no one else made it like her. It was only about eight in the evening, and they would leave for the church of SS Cosmo and Damiano at about eleven o'clock, to be there for the midnight mass. They could have left later, but they wanted some time to socialize with the neighbors and make plans for the following day. Uncle Pas went out to the barn, and brought in humongous pine cones, which he put in the coals of the fireplace. Luna said:

"Why is your father burning the pine cones?"

"He's not burning them, dunderhead! He's just cooking them, so we can get the pine nuts."

"Pine nuts?" Exclaimed Luna: "There are pine nuts in the pine cones?" Ivana looked at her amused:

"Where do you think they came from?"

"I don't know!" Exclaimed Luna: "From pine nut trees!" Ivana said, looking at her curiously:

"How do you think they were hanging on the trees?" Luna thought a moment and then said, brightening up:

"In little baskets, of course!" Ivana was laughing and rolling on the floor, to Luna's chagrin, and Aunt Esther said sternly:

"Don't make fun of Luna, dear, when you were younger you thought we picked up our dry figs from the dry figs tree." Ivana stopped and looked confused:

"That's true, I did think that! I'm sorry Luna; I shouldn't make fun of you like that!" Aunt Esther sat back, pacified, and Luna, looking at Ivana saw that she was smirking and did not look sorry, and pinched her leg that was sticking out in front of her. Ivana made a small squeaking sound, and tried to pinch Luna's leg. Luna rolled away from her, and Ivana lunged and tried to grab her. They were rolling on the warm, clean tiles to Uncle Pas' delight, and Aunt Esther's contrived nonchalance. Eventually Aunt Esther exclaimed:

"Stop now, girls! You are showing your limbs!" At that, the girls modestly pulled their skirts down and took their place again in front of the fireplace.

The pine cones were ready, and Uncle Pas took them out of the fireplace with a steel tongue. He deposited them on the edge of the hearth and let them cool down. Eventually they were cool enough to touch, and Ivana showed Luna what to do with them. The pine cones had opened up like flowers, and inside of every petal was a small brown nut. When picked up and gently thumped on the hearth, flower petals down, the little brown nuts popped off. The girls picked them up and filled a basket with them. After they were finished taking the nuts from the cones, Ivana said:

"These are the good kind, they're soft and easy to open, they have some that are very hard and you have to open them with a hammer. Papa' doesn't like that kind, so he replaced all of those trees with the soft nuts, and we have it easy as we can open these with our fingers." Then she went on to show Luna how she took a brown nut, she cracked it open between her thumb and forefinger, and a beautiful, white and tender pine nut popped out of it. At first the girls popped a few of the delicious, fresh nuts in their mouth, but they were really full, so finally they started to seriously clean the pine nuts, and when they were finished they had a big bowl full of them. Aunt Esther took the bowl, and spread the pine nuts on a cookie sheet. She set the cookie sheet on the fireplace mantle, and said that in a couple of days, when the nuts were nicely dry, she would put them in a jar to use for cooking and baking.   It was getting close to ten o'clock, and they all went to their respective bedrooms to rest and prepare their clothes for church.

On the way up the mountain, they saw people walking on the side of the road carrying lanterns, and other vehicles up ahead; church would be full. The girls were wearing their new winter coats, and Aunt Esther was wearing a nice plaid coat in many colors, the predominant color being green to match her soft wool dress. The girls were wearing their angora hats, which Uncle Pas picked up a few days before Christmas; they were very pretty, and the girls looked like fresh flowers with their fluffy hats in pale blue and soft white. They were all wearing their good shoes, and the girls carried their handbags, and had fixed their hair especially nice. Luna's hair had grown long enough to allow her some nice, soft braids, and she had tied them on top of her head, almost like Aunt Esther's hair do, and with her hat on, only her face showed, framed by a soft blue cloud. Ivana liked her braids down and swinging about every time she moved her head, and her dark braids came out of the soft white hat black and shiny with white bows at the end, made with the left over angora yarn. Luna secretly thought that Ivana looked like Dorothy in 'The Wizard of Oz', and at times she expected her to break into song and start belting out 'Somewhere over the Rainbow' just like that. She smirked at that thought, and when Ivana saw it she was always suspicious of her, but didn't know why. The church was already packed, and they were hailed by Anna, who had managed to save two seats for them, by spreading herself and her stuff all over the pew. Uncle Pas escorted Aunt Esther to the seats, and when she was seated, he helped the two girls squeeze in the other one, and then joined the men standing up behind the church pews. Anna complimented their hats and held the girls' hands for a few seconds, and then they all looked to the altar, where Don Attilio was officiating.

There was fresh holly, and red and green decorations everywhere, and a multitude of sweet holiday scents permeated everything. Someone had sent for greenhouse flowers, and others donated large, white lilies for the altar. There were chrysanthemums everywhere at this time of year but none in the church at this time as they were usually only used for funerals, since it was bad luck to use them for anything else. At the stroke of midnight, everyone got really quiet and the organ started playing beautiful and somber holiday music. A minute later, a procession walked slowly towards the altar, and the Baby Jesus was placed in the manger next to the Virgin Mary and San Joseph. One big difference from home, Luna thought, was that here the Baby Jesus was a real baby, and San Joseph and Mary were that baby's real parents. Every year the family with the youngest baby was chosen to play the holy family. During mass the baby started crying, and Mary put him at her breast, under her shawl, to quiet him down. It was all so holy, so sacred, that Luna felt immersed in her religion. For the first time in her young life, Luna truly believed. With this revelation came a great sense of peace and tranquillity, and for the first time ever, she put her young life in God's loving, capable hands. Kneeling down at the pew, she whispered:

"Thy will be done!" While a tremulous tear slid down her cheek. Anna, always attuned to her thoughts and emotions, reached over to caress Luna's shoulder. When Don Attilio started his sermon, they all listened attentively.

"Welcome my children to our glorious celebration, and thank you for coming on this holy day to welcome our savior amongst us. It is fitting that an innocent child represents our baby Jesus, for He was also an innocent child, as well as our savior! We should all bow our heads in prayer in His presence, and promise to love each other like Jesus loved us, always! He loved us so much that he gave his life for us! But that's another story, which we'll talk about on Easter! Right now let's just pray, and be together, safe and warm. Tomorrow we'll get up late and have a great Christmas dinner! Thank you for all the donations and all the grand food! We shall make joyful noises unto God while socializing with our friends and family. God bless you all!" And with that, Don Attilio stepped down and started walking among the people, smiling and joyful.

Ivana put her arm around Luna's shoulder for a minute, and together they inclined their heads over their hands and allowed God's grace and love to grow in their hearts. After the services, they emerged out into the night, punctuated with bright lights and excited chatter. Everyone stopped to wish everyone Happy

Holidays, talk to their neighbors and make plans for the following day. Don Attilio did very well in the donations department, and large baskets of goodies were on the table in the entrance. Several of the mothers, including Ada's, Concetta's and Luana's wanted to know where the girls bought their hats. Aunt Esther made sure to tell them the hats were a perfect copy of the ones in the American movies, and that the wife of the sexton at Saint Bartholomew's Cathedral had made them. Everyone exclaimed:

"Concetta? Cipriano's wife? What does she know about American fashion?"

"You'd be surprised!" Assured them Aunt Esther: "I'm not quite sure, but I think she has relatives in America. And did you know that she knits for the Ripetta store? And Ripetta sells nothing but the best as you all know!" And Aunt Esther walked away with a satisfied smile on her face while the women all got together and started to talk over each other in their excitement. Uncle Pas congratulated her:

"Well done, Estherina, very well done!" Aunt Esther inclined her head piously, acknowledging the accolade.

The following day they had been invited to visit the Merolli family, before the Christmas meal, and they invited various guests for after their own meal. The Christmas meal was private, to be consumed in the bosom of the family only, but socializing before or afterwards was especially sought after. Aunt Esther had prepared delicious treats to offer her visitors, and gifts were to be exchanged at these visits. The coffee had already been roasted, the cream was cooling in the pilone, and the fruit had been taken out and arranged in flat, stiff baskets. The Christmas capon was already stuffed, and it would be put into the Dutch oven overnight, as soon as they got home, and the fresh pasta was drying on racks in the kitchen. The pasta sauce would be made fresh in the morning, and the bread had been stored inside of Gargantua fresh and fragrant this very evening. The tender peas that would accompany the meal had already been shelled, and the small white potatoes were ready to be peeled and boiled. A large salad of hardy green leaves was cleaned and chopped, and a fresh batch of yellow creamery butter was resting in the milk box outside. They slept well that night, no dreams, good or bad, and woke up rested, peaceful and happy.

On Christmas day they woke up late, took care of small chores (the animals needed tending no matter what day it was) and then dressed and drove to the Merolli's farm. In the back of the truck they had big baskets of winter fruit (oranges, lemons, apples, dried figs and nuts) some large, colorful strufoli donuts in baskets lined with waxed paper and jars of Aunt Esther's scrumptious strawberry marmalade. The girls had made some crust crackers for the Merolli's Christmas dinner, and Aunt Esther kept admonishing them not to break little pieces off of the golden, crunchy sheets. The crackers were Aunt Esther's invention, and she wanted everyone to try them out so she could see if they liked them. Every time Aunt Esther made a simple crust of flour, anise seeds and water mixed with a little oil, for her Swiss chard pies, she would bake the extra dough in a cookie sheet, thin and flat, until it was golden brown and full of bubbles. Even before this cracker had cooled, it was always gone, so she began making extra 'crust crackers' so they could have a few sheets to enjoy with their everyday meal. The wonderful aroma of the crackers filled the truck inside and out, so once in a while a little 'crunch' could be heard from the back. But the girls steadfastly denied picking little pieces from the crackers.

"It's just the waxed paper!" Was their usual excuse, but Aunt Esther and Uncle Pas smiled knowingly at each other anyway. At one point Uncle Pas couldn't stand it anymore:

"Give me some!" He whispered, and to Aunt Esther's clucking disapproval, they handed him a big piece. So Aunt Esther said:

"Since you mangled one of the sheets, we can't bring it in anymore. We made a lot, so we have plenty left. Hand me some. Let's finish it and dispose of this misdeed." So they finished the sheet amongst themselves, and picked up all of the crumbs from the paper. At that point, Aunt Esther picked up the flat basket full of the golden sheets, and held it on her lap, while everyone huffed and Uncle Pas observed how it was awful not to trust your own family when it came to a few bits of crust. Aunt Esther did not relent, and the rest of the crackers arrived safely to the Merolli's, crunchy and fresh as ever. Anna was waiting for them when they arrived, running out with open arms. Mario came and helped carry the baskets inside, while Amelia pushed her arm through Aunt Esther's and directed her to the door. Inside, the rest of the family was seated in the fancy parlor, waiting for their guests, and Luna and Ivana sat with Mario's children. Anna also sat with the children, and asked them what they expected from the Befana, since it was only twelve days before the epiphany. The boys had all kinds of requests, from toy guns and toy trucks, to yoyos and soccer balls, the bolder ones asking for bicycles and roller skates. Anna sighed and told them:

"More likely you'll get sweaters and socks, dry fruit and an orange, maybe even a piece of coal, and if you're lucky a small cap gun, but you can certainly dream until then!" And they all sighed together. Luna and Ivana didn't have any idea what the Befana would bring them, especially Luna. She said, uncertainly:

"I don't think la Befana will bring me anything, although Aunt Palma is making us knit a big sock; the Befana doesn't know I'm here, I bet!" Anna embraced her and said:

"Oh, she knows you're here, Darling, don't worry! She doesn't know what you would like, but she has already prepared gifts for you and Ivana. So she has for the boys, although she already knows the boys won't be thrilled with their presents!" The boys guffawed and pushed one another off the chairs, and then they ran off to get some of the delicious looking things being passed around. Anna couldn't stop complimenting Aunt Esther on the crust crackers, and she handed out her Christmas baskets full of the brown wine donuts, jars of everything from artichokes in olive oil to julienned eggplants in vinegar, and best of all, handfuls of her sugar and almonds nougat, the brown Neapolitan kind wrapped in tissue of all different colors. Amelia's mother-in-law had made precious bottles of Limoncello, a delicious liqueur made with lemons, water, grain alcohol and sugar, and her father-in law handed out bottles of his best white wine. After about another hour, they all said good bye, wished everyone a wonderful holiday, and went home to start preparing for their holiday meal. When they had everything ready to go, Ivana and Luna went upstairs to change from their housedresses, and when they came down, Aunt Esther and Uncle Pas were waiting for them, and they looked solemn. Luna got scared:

"What's happened?" She asked Ivana:

"Nothing," smiled the girl: "It's The Benediction!"

"The Benediction?" Repeated Luna:

"Yes, let's sit down in our seat at the table!" They sat down, and lowered their heads like Aunt Esther, with their hands together in prayer. Uncle Pas slowly got up, picked up a small olive branch from a basket, dipped it in a small vessel of holy water and shook it in all of their directions:

"May God be with you all of your life, and may this benediction save you from hurt and pain. My love for you is freely given, and it will envelope you all of your life! Amen!" And then he sat down, smiled at them with moist eyes, and while Aunt Esther put the precious water back in the hutch, he exclaimed:

"Let's dig in!" Luna was moved; she asked Ivana if everyone did this. Ivana responded:

"Only the religious people, us who believe. Papa' does it at Christmas and Easter." A few days before, Ivana had told Luna about The Christmas Letter, and they each had made one. It was a letter decorated with glitter, flowers, rainbows and anything you could think of. In it you were supposed to write your desires and hopes, and what you expected from the Befana. The letters were now resting under Uncle Pas' plate, and he ate without letting on that he even knew why his plate was wobbly and there was a hint of glitter on the tablecloth. If he didn't read the letters, they were null and void, so the girls waited with suspense to see what happened. After the meal was over, and the plates were taken away, Uncle Pas looked down and feigned the greatest surprise:

"Why, there's mail under my plate!" The girls giggled, while he slowly picked them up and read them one at the time. Luna couldn't stop herself from thinking 'You've Got MAIL!!' from that stupid movie her Mom sometimes watched on cable, her eyes a little teary. Uncle Pas first read Ivana's letter, and when he was finished, he got up and kissed her forehead. He whispered something in her ear, and Ivana smiled up at him. The letters were supposed to be secret, so Uncle Pas didn't divulge what was in it or what he said. He just put Ivana's letter in his shirt pocket, and picked up Luna's. Luna had written a very short one. She didn't ask for anything material. All she wanted was to be able to keep all of them with her forever, because she didn't want to lose anyone anymore. She of course also wanted her own family back, if such a thing was even possible (she already knew it wasn't).

Uncle Pas got up and went to kiss Luna's forehead, like he did Ivana's, and whispered to her:

"You will not lose everyone, sweet girl, and you will have everything in life that you deserve. I promise!" And Luna smiled up at him with tears in her eyes. She believed him, she didn't know how, but she knew deep in her heart that what he had told her would indeed come true!

After the dishes were done and everything was back in place, the company started to come. The guests included Nannina, Giustina and Aunt Palma, Ada with her mom and dad, and Roffo, who was now back home and very happy. Great Uncle Biagio and Great Aunt Marianna were there for a little while, and Gianna, Uncle Saverio and the children were there as well. Great Uncle Biagio and Great Aunt Marianna held their grandchildren and spoiled them, while Gianna and Uncle Saverio made the rounds and handed out gorgeous Panettones to everyone. Towards the end of the evening, The Fool, his wife, Antonietta and Rodolfo were there. They excused their lateness but they had made the rounds, first to Antonietta's brothers, and then to Rodolfo's family. Thank God they rode in Rodolfo's truck, or they could never have done it! The families were all well and everyone sent their regards. Antonietta was hardly aware of her surroundings, just Rodolfo, and he was enthralled by her. They sat next to each other holding each other's hand and just looking into each other's eyes without saying anything. Ada, Luna and Ivana kept elbowing each other and whispering:

"They're in looove!" Everyone exchanged presents, ate everything delicious that was offered, and drank numerous cups of coffee. They talked about everything, except the wedding; they didn't want to jinx it and it was like the elephant in the room. Still, the wedding was on everyone's mind, since the big day was less than two weeks away and everyone knew there were still a million things left to do. Will they make it and will it turn out as they all hoped? Hopefully! The only ones who didn't care were Antonietta and Rodolfo. She was all in maroon velvet decorated with white lace, with black little pumps and a great mountain of shiny black hair and Rodolfo was all in black, with a corded sweater and corduroy pants; his only jewelry a great engagement ring on his powerful hand, given to him by Antonietta. She kept caressing his ring, symbolizing her possession of this magnificent male. Antonietta's jewelry winked in the midst of the soft dark velvet, and Rodolfo's eyes shined feverishly on the small figure of his bride. They had only eyes for each other or, in Antonietta's case, eye, since she still let her hair cover her face, but Anna had promised everyone that on her wedding day, Antonietta would be revealed in all her beautiful glory. Quagliozzi the photographer showed up for a few moments, took the betrothed's picture next to the nativity village, drank a small glass of Limoncello and started to leave, muttering something about his family disowning him if he didn't show up at home in the next hour, complete with presents. Gianna handed him a panettone and Anna handed him a basket of her cookies and a bottle of Limoncello. Aunt Esther handed him a bundle of her thick, white nougat, cut in large squares and wrapped in a piece of waxed paper covered by a white napkin tied on top like a flower. Luna and Ivana handed him a marzipan basket full of tiny marzipan fruit they made under Gianna's tutelage in school, wrapped in waxed paper. Quagliozzi beamed, smiled, bowed and finally left.

Aunt Esther always was of the opinion that there should be something extra for an unexpected, but not less welcomed guest at Christmas. She was well satisfied with her precautions and their result. After much talk, jocularity and communion, someone said:

"I for one am heading home. I want to be in top form for the painting." Everyone agreed, they all declared that they wouldn't miss it for the world, and eventually everyone left. Aunt Esther never allowed her guests to do any work, so the house was in some disarray. Uncle, well satisfied with his company, his family and their wonderful communion with each other, helped Aunt Esther and the girls, making short work of the cleanup. He worked harder than anyone, and when Aunt Esther urged him to go to sleep and let her finish, he observed piously:

"You know that I serve and serve, and when I'm done, I serve some more!" Aunt Esther swatted him with a kitchen towel:

"Ho, go on with you!" Uncle reprised his pious monolog:

"Only a life lived in the service of others is worth living!" Ivana whispered:

"I wish he never got that book about some American philanthropist, it really made an impression on him!" Luna asked:

"Who is it?"

"Some guy called Armand Hammer"

"I've never heard of him!"

"Neither had I, until he started to quote him every other step!" Luna was surprised all over again at how books were precious here, and how the information gleaned from them was used in everyday life. These people, buried somewhere in the Old Country, were more literate then highly educated professionals in her day. Even though you could find anything in less than a second, no one read much at home! She shook her head and kept working, and while they continued their work, Luna asked Ivana about the painting everyone kept talking about. Ivana said:

"It's the most beautiful thing everyone has ever seen. It's ancient, and it was painted by a blind artist hundreds of years ago. It's so fragile with age that now they keep it in a cave under the church. Once every year, they allow the people to see it, and I promise you it's an experience you'll never forget!" At these words, Luna felt a frisson down her spine, like a premonition. She asked:

"Will we see it?" Ivana said:

"My mother wouldn't miss it for the world; she says it's a wonderful tradition and you come away from it with a renewed sense of faith. I like it, it makes me feel good, and that's all!" That night it was another one of deep slumber, no dreams, no interruptions; only peaceful sleep.

The following day was very busy. Laundry, as well as other important tasks had been forgotten for the last few days, and now the chickens had come to roost, so to speak. The viewing of the painting would be in the afternoon, around 3:00 P.M., so they had a quick lunch of delicious leftover eggplant parmigiana and were ready to go by two o'clock. They wore somber clothes, and Aunt Esther said the rosary on the way up. When they reached the church up on the mountain, there were many, many people waiting in silence, with most praying. After a while the Monsignor of the sanctuary, flanked by Don Attilio and the younger priests, opened the church door, and after blessing everyone, he started to tell the story, like he did every year:

"In the year 527 after Christ, Theodoric the Great, king of the Ostrogoths, and his daughter Malasuntha donated The Library of Peace, and part of the temple of Romolus, to Pope Felix IV. The Pope united the two buildings and made the basilica of SS Cosmo and Damiano in Roma. The Pope had heard that in Arabia, where the saints originated, there was a great painting representing the birth of Jesus, made by the painter Parnasso. Parnasso was a young shepherd when Jesus was born, and he went to adore the child Jesus in his manger. When he grew up, Parnasso became a famous painter, and was well known for his religious paintings. When he was one hundred years old, and blind, an angel appeared to him. The Angel told him that he was an emissary of the Virgin Mary, and that she wanted him to make one last painting. Parnasso fell to his knees, and cried:

"I would be honored to fulfill the Virgin's request, but I am blind, and can no longer paint!" The Angel extended his hand to Parnasso, and helping him up said:

"Look around you, Parnasso!" Parnasso did so, and to his stunned amazement, he could see everything even better than when he was young. The Angel told him:

"You will see until your painting is finished, Parnasso. After you are done, all will be as it was. You will paint what you saw as a child when you went to adore the newborn Baby Jesus. Close your eyes, and describe the scene you saw as a child." Parnasso promised, and after the angel left, he ran around to everyone telling of the miracle of his sight. Parnasso was so happy; he ate, drank, painted and lived to the fullest, but did not start the painting the Virgin Mary had requested. He did not want to lose his sight again, and realized that if he postponed painting the scene, he could see that much longer. He took to wearing embroidered robes and consorting with younger women. After three years, the angel appeared to Parnasso again, and told him that the Virgin was sad at his trickery, and she withdrew her request. Parnasso fell to his knees and begged the Virgin to forgive him, but the Angel fell silent, touched his shoulder and disappeared. So did everything else, for Parnasso was blind once again. He had a great burden in his heart; because he had disappointed the Lady he had worshipped all of his life for his wretched selfish reasons. He fumbled around his studio, found all of his implements, and started painting. But instead of painting with his eyes, he painted with his heart. People came to see him, and they stood quietly by, while figures, places and things flew out of his brush; they whispered that it was a miracle. Parnasso did not stop, not even to sleep or eat. In a few days, the great painting was finished, and after he put down the brush for the last time, Parnasso lay on his pallet in the studio, closed his blind eyes, and whispered:

"I am done, Angel, I've done what you ask. Take me home now!" In a few moments, his breathing stopped, his face took on a peaceful expression, and he smiled and was gone from this hearth with a great sigh.

The pope had heard the story many times in his life, and he decided to get this famous and very old painting, for the two Saints he was building the Basilica for. After much deliberation, the painting was contracted, and then shipped to Roma. But it never arrived, and eventually it was declared lost and forgotten. Hundreds of years later, a young shepherd who was tending his sheep up on Mount Leuci, saw a very old, very large wooden box in the very spot where the church lies, and he told his father. The box had the seal of the Pope of ancient Roma on it, and the shepherd took it to his priest to decide what to do. The box was ancient, but sturdy, and no one wanted to desecrate it. It was finally decided to call the modern day Pope, and he traveled to Pontecorvo with his dignitaries. Finally, with the Pope's blessing, the box was open, and inside, tightly rolled up was the great painting. Everyone present fell to their knees, and after much deliberation, the Pope decided that it was the will of God that the painting had found its way on mount Leuci, and a new sanctuary for SS. Cosmo and Damiano should be built right on the spot where the box was found, and the painting should be displayed there. And so they did! But the painting was so ancient and fragile that it couldn't be displayed in the church, as it would soon crumble in the light of day so they made a cave under the church, where the temperature was perfect and the light was just soft and dim, and hung the painting on a wood frame, the frame on stilts, so the religious could see it, adore it and pray in front of it when the time was right. That is why every year on the day after Jesus was born this painting was on display for all to see."

After the story, there wasn't a dry eye in the whole group. Finally a small door on the side of the Sanctuary opened, and the people filed in one by one. They descended a small, dark staircase, down into the bowels of the hearth, and after a few minutes, they reached another door leading into a great, subterranean cave which was still and cool and lit in a mysteriously filtered half light. Everyone filed in front of the painting slowly, taking a place at the back of the large room. The painting depicted the inside of a large cave. In the forefront was a small manger, where the Baby Jesus was laying. On either side stood his parents, the Virgin Mary on the left and St. Joseph on the right. Behind them, a cow and a donkey lay peacefully, and a brilliant light coming from the back of the cave illuminated everything in a peaceful, golden light. Mary had her arms outstretched to a little peasant girl, who looked up with wonder. She had tears streaming down her face, the little bit that could be seen, and Mary was consoling her, looking like she was going to caress the girl's hair. The girl was wearing a long black skirt and wooden clogs on her feet. She was also wearing a white shirt and a blue shawl over most of her hair. On the floor of the cave, next to the girl stood a white, rectangular object with black buttons on the front, which looked remarkably like a small microwave. Luna stared, her eyes wide, and unknowingly stepped forward until she was very close to the painting itself. Up close, the white object was nothing but brush strokes, but the girl looked just like she thought. She whispered to herself:

"It can't be! It just can't be! Can it??" Looking up into the painting, she looked right into the eyes of Little Jesus, and that same look she remembered was there, but the Baby Jesus was smiling, right into her eyes, almost as if she was standing in front of him into that far ago and far away cave. Standing behind the girl in the painting, Luna could see the three Magi, their extended hands offering gifts to the Baby Jesus, and their golden robes fluctuating in the air. She was stunned and speechless, and tears were brimming out of her eyes. Inconsequently she thought:

"I'm becoming a crybaby, a watering pot, there's always something dripping down my face. I've never cried like this before; never!" Everyone else was crowding close to the painting, and Luna was pushed around in the shuffle without realizing it:

"It's not possible!" Her mind was screaming. A voice in her head whispered:

"Anything's possible if God wills it, Child!" And then: "Do you believe in God, Luna?" Luna whispered:

"Yes, I believe!" And the voice said forcefully: "Then, My Child, BELIEVE! Open your mind to His true love!" Luna fell to her knees in front of the painting, and in the midst of the other kneeling people, said:

"Thy will be done!" Before bending her head down. At that moment she felt a soft touch, looked up and saw Aunt Esther standing next to her:

"It's almost like we were standing there, in front of them in that cave, isn't it?" Luna smiled up at her:

"Yes, how very true!" Ivana reached them, and kneeled next to Luna, and they held each other, while Luna's trembling slowly stopped:

"What am I going to do without Ivana?" She thought. Suddenly, that same voice whispered softly again to her:

"Remember, Dear Child, anything's possible. Don't assume anything just yet. Just wait and see!"

Pontecorvo panorama looking down from the bus depot.
Photograph 1950

It was ten days before the Epiphany and the wedding. By now, everyone was running around like chickens with their heads cut off. Communications flew from one house to the other. The Fool had taken to walking over to the gravel pit, and working inside of Antonietta and Rodolfo's new home. It had been finished, and was just beautiful inside and out. Between Assunta and Rodolfo's labor of love, and Antonietta's brothers' bull work, the house was a heaven of comfort and beauty. There was a large office for Rodolfo, and a small, cozy one for Antonietta. The Fool used the small office as a hideout, so no one knew he was there save for Rodolfo. Antonietta hadn't been inside the house yet, she would first walk in as a bride! Rodolfo was not living in the house either. They would both move in as husband and wife. Still, he went to it almost daily to bring small things that Antonietta might like and to dream of a married life yet to come. Happy days were indeed coming, and they were pretty close. Anna was already working on a grand strategy for unveiling Antonietta's charms, and the dress stood on a dummy in Aunt Esther's spare room, looking sparkling, ethereal and unreal in the eerie light filtered through the fine lawn curtains. The girls were on vacation from school until after the Epiphany, and between chores and Aunt Palma's tyranny, they were kept pretty busy. They made the rounds a couple of times, finished their huge stockings and helped Aunt Esther iron and prepare their clothes for the wedding. The dresses were all beautiful, and the girls felt like little princesses when they had the last try-out. But on the end of the week, three days before the wedding, they found themselves at loose ends. Ivana suggested going to the river, but it was a halfhearted suggestion, as the river was turbulent and the air was uncomfortably cool, the ground slimy and slippery. Luna said:

"You promised to show me something, a long time ago, regarding our ancestor, and I don't know even what you meant, but you were so mysterious, I'd been thinking about it sometimes." Ivana's eyes sparkled right away, and she said:

"I forgot about that! Yes, I'll show you, but you have to promise me that whatever I show you remains a secret. Papa' doesn't like others to know about this, it's a family secret!" Luna was all excited as they ran together to the big barn.

Once in the barn Ivana pointed to a big box of hay, and with Luna's help first they emptied it and then moved it, revealing a trap door. After pulling the door up, they revealed dank, dark stairs that went straight down. Luna said:

"What if you're a crazed killer, you take me down there, then kill me and leave my body to rot?" Ivana laughed and said:

"No! I wouldn't do that! It's too much work! Maybe I'm a ghost and I'll haunt you down there in the dark!" And then she screamed: "Booooo!" And tried to grab Luna. Luna shrieked and ran down, followed by Ivana. Miraculously they did not fall to the bottom of the stairs, and stopped in front of an old, small brown door. Ivana went to a small crack in the wall, and pulled out a little black key. She inserted it into a hole in the door, turned it, and then pushed the small door open. She carefully put the key in her pocket:

"You don't want to be trapped in here without the key!" She exclaimed, and then pushed up a small switch and a wobbly light bulb, hanging in the middle of the room, went on. She said: "It was only a few years ago, after the war, when Papa ran some wires down here and put in the electric light bulb; before that you had to light a torch to be able to see." But Luna didn't hear her; she was speechless. All around the room were shelves full of stills, jars, long-necked glass containers, cruets, beakers and test tubes. The walls were covered by great murals painted on animal skins which depicted the human body in all its mystery, all of its secrets revealed. Ancient bundles of herbs hung from the rafters, and strange instruments were lined up on wide shelves which stood against the wall. Great big glass jars seemed to contain what looked like body parts, human and animal, in a whitish liquid. One entire wall was covered by books and rolled up parchments, and a strange medicinal, herbal smell permeated the room. On one side there was what looked to be a small kitchen, and pots in various sizes hung on the wall next to it. Next to the sink there was even an ancient-looking microscope, a large box of glass slides next to it. Great furs covered the floor of the room in various shades of brown and gray, and there was a pallet covered in more furs in a far corner. Luna looked around hardly believing her own eyes, and then whispered:

"What is this room? Whose is it?" Ivana replied:

"It belonged to our great-great- grandfather. People said that he was an alchemist, sorcerer and witch doctor. He practiced his craft in secret, but after he helped a man who appeared to have drowned by resuscitating him, he was persecuted as a witch and was forced to leave his native Sicily, coming over here to start a new life. In those days people were very ignorant of these things, and anyone who practiced the 'dark arts' as they called them, was persecuted and burned. Our great-great-grandfather was actually a doctor and a scientist. He died when he was over a hundred years old, and after he was buried, his children locked up this room, never to use it again; it is a family secret, so don't tell anyone about it. Please!" Luna's eyes were big and round and she asked in awe:

"What kind of discoveries did he make, and what's in those books of his?" Ivana replied:

"No one knows. Since the distant past the family has always kept this a secret. It will be passed on to future generations. Maybe in the future, when no one is afraid anymore, someone will bring this to light. But Papa' says it's too soon right now." They walked around the room, gently touching and examining things at random, afraid to move anything or knock any of it over. Surprisingly, there was little dust in here, and this room preserved the samples and other things in it as perfectly as if it was air conditioned. Luna felt eerie, touching objects which had belonged to someone in her very distant past. But then, she wasn't even sure this person was related to her. Balthazar dropped her here, but maybe these people weren't even her family! This thought depressed her, but somehow she felt connected to this place, and she knew in her heart that she did indeed belong with this family. Suddenly, a strong feeling inside told her that not only was she intimately connected to this room and this family, but that she would be back here again in the future! After exiting the 'secret room' the girls felt a little shook up, so they went over to Aunt Palma to retrieve their Befana stockings. The night after next, they would hang them on the fireplace, and Luna, with Ivana, would wait with trepidation for the following morning, when it would be revealed if the Befana knew she was here, and if Luna would receive anything. After the ritual of la Befana on that morning, Aunt and Uncle would go up to SS. Cosmo and Damiano to check on the preparations for the wedding banquet, and in early afternoon everyone would get into their fancy clothes and go to church, where Antonietta and Rodolfo would be married. The only question after that was how well the banquet went, before their labors were finally finished. Toscana, Lilliana and Inessa were stationed in the pavilion and had been working feverishly for a week, and The Wedding Consultants had been taking turns directing the women who were doing the preparations for the food. In high secret, Toscana was directing the assembly of the wedding cake, and Gianna was in charge making the pastry. She reported to Toscana when there was a question, and Toscana always smoothed everything in her calm and sweet manner, keeping everyone willing to work their butts off for her. Lilliana had a hoard of people decorating and beautifying the pavilion, and what she demanded of them was hard, painstaking work. But when they saw the results, they admitted that she was a bona fide genius and kept on going. Inessa had turned from a sweet, lovely angel, to a general marching her troops to exhaustion; she was choreographing everything like it was a ballet and everyone knew that without her, the wedding would not come together as a whole, instead being just a series of disjointed affairs. Out of the great pavilion's windows came orders, complaints, long suffering sighs and astounding noises, but no one was allowed inside, and the people working there were sworn to secrecy. Inessa kept reminding them of the fate of the people who built the pyramids; they were buried in there with their masters, to make sure they didn't talk. She stood in front of the bunch inside, turned sideways and exclaimed:

"Don't I look just a little bit like Nefertiti? I'll have you know that she could have been one of my ancestors, and I have no qualms about burying anyone who flaps their lips." People staring at her long necked, perfectly chiseled profile, the high cheekbones, the honey colored perfection of her skin and the slanted, slumberous eyes saw the truth of this statement, and decided against telling anyone anything; after all one never knew.

Someone had read in a book that in ancient China the emperors would bury the workers who built the Great Wall right into the walls themselves, and everyone was discussing this with chills going up their spines. Inessa was all-resolute, and no one wanted to take a chance. Besides, she had God on her side too, as Don Attilio followed her around like a puppy and agreed to anything she said. To give Inessa her due, she was deferent and respectful of Don Attilio. No cup of coffee or sweet bun was offered to anyone unless Don Attilio got his share first, and no prosciutto or mortadella sandwich touched anyone's lips unless Don Attilio pronounced it delicious.

Anna had been going to The Fool's house with various bundles the last few days, and she was also as close mouthed as can be. The day before the wedding, from Antonietta's room came cries and noises. Rodolfo paced outside, and was about to storm his bride's room any minute, held back only by The Fool's hard grip on his arm. More than once, The Fool had to hiss in his ear:

"Calm down, boy, she'll be fine. Remember it's bad luck to see your bride in her wedding finery before the wedding; why don't you go home and we'll see you at the church tomorrow." To which Rodolfo hissed back:

"I'm not leaving unless she tells me to. I'm going to kiss my bride before I go if it's the last thing I do!" Assunta stood in a corner twisting her hands, with tears ready to drop, and finally The Fool, with a sigh, knocked at Antonietta's bedroom door. Anna stuck her head out, and they talked quietly for a few seconds. A minute later, Antonietta came out with her head down, disheveled, her hair standing up straight and stiff. Rodolfo went to her and took her in his arms, in front of her parents and everyone. He whispered quietly to her, and she nodded her head and looked up into his wonderful, concerned face. In front of everyone, Rodolfo bent down, this time kissing her right on the mouth lovingly. The Fool grabbed Assunta, who was standing there with her mouth hanging and her eyes wide, and turned her away with him to give the betrothed some privacy. Rodolfo whispered:

"What are they doing to you, My Sweetheart? One word and I'll take you away right now!" Antonietta quivered first, and then raised a small hand and caressed his brow:

"It's just the wedding dress and hairdo. They want to make me beautiful for you, but I'm not used to showing my naked face."

"You're already beautiful to me, Sweetheart, you always are! You don't have to do anything more. Like I said, one word and I'll take you home with me!"   Antonietta looked at him, and whispered back:

"How did I get so lucky as to find someone like you? I made up my mind; for you, and for now, I'll let them do whatever they want.   The day after tomorrow, we'll be in our own home, together, and we'll be free from all this pressure. We have to honor your parents and mine. Tomorrow is for them, but the rest of our lives is for us." At that, Rodolfo held her to his bosom for long seconds and kissed her tenderly, before unwillingly pulling himself away and storming out the door. The Fool turned Assunta around, and she just caught Antonietta's back as the girl went back into her bedroom. She leaned her head on her husband shoulder and sighed:

"Oh Tarquinio, I hope everything's going to turn out alright." He smiled and replied:

"I'm sure it will! I'm spending practically all that I have, but for once I don't mind at all. I'll make more later. What counts is that the children will be set for life, even our beautiful Antonietta. Will you still be by my side if I'm not able to recoup my losses and we have to economize?" Assunta squirmed closer and replied:

"I'll be by your side even if we have to live in a cave. All I ever need is you!" The Fool laughed, and holding her with his strong arms, said:

"It won't ever be as bad as that. I have more than enough money for us to be comfortable in our old age; I was just worrying myself a little. This wedding made me a little soft. Seeing how happy Antonietta is, and seeing how happy all of these good people are for her makes me want to do even more for them. But I'm still a careful business man, no matter how old my age, and I have a scheme coming up with Carletto the Lawyer that should become very profitable; he's a genius when it comes to money schemes, but honest! Now that my children are all set, I'm going to use my money to make a real difference around here. After all, I'm still going to leave the kids plenty, more than they'll ever need. It just feels really good when I help others too. After I'm gone, I want to be remembered for more than just being rich." And they stood together holding each other tenderly.

In her bedroom Antonietta was telling Anna, in a scared little voice, that she was going to let her do whatever she wanted with her hair. Anna looked at her curiously:

"We've been battling back and forth about everything, and I understand that you may be shy, but your hair is something else entirely. What is it that you're trying to hide behind your hair, girl? You have nothing to be ashamed about, you're pretty and with the right arrangements you can be beautiful! Isn't it time that you tell me what's wrong? I won't tell anyone, I promise! We all have our quirks, but this thing about hiding your face tells me something's wrong. You can tell me, I'm old enough not to be surprised by anything, and I really want to help." Antonietta looked down at her hands, Arancio the cat climbing on her lap in one fluid jump:

"I was ten years old when my aunt, my mother's fancy sister, came to see us. She'd never been over to the house before, she only saw me on the day I was baptized in church, together with my grandparents. She came over to hide from her family, as she had had a big fight with my grandparents and didn't want to see them. My mother took her in and served her like a queen, even thought my father was not happy about it. She was going to run away from home, and marry some boyfriend of hers that her parents disapproved of, and when he didn't show up at the appointed place, she came to us. One day, I came from school and was sitting at the kitchen table waiting for my after-school snack, and my aunt got really mad because she had to wait her turn to be served and told my mother that I shouldn't be sitting at the table. I was nothing but a little black monkey, and I should be kept in the closet, away from normal people. She said I had the mug of a monkey and when I grew up I'd be a monkey proper, and if anyone saw my face, no one would want me. My mother cried, and when my father came home and found out, he told my aunt to leave. We never saw her again." Anna looked furious, but didn't say anything. After a while, she said:

"What happened to her?" Antonietta laughed, and replied:

"She was so desperate to get away from her parents that she ran away with the mailman. They married and had a lot of kids. During the war, my father helped them, he gave them money to move up north, and now they are doing very well. She writes sometimes; her parents lost everything in the war, and now they're both dead." Anna shook her head as she usually did:

"Why did your father help them?" Antonietta said:

"My mother asked him to." Anna replied:

"Your aunt was spiteful and hurtful, but you gave her power over yourself. Now just forget about her. You snatched yourself a good man, and a powerful, handsome one at that. Go to him in all of your glory, and see what he thinks. He already loves you, as you know, and no matter how you think you look, know that he only has eyes for you." Antonietta looked happy and hopeful, and while she was in such a good mood, Anna played with her hair as much as she pleased. The cat was happy and purring on Antonietta's lap, but Anna pushed him off to try on Antonietta's slip. The dress was going to be delivered on the following morning, and Anna was going with the dress. No mishap was going to happen on her watch to the dress or the precious veil. Antonietta had tried on the dress in various stages, first the bodice and then the skirt. The decorations were not on yet, but she had tried on the veil, and she was afraid of looking funny in all of that fancy finery. Anna had said:

"Wait till you see Rodolfo in his wedding clothes; he's resplendent!" Antonietta had blushed and Anna was thinking of sending someone down to Ripetta's to buy a small make-up kit. A little blush, a little pink lipstick, a little mascara! What harm could it do! If a girl can't go all out on her wedding day, when can she do it! Tomorrow she would ask Mario to run to town first thing, get Ripetta out of his bed and buy the kit. After that, she had to make a special trip to the Sargentos on Befana business; of course, she had to deal with la Befana in her own home, and off she was to The Fool's house for the showdown. She'd already taken care of la Befana at her other children's houses, and she would see everyone at the reception in the pavilion. She felt light on her feet, very busy and quite happy. Who said that old age had to be bad? If you were busy helping your family and everyone else around you, the Good Lord made very sure you forgot your aches and pains while you were taking part in someone else's joy!   After Anna had finished caring for Antonietta, The Fool walked her home.   Anna hung onto his strong arm in the dark, smelled his manly aroma of cigars and wine, and remembered how she and her Domenico used to take quiet walks at night before returning home together to love and cherish each other. Anna would dream of her Domenico tonight, if she was lucky!

Market stall up on the mountain.
Duclere Design

It was la Befana day! The night before, Luna and Ivana hung their big stockings on the fireplace mantle, neither sleeping very well as they waited for morning. At first light they woke up, since there was a lot to do before they took off for the day to attend the wedding. The girls ran first to the fireplace to see what la Befana brought them. Ivana jumped on her bulging stocking, while Luna stared with unbelieving eyes at the stocking she had hung. Last night it was flat and empty, now it was distorted and bulky, full to the brim. She slowly walked to it, took it down and then held it to herself like a treasure. Aunt Esther and Uncle Pas looked on with big smiles, and Aunt Esther had a little shine in her eyes at the way Luna was holding her stocking. Ivana elbowed her:

"What are you doing? Aren't you going to open it?" Luna shook herself, and then like Ivana, she tore into her stocking. They took their stockings to the table and emptied them, one on each side, so their stuff wouldn't get mixed up. As they did so, Uncle Pas went near the table and handed them each a bulky package. The girls looked up at him with questioning eyes, and he said:

"These were too big for the stockings, so la Befana asked me to hand them to you myself." Feverishly, the girls unwrapped the heavy bundles and to their surprise they each came up with a large book. Luna had a beautiful leather bound version of 'The Betrothed' and Ivana was holding a beautifully covered Italian version of 'The Grapes of Wrath'. Luna held her own copy of 'The Betrothed' to her chest like a treasure, but Ivana said:

"What is this book; I've never heard of it!" Uncle Pas responded:

"It's written by an American writer, I found it very interesting. It will teach you about that great country. You'll like it!" Luna added:

"I found it sad. It's all about a poor family from the American state of Oklahoma. They were trapped in the so-called 'Dust bowl'. There was no water and everything was dry and nothing grew, so they traveled to California, another American state, to find a better life during The Great Depression." Uncle Pas looked at her with understanding, but Ivana said:

"How would you know about this?" Luna responded:

"I learned about it in school!" Ivana laughed out loud:

"Good thing our teacher and The Fool aren't here, or he would have snickered at her, and we would have had to hold her off of him." Uncle Pas said seriously:

"I think you should start learning about the United States! It's very important." Ivana held her book to herself and whispered:

"I will Papa', I will!" Then they put their books down and checked on the other gifts. On the very top of each stocking, they found a small bundle. When unwrapped, a piece of coal popped out. The girls both giggled and Ivana said:

"The Befana always puts the coal first! Don't let it throw you, the good stuff comes after."

"What's it for?" Luna asked.

"That's to remind you that you're not perfect." Ivana said. "Everyone is 'bad' sometimes. What's important is that you're 'good' most of the time." Next from each stocking came a small burlap sack filled with dry figs, almonds and shelled walnut. After the dry fruit and nuts, they found little bundles filled with chunks of dark chocolate; they both squealed in pleasure. Next were bundles wrapped in yellowed tissue paper which, upon unwrapping, revealed the most wonderful pieces of tombola lace the girls had ever seen. Ivana whispered:

"Aunt Palma's hundred year-old lace! She said she was going to give it to you, but I thought she forgot! Instead, she gave me a piece too!" Luna gently picked it up and held it in her hands with reverence:

"I haven't seen lace more beautiful anywhere in the world!" Aunt Esther said:

"These days you see lace like that only in museums. It is very precious, priceless really!" They put it down carefully, not even questioning how the lace came to be in the Befana stockings, and went on to the next thing. This was a round object wrapped in tissue. It turned out to be a heart shaped, red velvet jewelry box, and when they opened it, they couldn't even breathe; inside each was a gold pin and matching gold dangling earrings, surrounded by a long gold chain wrapped around many times. The two sets were different from each other, and Ivana and Luna looked in shock at the expensive jewelry. Aunt Esther said:

"This is for when you girls get your very own original paisana costume." The girls whispered in awe:

"Are we going to get an original paisana costume? Will we look like Anna?" Aunt Esther said:

"I wouldn't know, but when you get one, you'll be all ready to wear it immediately." Uncle Pas said:

"We won't usually ask the Befana to bring such expensive gifts, but now Luna is here with us, and we don't know when we will be all together again, so we wanted to make this a special time." The girls were astounded at their good fortune, and in turn they hugged Aunt Esther and Uncle Pas with wild abandon. Then Ivana said:

"We might as well finish empting the stockings, there's usually nothing good at the bottom, but with today you never know!" They stuck their hands all the way down, and came up with a big orange from the toe, and a large pine cone from the heel. Ivana said:

"What did I tell you?" And proceeded to happily peel her orange and start eating. She handed Luna some of it, which Luna ate, while putting her orange carefully back in the toe of the stocking (At home, she never gave these things so much as a second look.) Ivana said: "Don't think you can save that all for yourself, we'll share it later!" Luna stuck her tongue out at her, and Ivana said:

"Yuck! Your tongue is horrible, all red and full of food!" Luna pulled it in, mortified, and Ivana said:

"Got you!" And they started to arm-wrestle on the table, being very careful not to drop their presents. They spent a little while wearing their jewelry and admiring each other, and then they put everything away preciously, and set up for breakfast. Aunt Esther said they should have a great breakfast, to celebrate the Epiphany and because they didn't know when their next meal would be. They ate scrambled eggs and home fries with soft olive oil rolls, sausages and peppers, maritozzi (filled with custard cream and almost as good as Great Aunt Marianna's), with orange juice and cappuccino to wash it all down. Ivana said:

"We almost never have orange juice." Luna asked:

"Why?"

"Do you know how many oranges have to be squeezed to make a glass of orange juice, and how much work it is?" Answered Ivana. Luna said:

"No, I never thought about it before. At home we buy our orange juice already squeezed, and we have it nearly every day."

"I knew you were lucky, your parents must be rich!" Luna did not make a comment, but looked up to see Uncle Pas look at her with satisfaction. Every time he gained some new insight about her and the time she came from, he seemed quite pleased. Aunt Esther looked at her curiously, in one of her rare moments of doubt, but she was soon distracted by a knock at the door. As she opened the door, there stood Anna outside:

"I'm here on Befana business!" She announced, and stepped inside unceremoniously. She nodded her head to Uncle Pas, and went straight for the girls. They were watching her curiously, and Anna said:

"La Befana was so overworked, that she asked me to help deliver presents, even with all of the things I have to do!" She deposited two bundles on the table in front of the girls, and said:

"She asked me to give you girls one of these bundles each, she marked them." Anna looked for special marks on the bundles, and then handed one each to Luna and Ivana. They said in unison:

"What's in the bundles?" Anna responded:

"Beats me! Let's open them up and see." Luna and Ivana, politely and gently, tried to undo the strings on their tightly-bound bundles, but when it proved too difficult, they, to the laughter of the adults, excitedly ripped the brown paper instead. When they were done, they pulled off some tissue paper, and lo' and behold! Embroidered corsets, silk aprons, black embroidered skirts and overskirts, white full petticoats and white lawn shirts tied in minuscule pleats, along with shawls of wonderful colors popped out. Two smaller bundles within contained the sleekest, daintiest, most colorful pair of Cioci shoes the girls had ever seen; they were fashioned in strong, light leather with flowers and leaves engraved on them in a multitude of bright colors. Inside the Cioci were folded white starched leggings and black leather laces. Luna and Ivana couldn't stop themselves; they were screeching and jumping up and down while holding various parts of their marvelous original paisana costumes. Luna's costume was all black felt, with a blue shawl and apron, white shirt and white petticoats, embroidered all over in wonderful bright colors and with bright fringes. Ivana's was all black felt with a red shawl and apron, white shirt and white petticoat, everything embroidered all over in colors very different than in Luna's, and bright fringes on the shawl. They couldn't believe these wonderful gifts! The girls jumped up and declared that they were going upstairs to try the costumes on. When they came down a few minutes later, the girls looked beautiful and fresh in the expensive and adorned old fashioned clothes, all of which fit them to a T, looking like they were custom made just for them. They both launched themselves into Anna's arms, and kissed her, saying:

"Your Befana was the most wonderful one of them all, even thought they were all just the greatest. We are so lucky, and we know it! Thank you, thank you with all our hearts! When can we wear these costumes to show them off to everyone?" Anna said, laughing:

"How about today, after the wedding, in the pavilion for the dance?" The girls screamed again in joy, and ran back upstairs to take off the beautiful costumes for later. After they came back down, Anna had to leave them; she had her work cut out for her, and she swore that they were all going to be bowled over by Antonietta's beauty if that was the last thing she ever did! The presents were all packed away, and the costumes with the jewelry were put in a cardboard suitcase for safekeeping and to carry them to the pavilion. It was still early, and they took care of the animals, as they were going to be left alone for long hours, and they needed to be fed, cleaned and set up for their absence. They had about two hours before they left for the little church up on the mountain, when they heard someone drive up. They all rushed outside, as a small black car stopped in front of their door and a middle aged couple came out. Aunt Esther ran to them, embraced them and cried:

"Mamma, Papa', I didn't know you were coming! I didn't get a telegram or anything!" The woman, looking much like Aunt Esther but older, said, caressing her hair:

"We didn't know we were going to come until yesterday, but something happened that made up our minds, and we didn't trust these telegrams; sometimes they arrive later than the people they are heralding!" The man embraced Aunt Esther, and then shook Uncle Pas' hand. Ivana ran to both of them, and they embraced and kissed her lovingly. And then they turned to Luna:

"We didn't know how you would be, Luna, but you are family as we can see! Welcome and thank you for reminding us that some in the family are far away, and we need to think of them also!" Then they both embraced and kissed Luna, Aunt Esther's mother extending her right hand to quickly touch Luna's forehead, the center of her chest, and her left and right shoulders. Luna realized that she had performed the sign of the cross on her, like a benediction, and a chill came over her as she felt this to be very familiar without even knowing why. She shook off the feeling as they walked into the house, with Aunt Esther's mother holding her hand. Luna felt strange, as if she knew these people, especially Aunt Esther's mom. But how could she? This was the most puzzling feeling, not entirely unpleasant, that she had ever had. She felt genuine love coming from them, as they all walked into the house. There was excited talk, they had a suitcase with them and a large box, and when all talk subsided, while Aunt Esther and Uncle Pas were serving some restorative coffee and red wine, they called Ivana and handed her a parcel. They said, smiling, that la Befana had dropped the parcel at their house the night before and they didn't know what was in it. Ivana ripped the paper eagerly, and she found the cutest leather handbag with shoes to match, and the shoes had little heels on them! Luna held the shoes for a short while, because Ivana took them right back, and exclaimed:

"Heels! You're so lucky!" Ivana said:

"I know, my grandparents are so wonderful! Now my parents can't say anything about me wearing heels anymore, they've been overruled!" And she smiled at Aunt Esther and Uncle Pas who were looking at the scene with great pleasure. For Uncle Pas they had a light blue, fine lawn, store bought shirt, which Aunt Esther loved immediately, and said that Uncle Pas was going to wear it for the wedding. For Aunt Esther they had the coveted tall and rectangular baking pan with a cover, used to make American bread with. After that, Aunt Esther's mother called Luna and said seriously:

"Luna, your Aunt wrote us everything about you, we know your name is Luna Marina Blue, and we have been following your stay here with interest. Just yesterday we came across something that, somehow, reminded us of you; maybe it's a sign, but that's what made us decide to come here today. We don't usually drive so far, except for something very important. This wedding is very important to everyone, we know, but it's not family, and we're retired and don't like to go away from home for too long. But what we saw yesterday was too eerie to ignore, and we think that this somehow involves you."   Ivana's grandfather then handed her the flat box, and she handed it to Luna with an uncertain smile. Luna held the box in her hands for a while, almost scared to open it, until Ivana cried:

"What are you waiting for? Open the box, why don't you? I'm dying to see what's inside!" Luna started to undo the string that held the box closed, and then gingerly took off the paper and folded it, while Ivana was chomping at the bit. Out came a frame with a picture in it. It was just a reproduction of an ancient mosaic, everyone could see that, but what the mosaic represented took their breaths away.   Ivana's grandmother explained:

"Not too long ago, an ancient villa was discovered buried underground on one of the hillsides of Roma. The archeologists who found it were marveled at the find. No one knew that a large villa had stood on that site. They excavated it, and they found treasures beyond belief. Everything left behind describes life in ancient Roma in very high detail, especially the life of the inhabitants of the Villa itself. They seemed very progressive people, and the lady of the house was renowned for her charitable donations. It's almost as if the people who lived there were preparing the villa to be found, and they took care to preserve everything as best they could. The owner was a proud Roman named Aurelius Micaenas, the Roman Empire's Chief Financial Minister. In his youth he had been a general in the Roman Army, and was rewarded by the emperor for his valor with this important job. His wife's name was Valeria, and they had three children: Luna, Marina and Balthazar. When the villa was excavated, they found in the center of it, and very well preserved, Valeria's private room, her zotheca, and on one wall a strange and beautiful mosaic that took up one entire wall. They made copies of this mosaic, and we bought one for you, Luna. We're not sure how, but we think that you're deeply connected to this discovery." Luna looked at the reproduction of the mosaic, and her eyes misted, and when she read the inscription on the mosaic, she started to sob, holding the frame to her breast. In the mosaic there was a family of two parents and three children. The mother, a beautiful, patrician lady with dark fluent hair, was sitting on a luxurious Roman couch, with her tall, proud husband standing next to her. On the other end of the couch, two beautiful girls of teenage years, who looked like their mother, and a boy of about ten, who looked like their father, stood holding hands. Next to the lady on the couch was a piece of clothing displayed like it was a very important piece to her; it looked almost like a small, modern robe, quilted, with pockets and large gold buttons, in a pleasant blue color. Under the picture a message was etched, saying: 'Ab antique, gratias, mea optima amica Luna.' Everyone was scared, and Aunt Esther remembering what her husband said the day she lost the baby:

"If Balthazar said it, you can believe it!" Stood transfixed looking at Luna with new eyes. Ivana said, impatiently:

"You don't have to cry for that, dunderhead! It's only a copy, you know!" At that everyone laughed, a little uncomfortably, and Ivana said: "What does that inscription means, anyway!" Luna answered, quietly:

"From the distant past, thank you, my great friend Luna!" Ivana exclaimed:

"How would you know what that means, anyway!" And as Luna was about to answer she added: "Wait a minute, let me guess; you studied some Latin at your school, right?" And as Luna miserably assented, Ivana reiterated: "I wish I was going to a school like that! On second thought, actually I'm glad I don't go to a school like yours; there wouldn't be enough hours in the day to learn all that! And just because some ancient girls carry your name, it's no reason to go all to pieces; I'm sure there were a lot of girls named Ivana in ancient Roma, yet you don't see me getting all emotional!" At that, everyone laughed again, relieved, and Luna said:

"I don't know what I would do if you weren't there to keep me grounded!" She kissed Ivana's cheek and then lifted the frame religiously, and carried it upstairs to her room. Over the girls' head, Aunt Esther signaled her mother something that meant:

"I'll tell you later!" And her mother signaled back:

"I'll wait!" Luna, for her part, was still reeling from what these people showed her, and later, before leaving, she planned to tell Uncle Pas all about it. He would understand and know why this was so important to her! Valeria had given her a sign from the distant past, saying that she, Luna, had rescued her in more ways than one, that Luna had saved her in a way that no one else could, given the time and place.

Woman frying goodies on market day up on the mountain.
Duclere Design

19: Wedding!

There was one hour left before they had to leave for the church, and everyone forgot about everything but the wedding. When they finally came down from the bedrooms, they were all in splendid attire, Uncle Pas in a beautiful grey suit with his light blue shirt, shiny, black pointed shoes and a sharp red tie, Aunt Esther in her cream suit with a long overcoat decorated with golden trim and golden colored leather pumps. But the shining ones were Luna and Ivana. Luna was a vision of loveliness in a shimmering, blue velvet Snow White-styled dress with puffy sleeves, and decorated in white lace. With it she wore her little, powder blue pumps with tiny heels and a bunch of flowers on top. She was wearing her hair down, curled under and shiny black; on both sides she had a pin with a small bunch of flowers holding her hair away from her face. Everyone admired her and kissed her forehead, and Uncle Pas kneeled in front of her, and kissed her tiny hand:

"You are wonderful, My Princess, may I reserve a dance with you at the party?" Luna giggled and hugged his neck, planting a kiss on his forehead. Then it was Ivana's turn; she was wearing her dark rose velvet Josephine dress, with a pencil thin skirt covered by a wider overdress open in the front. The high waist made her look even taller, and the tiny puffed sleeves which turned into thin long sleeves, were stylish and attractive. Light rose lace decorated her neck and waist, and the dark rose-colored satin shoes with gold buttons on the side, peeped glimmering out of her hem. She was wearing her hair braided and rolled on top of her head like a coronet. Everyone exclaimed about her too, and Luna hugged her and told her how lovely she looked. Uncle Pas kissed her hand also, called her his little princess, and asked her for a dance. Aunt Esther's parents wore nice, expensive store bought clothes, and they all made a bunch of beautiful people going to a beautiful wedding. They got into the truck, Aunt Esther and her mom sitting with Uncle Pas, and her husband sitting on cushions in the back with the girls. They arrived at the church early, and took their reserved seats with the other Wedding Consultants and the bride and groom's family. The little church was covered in flowers and everyone looked splendid and happy.

The outside started to hum with noise and music, and everywhere you looked, it was people, vendors and joy. The cars were parked well away, and most of the people had walked over, Anna reported. She was dazzling in her many-colored silk costume with the beautiful patent leather shoes decorated with buds and leaves. She wore her hair in two braids pulled up on both sides of her head, with many shiny ribbons falling and fluctuating next to her happy face. She was going in and out of the church, waiting for the bridal party to arrive so the girls could take their places behind the bride and hold her train. Everyone was curious about the Dressing of the Bride, but Anna kept MUM, saying simply:

"Soon you'll see how beautiful she is for yourselves!"

Finally the lookout ran into the Church and announced:

"The Groom is here! The Groom is here!" And in walked Rodolfo surrounded by his family. He was indeed splendid, like Anna said; he was wearing a black suit with a dazzling white shirt, a dark blue tie held by a tiepin of gold and blue topaz, with matching cufflinks and lapel pin which held a white carnation boutonniere. His hair was sleeked back, and fell a little over his shirt collar in the back. His eyes were black and intense, his shoulders wide and powerful. He was a majestic figure to behold, and all the ladies present whispered:

"Antonietta is sooo lucky! I don't know if she even deserves a man like that! So, she has money, but who cares, she's mousy at best!" And Anna, listening to that was cackling in glee, and saying to everyone:

"I know something you don't know! (I wonder how they'll take the red shoes Antonietta insisted on.)"

Next, the wedding march started, and from the church's front door, a beautiful vision entered on the arm of The Fool. A dream of iridescent, fluctuating white floated down the aisle. The dress and veil were the focus at first. The dress was made of heavy satin, beadwork covering the entire front, shimmering and winking, then encircling the tiny waist ending in a point right in front. The dress was shorter in front, the heavy satin floating in fluid waves above tiny, elegant ankles and high heeled, fragile red shoes. Red shoes? At first everyone gasped, but then they had to agree that the shoes gave the whole ensemble a touch of whimsy, which was a new idea to everyone. The dress fell to the floor in the back, producing a small train which was covered by the ethereal, floating veil cascading from an iridescent coronet over the bride's hair. The veil was like air floating around the bride, and the only reason people were even sure there was a veil was because here and there white dots punctuated the light-as-air masterpiece. Also, two beautiful girls, one in deep rose and the other in lovely blue, (Were they really those two scampers who followed everyone around, who ran around all day on their bicycles and stuck their noses into everyone's business?   And where did they get the wonderful dresses?) were gently holding the ends of the veil to make sure it didn't end up under anyone's feet. Enveloped in this beauty was a vision; the most beautiful, proud and sparkling brunette everyone had ever seen. Her dark hair was pulled severely back, forming a chignon contained by the shiny coronet on top of her head. She had a high forehead, eyebrows like a blackbird's wings, clear and shiny golden brown eyes with long lashes, a small nose and pouty pink lips. Her high cheekbones had a golden pink hue to them that resembled the pink on her lips. Everyone thought:

"The Fool is escorting the wrong bride, and poor Rodolfo is going to be heartbroken when the real, plain Antonietta shows up!" Ivana said:

"How can Antonietta be so beautiful!" And Luna thought:

"Anna, you sly fox, Antonietta has makeup on her face!" Only a touch, of course, but it highlighted Antonietta's dark beauty, on this, her special day. A stunned Rodolfo walked over like a sleepwalker to take his bride from her father's arm, and everyone whispered:

"It was love that turned a mousy Antonietta into a beautiful woman!" The whole church sighed, and they all turned a loving eye to their companion, their husband, their fiancé; everyone was well acquainted with the power of love, they saw it every day, in fact, no matter how wonderful Rodolfo looked, all of the women in that church secretly thought that their man was more handsome, and all the men secretly thought that no matter what they were wearing, their women were more beautiful. Rodolfo leaned over to his bride and said:

"I already loved you, warts and all, but you haven't any, you are the most beautiful woman I have ever seen; what did I ever do to deserve you?" Antonietta raised her head proudly and responded, loudly:

"You are you! That is all I ever wanted, you as my lifelong love! Will you still love me when I'm old and not so pretty anymore, Rodolfo?" And Rodolfo responded, also loudly:

"My heart and body are yours forever, my love; I declare this to you on our wedding day!" Don Attilio smiled, and everyone else did also, but Antonietta and Rodolfo had eyes only for each other. Suddenly a loud sobbing was heard, and everyone turned to the family's bench, expecting to see Assunta cry in her husband's arms. But it was not her crying loudly, but The Fool, whom she was trying to comfort by running her hand up and down his arm. When they saw The Fool, the most hardened man in the province, sobbing without restrain, they all had misty eyes and dabbed at them with handkerchiefs in excitement and delight.

As Don Attilio finally pronounced Antonietta and Rodolfo man and wife, everyone suddenly stood up and cheered as the newlyweds held each other in their arms and kissed.

Ancient little church up on the mountain.
Photograph 1950

After the wonderful ceremony, Rodolfo and Antonietta emerged from the church into bright afternoon light as husband and wife, to even more clapping and cheering. Rice flew overhead from every corner, and Luna and Ivana laughed in joy, saying:

"They will also have three hundred children, like the bride in Pontecorvo!" The walk to the pavilion was short and quick, but the newlyweds were asked to take the long way around the grounds, since there wasn't room in the church for all the people. Some of them came from far away and they had a right to see the couple after traveling so long. All around the perimeter of the large area, and down the mountain, vendors were lined up, and the items being sold were so varied, that it boggled the mind. At one point, taking her eyes off of the veil for a few seconds, Ivana said:

"Oh My God! Lulubean's is here! I can't believe it; I have to go there later!" Luna said:

"Why are you so excited over beans? We have all the beans we want at home!"

"Not those kind of beans, dunderhead! I'm talking jewelry. Lulubean's makes jewelry! She makes slave bracelets that are out of this world!" Luna was suddenly very interested:

"What do these slave bracelets look like?"

"They're wonderful! I'll show you later!" After a long time, as Rodolfo and Antonietta very gracefully stopped to thank everyone and talk to all of the well-wishers, some of which they never met before, they finally arrived at the huge front door of the pavilion. The wedding consultants had not seen the pavilion fully decorated this day, as they wanted to take part in the wedding ceremony, so they left the last minute preparations in the capable hands of Toscana, Lilliana, Inessa and the people hired to work at the wedding. As they followed the wedding procession inside, they knew that they were right to trust these wonderful people. Toscana, Lilliana and Inessa stood in the entrance, welcoming everyone in the wedding party, and they looked amazing; Toscana was all in gold, wearing an empire style dress with a beautiful neckline, decorated in shiny, golden sequins, a beautiful brown silk orchid pinned on her shoulder. On her neck she had a gold chain with a large, shining gold medallion and she had beautiful, shining dangling, gold earings to match; her hair was a shimmering coronet of golden brown, and she was wearing golden brown, high heeled pumps. Lilliana was all in black; she shimmered and shined in a dress of black satin decorated with a corsage of pink satin orchids with emerald green leaves. On her feet she wore high heeled, pointy pumps in emerald green, and what seemed to be real emeralds shone on her wrists, neck and ears. Inessa was all in deep rusty red, stiff watermark taffeta, her symmetrical dress going from a wide angle at the bottom to a small point just under her chest. The luxury of the cloth was enough to get everyone's amazed attention, never mind the progressive design. The top of the dress consisted of a reversed triangle, wide at the shoulders which sported raglan sleeves, and small at the waist, where it conjoined with the bottom by a slim black belt. She had black high heeled shoes, and simple black onyx jewelry on her neck, wrist and ears. Her long, black hair was pulled back in a large, shiny chignon decorated by a red silk orchid.

After enjoying this vision of the three lovely ladies, everyone looked inside of the pavilion to a scene so wonderful that they all exclaimed in awe. In the center of the humongous room was a stage done all in white. This went half the length of the room, the other half being reserved for dancing. On the stage winked linen ware, silverware, dinnerware and glassware. The centerpiece was a large, splendid carving of the bride and groom, its sheen winking amongst the food, and all around, space was taken up by long, white plates of hors d'ouvres. There were plates of mixed fried vegetables, mixed fried cheeses, small fried meat and vegetable pies, huge piles of tiny, golden rice balls oozing drops of red sauce and cheese, plates of sliced salamis, dry sausages, prosciutto and mortadella. There were plates of artichoke hearts in oil, eggplant in oil, mixed, vinegar-cured vegetables, plates of every kind of salad, plates of tiny ricotta cheeses and slices of Provolone and Parmigiano cheese, tiny fresh mozzarellas garnished with tomato slices and sweet basil and huge plates of mixed soft cheeses, prominent a sweet creamy Gorgonzola cheese, everyone's favorite. (No wormy cheese, to Luna's relief). Some things in the back were stuff Luna had never seen, but she was game to try a little bit of everything, slowly, as to have room for it all. Around the room were elegant, long tables that could sit at least twenty people each, and names of families and their friends were displayed prominently in the center of every table. The wedding table was on the end of the room, in front of the dancing area, on a platform, and the wedding party took their places, with Antonietta and Rodolfo at the center, facing all of the other guests. On every table a marvelous centerpiece, made by local artists, shined and added beauty to the proceedings. The centerpieces were mostly flowers, made of silk, paper, wood and pottery. There was a common theme to them, and after discussing it at length, all of the artists concurred that the common theme would be a cannata, the symbol of their region, and every creation in the room was arranged in a squat terracotta cannata with the word Pontecorvo inscribed on it. The centerpiece on the wedding table was a long, pottery terracotta creation which resembled a pool, overflowing with flowers of every kind, low on the table so as not to obscure the newlyweds and their families. The Cannatari from the Pastine quarters had done superb work, everyone agreed.

The food and the tables hit the senses first, but afterwards, when everyone started to look around, the room amazed everyone as much as the party. The floor was made of large, beautiful, white nonslip tiles and the walls were also white, except for the four murals, two on each long wall, of Vivaldi's 'Four Seasons'. These were made of individual painted tiles, like a giant mosaic, and the colors and designs were breathtaking. One wall had spring and summer murals next to each other, and the other had autumn and winter, also next to each other, copies of original canvas paintings by the French painter Nicolas Poussin. Spring depicted Paradise all green, fresh and beautiful, with Adam and Eve still innocent and happy, as Eve pointed to a tree full of apples. In the summer mural, colorful men and women worked around a glorious field of green stalked, yellow corn, while in the distance beautiful horses pranced and whinnied. In the autumn one, the ground was stony brown, but the apple tree still bore fruit. In the distance, small towns could be seen up in the mountains and in the foreground some Israelites carried on enormous bunch of purple grapes on a pole. In the winter mural, Nicolas Poussin depicted The Flood. In the distance could be seen the dim outline of Noah's Ark on tranquil waters, while in the foreground, thunder and lightning illuminated a group of stranded survivors who did not know yet what awaited them; near them a snake was seen slithering on the ground as a symbol of impending doom.

Above all of this, the setting sun shone through the pavilion's colored skylights, throwing rainbows on everything. The food, the people, the murals and the decorations were all bathed in wonderful rainbows of pink and blue, swaying from the ceiling, down to the flower-filled, cascading window boxes. It all looked Heavenly, as if a bright light shone down from on high. It had been decided, together with a local artist, that the skylights should not have anything painted on them, instead being made of squares of different colored glass joined by lead, to provide the effect of a rainbow of colors cascading over everyone and everything, changing as the sun moved through the sky. Everyone found their places and soon the pavilion was full of festive and happy people. Everyone who was anyone was there; Anna sat with her family and pulled Signora Bruno and her son next to her:

"You're my family too!" She told them, and they kissed her cheek and sat with her large family of children, in-laws, grandchildren, and some dear friends; Amelia, Angelina and Irma sitting amongst their family proud as peacocks that their work paid off so beautifully. Gianna was also proud as the fruits of her labors were so well received and enjoyed by everyone; wait till they see the cake and pastry! Aunt Palma, in a scintillating costume and great head scarf, her chest, ears and hands covered by a fortune in gold, sat at a table with Aunt Nannina, her two brothers, Uncle Saverio and Uncle Luigi and Giustina and their entire family, which included great Uncle Biagio, Great Aunt Marianna and Gianna the teacher with her children. Aunt Palma had an empty seat on one side, and Aunt Nannina on the other. At one point she started to gesticulate furiously, inviting someone over; a giant of a man in a fancy and expensive outfit approached the table. He was wearing a soft navy blue suit, snowy shirt and maroon silk tie. His feet were shod in expensive, black, pointy shoes and he exuded style and class all the way up to his neck.

Above his neck it was another story; he sported a mane of curly, glossy black hair, a luscious mustache and an irreverent, blindingly white smile; he had shaved his goatee. Ferdinando came close hesitantly, and Aunt Palma invited him to sit with the family, as Aunt Nannina looked around with her nose in the air ignoring them. When Ferdinando was about to sit on the empty chair next to Aunt Palma, the little old lady jumped up and moved agilely to the empty chair herself, and Ferdinando sat next to Aunt Nannina, wearing a big, satisfied smile. Then he leaned over and kissed Aunt Palma's wrinkled, tiny cheek, and whispered:

"Thanks, little princess!" And Aunt Palma, cheeks pink, leaned over and put her head on his powerful shoulder. Luna and Ivana were nowhere in sight. In fact, that very minute, they were checking out the bathroom, a favorite activity of theirs, wherever they went. It was glorious; all white, large, covered in tiles from top to bottom. It sported a toilet, with a large overhead tank of water fed by a water tank on the roof, bidet, sink and even a small, sitting-down bathtub. Fluffy towels were everywhere, and they had the initials AR on them, for Antonietta and Rodolfo. They had retrieved their bundles from the truck, and were eager to change out of their ceremony dresses and into their little, colorful and precious authentic costumes:

"We're giving everybody a great fashion show, aren't we?" Luna asked. They giggled. They ran out of the bathroom, two happy little larks, light as a feather in their wonderful Cioci and with their skirts swishing around their legs, and then stopped suddenly, a vision in front of them. He was steel slim, wiry, handsome and smiling, while wearing a beautiful silver grey suit in lustrous poplin. The silky poplin moved and shined with his every step and his black silk shirt and red tie gave him a rogue look. He opened his arms to the girls, and they both ran into them, screaming:

"Uncle Gaetano!" He picked up both of them, one in each powerful arm, and twirled them around briefly, their skirts ballooning and flapping, then put them down and exclaimed:

"But you are the two most beautiful little paesane in the whole place!" And then, looking towards the tables where Aunt Palma and Anna sat:

"No offense to you, my two beautiful big paesane!" He screamed, to their clapping delight. The girls said:

"Uncle Gaetano, you look so good in your suit, but we like you better in your sharp motorcycle clothes!"

"Well, my girls," he said, "I like me in my motorcycle clothes better too, but this is a fancy wedding, and we must observe the proprieties!" And at their laughter, he said:

"But I must say that you two are observing the proprieties quite nicely; you're both ravishing!" He then bowed to Ada, Concetta and Luana, who were standing on the side with a group of other girls, all beautifully appointed, and declared:

"There is an overabundance of flowers in this room, a man can drown in all this beauty and glamour; don't fight over me, girls! I'll dance with each and every one of you!" They all laughed and primped, and then Uncle Gaetano picked up Luna and Ivana's little hand in turn, kissed them and said, winking:

"Save me a dance, you two lovely little vixens, I'll come back when the music starts!" And he swaggered away. Luna and Ivana just stood there, heaving and smiling, their arms around each other. When they walked over to their table, Aunt Esther said:

"You've seen Uncle Gaetano, I see!" And Uncle Pas said:

"I think everyone has!" Then he smiled at them and complimented their outfits again; as did everyone else. They were sitting with Aunt Esther's parents, and also Ada, Concetta and Luana and their families, so all the girls came back to the table. Ernestina and Arturo were sitting close together, he was holding her hand, and Ada's eyes were shining because her parents were loving each other; Aunt Esther looked at them with approbation, and Ernestina smiled at her with a tremulous but happy smile on her pretty lips. Everyone was admiring the newest little paesane, and the other girls were touching the gold jewelry with awe, while for the first time in their life they were thinking of maybe adopting the costume for special occasions. Luna and Ivana's Cioci were certainly light and pretty, and the silk of their clothes was swishy, soft and colorful. Luna had her hair in braids, up on both sides of her head like Anna's, with long, multicolored ribbons hanging on each side of her face, while Ivana put her hair up and wore a silk kerchief tied behind her neck, with curls escaping on forehead and over her ears. The dangling earrings were so beautiful, and felt so good swinging against their neck, that they couldn't help moving their heads here and there just to make them dance; yes! The Befana had certainly done them right this year! Someone pointed to a table on the other side of the room, and they were finally able to set their eyes on the famous Stina Ciacia, there with her children, daughters-in-law and grandchildren. They expected to see an old hag with sparse hair and a large pimple on her nose, something like the Befana. Instead she was a nice, youthful looking older lady, a little plump, well dressed and very sociable. Luana's mom said:

"Before her husband died, you couldn't get a word out of her, now she's the epitome of friendliness and almost a social butterfly; go figure!" And the girls remembered what Aunt Nannina had said about her husband maybe being cruel to her, that day in Pico, and privately thought that maybe she was right, and her husband was not that nice to her, so they got up, ran to her table and pirouetted in front of her to show off their costumes. She exclaimed:

"Oh what wonderful girls, who do you belong to, you cute little paesane you!" And they exclaimed in unison, while pointing to their table:

"The Sargentos, and Anna, there on the table next to them." Stina smiled:

"I know them, good people; Pasquale Sargento helped me quite a bit when my Marco died!" A shadow passed over her face, and then she laughed out right:

"That Anna, she's got her finger in every pie. Did she have those costumes made for you girls?" And they said:

"La Befana brought them to her house for us!" And Stina Ciacia held out her arms and kissed them both on the cheek:

"She pretended to move away when she got married, but her Domenico couldn't keep her away from Pontecorvo. She knows everyone, and the Befana most certainly got names from her to order those wonderful costumes. At one time I remember her, she was on a gipsy kick, and ran around dressed like a real gipsy, golden coins hanging on her forehead and everything! I must say she did look good, though! Ah, the crazy days of youth! We went to school together, you know!" She then got up, held Luna and

Ivana by the hand and walked over to Anna. Anna got up and embraced the woman:

"Stina, long time no see! You've got my two wonderful girls!" And extended her arms to them. Luna and Ivana ran to her and she held each one in one arm, the three of them looking just like three peas in a pod in their beautiful costumes. Anna pulled up a chair and they left her happily talking to Stina Ciacia about their dear departed husbands, and Luna and Ivana went back to their table, unwittingly sashaying their little bums and showing off their authentic ensemble to everyone. In the middle of it all, of course, Quagliozzi, who came with his whole family, ran around, seeming to be everywhere. Unbeknownst to them, he took several pictures of the cute little girls, under the fabulous light, with their colorful costumes on and sashaying around the place with big smiles on their faces. All at once, the great door opened again and, lo and behold, la Befana was there! She cackled and pirouetted, she sported her big bag as she always did, her Roman hat, and of course her broom. All of the children in the room ran to her and surrounded her, and at The Fool's signal, the men at the door opened it wide again and let in a great bunch of people. They were quiet and well behaved, mostly parents with a lot of shy children. They filled up the room, but they stood quietly in their places and smiled uncertainly at the guests. La Befana talked to them, asked if they had been good children, and they all assented. Slowly the children got excited, and la Befana told them of the rough ride she had on her broom, and how her black cat Nasturzio had jumped ship over Pontecorvo, and she was sure he had gone back home to rest while she was doing all the work by herself. But she said she didn't mind, as seeing happy children was all she ever wanted. At another signal from The Fool, the door opened again, and this time it was men bringing in great wooden boxes. The Children looked with big eyes, their little mouths agape, and when the tops were pried off by the men, it was revealed what was in them; box upon box of toys, mostly dolls and shiny racing cars or military tanks. There were also cap guns, whistles, harmonicas and tin trains. All of the children were instructed to file in front of la Befana, and to point at what they wanted, and so after about half hour, just about everything was gone. La Befana then stood next to the kitchen and handed bundles to the parents. In the bundles were food, fruit and cookies. Everyone filed away a lot happier than when they came in, singing the praises of Antonietta and Rodolfo, and wishing them a hundred wonderful years together, and dozens of children.

Suddenly, the loud noise of a spoon being banged on glass made everyone turn to the wedding table. The Fool, who was no longer crying, got up, and lifting up a champagne glass full of amber liquid, said:

"I drink to my children, my beloved Antonietta, my new son Rodolfo, and his entire family; we are one now, and no young man can be more loved and accepted by us all. He is honest, straight as an arrow, and no slouch in the looks department. My Antonietta was lucky to get him; they have given me a new lease on life. Please lift your glasses to the new addition to my family." And as soon as everyone drank to the bride and groom, Rodolfo's father got up and lifted his glass:

"I drink to my children also. To my son Rodolfo and my new daughter Antonietta; I've come to love this girl as if she were my own, and not because she gave me a job, mind you!" Everyone, well acquainted with their story, laughed and he continued: "She's like a shy violet, but once she lets out her perfume, you can't help falling in love with her. My son was very lucky she'd have him, and so were we all; they are made for each other." Everyone toasted the bride and groom, and finally the permission to go up and take the delicious food was given by Rodolfo himself, who went to the food stage and filled two plates with the same food and took one for himself and one to his bride. Everyone went up to the stage, one table at the time, very orderly, but without lining up like Luna always saw at home. Eventually, almost all the food was gone, Luna and Ivana having taken only very small samples of everything, as they knew what was coming. When everyone was finished with the Antipasto, they all brought their plates to a table near the kitchen door, and after a while, the plates were wheeled into the kitchen, and another table was wheeled out. Everyone filed slowly to it, and they picked up the soup plates on top of the table. Some women in white with blue aprons quickly cleaned the food stage, carefully packing the leftover antipasto in cardboard boxes lined with sheets of oiled butcher paper and they were put outside, in the cold, on a special shelf to keep fresh. Next, giant soup tureens with ladles were brought out, and there were three kinds of soup: the original wedding soup of chicken with small meatballs, bits of chicken liver, and the most finely cut egg noodles ever, some escarole and whole, poached eggs floating in it. The second soup was beef, with bits of ossobuco meat floating in it, rice and lots of grated Romano cheese. The third soup was a very light, vegetable soup for the people whose stomach was at the time foolish and acting up. But it was also wonderful; it had little bits of all kinds of beautiful, colorful herbs, a golden broth, tiny almost invisible pastina and bits of scrambled eggs. When everyone was done with the soup, the leftovers were saved in large, deep aluminum tins with covers. After the soup, large, flat dinner dishes were put out. It was pasta time. Great bowls of ziti in red sauce, rigatoni in golden brown meat sauce, pasta al forno consisting of mezzani mixed with sauce, mozzarella, tiny meatballs and hard boiled eggs, mafaldine curly pasta Sicilian style, a la Norma, with sauce, strips of eggplant and lots of grated Romano cheese, and again a dish for people with weak stomachs; pasta Alfredo, very wide, homemade egg noodles, butter, cream and lots of parmesan. Someone saw Mimmo, Uncle Gaetano's father, walk back with a plate of the pasta Alfredo and hollered:

"Hey Mimmo, you had only three dishes of the red pasta, before you took the white, what's the matter with you!" And he hollered back:

"I've got a foolish stomach today, that's what!" And there was general laughter, as Mimmo was a lover of pasta, and he would usually have more than most, never coming close to the 'white' pasta. By the time he got to his table, his wife, Angela, petted his stomach and declared:

"Feel better soon, husband, we wouldn't want this old friend to disappear!" And she smiled up at him. Slender and dark, with black hair and green eyes, she had been known in her youth as the most beautiful girl in the county. She was still beautiful, in a mature way, and you could see who Uncle Gaetano had taken after.

By the time the pasta was out, big containers saved, it was getting dark outside, and lights went on everywhere around the pavilion. The Piece de' Resistance was coming out and everyone was ready for it; four men had been outside at the fire pit for hours, taking turns, and now they were called in with their masterpiece. Porchetta, roasted whole pig, was brought in by the four men, on a humongous wooden platter (made by Uncle Saverio no doubt!) and the aroma was intoxicating. The pig had a great apple in its mouth and its cavity was stuffed with herbs, Rosemary, thyme and sage. Its skin had been washed, scrubbed and rubbed with condiments, and it was crunchy, dark and delicious, the meat inside was fork-tender, white or dark, literally falling off the bones. After more than half of the pig had finished, the rest was arranged on the platter, cleaned and deboned, to join the rest of the food. There were steaks and chicken, but everyone just tasted everything a little bit, everyone was by now full to the gills and ready for salad and dessert. A great, mammoth salad of fresh arugula, lettuce, tomatoes, cucumbers and slivers of onions, was served in a giant wooden plate (again, Uncle Saverio!) and everyone dug in to clean their palate and taste the delicious vinegar and extra virgin olive it was doused with. Afterwards, when everyone just sat there in a slight lethargic state after all the food and excitement, everything was cleaned up, dessert plates were brought out, and coffee was served. The smell of coffee was intoxicating, and everyone's head popped up, eyes brightening and appetites returning, for dessert only. Huge towers of different kinds of cookies all mixed were put on the food stage, towers of white meringues with chopped almonds, towers of the puffy, white wedding cookies, towers of Anna's brown wine cookies, towers of dough knots sprinkled with granulated sugar, towers of soft, anise scented slices, towers of golden yellow, soft and puffy lemony donuts, and towers of crunchy white and chocolate biscotti. But the centerpiece was not out yet. Finally the kitchen door opened, and out rolled a table covered in white all the way to the floor, and on top was the most beautiful wedding cake Luna had ever seen. It was not a tower cake, like at home; but great and flat, taking almost the whole table, shaped like a heart (Toscana was listening!). In the center of the cake, a single castle tower stood, with intricate designs of windows and doors. On the top window stood the figurine of a bride with long hair and on the bottom of the tower stood the figurine of a man all dressed in black, with an accordion on his chest. Obviously he was serenading his bride way up in the tower, and she was in the process of throwing down her hair. The rest of the cake was all covered in beige hazelnut crème frosting, and swirls and designs in white colored buttercream frosting decorated every inch.   Antonietta and Rodolfo came down from the wedding table, and walked to the cake. Someone handed them a silver cake spatula, with a sharp edge on one side. Antonietta cut a sliver of the cake, and picking it up with her small fingers, fed it to Rodolfo. As she put it in his mouth, he closed his eyes and touched her fingers slightly with his lips. Afterwards, he took a little sliver of the cake and gently put it on Antonietta's tongue, touching her pink lips with his fingers. No smashing of the cake in the face of the bride or groom, thought Luna, here people had a lot more pride and dignity and wouldn't do anything that silly. After the cake ceremony was done, Antonietta and Rodolfo walked back to their table amongst clapping and cheers. They held hands, and looked at each other in a way that had every woman in the place sighing. The cake was taken back and soon plates of cake were being passed around to every table. When Luna and Ivana finally had a piece, they both agreed that it was the best cake they had ever had, and they've had pastries and cakes galore since Luna's arrival. The cake was two layers except for the tower, and it was a soft, moist, heavy cake base filled and decorated with hazelnut pastry cream and cream colored buttercream. It had a slight taste of rum, and a subtle hint of Strega liquor. After the cake everyone declared that they were not going to eat any other dessert, as they liked to keep the taste of that cake in their mouth as the last thing they ate. At that point, big trays of large lace bags were brought out, and everyone took one and filled it with the offerings on the dessert trays to take home. Luna and Ivana loved the bags, and put all of their favorite cookies in them, to eat later, at home, when they didn't have so many goodies to pick from.

The guests suddenly quieted down as a group of people walked into the room.   There was a man in a too-small, multicolored plaid suit, with brown shoes with white spats, red hair, red face, flat nose and a prominently exposed front gold tooth. Following him were three women in long, old-fashioned dresses. The man minced his steps in a funny way and was carrying a guitar, and each woman was also carrying an instrument. One of them had a concertina, a hexagonal small accordion, one had a violin and the third woman had a tambourine. They walked to the middle of the room and started to play. The man strummed some music and then started to sing a slightly nasty song about how some girl betrayed him and what he was going to do for revenge, accompanied by the women's music. They gyrated and danced as they played, and the man played the guitar between choruses of his song, going up to every table and accompanying his song with slightly lurid gestures; he made fun of everyone and laughed in their faces, but they seemed to like it and laughed uproariously with him. His dances and mincing steps were very funny, and his cartoonish painted face was expressive in a mocking kind of way, and the women also seemed very irreverent. After about half an hour of this, The Fool said something to one of the women working in the kitchen, and they signaled the group and offered them a meal at a table near the kitchen door. While they voraciously attacked the food, The Fool's three prosperous looking, humongous sons, got up and started to go over to their table, but The Fool stayed them with a gesture, and walked over himself. He approached the guy and quietly asked him who hired them. The man shrugged and said:

"No one, but we were hungry, not much money in this business, we heard about this rich wedding, so we decided to come in and perform, we figured we would get at least a meal out of it." Then he pointed to the women and said offhandedly: "My mother, my sisters!" The Fool inclined his head to them and then said:

"We understand, and we thank you for the fine performance, and you can have all the food you want, and I'll pay you your usual fee, if you tell me what it is, but the performance is over, we have some musicians we already hired for the dancing. Please eat, and when you're done, come to me, I'll pay you and wish you well on your way." They nodded yes, and the sardonic, derisive expressions left their faces; they looked tired and worn and ate with their heads down, and when Rodolfo heard the story from The Fool, he said:

"There, but for the grace of God, go I!" To which The Fool replied:

"No, son, you'd never be like that, you're an artist, and you could have had a splendid career in Roma, and if worse got to worse, you would have worked your butt off, but you would have never come to that." Antonietta, who had followed this exchange with interest, said:

"You're pretty enough, you could've always married a rich girl, Rodolfo!" and looked at him coquettishly. He leaned over and whispered in her pretty little ear:

"Later you are going to pay for that remark, my pretty!" To which she erupted into a tinkling laugh and then said:

"Promises, promises!" And they held hands and looked at each other with their hearts in their eyes, and prompting The Fool to give the migrant musicians more than he had decided on before. His daughter, the only person in the world he would gladly give his life for, well, maybe Assunta too, was happy, in perfect communion with her chosen mate, and already acting wifely to her new husband; yes! He had been lucky, and he was now disposed to help other people grab a bit of luck of their own if he could.

After all of the pastry had been disposed of, great trays of fruit were brought in, and large coffee pots were set onto each table. Everyone went to the serving table and picked up espresso cups and tiny spoons; sugar bowls were on each table and to everyone's delight, instead of regular granulated sugar, the bowls were full of sugar cubes. They also enjoyed a lot of exotic fruit imported from Sicily and other countries, like coconut meats, pineapples, grapefruits and bananas. From Sicily there were blood oranges, loquats, tangerines, persimmons, apples, grapes, strawberries, prickly pears and mulberries. There were cantaloupes, honeydews and winter, yellow flesh watermelons. Everyone found their favorite, and the girls were cruising the food stage like honey bees, chattering and laughing. Ivana said:

"We're so lucky la Befana came on Sunday!" Luna said puzzled:

"Why?" And Ivana explained:

"Everyone knows you get married only on Sunday, Dunderhead, unless you elope, and then nobody cares when you get married as long as you do! And if la Befana came tomorrow, we wouldn't be able to show everyone our costumes." And Luana said:

"I think I'll get a costume too, I'll ask for one on my birthday; I never used to like them before, but now that I've seen yours, I kind of like them; I think I'll be pretty in it." Ada and Concetta agreed, and they all had a big discussion about the merits of head kerchiefs versus leaving your head uncovered and decorating your hair. The adults were drinking rivers of espresso and talking animatedly among themselves, but Uncle Pas was looking at his girls with a sad expression on his face, and Aunt Esther put her hand over his and told him:

"Don't be sad, she'll be back in the summer!" At those words, Uncle Pas' face looked even sadder, and his eyes shined. Aunt Esther looked scared:

"Pasquale, there is something you aren't telling me about Luna, isn't there? Please tell me what it is!" He looked at her with pain etched on his dear face and replied:

"I'll tell you some time, dear, but not now. It's not a bad thing, you know, it's just that I'm very selfish and I want that little girl for our very own, and that's not possible!" Aunt Esther whispered:

"We have Ivana; we aren't going to lose her!"

"No dear, we aren't going to lose her, you can be sure of that!" Aunt Esther asked, so low that he could hardly hear her voice:

"When, Pasquale?" He looked at her and said, under his breath:

"Tomorrow………" They held hands, and looked at the two happy, chattering little girls, and just wanted to cry.

The wedding food was done, everyone was so full they could hardly move, and it was the perfect time to dance. There was a table with some gentlemen in suits who ate and drank happily and were now talking animatedly to each other, The Fool signaled them, and they got up, took their chairs and went to the end of the great room. They sat in a semi-circle and some people brought them instruments. While they were tuning their instruments and getting comfortable, trying to avoid Quagliozzi with his Eveready camera, The Fool walked over to the previous performers, and paid them some cash. The older woman cried quietly, and took his hand to thank him. The Fool said:

"Go to Roccasecca, see the hotel manager there, tell him I sent you, he'll let you play during dinner. He owes me one! I'm sure he won't pay you anything, but you'll get a meal every time and the patrons will throw some coins at you if you please them. Keep the jokes down, and try not to be too salacious, they're a puritan lot in Roccasecca and they frown at smut. Find out what kind of songs they like, sing those and you'll get business all around, maybe as far as Cassino. If you find yourself in dire straits, go see my friend Quirino and his wife Maria, they own the biggest store in Roccasecca, near the train station; tell them I sent you, and they'll help you. They are wonderful people, and you can trust them." They left holding bundles provided to them by the kitchen staff, and everyone got ready to dance. The Russo boys were hovering near the girls, and so were Luca from Pontecorvo and Remigio the Pilone boy, Roberto was standing off to one side, and no matter how much Ivana looked at him with longing, he didn't come any closer to her. All at once, the group started to play a song, 'My daughter', the father and daughter dance song. Antonietta floated to the middle of the room on her father's arm; the precious veil had been removed and carefully stored, and she now wore just the brilliant coronet which held her hair inside, forming a high, glossy chignon. Her swan neck was seen for the first time by everyone, and they were still impressed by her beauty, poise and elegance; although everyone still thought it was love that did it. Also, everyone was still marveling at seeing The Fool wear a suit, it was a first, but he looked dapper and happy, and he wore his black, shiny pointed shoes like they had been made for him. Of course no one knew how much they pinched, and how he wanted to get rid of them and put his wonderful Cioci on, but for his beloved Antonietta, he would even wear those instruments of torture. They waited, poised for the music, and when it started, they started dancing. As the rest played music, one of the gentlemen stood up and started to sing soulfully:

"You are beautiful my dear, because your mom is beautiful like the sun to me.

Again and forever, I'll tell you my dear, I love you little girl and I always will!

I'm happy, I'm content, and seeing you dressed as a happy bride is all I've ever wanted.

Nothing will ever change between us,

I'm still your daddy and please always call me Papa'.

I love you little girl and I always will."

Loud sobbing was heard, and Assunta collapsed into Rodolfo's arms. A lot of the ladies present started crying in their husband's arms in sympathy, and everyone had a jolly good time being sentimental. Eventually the father-daughter dance finished, and Rodolfo walked up to The Fool and claimed his bride. After they danced, they went back to the table, where The Fool was holding and comforting his wife, who was happy and rosy and no longer crying. It was time for the guests to dance! When the music started, a lively, beautiful sound, Luca extended his hand to her, and Luna accepted it, her cheeks pink. Marco and Marcello asked Luana and Ada, and Remigio grabbed Concetta and twirled her away. Ivana was just standing there, when Roberto walked over and said:

"Well, as long as you're a wallflower, I might as well ask you to dance!" Ivana didn't even bother with the snub; she just walked into his arms and danced with a smile on her lips. Now that everything was done, and things were under control, Toscana, Lilliana and Inessa finally let themselves be free of duties and danced with their husbands. Toscana's slim husband stood up and put his arms around her and guided her to the dance floor, while Lilliana had to pull her tycoon husband away from a group talking business, and Inessa had to look around to find her young, handsome husband who was having fun with some of the children and their toys. Nannina couldn't very well spurn Ferdinando in front of everyone, and she was dancing with him, eventually closing her eyes and gently laying her head on his chest. Uncle Saverio was dancing with a beautifully groomed and dressed Gianna, as she now reserved fancy dressing just for special occasions, like everybody else, and they seemed happy and looked striking together. They all made wonderful couples, and everyone else was also having a wonderful time. Even Arcibaldo, the old architect, was having the time of his life. He was usually alone, a widower and the owner of a peaceful and quiet life. But he was finding new excitement, surrounded by young, beautiful farm girls and wonderful people. He invited one girl to dance, and he found that he still had the energy to keep up nicely. He was thinking of starting a new life, while unbeknownst to him the girl, a serious, beautiful, older, ambitious but lonely lady had already designated Arcibaldo as her future husband, to love and honor while he would provide her with a prosperous life in the wonderful Roma. Yes! A marriage would be good for the both of them! She caressed his back lightly with her hand, and Arcibaldo looked at the beautiful girl with dreams in his eyes.   Uncle Gaetano claimed his dances, and first Luna and then Ivana danced with him, and he promised to come by in the next few days, and twirled them as they were dancing, making them feel light as air and beautiful as butterflies.   The entire wedding came off beautifully, without a hitch, and they all knew that if the occasion was important enough, there would be more good times and fun to be had in that wonderful place of theirs. Everyone had worked incredibly hard to bring about the perfect celebration, and they intended on doing so again and again in their life.   Over the coming years, the wedding of Rodolfo and Antonietta would be one of the myths of that wonderful place, the tale getting better and better with each retelling. Quagliozzi's pictures, showing not only the wonderful event itself, but the hard work that went into its preparation, would provide a complete chronology, showing just how a group of 'simple' backwater folk living on the farm in Old Italy managed, with no help or guidance of any kind, to create something truly unforgettable, thus cementing this event as part of Italian legend. The church and 'The Pavilion', as the pavilion became known, would become quite famous as well, the place where the rich and elite would come from far and wide to hold their own events. While some would wonder what made a 'so-called' nondescript back country church and parlor hall so unique and special, they would soon get their answers, and see for themselves what, or more accurately who, made it so. For the skill, talent, and sheer artistic creativity of these people were a wonder to behold. Others would try to emulate them, never quite understanding what made them all so great at what they did. But in reality it was all very simple: Hard Work, Doing a Good

Job, Caring for Others, and being Honorable in all things. As for the original group of musicians The Fool had spoken to, they would end up taking his advice, cleaning themselves up, and becoming famous themselves, even performing at 'The Pavilion' to great applause. And throughout all of this, a 14-year old little girl, named Luna Marina Blue, would be remembered for her truly original ideas, which helped make this event the best it could ever be!

At the end of the party, the ladies working in the kitchen brought out large baskets full of party favors. Just as Inessa had wanted, the party favors were certainly the best saved for last. They consisted of two beautiful, white intertwined swans in almost transparent ceramic, and in the center there was a cavity. Into it was a bundle of white lace filled with sugar coated white almond candy, the official wedding candy in this place, out of the cavity spilled white lace, gold ribbons, and a myriad of tiny, handmade silk flowers decorated with shiny sequins and seed pearls. Hanging on a gold ribbon was a folded, shining tag, outside the tag said 'Wedding' and inside it said 'Antonietta and Rodolfo; January 6th, 1951'. Every one of the party favors was a work of art, no two exactly alike; they must have taken days to make, and they were a precious and welcomed gift. Some of the ladies present were declaring that this party favor would take the place of honor in the hutch of their good dining room. When the bride and groom left, Antonietta stopped at the door, turned around, and threw her bouquet of roses into the group of people waving at them, wishing them well. With a good nudge from Aunt Palma, Nannina was at just the right spot, and she caught it in both hands. She colored, her eyes going unwittingly to Ferdinando, and as Aunt Palma cackled and danced, Ferdinando went over to Aunt Nannina, quickly bent down, kissed her cheek and swaggered away surrounded by his friends. Antonietta and Rodolfo were whisked away by one of her brothers, who had rented a big car for the occasion, and the rest of their families were taken home in various trucks. The guests spilled from the pavilion in the soft dark, barely noticing the large plaques in front with the names of the donors of the pavilion and everyone who had taken part in creating it. That was a pleasure reserved for later during the daytime, when people were not tired and they could mill around and see the plaques well in the sunlight. Ivana couldn't wait to go outside, and when she saw most of the market stalls still there, twinkling lights in the dark, she pulled Luna by the hand:

"Let's go! Hurry up! We don't want to miss her!" Luna didn't know what she was talking about, until Ivana said: "Lulubean's!" Luna remembered and said:

"Right! I forgot! The slave bracelets!"   And they ran until Ivana stopped in front of a tall, colorful stall with a light inside of it, with a tall, beautiful girl standing in the back of a table. She had long brown hair, lovely eyes and Madonna like features; she smiled and patiently showed them the twinkling jewelry in the light of the lamp. They were marveling at the slave bracelets, with a ring for each finger, chains from each ring to a spot on top of the wrist, where they were attached to a matching bracelet. The chains and the bracelet were quite beautifully designed, links intermingled with stones and pearls, and you could see how expensive they were to make, considering the work and the materials involved. They asked Lulu if she made them, and she said that she designed and made everything you could see on the table. The girls wanted a slave bracelet more than anything, but they remembered suddenly that they had no money with them, and looked at each other in consternation. Aunt Esther and Uncle Pas had followed them to the stall, and smiling, Uncle Pas bought the girls what they wanted. Aunt Esther's parents drove home with Aunt Esther's aunt, her mother's sister, and they were coming back late the following day to stay a couple of days with their daughter, so the Sargentos drove home with just the girls chattering in the back, and Uncle Pas and Aunt Esther holding hands quietly in the front.

On the way home, Assunta had said to her son:

"Drop me off at Antonietta and Rodolfo's house!" And The Fool had said:

"Whatever for?" Assunta replied:

"You know!.......I have to make sure everything is alright with the newlyweds, I'm her mother, after all. It's my duty!" To which The Fool said:

"Everything is alright with the newlyweds, believe me! I trust Rodolfo! Let's go home!" Assunta heaved a sigh of relief and they drove home. The following day, very early in the morning, The Fool sneaked out of bed quietly, dressed and went out. He turned towards the sand and gravel pit and had a long walk to the fancy house on the hill, where he sat on the porch bench and waited. He didn't have long to wait, as Antonietta was an early riser like himself. When she came out in a robe to let out Arancio the cat and sit and look at the rising winter sun, she saw him and sat down next to him:

"What are you doing here, Papa'?" She asked, and he said, looking her in the eyes:

"I just wanted to make sure my little girl is happy!" Antonietta colored and answered truthfully:

"I've never been better! Rodolfo's a gentleman, but not too much of one, just as I wanted. I'm going to be happy, I never knew being married was this wonderful, and I'm not just talking physical attraction. He loves me, and I love him, and we're part of each other now; we'll live together and share everything, and have babies we'll love to pieces. And now, if you ask me any more questions, I'll have to boot you off my porch." The Fool laughed out loud, got up, kissed her forehead, and said:

"Hurry up! I can't wait for those babies; don't make them too big, please!" And then walked away, happy. Antonietta, singing to herself, went into the kitchen and decided to make Rodolfo some breakfast:

"I hope he likes hard boiled eggs with his toast for breakfast, that's all I know how to make, I'll give him some fruit to go with it; I think I'll ask my mother how to make an omelet one of these days. For now this will do." And thus she started her married life, with joy and wonderful feelings of love towards her other half, beautiful and loving Rodolfo.

39. *Piazza Annunziata*. Cartolina color seppia, bollo post. 30/VIII/1916. Retro: "42160 Editori F.lli Danella".

Pontecorvo 1916, church in the Pastine quarters, just after the bridge, to the right.
Danella Bros.

In the Sargento household, everyone was up early, even though there was no school this week. Everything would go back to normal on the following Monday. The countryside was quiet, with everyone tired from the past few days, but as usual, the animals needed tending, and there was work to be done early in the morning. Luna and Ivana went to the pilone to wash, and after hanging their clothes on the line in the barn, they went inside for breakfast. Aunt Esther was in the kitchen and made them some scrambled eggs, toast, fresh churned butter, marmalade and fruit. The girls were amazed, as they always made their own breakfast, but Aunt Esther said:

"It's not right to travel on an empty stomach; one feels much better all day if one has had a good breakfast!" The girls stopped eating and looked at her:

"Who is traveling?" They asked, and while suddenly Luna's blood froze, Uncle Pas entered the kitchen and said:

"Today Luna is going back home!" Suddenly, Ivana screamed:

"No! I'm not going to let her go!" And ran upstairs crying. Luna, stricken, looked at Uncle Pas and Aunt Esther, and said:

"Can't I stay a few more days?" At that, Aunt Esther started crying in her apron, and also ran upstairs. Uncle Pas looked at the girl's ashen face, her trembling hands and piteously dilated eyes, and suddenly turned away and said:

"Look here, Luna, we did everything for you for months, we changed our lives to accommodate you, we took your tantrums and bad behavior and we tried to help you! Frankly we're sick of it, we want to go back to our regular life, and you need to go home. You don't belong here, and the sooner you realize this, the better it's going to be for all of us." Luna's eyes dried up, she felt a heartache like she had never felt before, and with her head down started to climb the stairs to go pack; she wasn't wanted here, and they were right, they did a lot for her, but it was time to leave them alone. She continued to climb the stairs, but she wanted to see her Uncle Pas' dear face one more time, she wanted to say:

"I'm sorry for everything!" She turned around slowly, and saw Uncle Pas rub away what seemed like tears from his face.

She suddenly understood the depth of his love; he was acting mean so that she wouldn't feel so bad anymore at leaving. She turned around, ran to him and threw her arms around his waist. She hugged him as if her life depended on it, and finally his arms went around her and he hugged her convulsively. They stood like that for a long time, and eventually, when both of their tears had dried, he pushed her a little away from himself, and looking at her said:

"It's not so bad, my Sweet Little Luna! Your parents love you, and they would miss you and be too hurt if you didn't go home to them. You've learned a lot here, and you're a different little girl now. Go home and show them your love. You have a long life ahead of you, and I'm sure we'll meet again someday!" Luna looked up and said:

"I'll go upstairs and pack, Uncle Pas! I'll try to remember what you taught me, and every time I need to do something, I'll think of you and try to do the right thing always!" They hugged again, and Luna went up to pack for the last time. She had acquired a lot of stuff over the past few months, and her suitcase could hardly fit it all, so she left all of her clothes and shoes behind. She couldn't wear them in the future, except of course for her blue Snow White dress and original paisana costume, and the shoes that went with both outfits; she wasn't going to leave them for nothing! At one point, she heard a noise. She looked up and there was Ivana at the door. They flew into each other's arms, and Ivana said:

"If you don't come back, I'll come and find you! I've already told you; whenever and wherever you are, I'll search for you! I will not lose you, Luna Marina Blue, no matter what happens. And that's a promise!" She then hugged her as if she was never going to let her go, turned around and ran downstairs. When Luna, in her soft blue coat that Aunt Esther had made for her, came down, Aunt Esther was waiting for her, and hugged her, crying. She smoothed back her long, black hair and told her:

"We will never forget you, Sweet Luna! You're in our hearts and you'll always be part of us!" Uncle Pas picked up her suitcase while Luna just held her golden yellow felt handbag, and sadly went outside to the truck. Before leaving for the last time, Luna knelt under the giant mulberry tree in the front yard and carved her name and the year in the bark, near the bottom. That way there would be something to prove that she had been there. Luna was sobbing quietly as they drove away from the desolate, but oh-so loved, farm and said in anguish:

"I haven't said good bye to anyone!" Uncle Pas broke his reserve for once, and said:

"That's how Balthazar wanted it to be!" Luna's head shut up and she asked:

"What else did he say?!"

"He said that we should tell everyone that your parents sent for you, and there wasn't any time for farewells. We will convey your goodbyes to everyone for you. There would be too much confusion otherwise. They would ask you for your address, and they would want to come and visit you too. Everyone loves you, you know! This way they will be told that you'll come back next summer, and by that time, there will be another story, and eventually everyone will move on. They won't forget you, of course, but they'll stop expecting you. You have made an indelible impression on everyone here, Young Lady, and you taught us so many things. We were so very blessed to have you!" Luna looked out the window, and tears slowly ran down her cheeks again:

"I haven't seen Benito dance!" She said inconsequently. Uncle Pas smiled his dear smile at her, and said:

"It's Monday, Luna, and we have a lot of time to spare!" She leaned her head on his shoulder and cuddled to him quietly. When they got to Pontecorvo, they could see it was market day. They drove all the way to the Civita quarters, left the truck at Piazza Duomo, right between the Cathedral and the hatter's house, and walked the rest of the way. A lot of people saluted them, everyone knew Luna by now as well as they knew Uncle Pas. A gentleman tipped his hat at them and told Uncle Pas:

"Nice little girl you have there, Sargento!" Uncle Pas put his hand on Luna's shoulder and replied:

"Yes! I know!" When they passed Town Hall, they started to hear music. There was a large group of people in front of Uncle Master's Shop, and Uncle Pas led Luna so that she was in front. No one minded, since they could see that she was shorter than all the adults. Benito was there, tall and dark, with smoky, sultry eyes and black curly hair. He looked at his audience with half-closed eyes and a slight smile on his full lips. He was wearing black, tight pants, pointy black shoes and a white, loose shirt tucked in, and Luna whispered to herself:

"Elvis!" Suddenly, he grabbed a little black sombrero with white puffs all around the edge; he put some castanets on his fingers, and with his body erect, he lifted his hand to the back of his head and pushed the little sombrero up and down over his eyes. As everyone waited in suspense, he moved his fingers and the castanets started making noise. At the same time, Uncle Master coaxed a seductively sensual sound from his guitar and Benito started to move his hips languorously to the rhythm; he was a wonderful dancer! Everyone held their breath, you could have heard a pin drop, and suddenly a sob broke from Luna in the silence. Benito stopped and looked down into his audience, then walked to the front of the store, put a finger under Luna's chin and seeing the tears run down, said:

"Hi there little girl! Why are you crying? Do I dance so badly?" Luna looked into his dark, unfathomable eyes and whispered back:

"I'm leaving Pontecorvo and all the people I love, today, I have to go back home!" And as a tear rolled down her cheek, Benito smiled:

"Now now, little girl! I'm away from home myself, and I'll soon have to go back there. Didn't anybody ever tell you that there's no place like home?" Luna answered, smiling and crying at the same time:

"Yes, a girl named Dorothy!" Benito smiled back and said:

"Yes, I saw that American movie too; smart girl!" Everybody screamed:

"Which American movie? We don't know anything about it!" Benito answered:

"It's called 'The Wizard of Oz' folks! I saw it in Roma; go see it, it's wonderful!" Everyone shouted:

"Let's ask Giampiero about that; if anyone knows, it's him!" Then Benito bent down, deposited a light kiss on Luna's forehead and said:

"Go home, Little Dorothy, and be happy! Remember how sad Dorothy was at leaving her friends, yet how glad she was when she got back where she belonged? Everything will be alright for you. I promise!" After that, Benito gave Luna a hug and then started singing 'O sole mio', low and sultry at first, and then growing to a golden crescendo. Suddenly Uncle Pas was there, pulling her arm gently and whispering:

"Let's go, Little Dorothy. It's time to go home!" They walked away, to everyone's cheering applause, and as she went, Luna turned around and waved good bye shyly. Everyone shouted:

"Good bye, Little Dorothy, Be Happy! We Love You!"

They drove to Aquino in silence, Luna taking in the sights and sounds of the lovely, familiar countryside, thinking of how strange it all was to her at first, but how familiar and homey it was now. She was sad all over again, knowing she would never see this wonderful place ever, especially the friends and family she had grown to love. Luna again wondered why her family couldn't come to live here, or why couldn't everyone come to live with her? But then she remembered all the things that Balthazar told her about people and their time and place.

"Luna, this is the way of life. There will be other times when you have to leave a beloved place, with no choice in the matter. I am sorry, Dear Luna, but there's no other way. Uncle Pas and the rest of the family know this, and although it's just as sad for them as it is for you, they understand that it's the way of things." Balthazar's voice whispered softly to her. When they arrived at the little train station, they walked inside the small, dark, and dusty waiting room. It was like yesterday when Luna first arrived here, not knowing what to expect and desperate to get back to her bedroom back home. Now that she was finally getting her wish, she was unbelievably homesick all over again, just like before. Things were totally different now: Luna had an entire family, not to mention lots of wonderful friends, whom she might never see ever again! All she ever wanted was to have everyone she loved together in one place, even knowing how impossible this was! They were about half an hour early for the train, so they sat down to wait. The lovely smell of espresso was still there, and so was the girl behind the small counter in the alcove, but neither of them wanted anything. Uncle Pas looked at Luna's sad face and said:

"You'll be in the future in a few minutes, Dearest Luna. It's very exciting, if you think about it, and I would really love to know a little more about it, if you feel like talking." Luna slipped her hand inside of his, and replied:

"I thought that you weren't supposed to talk about what's yet to come!"

"That's true; it was the fear of 'Them' pulling you away sooner than they were supposed to. But now that you're going away, Balthazar trusts us. He said I can ask you a few general questions." Luna smiled sadly at him:

"The future is not that exciting to me, because you all won't be there. I finally realized that it's the people that make us happy, their love and caring. What will I do without you? I won't be able to tell anyone about you. What good are computers and portable phones and MP3 players when the people I want to talk to aren't there?" Uncle Pas smiled down into her earnest little face:

"There will be people for you Luna, believe me! Never forget that wherever you go, there will always be those who will get to know and adore you! But now, tell me a little more about what's to come." Luna told Uncle about the stock market:

"I don't know much about it, they say people got rich buying stock pertaining to electricity, cars, phones, television, computer companies....." Uncle Pas said:

"I know about phones, even though they aren't portable yet. But what are these computers exactly? I heard a little about these so-called 'electronic brains', but I don't understand them very well!" Luna told him she didn't know how they worked, they could be used to find out anything you want, people write to each other with them, and the messages are received instantly no matter what part of the world you're in, they're used in schools to study, and you're always connected with the world when you have a computer. Then she looked up into his wonderful eyes, and said:

"I have just realized, though, that having a computer is no substitute for being with real people; I have never missed my computer the entire time I was here." Uncle said:

"I hope they hurry to invent them, I sure would like to see one, someday! I would love to be able to read anything I want and talk to those far from me!" And then he asked: "Is there something to this Television machine they have in Germany? Is it still around in your time?" Luna was surprised:

"I wasn't sure they had television this far back! Yes, television is a great part of life in my time; you can see events from all over the world, but again, people mostly spend a lot of time alone and locked in the house watching television instead of doing things with other people." Uncle Pas thought a little, then said:

"It seems that people are forgetting the art of socializing, and of helping each other, and they've forgotten that you're only happy and fulfilled when you make a difference to each other. You're going to have to do something about that when you're all grown up, Little Luna. You know how things are now, and you know how they will be, and you have to make people understand good morals and real values."

"How can I do that, Uncle? No one will listen to me; they don't care about anything, just their Facebook and their soap operas and their Internet!"

"You'll find a way to wake them up out of their apathy, I know you will! If anyone can do it, My Wild Little Luna, you can!" They hugged each other for a moment, and then Luna said:

"They've made a lot of new discoveries about medicine, but mostly, they found that if you take care of yourself and eat well and natural (like we do at the farm) it's very hard to get really sick. They say that hygiene is also very important, as well as getting enough sleep, and not smoking, which I've already told you. And if anyone has a cold, or other catchy stuff, wash your hands whenever you touch something and stay away until they are better. That's really all I know! Oh, you must brush your teeth very well every day, or they will get rotten, but you already do that! And Be Happy. Being mad and sad can hurt you more than you know! Many people at home are unhappy and they get sick very easily because of stress! It's the biggest reason for seeing the doctor there. There are too many things to worry about, and people are always getting heart attacks! My parents have no time to spend with Kyle and me, and it gets even worse during the holidays, which the Grown-Ups can't wait to be over, so things can 'go back to normal'!" After a minute, Luna burst out:

"I'm so afraid, Uncle! What if Balthazar makes a mistake and I disappear forever?" Uncle Pas laughed out loud at that, and held her tightly for a few seconds, saying:

"Don't worry, he'll be very careful. After all, he doesn't want The Powers That Be to be mad at him, does he?" Luna laughed too, and said:

"You're right, he's so scared of them, it's almost pathetic." They hugged in silence, and when the whistle from the approaching train suddenly blared, Luna hung on to her uncle desperately. He held her and said:

"Remember your Uncle Pas and remember what I'm telling you; Wolfgang Von Goethe once said 'Whatever you can do or dream you can, begin it. Boldness has genius, power and magic in it.' And you have proved that to us many times over these past months; you shook us up and made us do all kinds of new things. Now go home and do the same, I believe that you can change the world, if you want to!" And with a last kiss on her cheek, he pushed her up into the train, handed her the suitcase, and stood on the ground waving while the train, with a loud whistle, started slowly chugging as it picked up steam and moved away. Luna, her little face pushed against the train window, looked at her unassuming, quiet, successful and self-educated Uncle until his dear figure blurred and disappeared. She then turned around and slowly walked into the next compartment, her head down.

When Luna entered the compartment, she thought about the first time she was on this train, so recently, yet so long ago. The same wobbly motion made it hard to walk. The same hard wooden seats were located on both sides of the narrow middle isle. The wide wooden planks on the floor had the same large gaps in between, where the tracks could be seen flying below. The overhead racks were again filled with bundles, baskets and cardboard suitcases. And yet the compartments were somehow bare and drab-gray, as if all the recent joy had gone out of everyone and everything. As Luna continued forward to find a seat, she saw a pair of ...Cioci. She looked up, and lo and behold, she took a flying run to someone's loving arms:

"Anna!" She cried, and the old lady enveloped her in all her love by gathering her to her bosom. Luna sobbed noiselessly for a few seconds, and then looked up into the dear old face:

"I didn't know you'd be here, I didn't think I'd ever see you again!"

"How could I let you go without saying good bye, My Angel? That old Balthazar knew better than to take you away from me without a last kiss!" Luna held Anna tightly and slowly started to feel a little better. She said her voice muffled:

"What am I going to do, Anna? I'm going to lose everyone, I'll be all alone, and I don't know what I'm going to do!" Anna looked at her seriously:

"You know, Luna, life is what it is; it's mostly hard, it has its moments of joy and its moments of pain. The joy is few and far between, but when it's here, it's the best feeling in the world! We have known quite a few joyful moments together, haven't we? Ultimately what counts is how happy we make those close to us. We all possess tremendous power, you know. It's the power to give a great gift to everyone connected to us. It's the gift of love, giving and receiving, and it's what makes life worthwhile, when everyone feels happy and secure.   If you put a smile on everyone's face, that is the greatest gift of all. And to make ourselves feel happy and safe, we have to know in our hearts what we leave behind. I know what I'm leaving behind, Dearest Luna, and it makes the rest of my life worthwhile." Luna said intrigued:

"How do you know what you're leaving behind?"   Anna tweaked her nose:

"That's for me to know and for you to find out, nosey girl! But you'll find out, eventually, and when you do, think of your Anna who loved you!" Luna felt all at once very calm and very tired, as if she knew she had nothing to worry about, like someone she loved was looking out for her. She curled up into Anna's safe and loving embrace, and letting the gentle rocking of the train lull her, fell asleep serenely.

41. *Scorcio*. Cartolina non viaggiata. Retro: "Ediz. Cartoleria Quagliozzi - Ripr. vietata / Stab. Dalle Nogare e Armetti - Milano"

Pontecorvo, looking up from the bridge to the back of Santo Stefano quarters.
Quagliozzi-Dalle Nogare & Armetti

A few seconds later, there was a small, silent shimmer at the end of the train compartment, and Balthazar appeared in from of Anna and the sleeping Luna.

"Anna, I wanted to come and tell you that Luna will soon be seen safely to her rightful home, where she will reunite with her family." Anna asked:

"So she'll finally go home then?" Balthazar responded:

"Yes. Once she returns to the time and place where she belongs, she will begin her future."

"Thank God!" Anna said, relieved. "It's just that I love her and will miss her so very much!" She said, tears in her eyes. After several seconds of hesitation, Anna asked:

"Balthazar, tell me, what's it like in Luna's time? Are things really bad there?" Balthazar responded:

"Anna, you would be amazed at the advances that have been made in everything from science to medicine, some of which would be totally new to you. But there are some things that would seem quite strange to you as well, and still others that would very much sadden you. But even with all of that, Anna, the basics of life have not changed so much that you wouldn't recognize them for what they were." Anna asked:

"Could I live in Luna's time, Balthazar?"

"Yes, you could, Anna. There would be challenges of course, but it would not be that difficult for you. But you would not be very happy there, however. Many things which you take for granted are now different. For example, very few people go out just to enjoy life, preferring to stay indoors day and night, alone with their computers or TVs." Anna, looking astonished, asked

"Does no one talk or socialize anymore?" Balthazar answered:

"There are many people who enjoy that, but they are fewer all the time; everyone is so incredibly stressed out and busy that there's simply no time for such things." Anna said:

"Don't good values, friendship, family, and the sense of independence mean anything anymore?"

"Not like they do for you, Anna. Many people wait for the TV to tell them what to think or how to feel, while relying on others to do the simplest tasks. Where Luna is from, life is basically a mad dash to get up early in the morning, be on time for work and school, and then come home to sit in front of the TV, until bedtime; at least for most people." Anna asked amazed:

"Why did things change so much, Balthazar?"

"I don't know," he admitted, "there are many reasons for this, Anna, from the breakdown of basic morals and values and the fact that money is all-important, to the allure of technology, which has replaced the desire to be with people."

As the train quietly rattled down the tracks, Balthazar continued:

"Remember how badly Luna felt about her parents not paying attention to her? Few parents from Luna's time take the time to actually know their kids, despite the advice from numerous books on the subject. As daily life moves faster and faster, everyone simply disconnects from each other. In truth, Anna, many parents have little experience in raising children, and even fewer worry about their emotional well-being. They would rather think about school grades and getting them into the best colleges instead. They lack your insight and experience, and as a result, these kids feel sad, lonely, and uncared for. I'm sure you realize how this can affect them as adults."

Nodding sadly, Anna said:

"Balthazar, I'm nothing special, just an old woman. All I do is actually listen and take children seriously." Balthazar responded:

"That's basically all a child needs, Anna. Need proof? Just how quickly did Luna, scared and confused as she was at her arrival here, 'fall in love' with you?"

"Balthazar, I just tried my best to show her some love and caring. It was obvious from the first moment that she got little or none at home." Balthazar said:

"Anna, This leads me to the whole reason I'm here talking with you now. I wanted to tell you as a certainty, that you've given Luna the most wonderful gift it's possible to give, the gift of your love and understanding, your morals and your values. In other words, Anna, the gift that a loving Mom gives her kids, your heart! Anna, Luna will never forget you as long as she lives, just as she'll never forget the family she grew to love while here. You will always be part of her, and she will love you forever!" With tears in her eyes, Anna caressed the sleeping Luna and responded:

"Balthazar, I love her too, more than you could ever know. I wish I could have been her Mom! I would never have ignored her the way her parents did! If only I could go with her just to keep her safe! I know it's not possible, but I'll miss her so very much! I still don't understand how anyone could treat their kids that way – for ANY reason! If your kids are hurt or sad, does anything else even matter?!" Balthazar said:

"Anna, I have no answer for that. I cannot help the way things have become, especially in Luna's time. All I can do is thank you for making all the difference in the world to her, and warn you of what's to come, and to assure you that your love and devotion to Luna will mean everything to her!" Anna replied:

"If things are going to be so bad, let Luna stay here and I'll take her in like one of my own." Balthazar hesitantly responded:

"Anna, you know that is impossible. Despite everything, Luna wants very much to go back to her home, and she'd be very sad at never seeing her family again. But I want you to know that all of your love and devotion made a very big difference in her life." Anna, crying, said:

"Balthazar, thank you too. Thank you for bringing Luna into my life, and thank you for letting me make a difference to one more lost little child! I know that I must leave now, but I will pray for her always, and I truly hope that her family will start to appreciate the wonderful little girl I've come to know so well! Luna Marina Blue will always be in my heart!"

At this time, the train started slowly reducing speed for the next stop, the wheels squealing on the rails in a soft, sad refrain. Anna caressed and kissed Luna one final time, whispering:

"Luna, I love you, and always will love you! You are such a wonderful little girl, Little Luna, and you'll carry me inside you always! Go home, God speed, and show everyone your wonderful heart. You'll go far, My Beautiful Little Luna! Remember, I Love you!!"

The train slowed down and was almost to the next stop, its rocking subsiding quietly. Gently setting Luna down on the seat in a comfortable position and covering her with her shawl, Anna slowly got up and walked out of the cabin as the train came to a complete stop. As she was walking out, Balthazar handed her Luna's prized possessions; her yellow handbag and her cardboard suitcase. Crying visibly, she looked back at Luna and Balthazar for the final time, blew Luna a soft kiss, gave the sign of the cross, and then silently exited the train, leaving Luna's life forever.

42. *Scorcio panoramico.* Cartolina, bollo post. 20/1/1930. Retro: "105678 Tip. e Cart. Nora Pietro - Ripr. viet.".

Pontecorvo panorama 1930.
Pietro Nora

Eventually, Luna woke up feeling somehow rested and relaxed. She found herself alone on the hard wooden bench of the train compartment. Had Anna really left her while she slept? Looking up, she saw Balthazar standing in front of her with his fancy, shimmering robe shining brightly and eerily. Extending a hand to her, Balthazar gently said,

"Luna, wake up. This is the moment you've been waiting for since you first stepped into that light! Ready for your trip home, Ms. Blue?" Resigned, almost content, Luna nodded, got up, took Balthazar's hand, and slowly followed him to the very end of the compartment. As they approached the silently shimmering portal, Luna noticed that it was exactly like the one she went through at her arrival here. As she slowly walked through, leaving 1950's Italy behind for the final time, Luna turned and looked back through the portal as the wheels of the train made one final squeal on their rails in a sad farewell. Reentering The Machine of Time and Space, Balthazar led Luna through the same dark chamber that frightened her when she arrived, before going through the silent and scary portals that led to the twisting hallways, this time in reverse. As they walked through the halls that Luna remembered so well, she asked with tears in her eyes:

"Why did Anna leave without saying goodbye?" Balthazar responded, suddenly much less businesslike, with what seemed like sincere compassion in his voice:

"Dearest Luna, I am so very sorry, but Anna had to leave. If she had stayed, it would have been much harder to get you back home safely. You would not have wanted to leave her, and it would have been impossible for her to come with you. Luna, Anna was sadder than I've ever seen her, but like Valeria, she came to realize the need for you to move forward instead of staying in the past." As Luna walked slowly along the familiar cold, silent corridors, she saw Balthazar's robe and turban glowing ever so brightly and eerily, making strange shadows all along the silent stone walls. She also realized that she had survived her 'Grand Odyssey', and just as she had wanted all along, she was finally returning home. But everything was different now! She had learned so much, and fallen in love with so many wonderful people! Suddenly, a tight knot formed in her stomach as all the terrible feelings of loss and sadness finally hit her. Crying openly, she rounded on her still-mysterious guide:

"Balthazar! I'll never see Uncle Pas and Aunt Esther, Ivana, Anna, or any of the others ever again! I even miss The Fool! Everyone and everything I've ever loved on my trip will be gone when I go home, and I'll be all alone! I'm afraid that in a few months, this whole 'Odyssey' as you called it will seem like nothing but a dream!" Tears flowing, Luna cried,

"Why can't I have everyone with me? Please help me! I don't know what to do anymore!" Suddenly compassionate, Balthazar asked her:

"Luna, do you trust me?"

"Y-yes, I do. Sometimes I can't stand you, but I do trust you."

"Luna, know that throughout your Grand Odyssey, I've been your guide and messenger. I don't make the rules, however." After another minute of walking, Luna stopped and leaned against Balthazar. Gently, he continued: "Remember when you had to say goodbye to Valeria when you first arrived here? Seems long ago, doesn't it? Remember how you felt like you would never survive without her? Even after all this time, Valeria holds a special place in your heart, doesn't she?" Mutely, Luna looked up at him and nodded. "Luna, by now you should have realized that it was impossible for Valeria to stay with you. She needed to go back to her own time to begin her own future and live a full life. It was necessary for her to 'go away', and even though she was very sad for a long time afterwards, she came to realize the wisdom of this in the end. By now, you should also know that, even though you only had a brief encounter, she loved you as much as you loved her! After all, she named her children after you, amongst other things." Again, Luna silently nodded, tears welling in her eyes all over again.

"I miss her so much!" She finally said her voice breaking. After several seconds, they started slowly walking again, Luna still leaning on Balthazar's tall frame.

"Luna, Valeria never stopped thinking of you. Throughout her entire life, she held on to that robe you gave her, and once in a while she would get tears in her eyes from missing you and thinking about the world you lived in and where you came from."

"I'm glad she didn't forget me." Said Luna.   As she and her guide continued down the corridors, the deathly silence fell away, replaced by a low rumbling, and then soft running water. Peering out of a porthole, Luna saw that the sky and stars were exactly as before: dark violet-blue with occasional pinpricks, some faint, others bright:

"Luna," Balthazar said in a gentle voice "Do you understand what I've been trying to tell you?" She answered him flatly:

"That sometimes people you love go away and there's nothing you can do about it."

"Luna, I know this is a lot to take in for a little girl, but remember that change is a part of life. Nothing is eternal, and anything that stagnates for too long withers away and dies. Do you remember why Emperor Nero burned down Ancient Roma? Everything, even giant cities, must go through this. Change and renewal are part of the universe, and nothing is immune to those effects." Eventually, Luna and Balthazar reached the end of the corridor and came out into the large room with waterfalls, ponds with lily pads floating on them, and the weird portals she saw the first time she was here with Valeria, back before her Grand Odyssey had begun. Although it was the same room as before, it was darker, the lights down low as if it was night. The water was also quieter, making restful sounds, and all the children were fast asleep in their alcoves, covered with blankets and silently watched over by the younger guides from before. As they walked quietly through the room, Balthazar put a finger to his lips and said softly:

"Please be quiet going through here." Realizing what she was seeing, Luna asked in a whisper:

"Are these more children who need help finding a home?"

"Yes, Luna, they are. As you can see, our purpose never ends. Somewhere there's always another disaster, or more tragically, a truly bad home situation, requiring our intervention."

"Will they be okay in their new homes?" Luna asked softly.

"Yes. Just like with you and Valeria, each of these children will arrive at the proper time and place so they can complete their destinies." As they walked across the huge room, Luna started to understand the simple truth behind Balthazar and the Machine of Time and Space, aka, the McMachina. Her guide, and all of the other guides, was charged with an awesome responsibility; to rescue, protect and help children in need, to get them to a place they can safely call home. Since this required taking them away from their place of birth, helping them through the sadness and feelings of homesickness was all-important. Of course, before going through her Grand Odyssey, Luna had never truly been away from home and all she knew, and she'd never felt truly alone. She tried to imagine what any one of these other children must be feeling right now, and realized that Balthazar had spoken the truth from the beginning. These poor souls ALL had it much harder than she! Instead of running away from a stupid family argument like an immature child, they had to deal with losing everything they knew to start a new life in a totally strange place. Yet there was simply no other way to handle these situations. To leave these children where they were would inflict great harm, and even in their new home, survival was not guaranteed. Luna finally understood that loss and change were inevitable parts of life, and that the manner in which one came to terms with those changes was one of the best judges of one's character. Feeling bad for how she treated her parents, teachers, and even her little brother, Luna then resolved to behave better in the future. Instead of getting angry and loud, she would solve problems by using her intelligence and creativity, because nothing was more effective in conquering the impossible than an intelligent and dynamic mind!

As Luna and Balthazar reached the end of the huge, dark room, she took one last look at the place where she'd met her dear friend. Waving good-bye, she said a silent prayer to the poor sleeping children who were hurt, frightened, and looking for their new home.

Leaving the huge room behind, they traveled through more winding stone corridors with large windows, until arriving at the large, brightly-lit room with the circles carved into the floor, from which she first arrived at the McMachina so long ago. Turning to face Luna, Balthazar took her hands and, looking down into her sad face, said:

"Luna, I know that even going home, where you've wanted to be, won't be easy for you. You lost some things on this trip, but you've gained so much more! Soon, you'll be back with your rightful family, and there will be wonderful things for you in the future, just wait and see!"

"But I won't have anyone from Pontecorvo! They're all gone by now! I'll never see any of them again!"

"Luna," Balthazar said gently, "trust me on this, you have not lost nearly as much as you may believe. Just remember that life is full of both opportunities and challenges; wonderful things are just around the corner."

All at once Luna suddenly cried:

"Balthazar! We have to go back! I forgot my suitcase and my handbag on the train!" He looked at her with sorrow:

"No, Luna, you didn't forget them! They were not there anymore when you left! Anna took them!" Luna was bewildered:

"Why would she do that?" Balthazar said softly:

"If you brought them here, they would have disappeared on you. You can only take what's in your head, nothing more. The rest will be there when you get home, only the proper way." She didn't understand:

"What's this 'proper way'?" He stated:

"The passage of time, Dear Luna, the passage of time!" She still didn't understand:

"What do you mean?"

"If someone saves those things for you, properly preserved, they will be there for you when you get home." Suddenly, stunned, Luna realized that she was no longer wearing her outfit, nor her soft, blue coat, but her pajamas and slippers; the precious friendship gift from Ivana was not on her neck anymore! Touching her hair, she realized that her long braids were gone, replaced with the short, unruly hair exactly as she had when she first came here. Balthazar laughed out loud:

"Not to worry, dear, your hair will grow back. And you have plenty of clothes in your closet at home." Suddenly, Balthazar took on a worried expression:

"Luna, we have a problem! You've been talking to me in Italian this entire time. There must be something wrong! Wait just a minute." Luna looked up at him and waited. A few seconds later, he stared at Luna with some surprise on his old face, and stated:

"It seems that there has been a glitch with the language apparatus, and all the languages we channeled through you are there to stay; no fault of your own. It seems that whenever your mind gets a hold of something, it never lets go!" Luna laughed:

"You mean that now I speak Italian forever?" And Balthazar said, lugubriously:

"And Latin, don't forget Latin!" She said:

"What are you upset about? What is the problem with me speaking Italian and Latin?" Balthazar sighed:

"It's an infraction of the first order! If you suddenly start speaking fluent Italian and Latin, everyone will want to know what happened, The Powers That Be are very displeased with me, as if it was my fault!" He added sottovoce. And then he said:

"You, Miss Luna Marina Blue, will have to cooperate, and restrict this situation so that no one will ask questions!" Luna said:

"But what can I do!" And then, at Balthazar's dismayed expression, she said:

"I'll find a solution, I actually have already thought of one. All I ask is to be able to take one small thing with me when I go home." Balthazar looked scandalized:

"Miss Blue! Are we resorting to blackmail, now?" She smiled:

"Call it what you want, if I don't have the one small thing I want from my trip, I'll start giving speeches in Italian and Latin everywhere I go! I don't think The Powers That Be will like that very much, will they?" Balthazar looked trapped, and then he furtively approached her and whispered:

"What do you want to take with you?" And Luna whispered back:

"The silver chain with the half friendship heart, that Ivana bought for me in Pico." He looked around apprehensively and whispered:

"Done!" Luna's hand shot to her chest, and suddenly there it was! It felt so good! Like Ivana was right there with her. Then Balthazar pressured her:

"Well? What is this solution?" Luna said:

"I'll start taking classes in Italian and Latin as soon as I get home, and I won't let on that I already know these languages; I'll be very precocious and learn them fast, though! I'll say that I want to become an historian of Ancient Italy, and need these languages to read the original scripts. In fact, I think that that's just what I'll do when I grow up." And Balthazar clapped his hands and exclaimed:

"Brava! Brava! Miss Luna Marina Blue! The perfect solution; you are a very smart girl and I know you can carry on this assignment very well." And then he said:

"You know, Miss Luna, I really do believe what someone once said, that alone we're a drop and together we're an ocean." Luna laughed:

"Why, Balthazar, you're a veritable source of platitudes!" And he replied:

"When you've lived as long as I have, Miss Blue, you acquire quite a few of them." Luna sighed:

"Why can't The Powers That Be understand these things?" Balthazar sighed too, and replied:

"You have to forgive The Powers That Be, my dear, for they have lofty ideals." Then he looked up, at The Powers That Be, and smiled with a somewhat smug expression on his wrinkly face.

"So, Miss Blue, ready to reappear back in your bedroom?" All at once, Luna threw herself at the guide she had hated and for some strange reason, grew to love, and cried:

"Balthazar, please help me! I don't want to go back to 1950's Italy because I don't belong there, and I hate going back to my bedroom because no one wants me there! I beg you, let me stay here with you so I can help the children, the way I helped Valeria!" Balthazar, looking at Luna with genuine respect, said:

"Dearest Luna, that's really sweet of you to offer yourself like that. And I'm sure you would be wonderful with the children! Yet, Ms. Blue, I cannot take you up on your offer. Your destiny is far more important than that, and with this, I'm in total agreement with The Powers That Be!"

"What destiny, to go back to school and be laughed at by kids and teachers alike?"

"I do not know for sure, Ms. Blue. But there's one thing I CAN say. I know you want to stay here, but you may find that having is not so pleasing a thing as wanting. This is not logical, but it is often true." Balthazar said with a smile. Suddenly Luna perked up, smiling herself:

"Why Balthazar, you watch Star Trek?" To which Balthazar replied:

"Only the Original Series, Dear, only the Original Series!"

"Balthazar, you're a Star Trek Snob, aren't you?" Balthazar responded:

"Luna, many of the ideas in that show are far truer than you realize, especially the Prime Directive. As for now, Ms. Luna Marina Blue, it's time for you to go back to your rightful home and start your Ultimate Grand Odyssey, your life and your destiny!" Sighing, knowing that this was the very moment she had been waiting for since first stepping into that light, Luna stepped back into the same floor circle she had arrived on and Balthazar gave her the two-finger Vulcan Peace Sign:

"Live Long and Prosper, Luna, Live Long and Prosper! We'll probably see each other again someday!" And then he said: "Energizing!" And as the white light slowly enveloped Luna, she waved goodbye and said to herself,

"Beam me down, Scotty!"

Pontecorvo, May Street, 1950's.
Photograph

Luna stumbled out of the blindingly white light, and for a few seconds, she didn't know where she was. As the light slowly faded away, she began to recognize her surroundings; at long last, she was in her bedroom back home! Everything was the same, just as Balthazar had promised. But now it looked strange to her: too colorful, too bright and too gleaming. The colors and light hurt Luna's eyes at first, and then slowly she adjusted to them. As she did so, she realized she didn't like them very much. It was all tacky and fake, like too-sweet candy. She looked at the clock on her wall, and realized it was early, the same time she originally ran up here, angry at her parents. She didn't know what to do next, but she was quite exhausted! Her head pounding, her stomach hurting and her eyes stinging, Luna walked over to her bed, climbed under the covers and went to sleep, her hand on the keepsake hanging on the chain around her neck.

All at once, Luna's eyes popped open. The sun was high in the sky, and she knew she had overslept. Climbing out of the bed, she looked around for some clothes. But all she could see on the chairs and floor were jeans, pants and shirts, and like everything else, they too looked strange and tacky. Many were too tight, and most had big rips or bleach stains on them. She went to her drawers and found underwear, then went to her closet and rifled through her other clothes there. She finally found a little brown dress, a bit short and tight, but not too bad. She walked slowly into the hallway, but there was no one in sight, and it was the same in the bathroom. She sat in the tub, ran a little water, then picked up a piece of soap and a washcloth and washed herself carefully. As she did so, slow tears ran down her cheeks, as she remembered Aunt Esther's loving hands rubbing her shoulders and then her hair, before combing their wet length slowly, and wrapping her in a big, warm, fluffy towel and letting her go with a fast, warm hug. But now, her hair was short again, not too much trouble to wash, and she did have big fluffy towels. They had not been warmed up in front of the fireplace, but here it was warm anyway, so there was no need. But there was no fast, warm, loving hug. She did her solitary ablutions, threw her clothes on

(It felt funny to wear sneakers, they were so light and strange) and walked downstairs. There was still no one in sight, the whole downstairs still and quiet. She felt hungry for she had slept a lot of hours! Slowly she opened the refrigerator, the offensive white light making her blink. As far as she could see, there was nothing appealing there, except for some eggs, and she smiled when she saw 'American Bread'. Aunt Esther would have picked it up, examined it, and tried to come up with a facsimile. But this soft, mushy stuff didn't appeal to her anymore; she wanted something a little more substantial, something hardier and healthier. She didn't realize that, of course, but she didn't see anything she wanted. There were a few dishes in the sink, and more on the table. It was already six, and still no one was around, so unthinkingly she put her mother's apron on and did the dishes. Then she cleaned up and wiped the table, and eventually went downstairs to the washer and drier. There were clothes on the washer, mostly hers, as well as some linens, and Luna filled up and started the machine, guessing as to the amount of soap to use, then went back upstairs, and looked for a broom to clean the kitchen floor. Not finding one, she remembered that her mother always vacuumed the floor instead of sweeping it. She was sitting disconsolately on a chair when she happened to look up, and there on top of the refrigerator she saw a bundle. Her heart started beating fast, for this bundle looked exactly like the ones that she and Ivana took to school every day. She reached up and brought it down, and she noticed that next to the bundle was a small basket. She brought both down, and she opened the bundle. When she saw what was inside, her eyes watered and she couldn't stop a sob. Italian Fast Food was in the bundle, the hard, round rusks of dark grain and in the basket were a few large, round tomatoes. She didn't know where her mother got this stuff, but she remembered all the hurried breakfasts on the days when they were late for school, and smiled. She put a large rusk in a plate, ran cold water on it, let it soak for a few seconds, then poured the water out and broke the rusk in a few pieces. Next she cut up one large tomato and piled it up on top of it, she sprinkled the whole with a small amount of oregano she found in her mother's spice shelf, and she drizzled olive oil on top of everything from the little can her mother kept next to the stove.

She put a napkin on the table, gently put the plate down on it, and sprinkling a bit of salt on everything and picking up her fork, she started to eat like Aunt Esther always liked them to do, 'like a lady'. She was almost done, when she heard a noise. She looked up, and there was her mother; she didn't remember how small, cute and stylish her Mom was! Luna didn't know what to say, so she just said:

"Good morning, Mom!" Her mother paled, then looked at her plate and gasped:

"What are you doing, Luna? And why did you just speak Italian to me? Are you alright? You look thinner than usual, and darker. Are you sick? My baby, we're not mad at you anymore, we love you dear, and I hope you realize that!" Luna was shaken, she didn't know she spoke Italian, and to remedy the situation she announced, making very sure she was speaking English:

"I'm not sick, Mom, I've just decided that I'm going to learn Italian, and I was trying it out. I hope I didn't scare you!" Her mother walked over to her, and felt her forehead with her hand. She looked down, and said:

"Why are you eating that?" Luna responded, quickly:

"I want to do Italian things to get into the spirit, and I saw this bundle while I was cleaning up, and decided to try it out!" Her mother just stood there, and gaped:

"But you fixed it just like my mother does!" And then she said: "You were cleaning up?" And took a look around the kitchen, noticing the pristine condition that was not there the night before. Luna looked down:

"I know how hard you work, Mom, and it's not fair. Now that I'm fourteen, I'm going to help. I hope it's alright!" Her mother looked around the place again, then at Luna suspiciously, and when she heard a noise, she opened the cellar door, looked down into the basement, and said:

"What is that noise? Did you do something down there too?" Luna smiled:

"I put a wash on; it was mostly my clothes anyways. When it's done I'll put the clothes in the drier, they should be done, folded and put away in about an hour and a half; don't worry about them at all, I'll handle them myself." Her mom looked at her with moist eyes:

"My poor baby, you're working so hard! They did a real good job on you, didn't they! You're going crazy, and I'm just standing over here and don't know what to do." Luna laughed:

"That's not work! Doing the laundry nowadays is the easiest thing. In the olden days people really had to work to do it, the way we do it it's almost fun!" Her mom sidled away from her:

"I'm going to wake up your father, maybe he can help! For some reason you're talking almost like my mother, always complaining and telling me how hard life was in the 'Olden Days' and how easy we have it now." Luna walked over to her and embraced her:

"I love you, Mom, please be happy, I just want to help. I was alone for a long time last night, and I thought about everything, and I just realized how spoiled and selfish I was, and decided to change and become a proper daughter that you can be proud of." Her mom started to cry:

"The stress of that situation was just too much for you, poor angel; they have just made you crazy!" Luna laughed out loud and said:

"Come on, Mom! I know how bad I was, and frankly I was sick of myself, that's why I decided to change! Please don't wake up dad, I don't want to worry him, he has to go to work and needs his mind clear." Her mom was not convinced, and while Luna went downstairs to the basement to put the clothes in the drier, she walked up to the phone and dialed. When Luna came up, her mom said:

"I just talked to my mother, and she wants me to take you over there. She wants to talk to you; she sounded real happy, for some reason, and said that she wants to talk to you alone. I know you don't like to go over there usually, but she insisted!" And then she said: "I'm sorry I called my mother, but I didn't know who to call for some advice, I don't want it to get around that you're having problems." Her mom looked almost anxious, like she wanted to get rid of her, but was afraid to say so. Luna said:

"But what about school....." And then remembered and colored: "I forgot, I'm suspended for a week. I'll help with breakfast, I'll dry and put away the clothes, and then you can drive me over." Her mom was as nervous as a cat on a hot tin roof all morning, and her father gave her a few inquisitorial looks, but didn't say anything.   The only one unaware of anything different was Kyle; he tried to pull her hair to no avail, as Luna sidestepped him neatly, and tried to get a rise out of her by sticking his tongue out behind their mother's back.   But she smiled at him instead, thus stealing his thunder, and when he tried to trip her, she jumped out of the way and cuffed him slightly on his ear. He said, weakly:

"You got cooties, Luna!" And she made the motion of picking one out of her head, and putting it on his blondish spikes. By the time he had to leave for the bus, even Kyle was looking at her funny, and Luna almost felt some kind of tenderness for her bratty little brother; he was only a cute little boy after all. Luna's father kissed everyone, approved of Luna's dress with a smile and a nod, and rushed out. Kyle took the lunch Luna prepared for him rather gingerly, like there was a bomb inside, and left for the bus. Luna would much rather have stayed home and quietly reflect on her 'Grand Odyssey' and decide what her life would be from now on, the loss of her beloved family and friends in Italy still acute and painful. But she realized that her grandmother was old, and she should respect her and do what she wanted, and postponed her musings for later. Who knows, maybe she had something to say to her that would help! She was at loose ends; what should she do first? Thank God for the work to be done around the house, without it she wouldn't know what to do!   It never downed on her to use her computer, watch TV or make phone calls. It was still amusing to see her mother recoil every time Luna decided to do something, but a while ago, after the kitchen was cleaned again and the wash properly folded and put away, her mom said:

"As long as you're on this kick, I might as well take advantage of it; while you're at my mother's I might go to the library and find a book I wanted to read. Maybe I'll even have time to read it, if you continue like this until you go back to school!"

Pontecorvo, bridge 1950's. Cathedral way on top in the
background.
Photograph

On the way to her Grandmother's house, Luna looked around curiously; so many cars, so much noise, and so many people around! She almost felt a little confused, but she was getting used to it quite fast. She knew the way to her Grandmother's house, but she never quite realized what a nice part of town this was. They stopped in front of Grammeva's house, and though Luna had been there many times, all of a sudden she saw the house with new eyes:

"Grammeva's rich!" She thought. They parked in a spacious, horse- shoe-shaped driveway, as the house itself was set far back from the street. It was a great old colonial with white columns in the front, and a big wraparound porch in back. It had red shutters and it was painted.....dark rose? Luna stared, remembering how this was Ivana's favorite color, until her mother touched her arm hesitantly:

"Dear, I hate to tell you this, but be careful, will you?" Luna turned to her, and noted her worried expression:

"Be careful of what?" She asked curiously. Her mother looked a little ashamed, but went on courageously:

"Of my mother!"

"Grammeva?" Asked Luna surprised:

"Yes, my mother!" Luna couldn't understand:

"What do you want me to be careful of?"

"Well, you see dear, my mother has always been a little strange, but I always attributed it to the fact that she came here when she was twenty-one years old and already married, didn't know any English and coming from a farm in Italy, found life here a little too fast. But lately she's acting just like she's off her rocker; I had a talk with my father, but he only laughed and said:

"Your mother knows what she's doing, don't worry about her!" Luna, now a little worried herself, looked at her mother and asked:

"What has she been doing to cause this anxiety?"

"Well, for one thing, she has been wearing strange clothes, like some kind of costume; she doesn't go out in them, mind you, thank God! But she wouldn't tell me why, and she's been wearing her hair in braids, like a young girl. She's fixing up a room in her attic, under the eaves, and she wouldn't tell me who it's for, she just said that it's for a dear little friend of hers, one she knew as a child. She asked me about you many times lately. When I told her you were being very difficult, and you were doing housework, she just laughed like it was a good thing and said, 'Good girl!' Two weeks ago, just before Labor Day, she took a trip home to Italy, at the wrong time of year, and when I asked her why she was going, she said she had to retrieve some treasures she had over there; when she came back she had, among other strange things, an old bike. And only yesterday, right after you went to school, she came over and brought that bundle and basket. She knows we hate that stuff, but she insisted and stuck it on top of the refrigerator. I would have thrown that hard bread to the birds, but right after, they called us to the school and I forgot all about it." Luna was perplexed:

"It doesn't seem like she's doing anything that bad."

"You don't know her as well as I do! Lately she's been making snide remarks about things I know nothing about, and predicting dire consequences if we're not nice to you! Actually, it always scared me the way she's attached to you; when Kyle was born she was happy, but not the convulsive joy she exhibited when we had you." Luna patted her mother's arm:

"Don't worry, I'll calm her down! Are you coming in?"

"I can't! She told me I'm not allowed in the house, just you, alone!" Luna smiled at her mother and got out of the car, waving her away. When she walked in the house, she couldn't help feeling some kind of déjà vu; the inside was all bricks, tiles and stonework. In the entrance, a big tiled staircase went to the second floor, and the first door after the entrance, that Luna knew was the door to the kitchen, stood ajar. She felt eerie, and called out:

"Grammeva?" A voice answered:

"In the kitchen, Luna Dear!" She walked into the kitchen, and saw a woman in front of the sink; the woman had her back to her. Luna called:

"Grammeva, is it you?" The woman turned around slowly, and a gasp escaped Luna's mouth. She stood rooted to the spot, and then said:

"You're....You're.....Aunt Esther?" And then:

"No, you couldn't be, Aunt Esther was young, and you're......old." The woman smiled, adjusting the coronet of braids on top of her head:

"Your Aunt Esther was my mother, dear!" Luna stared:

"I know you, you're my grandmother, and how can Aunt Esther be your mother? You're older than her!" The tall, thin woman in a shapeless cotton dress, walked towards her, but Luna pulled back, worried. The woman stared at her seriously, and said:

"Whenever and wherever you are, I'll find you! I will not lose you, Luna Marina Blue, and that's a promise!" Luna's heart started beating a mile a minute, tears fell from her eyes, and she whispered:

"Ivana? Is that you? But you're an old lady; yesterday you were only fourteen, like me! It can't be, you're just making fun of me, my mother told me you were going crazy, and it's true!" And then she spouted: "How can you know about Ivana? Who told you? Was it that Balthazar? Because if it was, I'll.....I'll......" Her grandmother exclaimed:

"Oh, Dear, I've never heard from him. When you left, his job was done, that chapter was closed. He had other things to do; a lot of people needed his help, I guess." Then she walked to Luna again, and while she did, she pulled a chain from the neck of her dress and showed it to her. The other half of her friendship heart! As Luna looked at it, dumbfounded, the woman said:

"My name is Grammiva, short for Grammivana." Then she extended her right hand and touched Luna's forehead, the center of her chest, the left shoulder, and then quickly her right; the sign of the cross, like her mother's mother used to do. She had done so to Luna since she was a child, but before now Luna didn't know what this meant. She threw herself into the woman's arms, and sobbed:

"But how come you're so old! What happened to you?" Ivana laughed:

"Time happened to me, Luna, time! I've been waiting for you for over sixty years, Dear, and I didn't know who and where you were going to be, until my daughter met and married a nice young man called John James Blue. You were my own granddaughter, fancy that!" Luna started to see Ivana's traits in her grandmother, and hung on to her with all her strength:

"The last time I saw you, it was only yesterday, we just woke up after the wedding!" Ivana said:

"Oh yes, the wedding, I remember it well! It was the talk of the region for years after that. It still is, and there hasn't been one like it since." Luna still couldn't believe that her grandmother was indeed Ivana. She felt shy all at once, and said:

"Can I call you Grammivana from now on?" Her grandmother laughed:

"You can call me anything you want; you have been my favorite person since I was fourteen years old, Dunderhead!" Luna threw herself at the woman again and sobbed:

"It has been so long, how could you wait that long? And how could you lose everyone to come over here to find me?"

"I didn't lose anyone, silly, I came over here when I got married, and went back home every summer, at least until my parents were alive; now I go once in a while." Luna stiffened:

"Your parents died? You mean Uncle Pas and Aunt Esther........." Ivana sighed:

"Yes, Luna, but I want you to know that they had a long, healthy life, and they knew who you were. My father credited you for his long, healthy life, he said that on your advice he stopped smoking and turned the tobacco farm into a wheat and corn farm. A lot of his friends who kept the tobacco died young, and he knew then that you were right. Of course, now I know what you knew, and I thank God every day you were there with us at that time. Your mother didn't let me take you home to Italy when you were a baby, and I don't blame her, but I took movies of you, and showed them to everyone who knew, and I used to send pictures all the time. Just before he passed, my father used to say that in about ten years you would be fourteen and would go back there to us and we would be together all over again and we would take care of you and be happy all over again. He used to say that time was like a loop, it went around and around, and if we went on a train to it, we could stop anywhere we wanted and hop back on when we wanted to leave; I guess he got that from Balthazar and his adventures. In his last years he even had a computer, I gave it to him, and he loved it and said it made him feel closer to you! Your Uncle Pas died when you were four years old, and your Aunt Esther followed him a year later. I was with them each time, as it happened during my summer vacations at home, but they also had their other children and grandchildren with them" Luna asked:

"They had other children?" And her grandmother laughed:

"As if you didn't know! They told me what happened the time my mother had the miscarriage, you said that Balthazar predicted that they would have two boys, and they did; twin boys, my brothers, Marino and Gaetano." Luna looked at her with moist eyes:

"Remember the river?"

"You saved my life!"

"I was terrified; I didn't want to lose you! And how do you know about Balthazar?"

"Oh Luna, we have so much to talk about!" They embraced again, and then Grammivana said:

"Call your mother and ask if you can spend the night, I have so much to show and tell you, it's going to take days, but stay at least today and tomorrow for now!" Luna said:

"She went to the library to get a book; I'll call her when she gets home!" Grammivana looked at her surprised:

"What's wrong with her cell phone?" Luna laughed:

"I forgot about them! I left mine home!" Silently, Grammivana fished a cell phone from her apron pocket, and handed it to her. Luna scrolled until she saw her mother's name, and pushed 'send'. She talked to her mother for a few minutes, received permission to stay, as long as she called that night before she went to bed, and handed the phone back. Just then, a car stopped in front of the house, and someone came in. Grammivana called:

"In the kitchen, Robbie!" The kitchen door opened, and Luna looked at the new arrival, stunned:

"Carlo? No, you're Grandpa! Who are you? I'm confused!" The handsome, stout, grey haired man smiled and opened his arms to her:

"Come here, Pumpkin! Grandpa wants a hug!" But Luna stubbornly held back, and she actually looked spooked. Grammivana gave her a little push:

"Go to him, Luna, you know how much he loves you, when you were younger and we baby sat for you he used to read you to sleep all the time!" Luna said bewildered:

"He's not Carlo?" And the man said:

"Carlo was my father, Luna, I used to know you way back then; I'm Roberto."

"Roberto? The one Ivana was always looking at like she was going gaga?"

"The very one!" Said Grammivana. Luna said:

"The last time I saw you was the day before yesterday, at the Fool's daughter's wedding; you called Ivana a wallflower." He said:

"I didn't want her to know I was interested, I was afraid she would laugh at me; she was taller than I was, she still is." She flew into his arms:

"Oh Grandpa, I love you! Do you still love Swiss chard pies?" Grammivana laughed:

"He can't ever get enough! I've provided this man with Swiss chard pies for almost sixty years, and he still hasn't got sick of them."

"Do people make them over here too?"

"Sure," Grammivana said, "people from the same region as us, although I've heard that some tasteless people put anchovies in them." Grandpa Robbie said:

"I'd eat them with anchovies!" Grammivana said, smiling:

"You don't count, Robbie; you'd eat them with anything!" And Grandpa said:

"But I prefer yours, dear!" Luna looked at the two of them, and realized how happy they were with each other, and told them:

"You two remind me of Aunt Esther and Uncle Pas!" Grandpa said:

"That's a compliment and a half, they were wonderful, you could see how much they loved each other and everyone around them; so did my parents, though." Luna whispered:

"Wonderful Carlo and Angelina." Her grandfather said, his eyes moist:

"I'm so glad someone is here who knew them!" And Luna said:

"Every time I looked at Carlo, I felt so much love for him, and didn't even know why; now I know I was remembering my grandfather." Grammivana accosted Roberto and put her hand through the crock of his arm:

"My Roberto is just a wonderful man; I would have never made it over here without him; believe me, he's the taller one. We did everything together, and of course, without him you wouldn't be here!" And she blushed. Luna laughed out loud in joy, and then sobering up she said:

"But if you're my grandfather, then Anna was......." Her grandfather supplied the answer:

"She was your great-great-grandmother, and she knew it; Balthazar told her. She lived to a ripe old age, and she talked about you all the time, to the ones who knew, of course!" Luna was quiet for a while, then to lighten the mood said:

"I can see that you're quite well off, you were smart!" Grammivana told her:

"Yes, he was smart, he worked in construction and took very good care of me, but you know no one ever got really rich just working; you are the reason we are as rich as we are, you and Aunt Palma." Luna smiled:

"Aunt Palma? Dear Aunt Palma! How could she help you over here?" Grammivana smiled:

"That's a whole other story and I'll tell you everything tomorrow, after you have had a chance to rest; in the morning we'll have our espresso with some goodies, and I'll tell you everything. But regarding your help; my father told me your exact words: To get rich in America, people invest in the stock market; they buy stock in electricity, cars, phones, televisions and computers. And that's what we did. My father left the farm to the twins, and he gave me my share of the money when I got married. Roberto and I married when I turned twenty, he was twenty-two, it took a few months for the paperwork, and we came over here and set up housekeeping with that money; it seemed like a lot back in Italy, but when we arrived over here, we realized that it was just enough to get started." Luna asked, curious:

"Why did you come over here, Grammivana?" She said simply:

"My father told me that was where you came from, and I came over here to find you!" In unison they both picked up their chain and caressed their half of the heart, before embracing under the benevolent eyes of Grandpa Robbie. Luna said:

"But how could you wait so long, Grammivana? It must have been terrible!" Her grandmother laughed:

"No, it was wonderful! I did love the farm, but I would not have been satisfied being a farmer's wife. After knowing you, I somehow wanted to go places and do things. When we got married, I told Roberto everything, and he asked what I wanted, and I said I wanted to come over here and search for you; he said that whatever I wanted was fine. I have to tell you, though, that it was an exciting time for both of us. We know so much more, and we've done so much more; we feel that the move opened our eyes to the world around us. This is a wonderful country to be in, and even though we still love our birthplace, we are very grateful to you for drawing us over here. We're both American citizens, you know! All the years we had over here, even before we knew who you were, are the best of our life; no! We did not just spend time waiting for you, we knew you'd be here someday, and in the meantime we just lived loving and happy lives." Luna hugged both of them at the same time, and then she helped Grammivana make supper; they had homemade noodles in red sauce with cheese on top, thin, wrinkly beef steaks fried in olive oil and sprinkled with oregano, and a beautiful mixed salad dressed with sweet smelling olive oil and vinegar. Even though Luna had been in Grammivana's kitchen many times before, she just noticed now how it was large and sunny; it contained a great table topped by a humongous slab of marble covered by a snow white tablecloth, a large hutch filled with plates and glasses and, to Luna's amazement, a large wooden chest on four chubby feet:

"Gargantua!" Said Luna. Grammivana went to it, opened the top and pulled out a large bundle wrapped in a white napkin. Inside was a golden loaf of bread that she handed to Grandpa, and Grandpa took it, cut some large slices from it and put it back. Sitting down, Luna looked at her plate of pasta and said:

"Is this all mine?" Grammivana answered, with a smile:

"Of course, you're a growing girl, you need to eat!" And they both started laughing, with Grandpa looking at them with pleasure and determining to get in on their inside joke later. Sometime later, Luna looked up from her plate of salad and asked:

"How did you bring Gargantua over here?" Grammivana told her:

"It's not the same one, dear! That one is still at home, but it's too fragile to carry around. Your Grandfather replicated it for me; he's very good with building things, you know!" Luna looked around at the great fireplace against one of the walls, complete with a hanging iron pot and various size tripods, and she felt at home again. Of course there was no fornacella cooking apparatus here; Grammivana was the proud owner of a huge, commercial stainless steel stove, a huge stainless steel refrigerator and all of the other modern conveniences to be found in a well-appointed American kitchen. She did have one wall decorated with huge copper pots and a small copper bathtub. While they loaded the big stainless dishwasher, Luna felt so good, that she wanted to cry. She had everything! The past and the future melded together to form her new world, and she knew now that she would be happy and strong with her family to support her and her future in front of her.

Around eight thirty, Luna felt exhausted. They had a small supper of bread and cheese and tomato salad at seven, and for dessert they had some of Anna's brown anise seed cookies with coffee; Luna cried a bit over the cookies, but then she enjoyed them very much and decided to have Grammivana teach her how to make them. She called her mother, and told her she was going to bed in an hour, and she would call in the morning after breakfast. She told her mother that her grandmother was fine, and they had cooked supper together, as Luna wanted to learn how to cook Italian. Her mother was relieved, and said to tell her parents good night. After that, Grammivana told her that she looked very tired, and she should get ready for bed. Luna kissed her grandfather good night, and followed her grandmother upstairs. Instead of stopping on the second floor, her grandmother kept going, way up to the attic. On top of small, wooden stairs there was a small lending, and there were two doors, one on each side. Grammivana opened the one on the right, and Luna entered, flabbergasted; she was in a small, whitewashed room with a small window. Luna looked outside and saw a peaceful, large, green garden. She then looked around at the plain, almost Spartan room that looked almost like a nun's cell, with an austere small bed, a small table and chair and a small bureau. On the wall a large picture of Saint Maria Goretti, the child virgin saint, was the only decoration in the room. Luna threw herself in Grammivana's arms and sobbed:

"My room, this is my room at the farm! Thank you, thank you so much! How did you know that that's what I needed! I love you Grammivana, I really do." Her grandmother held her silently for a while, and then told her to look under her pillow. Luna did, and she found a nightgown exactly like the ones she used to have at home on the farm. Laughing and hugging it, she was pushed into the door across from her bedroom. In there was an old fashioned bathroom, with white sink, white toilet bowl, white bidet and a claw footed cast iron bathtub. Grammivana put some bath oil in the tub, ran some hot water and helped Luna get out of her clothes. Luna sank into the perfumed water with a sigh, and while she soaped herself, Grammivana sat on a small stool and waited. After Luna was done with her ablutions, her grandmother put some shampoo on her hair, and gently soaped it and washed it. Luna closed her eyes and relaxed. When her hair was clean, Grammivana rubbed it dry with a small towel, and then wrapped another one like it around her hair like a turban. She then handed Luna a fluffy, white cotton robe and she stepped into it from the tub. Luna thought she was dreaming, but her grandmother's soft and strong hands helped her dry up, and then she dropped the robe as her grandmother put her nightgown over her head. They cleaned up the bathroom, hung the towels and the robe on a rack, and Grammivana left to give Luna a bit of privacy:

"No black hole here." Thought Luna. When she came out and went into her bedroom, Grammivana sat on the bed with her, and told her how after she left, some months later, Carlo had installed a bathroom very similar to this one in the farm, upstairs, in what used to be Ivana's room, and from then on she slept in Luna's room until she got married, six years later. Luna was very pleasantly drowsy, and Grammivana helped her to get under the covers. She tucked Luna in, and Luna was asleep before her head hit the pillow. Grammivana tenderly caressed her unruly, moist curls, and smiled:

"My sweet Luna is back. After all these years I'm with Luna again; thank you God, for answering my prayers!"

That night, Luna dreamt that she was back at the farm, and Uncle Pas and Aunt Esther were there, but Ivana wasn't with them. Aunt Esther said:

"Dear, Ivana went to America, to wait for you, she'll see you there when the time is right." And Luna gladly sat between them and accepted their love and caresses. Two cribs stood near the fireplace, in the warmest spot, and two beautiful babies, one with brown hair and the other with black, were in each of them. Uncle Pas followed her glance and commented:

"I must say that Balthazar never lied to us, he told us about the babies, and lo and behold, there they are." Luna asked:

"Did you feel bad when I left, Uncle?" He responded:

"Balthazar came back to me and told me how you got home, and you were very happy, because Ivana was there waiting for you. That's why I let her go. She married a good boy, anyway, and he would take very good care of her." Aunt Esther said:

"Our boys kept us very occupied and happy, and of course, Ivana is almost always here, we can't get rid of her, you know!" And she laughed in pure joy. The farm faded and Luna knew she was back in her bed at Grammivana's, and she slept dreamily on.

In the morning, at five thirty, Luna opened her eyes, and looked around the room with pleasure. She hadn't dreamed it, she was really here, at Grammivana's, in a bedroom created just for her to remind her of her time on the farm! She walked to the bathroom across the small hallway, made very good use of it, washed up, brushed her teeth, and noticed how her hair was soft and curly after she went to bed looking like a chick with her damp hair. She was going to wear her clothes from the day before, but on the back of the chair, she found a wonderful outfit; she had a white blouse, a blue pleated skirt in soft wool and a grey cashmere sweater to go over the blouse. It seemed a very simple outfit, reminiscent of what she wore on the farm, but it was a very expensive brand and very expensive material. When she wore it, it looked chic without being ostentatious and it made her feel comfortable and warm. There was a decided chill in the air, even though it was only a couple of days after Labor Day; this was not sunny Italy. Luna knew that later on during the day she would be warmer, and would take off the sweater, but she loved everything about her outfit. A small knock at the door, and Grammivana stuck her head inside of the room:

"You're up already, I see! I'm glad you're keeping up the farm's hours; there is so much time to the day if you get up early! Of course, at night you have to go to bed early too, but you know what they say, 'Early to bed and early to rise makes a person healthy, wealthy and wise'." Luna smiled:

"Grammivana, you talk like a New Englander!" Grammivana smiled back:

"Luna, I AM a New Englander! I've been here well over fifty years, and I love everything about my new home! I was so lucky that you came and pointed the way for me, I don't think that I would have been happy just being on the farm." Together they made the bed, straightened up the room, and took Luna's dirty clothes to the washer downstairs. Finally back in Grammivana's wonderful kitchen, they made a large pot of coffee and brought out a covered dish from Gargantua. Grammivana put it in the middle of the table, and took the cover off. In it was a pile of Great Aunt Marianna's maritozzi sweet buns. Luna's mouth watered, and she exclaimed:

"Where did you get those? I didn't think I would ever see them again!"

"I made them, Dunderhead! They have every wonderful thing that you want over here, but these are a very local thing, just like Anna's cookies, and stuff like that is hard to find, so you have to make it yourself." Luna said, with a sight:

"I am going to miss those wonderful, humongous pastries, though; I don't think those are easy to make!" Grammivana replied:

"You don't have to miss anything! Next weekend we'll take a shopping trip to the North End of Boston and I'll take you to Mike's Pastry; you'll see!" Then she opened the window and called:

"Robbie, come, coffee's ready!" And after a few minutes, Luna's grandpa walked in from the back yard. He was in his work clothes, and walked over to Luna to kiss her cheek. She exclaimed:

"Grandpa, I thought you had gone off to work!" He responded:

"No, no Luna! I don't work anymore. I retired at sixty and decided never to work again; when you have enough money to live, it's fun to be home. I love my garden, it reminds me of the farm, and I love keeping it nice for your grandmother." And she said, laughing:

"And keeping it full of his Swiss chard, tomatoes, peppers, basil and other herbs, all needed for his food, naturally!" And then, seriously:

"Robbie's been working since he was seven years old, he deserves to enjoy himself, now." Grandpa put his arm over Grammivana's shoulder, and kissing her lightly on the forehead said:

"Don't forget that I also tend the flowers for you, dear!" Grammivana hugged him lightly and replied:

"I do love the flowers! Remember, Luna, how nice Assunta kept her garden, when we went to Antonietta's gold party?" Luna smiled:

"Of course, to me it was only a few weeks ago!" Grammivana sighed:

"I don't think I'll ever get used to this time traveling, but I'm so glad I can talk to someone about my past. I always wanted a beautiful garden like Assunta's, but at the farm there was too much to do, no one really had time for a flower garden, and while he was working, Robbie didn't have too much time for it either; beside, we only had a small yard the first years over here. After we made our money, we took the longest time to find a house that was right for us. This house is my refuge; it reminds me of the farm so much, and of course Robbie changed a lot of things after we bought it. I'm so lucky he worked in construction with his dad since he was a child!" They sat at the table, and at first they ate a delicious grilled cheese sandwich, and then some of the airy, yellow, soft maritozzi rolls, and finished the huge coffee pot of espresso between the three of them. After breakfast, they cleaned up the kitchen and Grandpa said:

"Dear, I'll be in the greenhouse if you need me!" And left the room. Luna said:

"Grandpa has a greenhouse?" Grammivana replied:

"In New England we have long, cold winters, as you well know. Robbie wouldn't be able to stay inside all winter long, and he's not big on shopping, so he built himself a huge greenhouse, and he has lemons, oranges, palms, figs, flowers, lettuce, herbs and other things that could grow in the winter. It's a veritable paradise in there, we have benches to sit on and spend time among the plants. In the long winter days I join him while he's working in there and I work on my tombola lace." Luna said, happily:

"You still make the lace?"

"Of course, Dear, I belong to a lace club, we have shows and everything. If you're interested in joining it, you'll be the youngest member and everyone will be surprised at your talent; Aunt Palma always said that you were a natural when it came to tombola." Luna hugged her:

"How can I be so lucky? You're the best grandmother in the whole world!" Grammivana smiled:

"You didn't used to think so before your trip, Dear!"

"I didn't know you, now you're my Ivana, and I don't think you're weird anymore, I know why you do the things you do!" Grammivana said:

"Many children don't realize what treasures can be found by getting to know their grandparents. Well, my dear, come with me, I have a few surprises for you." Luna said:

"Just let me call my mother first, or she'll run down to see if I'm alright!" After Luna reassured her mother and told her a bit of what she did, she followed Grammivana to the basement. They stopped in front of a small door. Grammivana pulled out a key and opened it, and they stepped into a very small room. The room was air conditioned, and it had shelves and a large closet. The first thing Luna saw was two bikes, one blue and the other red. They looked old fashioned, but they were freshly painted and in perfect condition. Luna cried:

"Our bikes! Oh Grammivana, how did you get them?" She smiled:

"I took mine with me when I first came here; we came on a boat and it was easy. I went to get yours a few weeks ago, and it was not easy to bring it back, but I made it." Luna was speechless:

"But they look brand new, it's been so long!"

"Robbie repaired and painted them, and they were actually well preserved, as I stopped using mine after you left." Her grandmother responded. And then she said:

"But now look in the closet." Luna looked, and cried:

"My stuff! Everything I was taking with me in my suitcase is here!" She fingered her piece of ancient tombola lace that Aunt Palma had given her, the Snow White dress from the church ceremony for the wedding, and her paisana costume that la Befana gave her at Anna's house. There was a jewelry box, and inside Luna found the gold Uncle Pas and Aunt Esther had given her, and the silver slave bracelet they bought at Lulubean's the night of the wedding. Everything was perfect, even her yellow felt handbag with the bunch of violets on top. Inside she found her wallet and the papers she carried in Italy in the 1950's. Her blue suede shoes were there, the shoes for the wedding and her small, light and colorful Cioci too. On top of the closet there was a heavy box, and when she brought it down, inside she found the book that Uncle Pas gave her; 'The Betrothed'. Luna laughed out loud:

"I didn't finish reading it, what with the wedding and all, I had only a few pages and I expected to read it all before I left, but I left so suddenly! Now I'll be able to finish it in my own good time." Grammivana said sadly:

"It's in Italian, dear, I think you'll have a little problem; I understand that they only gave you the gift while you were there." Luna hugged her and said in Italian:

"Let me tell you a little secret, Grammivana!" And after Luna told her grandmother what happened, they both laughed until they cried at the dirty trick she played on Balthazar. The last thing Luna saw, in the back of the closet, was the picture Ivana's grandparents brought her from Roma. She traced Valeria's features gently with her fingers, and silent tears fell from her eyes. Grammivana said:

"There's something you're not telling about that picture. Maybe at a later time you can tell me what it's all about." Luna promised, and then asked how everything was preserved so well. Grammivana told her that everything was packed away and put in their ancestor's secret room, underground, where the temperature was always the same, and where no one could touch and ruin anything, with Uncle Pas guarding her stuff all his life, until he knew who she was and that Ivana would be able to return everything to her.   Luna was overwhelmed at how, over these many years and decades, everyone took care of her and her things, and felt a wave of love so great for everyone, that her heart could hardly hold it.   At this point, Grammivana took a bundle from a box and gave it to her.   Luna unwrapped it, and the first thing she saw was the name Quagliozzi on top, and under it, in golden letters, 'Antonietta and Rodolfo, married January 6, 1951.' With awe she looked up at Grammivana:

"The wedding album?" Grammivana said:

"Yes, it belonged to my mother and she wanted you to have it.   When we have time we'll go through it and remember everything and everyone, especially two young girls sashaying around in their cute paisanella costumes.   It will take us wonderful hours, so for now put it back." Luna handled the album like a great treasure, and held it to herself before putting it back in the box safely.   Then Luna and Grammivana took a bike ride around their quiet neighborhood, and chased each other like they used to, with Luna winning every race.   Grammivana protested:

"No fair, I haven't used a bike in ages, while you have been riding up until a couple of days ago!" And Luna showed off her prowess as a bike rider, laughing and cavorting, to her grandmother's applause.   It was much easier to ride on the beautiful roads here, but they both thought with longing of the well-known country roads they used to ride on. When they went back to Grammivana's house, she asked Luna if she wanted to take her bike home, but Luna said her family wouldn't understand, and they would probably try to buy her a new one; it was much better to leave the bike at her grandparents' house and just use it when she was here. Afterwards, Grammivana and Luna went to the kitchen and worked together on a light lunch, and when everything was done, they sat at the kitchen table and Luna asked Grammivana how she had found out everything.

Grammivana's eyes were very sad as she recounted those first days:

"I couldn't wait until next summer, when you were supposed to come back, and I didn't get anything from you, not a letter or a card, and when I asked my father for your address so I could write you, he told me that I couldn't. I didn't understand, but he said that was all there was, and I should just go on with my life. I asked Anna, but she said the same thing; I was terribly afraid that something bad had happened to you, and you know how stubborn I am, so I decided to come and see you, to make sure. I looked in my father's papers, and found a letter from his sister, your supposed mother, she lived in Milano. Instead of going to school one day, I took all the money that I had been saving, left my parents a note that I was going to find you, walked to Pontecorvo, got an a bus to Aquino, there I took the train to Roma, and from Roma took a direct train to Milano. When I arrived there, that evening late, I slept in the train station, and in the morning, I found a bus that would take me close to your apartment, and walked the rest of the way. When I arrived at this apartment on the outskirts of the city, I knocked at the door, said who I was, and asked for you. They looked at me strangely, but after a while, they went to get you. But you weren't you; it was a strange girl in strange clothes. She told me she was my cousin but she didn't know me, although she had heard that they had hick relatives on some farm somewhere, but she had never been there and she would never go either. I was stunned, they said that she was the only cousin I had there, and they didn't know who I was talking about. They said that I fainted; they put me to bed, and went to send my father a telegram. I was scared and exhausted; I just slept and slept, and when I woke up the following morning, my father was there. He had left as soon as he received the telegram and had traveled all night long. I threw myself at him, and cried my heart out, I wanted to know what happened to you, and I asked him to forgive me for worrying him. You know what kind of man your Uncle Pas was! He fixed it with his sister somehow; he gave them a large suitcase filled with expensive Pontecorvo delicacies, a silk shawl that my mother sacrificed (the one he bought her at the feast of SS Cosmo and Damiano) a Caramella prosciutto ham, and a big container of marzolline.

They were very happy with all the goodies that they couldn't get in Milano, and asked us to dinner. My father told me that you were just fine, and that we would talk when we were alone. After dinner, we left and my father said that I would know all of it when we got home. At home, Anna was there, keeping my mother company, and when we arrived she held me and consoled me. She said that she missed you too, but that we would never be able to see you again; you were out of our reach. I couldn't believe it, and all the mystery was driving me crazy, so my father finally said that he would tell me everything. He held both my mother's hand and mine, and told us how Balthazar came to him and asked him if he wanted to host you, that you were a descendent of his, and of Anna, and you were being catapulted back about sixty years for a short while, to learn about your past and your origins, and to change some very bad traits that you were developing. If he didn't want to do it, Balthazar would have erased his memory of the encounter, but my father said he would do it gladly, and so you came. Balthazar had also talked to Anna, and she was happy to do it. He told Anna more, but she couldn't tell us, as she had to let life take its course, and if she told all we might have messed up and changed things. My mother cried, that we had lost you forever, but she also was happy you were going to be a descendent of ours; she loved you absolutely. I was inconsolable. I had realized that you were different than us, and now I knew why. I asked my father where you came from, and he told me Balthazar only said 'America' and named a town near Boston. I was desperate, and when my father and Anna told me that I couldn't tell anyone, or I would jeopardize the whole operation, I didn't know what to do. The Powers That Be and Balthazar helped countless children, they saved their lives and they helped them to become better people, and I didn't want to hurt anyone, but I had to talk to someone, and so I went to Aunt Palma and told her everything. She told me that she knew you were different, but she didn't know why. All at once everything made sense to her, and she sat me down and told me what to do. She said that it was too late for her, but she had her life and she was very happy with it, and she felt privileged to have known you. But it wasn't too late for me. She said that in about sixty years I would still be a spring chicken of seventy-four, and I could have a lot of life left in me if I believed I did. She told me to grow up, go where you came from, and wait for you. It was not just a coincidence that you came to us, she said, there is a connection somewhere. She gave me hope, and she told me to lead a happy life in America until I met you. She was at my wedding, she lived to be over a hundred years old, and at my wedding I wore a dress similar to Antonietta's; my mother made it, your mother got married in that same dress, and it's being preserved for your wedding. When you designed Antonietta's wedding dress, you were recollecting my own wedding dress which I showed you many, many times, so that when you did go back there, you would remember it. As you can see, your Uncle Pas was right; time is a circle, the circle of life." Luna embraced her dear Grammivana, who was not just her grandmother but her childhood friend as well. She then asked:

"You said that you have money thanks to Aunt Palma." Grammivana said:

"When Aunt Palma died, she left us something more precious to her than gold; her travel album and her mutandies. She also left us her money and her house; she left her gold to Giustina. I have never changed a thing, when I go there I stay at Aunt Palma's house, my brothers take care of it for me. She said that when I found you, I was to give you half of everything, and to leave the house to you, so that you would always have a place to stay when you went back home. I'll have you know, Dear Luna, that you're a very wealthy little girl. What belongs to Robbie and I will go to your mother, with a large gift for your brother, and half of the fortune that came from investing Aunt Palma's money has been in your name since you were born. I told your parents that it was an inheritance from my parents, and when you got it, your brother was not born yet, but we are giving him an inheritance, so there wouldn't be any Jealousy." Luna was amazed:

"Did Aunt Palma have a lot of money?" Grammivana laughed:

"She was very old when she died, and she had lived simply all her life, so yes! She had a large fortune." Luna put her head down on her arms, and sobbed. After a while she said:

"What happened to The Fool?" Grammivana smiled:

"Antonietta had five children, they were small babies, and The Fool dandled them on his knees for years. He was a very happy man. He became mellow and did a lot of good until the end of his life. They're all gone now, but Antonietta's children are big shots around those parts. A couple of them still run the Sand and Gravel pit, the rest are bankers. Anna's children have multiplied and you have so many cousins, aunts and uncles that you won't be able to remember their names. Gianna the teacher and Uncle Saverio lived to a ripe old age, their children have also multiplied; Uncle Saverio became a renowned artist, his pieces are in galleries and museums and are very valuable. Next summer we can go back home and I'll show you everything." Luna asked:

"Whatever happened to aunt Nannina?" Grammivana said:

"About five years after you left, Aunt Nannina retired from teaching. When she was free from working, since her job had been her life, she didn't know what to do with herself, so she thought magnanimously that she would make a gift of her free time to her beloved school; so she kept going back to her school, offering to help as a volunteer. She liked being the beneficial godmother to all the younger teachers, and she thought that they all waited for her to show up to help and to spread her sunshine. But after a time, she noticed that people were not happy to see her, and she asked why. They told her that by working for free, she was taking bread out of the other teachers' mouths, someone was going to lose their job because of her free work and frankly she should stop hanging on, she should get a life, just retire and leave them alone. Aunt Nannina was crushed; she went straight to Aunt Palma's and cried with her head down on the kitchen table. Aunt Palma hollered at her, she told her:

"Get out of here, you pusillanimous, fainthearted woman! You have a warm, handsome, willing man waiting for you, and you're letting him get away; he's starting to court Stina Ciacia's unmarried daughter, you know! Show some guts and go to him, he's not going to wait around for you much longer!" And Nannina went to Ferdinando's house and asked him to marry her. They got in the car, drove to San Giovanni Incarico, went to Ferdinando's Uncle who was a priest, and he married them right then and there. They went back home to Ferdinando's house, posted their marriage certificate on the front door of the sprawling farmhouse, locked the door and didn't come out for three days. After that, everyone was used to the idea, and when they emerged, they went to Pontecorvo to shop and eat; Nannina was not wearing her eternal business suit but regular, plain clothes, and looked the happiest anyone had ever seen her. Ferdinando was also wearing regular clothes. They made a pact that when they went out together, they would wear regular clothes, and the rest of the time they would wear whatever they wanted. Aunt Nannina did confess to Ferdinando that he looked very handsome and sexy in his costume, and he confessed to her that he was very proud of her when she was all important, while wearing severe and classy power suits. They enjoyed many long, happy years together, and went to their rewards only a few days from each other." Luna asked, with a few tears in her eyes:

"What about Uncle Gaetano?" Ivana's eyes watered too:

"His Vanna came back for him, they married, we went to the wedding and it was gorgeous; after the honeymoon he went with her to America. They lived happily for many years and had a lot of beautiful children and grandchildren. They say he died some years ago, but only his body is in that crypt; in Pontecorvo we know better. His spirit didn't die; he went back to his beloved countryside to wait for his beloved Vanna. In the meanwhile he rides the countryside on his beloved motorcycle, enjoying himself and helping travelers." Luna said, both smiling and crying:

"How do you know?" Ivana responded:

"They say that on sultry, quiet summer nights, if you stand still long enough, you'll hear that noise, you know which one!"

"Yes," said Luna: "the Gilera eight bolts!"

"They say he rides his Gilera in his black clothes and helps anyone who's in need or who's lost. A family whose car had broken down between Pico and Pontecorvo swears that a man on his motorcycle, all in black leather, appeared out of the pitch dark, stopped near them and fixed their car so they could go home; they never did quite see his face, he was wearing a helmet, he never said a word, and when he was done he just did the thumbs up sign and drove away in a puff of smoke." They embraced, and remembered dear, handsome, fun and daring Uncle Gaetano; a man in a million! Luna felt sad, happy, all shook up, and really kind of exhausted. Grammivana told her to go get some rest, and she would call her in an hour for their meal. As soon as Luna fell asleep, she was back on the farm. A party was going on, and it was a Good Bye party for her. Everyone was there, Anna, Angelina and Carlo, Irma, Amelia and Mario, great Uncle Biagio and great Aunt Marianna, Aunt Palma, Gianna the teacher with Uncle Saverio, The Fool and Assunta, Antonietta and Rodolfo, even Remo, Romolo and Romano. The Russo boys were there, Ada and her parents, even Roffo, Concetta and Luana, Nannina with Ferdinando and Giustina, Luca and the boy from Roma, who had eyes only for Ada; everyone was there, and Quagliozzi was running around taking everyone's pictures. Aunt Esther, Uncle Pas and Ivana had given the party for her, and Roberto was also there. Of course, having done all the planning, Toscana, Lilliana and Inessa were there to make sure it went perfectly, even embracing Luna in turn! Everyone loved her, they were going to miss her and Ivana and Roberto, holding hands, said:

"See you soon, Luna; we'll be looking for you at home!"

29. *Panorama*. Cartolina postale colore azzurrino; timbro 30/VI/1942. Retro: "41218 Ed. G. Quagliozzi - Studio Fotografico / Pontecorvo / Visto ufficio stampa R. Prefettura - Terni / Riproduzione vietata / Fot. Berretta S. A. - Terni, XIX".

30. *Panorama*. Cartolina, bollo post. 16/IX/1908. Retro: "1522 Fot. L. Macioce".

Pontecorvo, view from Cathedral, 1908.
Lorenzo Macioce

Luna walked very carefully into the building on the first day back at school. She had gone shopping with Grammivana at the Wrentham Outlets, with her parents' permission, and had bought some nice skirts, blouses and sweaters, in lovely colors, very fashionable styles and of first quality materials. She loved her soft, casual-dressy clothes in muted colors and modest styles; they fit beautifully, didn't attract too much attention and were just right for her age and figure. She had wanted something else rather than sneakers for shoes, so she found some nice leather shoes that reminded her of what she wore back home on the farm. So she bought two pairs of them, one black and one brown. When Grammivana brought her home after the day of shopping, her mother inspected what they bought, very surprised:

"Luna, dear, these clothes are so different from what you usually wear! Most of this is imported from Italy! You have changed a lot all of a sudden, haven't you?!" Luna said:

"You know, Mom, just a few days ago I had an Epiphany that completely changed my outlook on life!" At that, Grammivana's throat started to gurgle, but she stifled the laughter by disguising it as a chocking sound, and Luna pretended to help her by thumping her back. Luna's mother shook her head:

"I used to think that my mother was off her rocker, but now I think that you both are!"

Before she entered the school building on her first day back at school, Luna looked around and the first person she saw was Mr. Wheeler, her English teacher. He passed her on his way inside, and when she said 'Good Morning' to him, he turned around, smiling and commented:

"Thank you, Ms. Blue! I do believe that this is the first time that you were actually polite to me; you adopted the preppy look, I see! Well done!" Luna dreaded going inside herself, but thought that maybe it wouldn't be so bad. Inside, her friends were waiting for her. Myrna and Maria flanked her just in case, but no one said anything. The good kids were too polite to comment, and the not-so-good kids knew how hard it was to go back to school after suspension, so they refrained from opening their mouths. Luna went to her classes as usual, trying just to blend in and be unobtrusive, and she realized that if you refrain from acting up, no one pays any attention to you, and that she liked it better that way. At lunch time in the cafeteria, Luna looked at all the options, and chose a hardboiled egg, an apple and a large salad. She was surprised at the beautiful salad greens that were available; she had never made it a point to look before. She looked for oil and vinegar, but didn't see any, so she went up to the Lunch Lady, and Helga looked at her with enmity:

"Well, well, well! Look who we got here! Welcome back, Miss Nasty, and how was your little vacation, hmmm?" Luna looked at her and politely asked:

"Where can I get some oil and vinegar, please?" Helga answered, sarcastically:

"The Concierge just stepped out; I'll ask him as soon as he comes back --- NOT! Where do you think you are, Missy, the Grand Hotel? Putting on airs, are we?" And then she screeched:

"All we have is generic Crap-Dressing; take the stupid slop and shut up like everyone else! What, cat got your tongue? I guess suspension was good for you; you deserved it and you got it!" And in so saying, she dipped a ladle into a large metal bowl in front of her and dropped a great amount of undulating, bright orange goop all over Luna's clean, crisp salad with a loud PLOP!! Luna smiled at her sweetly, while from under the counter, she hooked the top of her pen under the edge of the large bowl, and lifted quickly. As Luna casually walked away, the bowl tittered for a bit, and then overturned, and a great amount of the alive-looking, bright orange goop splashed all over the front of Helga's apron, oozing like a glowing version of the Green Slime. As the Lumpy Lunch Lady screamed and screamed, Luna sat quietly at the table where her friends were waiting for her and started to eat, gently and ladylike of course, just the way Aunt Esther always liked. Balthazar, who was watching over Luna's first day back at school from above (she was one of his favorites, after all), saw the whole production, and started to laugh uproariously. As he was guffawing, he heard a grumble of displeasure from The Powers That Be. Looking up, unrepentantly, he said:

"Well, what did you expect, perfection?   After all, Luna is still Luna! And she STILL has the temper and disposition of a sailor (with the manners and the language to match)! But hopefully, since awakening to the world around her, she'll be a little more careful from now on!   Remember, there are many more adventures ahead of her; and ahead of us too!" And for once in the longest time ever, The Powers That Be made an approving noise, and actually sounded happy for a change!

How Good Can it GET?

The End

29. *Panorama*. Cartolina postale colore azzurrino: timbro 20/VI/1942. Retro: "41218 Ed. G. Quagliozzi - Studio Fotografico / Pontecorvo / Visto ufficio stampa R. Prefettura - Terni / Riproduzione vietata / Fot. Berretta S. A. - Terni, XIX".

Pontecorvo, panorama of the river 1942.
G. Quagliozzi-Berretta

About the Authors

G. A. Costa was born in Pawtucket, RI. He grew up in Seekonk, MA and now resides near Boston. He attended The Perkins School for the Blind until Junior High, where, as a child, he started learning how to sing and play the keyboard. After outgrowing Perkins, he attended Junior High in Watertown, MA. He then came home to Attend High School in Seekonk, MA, where he received High Honors and was inducted into The National Honor Society. While at Seekonk High, he joined 'The Verdandi Male Choir for Swedish Singers' with whom he traveled the country singing in concerts. After high school, he was accepted at SMU (now UMASS Dartmouth), and graduated with a B.S. in Computer Science and with a minor in Sociology. After graduation, he wrote for a computer magazine and designed computer games. Besides writing, he now plays various instruments, including the guitar and drums, while continuing to sing and write music. Other interests include any and all kinds of science and physics, reading, listening to music, and electric trains.

A. R. Costa was born in Milan, Italy, just before the Second World War, and was raised in Pontecorvo, Italy, in the Province of Frosinone. She obtained a teaching degree from 'The Fancy School in Town' when she was twenty, and soon after she was married in The San Bartholomew Cathedral, right across from her house. Since her mother was born in Fall River, Ma, and always talked about her life in America, Alessandra decided to 'come home' to the USA, and her entire family came with her and her husband. Now the author and her two children, her brother, sister, their children and grandchildren are all spread out very close to their roots, in and around Fall River, Massachusetts, in the Good, Old U.S. of A. Her parents, Nonno and Nonna, lie peacefully next to each other, near their family and together forever.

In. Cartolina postale color verdino - timbro 23 VIII 1926. Retro: "Prop. rs. Raff. Longo - Coloniali Liquori / Pizzicheria Generi alimentari - Corso Garibaldi - Pontecorvo - Editore / Garioni - Piacenza".

Greetings from Pontecorvo 1926.
R. Longo, Pontecorvo-Garioni, Piacenza

Our Ancestors – Nonna's Side

Our Ancestors – Nonno's Side

CPSIA information can be obtained at www.ICGtesting.com
Printed in the USA
BVOW03s1842310314

349313BV00012B/223/P